HOUSE
of MANY
ROOMS

MARIUS GABRIEL

HOUSE of MANY ROOMS

BANTAM BOOKS

NEW YORK TORONTO LONDON
SYDNEY AUCKLAND

HOUSE OF MANY ROOMS

A Bantam Book / May 1998

LIBRARY OF CONGRESS CATALOG CARD NUMBER: 97-46990

ISBN: 0-553-09653-2

Published simultaneously in the United States and Canada

Bantam Books are published by Bantam Books, a division of Bantam Doubleday
Dell Publishing Group, Inc. Its trademark, consisting of the words "Bantam
Books" and the portrayal of a rooster, is Registered in U.S. Patent and Trademark
Office and in other countries. Marca Registrada. Bantam Books, 1540 Broadway,
New York, New York 10036.

PRINTED IN THE UNITED STATES OF AMERICA
BVG   10 9 8 7 6 5 4 3 2 1

For Linda, Teddy, Tom, and Emma

My heartfelt thanks go to Beverly Lewis.

PROLOGUE

San Francisco

Father Tim pulls up at the gates of the Florio place. The electric window whirs down, and Father Tim presses the button. This is a ritual he enjoys.

"Father Timothy Dean," he says, in answer to the squawk from the speaker.

While he waits for the gates to swing open, Father Tim stares at the view of the house afforded through wrought-iron curlicues. It is called the Florio place in deference to Barbara's husband, but since he has moved out to a downtown apartment, people have started calling it the Montrose place again. It is an imposing 1870s mansion, with lots of Mediterranean balconies and arches, cream marble columns holding up a portico over the front door. The windows and parapets are picked out in the same pale marble. It has been impeccably restored, and given an Italianate flourish, complete with pink stucco and striped awnings. It is the kind of house that tourists love to photograph, a major chunk of sumptuous prefire San Francisco. Father Tim has given up a lot to serve the church, but he has not given up the pleasure of driving through the portals of houses like this one.

He parks his convertible behind Barbara's Rolls. Before getting out of the car, he flips the mouthpiece of his mobile phone and calls the bishop's office. Father Tim's position—director of material resources—has been created especially for him, and he savors every drop of privilege and prestige the job affords. Well, he would be wasted taking grimy confessions in a grimy confessional someplace down on the docks.

By the time he has finished his murmured telephone conversation, Barbara Florio herself has appeared at the top of the steps. She waves prettily, and Father Tim jumps out. He takes the steps two at a time, every inch the college athlete in his black designer denims, black gym shoes, black shirt and blazer. The white collar looks almost jokey, a fraternity prank. His tan face is split in a brilliant grin.

"Barbara. How are you?"

"So good to see you, Father." They clasp all four hands. She pulls him to her. "I've taken a big decision," she says dramatically, her glossy red lips close to his ear.

"Have you?" he asks. He sniffs her moist breath surreptitiously. Sinful female breath, but today there is no overlay of whiskey.

"Come in. I can't wait to tell you." She pulls him inside the house, all twenty fingers still entwined. Her face is solemn, but her eyes are sparkling.

In the hall, they come across Barbara's younger daughter, Therese. She is hurrying down the stairs with an armful of dolls. She is so intent that she cannons into Father Tim's athletic buttocks. Dolls spill, *clonk, clonk,* onto the hardwood floor.

"Why, Therese," sings Father Tim, turning. "How are you, young lady?"

Therese does not answer. Her face has a blind look, and when Father Tim touches her arms, he can feel her whole body trembling. He pats Therese's curly head, and helps her pick up the dropped dolls.

When he rises, he looks up and sees that Devon, the older daughter, is looking over the polished banister at him.

"Hello, Devon," he calls out. "Enjoying your vacation, honey?"

But Devon just stares back at him coldly and gives him a flat "Hi."

Father Tim is quite aware that both of Barbara's daughters detest him cordially. And he is no devotee of children, so that makes it even.

Barbara takes his arm possessively. "Come into the dining room," she urges, fingers kneading his biceps.

It is a long, cool room housing a long, polished table. Spread out on the table is a large ground plan, unrolled and held down at its four corners with books.

"I'm going to build a church," she says, a gurgle in her voice. She looks deep into his surprised eyes. She reaches for his hand and pulls him to the table. "Come and look."

Meantime, Therese Florio is carrying her dolls out into the garden. Dolls by the armful. She has so many of them that she has to keep them in a big box in the playroom, so many that she can make a whole classroom of dolls, and make herself their teacher. Today's class is a special class. Today's lesson is a special lesson.

The household staff see the child trotting intently up and down the stairs, but pay her little attention. She is a strange one, wild and untidy, and full of inexplicable twists. They have learned not to try and thwart her.

Her sister, Devon, sticks her head over the polished banister again. "Whatcha doing, Tree?" she calls.

Therese does not reply, just hurries on down the stairs with another armful of dolls. So Devon turns her glossy head to address Mrs. de Castro, the Venezuelan housekeeper, who is picking through the morning's mail.

"What's she doing with her dolls, Mrs. de Castro?"

"I don't know, honey," Mrs. de Castro says abstractedly.

"She's going to mess them up," Devon predicts.

"Time she grew out of them, anyhow," says Mrs. de Castro. Devon agrees sadly, and goes back to her own neat room. Therese is a very young twelve, but Devon is nearly fifteen, and already, as Mrs. de Castro says, quite the lady. It is high summer, and although the weather is glorious, and Devon is on vacation, she is working on a school project: Jurassic Animals. Her father has bought her a multimedia computer of her own. She has been browsing a new CD-ROM, *Microsoft Dinosaurs*, which she thinks is the coolest thing she has ever seen. She has been watching an animation where a huge T. rex stalks and kills a triceratops, as good as a movie, and really gross where the T. rex crunches up the smaller dino.

Out in the garden, Therese is hurrying, hurrying. Her heart is pounding, her ears are deaf with the beat of her own blood. All the dolls, she wants all the dolls. None must be absent.

She has made her schoolroom in the garden, behind the shed where the gardeners keep their tools. It is one of her special places. The dolls are piling up in a ragged semicircle, jumbled without much regard to their comfort, pink limbs jutting at the sky or the ground, evasive blue eyes staring glassily, mouths pressed tight as clams.

At last they are all present. She squats for a moment in the semicircle, panting a little. She has been running up and down the stairs at a good lick. Now she is ready. She arranges them, putting her favorites to the front. Then she steals into the gardeners' shed, using the key that is always hidden under a flowerpot.

It is a big, dark structure that smells of tar and oiled machines. Here is the riding mower that keeps the huge lawns like green velvet, here are the spades and forks and rakes, the chain saw, the lines trimmer, the hedge trimmer, and all the other machines for slicing and chopping and slashing nature.

Here, at the back, are the greasy red jerricans. The ones marked D have diesel oil in them, the ones marked 2-stroke have oil mixed with gasoline, the ones marked 4-stroke contain pure gasoline. These are the ones Therese wants. There are three of them. One of them is full, and so heavy that she cannot lift it, and has to lug it along with both hands. Her T-shirt and shorts are getting filthy, but that is quite usual.

The dolls stare glassily. The gasoline is like ice when it splashes over her hands, and the stink of it rushes into her lungs, making her cough. The jerricans get lighter. The dolls glisten brightly. In some cases, the gasoline seems to be melting hair and eyelashes. As she pours it over Miss Lucy, she sees Miss Lucy's painted face stream away, leaving a blank.

Soon the jerricans are empty. The heated summer air has an evil shimmer, and Therese is ready. Now is the baptism of fire. She has the matches in her pocket. Her hands are shaking as she fumbles open the box. She knows it is bad, bad. But it is all she has left.

In the dining room, Barbara shuffles through old photographs. They show a Victorian factory building bearing the legend, "Ranolph P. Montrose Inc., Clothing Manufacturers."

"My great-grandfather built the first factory in the 1860s," she says. "In those days, it was called South of the Slot, because the cable cars didn't go there yet. Of course, it all burned in 1906. My grandfather rebuilt it a year later." She shows him some more photographs, of a later building, long lines of doleful employees standing outside. Father Tim nods and nods, and murmurs replies as she goes through it all. How the business boomed during the wars, how for every drop of youthful blood that soaked into Montrose-stitched uniforms, a dollar poured into Montrose-owned bank accounts.

"When we modernized and moved downstate in 1973, all the machinery was sold off. The place has just been a warehouse since then. Now that South of Market is developing so fast, I've had more offers for the property than I can count." She pauses. "The last offer was for twelve million dollars, and our people told us it was undervalued at that."

Father Tim shakes his smooth head slowly. "I can't remember," the young priest intones, "such a generous bequest. Not in my time. Maybe not ever. The bishop will be overwhelmed."

"I wanted you to be the first to know, Tim."

"God bless you, Barbara. God bless you."

Barbara Florio accepts that graciously. "As to the actual design of the church itself," she says, "I thought maybe an open competition. The big firms might not be interested. But we could let all the young architects submit designs, and choose the best one. After all, this is to be a young person's church. A *people's* church."

"A *people's* church," Father Tim repeats, nodding vigorously. In the coming weeks and months, he will have to gradually break it to her that no church is ever likely to be built on the plot she is giving, welcome though the gift is. But for now, he knows God will understand if he temporizes a little. Until she signs the bequest, at any rate. "So this," he says casually, tapping the plan, "this is your own personal property? I mean, it isn't part-owned by anyone else in your family?"

"It's all mine," she says. "My grandfather left it to me in his will. I have the deeds right here."

"I didn't mean—" But he takes the deeds from her fingers nevertheless, and looks over them. He cannot help raising one final point. "And your husband?" he asks delicately. "He doesn't have any . . . ?"

Barbara's eyes turn very hard. They gleam stonily, pebbles on a riverbed. "My husband," she says silkily, "doesn't have a damn thing to do with this. Look at the deeds."

"Yes, I see—"

"Not a damn thing," she repeats. "It's mine. Don't worry about my husband, please."

"I won't," says Father Tim, with a giggle, not sure why he is giggling.

Out in the garden, Therese strikes the match, and watches it spurt. She is panting a little. Now is the moment of decision. In the bright sunshine, the flame is invisible. But the matchstick blackens and curls as it is consumed, and she feels a sudden wicked pain in her fingertips. She flings the match onto the soaked dolls. The gasoline ignites with a hard *whump* that is heard all over the house.

Nobody pays it much attention except Devon, up at her computer. When she hears the *whump*, Devon looks up from the dinosaur animation. She cocks her head. There is a shrill sound on the afternoon air, like the whine of some small machine. She listens, frowning slightly. Then she realizes the sound is not a machine, but the pitched, endless scream of a child. She runs to the window. An oily black shimmer is billowing from behind the garden shed.

"Tree," she whispers.

Devon flies down the stairs and through the house. She flies out into the sunshine.

"Tree," she yells. "*Tree!*"

She rounds the shed. The blast of ferocious heat stops her in her tracks. The explosion has flung dolls and dolls' limbs everywhere. The shed is blazing, the tarred wood roaring and spitting red gobs. The laurel bush is crackling merrily, too. Up in the trees, flaming dolls' heads are caught in the branches. The grass is burning, flames licking outward, fanned by superheated air. The fire has a deep, inhuman voice, which chants triumph.

Therese is screaming so high, it is not like a human sound, either. She stands caught in a triangle of fire, between the molten pile of dolls and the blazing shed and the pillar of flame that is the laurel bush. She no longer looks like a child. Her face is the blank face of a doll. Devon realizes that she has no eyebrows, no eyelashes. Her face is an oily red mask, wide open to let out that dreadful shriek. Her bare arms and legs are turning red, too. She has nowhere to run. Fire is all around her. She stands in a tiny space that is swiftly growing smaller as the fire devours the earth and the air.

"Tree!" Devon screams, holding out her arms. "Run to me, Tree!"

Therese's head moves fractionally. Her eyes seem to meet her sister's, but she makes no move, and does not cease her endless scream. She is paralyzed. And then the scream rises an impossible octave. Devon sees a halo of flame forming around Therese's head, turning her into a terrible doll-angel.

Without hesitating, Devon runs into the flames. The ravenous heat envelops her. She is running into a furnace. Her jeans and long-sleeved shirt protect her for a moment. Then she feels the heat reach her skin.

Somewhere in the world that is consuming itself, the sisters meet. Devon's hands claw at Therese's, grasping her, pulling her with violent desperation. Therese is smaller than Devon, and Devon has a kind of mad strength. She clutches her sister to her breast and runs with her, dragging her out of the furnace. She crushes Therese's face against her breastbone, knowing if the child breathes, the blistering air will shrivel her lungs. Her own lips are pinched shut. She can smell skin and hair burning, and does not know whether it is Therese's or her own.

And then she bursts from the flames with her sister in her arms. One of the gardeners is there by now, and so is Mrs. de Castro, and one of the maids. The gardener has his arms outstretched to clasp the two girls. But when he sees that they are burning, literally on fire, the man jumps back with a cry of fear.

Devon hurls herself on top of Therese, trying to smother the living flames with her own body. And brave Mrs. de Castro throws her own self on top of them both, using her hands and her broad body to crush the flames. Everybody is screaming. Mrs. de Castro beats at Therese's smoldering hair, crushing the embers. The child is no longer burning. Her scream has become a wild sobbing. Her eyes have rolled back in her head.

"We gotta get away from the shed," the gardener yells. "Move, for Christ's sake!"

The man's courage does not extend to helping anybody else. He runs back to the house to call the fire department. Between them, Mrs. de Castro and the maid drag the two children away from the shed, which is now a house of fire. As they stumble away, the first can of gasoline goes up like a bomb, blowing one side of the shed clean out. Inside, a whirlwind of fire dances around the machines. Another can goes off, a yellow blast that sends debris high into the air; then another.

Outside the kitchen door, Devon crouches over her sister. She cannot see just how badly Therese is hurt. Therese's hair is a wild muss. Her arms and legs are filthy.

And then, at last, their mother is there, Father Tim in her wake.

"What have you done?" Barbara screams at Therese. Then, to Father Tim's utter horror, she starts slapping her daughter.

The blows are wild, but several of them land on Therese's face, which is already burned and swollen. The child is still making that awful sobbing noise as she cowers away from her mother's onslaught.

"Mom, *no!*" Devon screams, trying to intervene. One of her mother's fists catches her in the mouth, splitting her lip. Devon reels away, clutching at her face.

"Barbara, for God's sake," Father Tim pleads, grabbing Barbara from behind.

Her arms hampered, Barbara is clawing at Therese's hair, fingers tangling in the blackened curls. Therese's head jolts as her mother tries, apparently, to pull her hair out by the fistful. The child squeals and writhes.

"Oh my God, oh my God, oh my God," Father Tim gasps, barely able to restrain Barbara's mad strength. The others join him at last, pulling Barbara away from her child.

But Barbara is still screaming, clawing at Therese. "What have you done?" she screams, again and again. "*What have you done?*"

The family doctor, Evan Brockman, is the first to arrive; he lives just around the corner. He is a distinguished-looking man, with a wonderful bedside manner. Barbara Florio's frenzied call has caught him on his way out to a golf game, and he is nattily dressed for an afternoon on the links.

Shortly after him, the fire department comes with a truck. The firemen run with a hose into the back garden, and start spraying the shed, which is already a blackened shell. A couple of police cars pull up, sirens yowling, lights strobing blue and red. The neighbors are crowding the street. It is one of the smartest streets in Pacific Heights, but even rich people love to gawk.

By this time, Dr. Brockman has both Devon and Therese in a cold bath, with every ice cube in the house floating around them. Mrs. de Castro is also in the bathroom, both her blistered hands held under running water in the sink. She is muttering in Spanish, shaking her head.

Devon wears only her underpants. Therese lies with her head cradled in Devon's arms, inert, glazed eyes staring at the ceiling. The doctor squats beside the bath, carefully peeling off Therese's light summer clothing.

Therese's monkey face does not even flinch. There is scorching and some blistering, but the younger girl has been incredibly lucky. Again. It is not so long since he was last in this grand house, treating the same child for shock and light burns. That time it was a kitchen accident, a pan of oil that caught alight and sent a river of fire up the walls and across the ceiling. This time is much more serious. In every way.

He glances up at Devon. "I don't think she's too bad," he tells her. "How are you feeling?"

"Okay," Devon says. But she is shaking, and evidently in shock.

"You did something very brave," the doctor says quietly. "You saved her life."

He sees a tiny smile move the grimy lips. This is a dysfunctional household, in his view, and Devon is the one sane creature in it. He can hear the girls' mother in the next room, screaming into the telephone. She is speaking to their father, who is in Los Angeles on business.

"I don't *know*," she yells. "She went to the shed and got a can of gasoline. How the hell do I know? She's crazy! She belongs in a mental hospital!"

Father Tim is at her side, his tan face pale and tight with worry. He can see that magnificent bequest, fruit of months and years of work, sliding away from his grasp in the chaos. He has always disliked both of Barbara's daughters. Now he positively hates them.

An ambulance has come howling up the hill from the closest hospital. A four-person team hurries into the suite, carrying big white boxes. They fill the bathroom, pushing aside the GP. He explains what has happened, then gives way to their expertise. Now sodden and shaken, he goes into the bedroom.

Barbara Florio is sitting on the bed, the telephone in one hand, a glass of scotch clutched in the other. The good-looking young priest is sitting beside her, looking sick. Dr. Brockman prescribes most of Barbara's drugs himself, and knows she should not drink alcohol. He also knows she is a borderline alcoholic, ready to plunge into full addiction any day now. He watches her gulp at the scotch and spit venom into the phone.

"*Of course it was deliberate, for Christ's sake.* Aren't you listening to me? She was trying to torch her toys. She's a fucking menace, Michael. She's gonna kill us all. Last time, she almost burned the kitchen down. This time—"

The doctor is making stealthily for the bottle of Glenlivet, not sure whether to take a swig himself before he hides it from his patient. Barbara's head swivels, and her eyes, bulging with panic and anger, fix on him.

"Yeah," she says. "He's right here." She thrusts the telephone at the doctor. "Michael wants to speak to you."

The doctor takes the telephone. "Michael? It's Evan Brockman."

Michael Florio's voice is urgent. "How are the girls?"

"A paramedic team is with them right now. They've both been extraordinarily lucky. Therese is in shock, and a lot of her hair got burned. Devon's in shock, too. Michael, she pulled Therese out of the fire single-handed. It's the bravest thing I ever—"

"Evan, please. What are their injuries?"

"Very light, as far as I could tell. Hair and eyelashes singed. Blistered hands. Basically, they got scorched without getting seriously burned. The paramedics will have a better idea in a quarter-hour or so." He does not mention Therese's catatonic state. That can wait until he knows more about it. The doctor watches Barbara grab the bottle of scotch and head out of the room. The young priest hurries after her.

Out in the corridor, Father Tim tries to soothe Barbara. But she is past soothing. "Leave me alone," she sobs.

"Barbara, please try to calm down—"

She wrings her hands. "Oh, God, it hurts so much!"

She is talking about herself. She has shown little concern for either of her daughters so far, and is certainly not getting herself involved in caring for their injuries. She is a strange kind of mother, Father Tim thinks, self-absorbed and blind. But there is no doubt about her suffering. "Can we go somewhere and pray quietly for a moment?" he suggests.

"I was so happy." Tears stream down her face. "I finally thought I was getting to do something *good* in my life."

"You were!" he exclaims anxiously. "You are!"

"They hate me," she blubbers.

"Who hates you?"

"*Them*," she says, jerking her blond head toward the bathroom, where her two daughters are being treated. "Christ, I wish I was dead."

"Barbara, don't let this happen to you. Let's pray together."

"Leave me alone," she shrieks at him. "Please, please leave me alone. Just go. Go away."

"Don't let this derail your intentions," he urges her. "You're under divine guidance, Barbara. Just listen to that still, calm voice in your heart. You're doing the right thing, please believe me!"

She stares at him, her eyes hardening again like wet pebbles. "That's all you care about, isn't it?" she accuses him. "The land. The money."

"No," he bursts out with a fine show of feeling. "I care about *you*, Barbara. I care about your soul."

She stares at him hotly for a moment longer. Then she sags away, groaning. "Get away from me, please."

"Barbara, let's go somewhere quiet and pray."

"Don't worry about your fucking land," she yells at him, anything to get him to leave her in peace. "It's yours. Don't worry about it. Just go."

And finally, he leaves, backing his GTi through the crowd, still sick with worry. Barbara Florio is a pathetic, tormented soul. She has tried hard to do good in her life, and he is eager to help her succeed, for all kinds of reasons. But he cannot help feeling she is doomed.

Back in the bedroom, Dr. Brockman is still talking to the girls' father on the telephone. "The housekeeper helped put the flames out. Her hands got burned, too. The shed is gone, and it looks like half the garden—"

"I don't give a damn about Barbara's garden. I want to speak to Devon."

"The paramedics are with her right now, Michael—"

"Are you on the cell phone?"

"Yes."

"Take it in to her. Now."

Dr. Brockman knows that tone. Michael Florio is not a man to argue with. He takes the telephone into the bathroom and passes it over the backs of the busy paramedics to Devon, who is having both her hands painstakingly examined. Devon tucks the telephone between her slim shoulder and her ear. She has a Madonna face—Botticelli, not Ciccone—which has been twisted in pain. Now it eases into a smile.

"Daddy? Oh, Daddy!" Her eyes close as she hears her father's voice. "I'm okay, Dad. Therese is, too. It wasn't her fault."

It suddenly occurs to Dr. Brockman that he should not have let Barbara Florio slip away with her pills and her booze. There have been incidents in the past. He has been called out to this house many times, especially since the marriage started breaking up. None of Barbara's "suicide" attempts have been genuine, he feels. Personally, he is much more worried about her outbursts of violence. He wonders whether Michael, surrounded by his busy, busy life, knows that Barbara occasionally gets tanked up and whales the two little girls with anything that comes to hand. But with the pills Barbara favors, even a mild overdose could be serious. It's a crazy household, he thinks, as he hunts for Barbara.

The house is swarming with people: family friends, servants, fire officers, police, paramedics. A second ambulance has arrived. There is a Valkyrie-looking woman in a blue ATF uniform, picking through the embers of the shed, even before the fire is all the way out. Even Michael Florio's lawyer, Paul Philippi, has turned up, prowling through the mob like the pit bull he is, growling into a cell phone. The doctor finally locates Barbara Florio in the laundry, a room he suspects she wouldn't normally visit. Among the big, expensive, gleaming machines, she is slumped, chomping pills and swigging Glenlivet.

"Barbara, for heaven's sake," he groans. He wrests the pills from her fingers and checks the labels. "How many of these have you taken?"

"Oh, God, Evan. What am I going to do?"

He is trying to read when the prescriptions were filled out, trying to get some idea of how many of these multicolored goodies have been gobbled in how short a time. He gives up the calculation. "Calm down a moment, Barbara. How many pills have you taken? How many of these?"

"Six or seven. I don't know."

"And these?"

"I don't know." She thrusts rose-pink fingernails into her gleaming blond hair. She is an attractive woman, though excess is attacking the soft parts of her face and making them puff up. She has a fleshy, full-breasted figure and a flirtatious manner, and she has had no shortage of swains since she and Michael separated. No man, however, seems able to fill whatever void rages inside her. Not even Michael could do that. The marriage that started out so beautifully fifteen years ago has ended up in much the same condition as the garden shed is right now, blown apart and burned out. "She wants to kill us all. She wants to burn us up."

"Who, Therese? Don't be silly."

"She does. I never thought the kitchen thing was an accident. Now I know."

"She's just a child," he says gently. He is taking her pulse, checking her pupils. "Barbara, please try and remember how many pills you've taken."

"Why shouldn't she hate me?" Barbara asks suddenly. "I'm such a fucking failure," she adds, in a broken voice that fills him with sadness. "I tried so hard. I tried so hard."

"I know. If you could just see it, you're succeeding. You're just too hard on yourself."

Her bark of laughter surprises him, blasting scotch fumes into his face. "I'm a rotten, self-indulgent bitch, and you know it," she mocks.

"Maybe you need some space, Barbara," he says carefully. "Maybe you should let the girls go to Michael for a while."

Her head whips around, eyes furious. "*Never,*" she says. "Never. Keeping them away from him is the best way I can hurt him, Evan."

"You really want to hurt him?"

"I'd cut his balls off if I could," she spits.

"That's whiskey talk. Where's Father Tim?" he asks, hankering for some spiritual assistance.

"He left."

"He left?" the doctor asks in surprise.

"You're all the same, aren't you, Evan? Doctors, priests, husbands. All the same. You only want one thing, and Christ knows it isn't me."

"Come on." He slides an arm around her shoulders to lift her to her feet.

"I'm gonna fix him this time," she says, rolling her eyes at Dr. Brockman.

"Upsy-daisy." Her flesh is soft, and ought to be alluring, but her skin suddenly feels clammy to him. Her temperature is dropping fast. She is heavy, and she resists being lifted. He sees her pupils start to dilate.

"Fix him," she repeats. "Gonna fix him good." Her voice has grown thick, her tongue lolling. Her head drops forward, her hair spilling around her face.

"Oh, shit," the doctor groans. He hauls Barbara to her feet and drags her out of the laundry, calling for help. A frightened maid comes to his assistance. They get Barbara into the hallway. At the same time, the paramedics are coming through with both girls. Therese is strapped on a wheeled stretcher, pale-faced and with closed eyes. Devon, wrapped in a blanket, is being helped out on a stretcher as well.

"We'll take them both in overnight," the leader tells the GP. "Physically, they both seem to be in good shape. But they're in shock, and they could do with observation." His eyes stray to the slack figure of Barbara, drooling and moaning, draped between the GP and the maid. "Is she okay?"

"Overdose," the GP says succinctly. "Tranquilizers, antidepressants, and alcohol. I don't know the quantities, but she's just ingested."

"Okay," the paramedic says calmly. "Let's take a look."

So, after a stomach-pumping and a fast puke in the guest john, Barbara joins the caravan that is heading downtown. The last the GP sees of her is in the back of the ambulance, rose-pink nails raking languidly through her gleaming blond hair. She lives in a fantasy of being Marilyn Monroe, he thinks suddenly. She has even cultivated the same vulnerable quiver of the lower lip as she tells you her problems. He manages to have a quick word with Devon before they go.

"Daddy's coming," she says. She is in pain, but she is calm. "He'll be here tonight."

"Good. I'm glad."

"Therese just needs Daddy," Devon says, as if apologizing for the whole sorry mess. "We both do."

Dr. Brockman kisses Devon's brow gently. "You're very brave," he tells the girl. "Just keep being brave."

She smiles up at him. "Are you coming with us?"

"Of course," he says. "I'll follow you in my car."

"Thank you," she whispers, her eyes closing.

Her stretcher slides into the ambulance. The doors close. The ambulances roll away. The lead driver has to tweak his siren to get a passage through the crowd.

Wearily, the family doctor leans against his own car and looks up at the house. How deceptive appearances can be. Life in there should be gracious, tranquil. Nothing should happen to fill the place with sirens and strangers and pain. But it does.

Dr. Evan Brockman rubs his face, then gropes for his cell phone to call his golf partner. His clubs are in the trunk of his Volvo, but he will be spending the afternoon in the hospital with two burned, traumatized children and a woman who describes herself as a rotten, self-indulgent bitch.

He looks up. The sky is blue, but the air still reeks of burning.

NE

AIR

KATHMANDU, NEPAL
TWELVE MONTHS LATER

"I want my baby."

Her throat was raw and dry. Her words were no more than a croak. She swallowed painfully and tried again.

"Please."

A hand touched her brow. Rebecca opened her eyes. The light stabbed into her mind like daggers of ice. She tried to focus on the figure above her. The nurse's face was brown, her eyes dark. She was saying something, but Rebecca could not grasp the words.

"Please," she whispered.

A slim arm curled around her shoulders, lifting her. Rebecca's head lolled; she could not seem to summon the strength to keep it upright. A glass of water touched her lips. She drank gratefully. Her throat hurt so much. The rest of her body was weightless, numb.

She was focusing a little better now. "My baby," she implored. "Bring her to me. Please."

The nurse shook her head, murmuring the same incomprehensible words. Something was wrong.

"My baby. Bring her to me!"

Again the nurse shook her head. She made a negating gesture with her hands. Something was wrong with the baby. It was sick. It had died.

They had taken it away already.

She clutched at the nurse's white sleeve. "What have you done with her? I want her!"

The nurse laid her gently back down on the pillow, but Rebecca struggled upright again. Everything was wrong. She was in the wrong hospital, in some strange country, where nobody understood her. Rebecca mimed holding an infant in her shaky arms. "My child. Please bring her to me!"

The nurse said something in a warning tone. She showed Rebecca the intravenous line that had been taped into her arm. The bottle of serum was swaying wildly.

Someone else appeared beside the nurse, a tall Asian man in a white coat. He bent over Rebecca. A flashlight dug into her eyes, searching, excavating the echoing hollow that was her skull.

"Where is my baby?" Rebecca pleaded. "Are you a doctor? Can you bring her to me?"

The man straightened. He smiled down at Rebecca, showing white teeth in a mahogany face. "This will help you sleep," he said.

She saw the needle going into the intravenous line, saw the drug sliding down the thin tube into her vein.

"No!" she screamed. "Don't!"

But the scream was only in her own mind, because blackness was pouring into her.

SAN FRANCISCO, CALIFORNIA

Far away, across the world, Barbara Florio was dreaming, too.

She must have taken more pills than usual, or perhaps it was some hallucinogenic power in the tequila, but her dreams were vivid, gorgeous Technicolor. She dreamed she was a girl, up at the summer house in Oregon, lying on a warm ledge by the sea, watching the sea lions.

There were twenty of them on the rocks below her, basking in the sun. There was only one adult male, huge and battle-scarred. His head and shoulders, covered with a shaggy mane, were propped upright. He was keeping guard over the others, who were all females or immature males, their sleek bodies sprawled around him. She was filled with love for that big, protective male beast, father and lover to all the herd.

How beautiful, she thought, how beautiful her childhood had been. Beyond the sea lions' rock, the Pacific surged turquoise and creamy-white. Sea stacks rose out of the water, giant colonnades of rock, whittled and sculpted by the waves. Some were big enough to support firs and other trees, clinging grimly to footholds in the stone. Others were stark pillars and stumps. The sea and wind had given them strange shapes like barns, haystacks, or sugarloaves.

Something pulled her away from that vision, half waking her. She knew someone had come into her room. Oregon receded. She tried to move, but her body was like a log. She was normally a light sleeper, even with the alcohol and the drugs, but tonight she was oppressed by a huge, pain-less weight. She could not even speak. She wondered whether she had had a stroke, something she had always feared. The thought normally filled her with panic, but not tonight. It was a vast effort to roll her head an inch to the side, another vast effort to open her eyes. She always slept with a bedside light on, but her vision was blurred. Then she saw who was standing there, looking at her. Her tongue quivered in her mouth.

"Please . . ." she said.

A shadow fell over her face. She felt fingertips lightly touch her eyelids, closing them. She slid back into her Technicolor dream.

Seabirds soared in the luminous spaces between the stacks. She could hear the waves grinding at the rocks. Sadly, she wondered just what it was that had always gnawed inside her, as this restless sea gnawed at the solid land. The sadness drifted away on a warm breeze.

She could feel the breeze rippling her hair. She gazed at the creaming surf and the towering rocks. In her dream, the morning was growing hot, and apart from the crash of the sea around the platform of rock that the herd had chosen, not a thing stirred. There was barely a movement among the slick, golden-brown hulks. The bull's imperious, watchful gaze was turning to a sleepy blink. As Barbara watched, the sea lion shrugged his vast shoulders and opened his mouth in a cavernous, pink yawn. Then he flopped down onto the rock. The breeze carried the thump of his two-thousand-pound body, and his lazy groan, to her dreaming ears. In the heat, the sea lions' coats had dried slick and greasy, their eyes had become sticky. The sea stretched hazily into a perfect midday, the sun blazing on the waves. Barbara floated, remote from regret or sorrow.

Another sound from the ugly present intruded into her visions, anger-ing her. Her beautiful male sea lion had heard it, too. He lifted his massive head, looked around. His almond eyes gleamed. The animal's nostrils flared as he sucked in air. He was smelling the breeze. Perhaps he had caught some scent of danger. He opened his mouth, showing sharp teeth against a blotchy pink palate.

Barbara drove herself to surface. Why were her limbs so leaden? Why could she not even open her mouth to speak? She could barely get her muscles to move. With an agonizing effort, she got her elbow beneath her, and pushed herself up a few inches. Her blurred eyes opened. She could feel saliva trickle from her lips down her chin.

The doors of her closet were open. She saw the hands sorting methodi-cally through her clothes, turning up each label to study it. She tried to speak, but she had so little control of her muscles that her jaw just fell open with a click, and her tongue lolled.

"Whaddaya doing?" she slurred.

"Nothing. Go back to sleep."

"Whaddaya want?"

"Hush. Go back to sleep."

Barbara slumped back into the pillows, her eyelids fluttering. She couldn't get any more words out. She wanted to go back to her dream, but she was disturbed, frightened. Her eyelids kept closing, blotting it out, then flickering open erratically.

What are you doing? she wondered. *Why are you sorting through my clothes? Why are you reading the labels, like a careful shopper at a sale?*

Then the truth started to dawn on her.

You're so clever, she thought. *You want to know what they're made of. You have to know something about man-made fibers, what they'll do and what they won't do. But the knowledge isn't hard to pick up. There. You've found the two garments you want. You hang them side by side. You tear a long strip from one of the garments. Then you light it with the little plastic lighter in your pocket.*

Barbara saw the yellow flame flare. Her eyes darkened. She watched, floating somewhere between her escapist dream and the terrible present. Reality was another kind of dream, a nightmare she had visited so often. As she watched, she knew what was happening, how it was going to work.

Now it's so easy. You push the smoldering strip of material up the sleeve of the second garment. Then you make sure all the hangers are straight, so it looks like nothing disturbed them. Then you close the closet doors. But not all the way. You leave a couple of inches, so air can get in and feed the little system you've set up.

She tried to call out, tried to wake the sleeping house. It was no use; she could not move her body. She could not even cry, but tears came sluggishly from beneath her lids.

"Why?" she whispered. "Why?"

She heard the pad of feet. "Hush. This is for you." Something pressed into her chest, something alien. A hand lifted her arm and rolled it over the object, making her clasp it to her breast.

"Sleep now." Lips touched her brow gently. She was alone. She started sinking back into her dream, hearing the roar of the sea, feeling the far-away sun on her skin. It was better to go there, escape there, than face what was coming. In the other world, her numbed fingers stretched, ex-ploring the thing she had been forced to clasp. Smooth, small, familiar. Hard here, silky there.

Then she realized what it was, and screamed.

It was not a real scream, and nobody in the real world heard it. But the sea lion bull heard it. She saw him surge upright, swinging his head from side to side. The younger males followed his actions, almond eyes searching for danger. The bull swiftly made his decision. He uttered a sharp bark and floundered into the midst of his harem, scattering them. The corpulent bodies jerked into action. Cumbersomely, the herd started flippering its way across the slab. Barbara watched them leave, seeing the fat clumsiness become instant grace as each animal hit the water and glided away. The bull, like a courageous ship's captain, was the last to leave. Before he slipped off the rock, he turned and seemed to stare into Barbara's eyes, whiskery muzzle gaping. With an explosion of spray, he was gone, herding his family to safety in the turquoise water. The slab was empty.

Black fog came creeping across the surface of the water. It blotted out the blue. It spread and swirled, heavy and toxic. She knew it was not fog, but something else, something that poured from her closet, heavier than air, hugging the ground. It would not get as high as the smoke detectors in the ceiling until it was too late, much too late. It rolled steadily, efficiently, implacably.

She cracked her eyes open once more and saw the fog starting to curl over the end of her bed. She was floating in a black sea, a fairy princess cast adrift in a terrible spell. Then she closed her eyes for the last time.

KATHMANDU

The drug did not put her completely under. It helped her start to remember. In a half-dream, she recalled being on the mountain. She was plowing through the screaming white wilderness, connected to Robert by a rope. She kept stumbling, and the rope kept jerking tight.

The blizzard was an icy furnace in which she could feel her strength being consumed. She fought onward, clutching the rope that was her salvation. As long as she could clutch that rope, she would keep going.

She felt herself sliding, falling, battering herself against rock and ice.

She felt the rope snap tight around her waist. She lay waiting for him, her strength almost gone. Then he was looming over her, squatting beside her. She felt his hands grope for the fastening.

"What are you doing?" she heard herself ask him, her voice bewildered.

"We can't go on like this, Rebecca. Neither of us will make it."

"Robert, no!"

"We both have to go at our own pace." The wind was tearing the words from his lips, so she could hardly hear him. "Try and keep up."

"Robert, don't leave me!" He had unfastened the rope from her waist. She was defenseless, disconnected, in this howling whiteness. He rose to his feet.

"Try and keep up," he repeated. He was looping the rope into a neat bundle. He clipped it to her waist. Then he turned and started clambering down the scree again.

"*Robert!*"

She dragged herself to her feet. Without the rope, she was doomed. Desperately, she flung herself after him. Her boots slid in the ice and she crashed down onto her side. He was already far away, receding in the blizzard.

She was so afraid of dying, so alone. She stumbled onward, calling his name. He turned once to look back at her. She caught only a glimpse of his goggles. No human feature was recognizable. Then he rounded a white shoulder of rock and was gone.

She stumbled after him. The rope, coiled and useless, flapped mockingly at her waist. She was alone and dying. All her strength, all her instincts for self-preservation, were useless now.

She was still screaming when, from another world, she heard voices. They spoke some language she could not recognize, a tongue of angels or demons.

Then she felt more darkness pour into her veins, and knew the doctors had increased the dose.

This time, the darkness was complete.

San Francisco

Somewhere in the world that is consuming itself, the sisters meet.

Devon clutches at Therese as she has done once before, dragging her sister away from the stairwell, which has become the open door of a furnace. The fire howls like some huge creature in agony or rage. The girls crouch on the landing in each other's arms, staring with eyes stretched wide at the flames that are ascending the staircase toward them. The very floorboards beneath their naked feet are hot. The air is searing skin, blistering lungs, scorching tender eyes.

"Mom!" Therese screams into the flames.

Devon echoes her. "Mom! Mom!"

"Where is she?" Therese babbles.

"I don't know."

Both girls scream for their mother for a while. But between the roar and the wild clamor of the alarm, they cannot hear their mother's voice. And nobody can hear them. They are alone up here.

Therese lurches forward, as if to throw herself into the furnace. Devon grabs her again and drags her back. "We can't get down that way," Devon screams into her sister's ear.

Therese is whimpering like a baby, clutching at Devon's arms. "What are we gonna do?"

"The bathroom," Devon decides. "Come on."

They stumble back to the bathroom, coughing, clinging to each other. The mirror shows them their own terrified likenesses. Therese's curly brown hair has tumbled over her face, hiding her features. Devon's normally shiny mid-blond mop is a bird's-nest tangle. They smell of singed skin and hair. Hot air buffets them, the breath of something hungry.

"Fill the bath," Devon croaks. "I'll get towels."

Therese turns the cold tap open wide. Water gushes into the marble bath. She fumbles the plug into the drain. Her body is trembling, her joints weak with terror. Her chest feels horribly raw and painful, as though there were a fire in there, too.

Devon flings an armful of towels into the bath. Both girls climb in.

Devon is coughing violently. Therese is sobbing like an animal that has been hunted down to its last corner.

"Whadda we do now?" Therese whimpers.

"Wait for Daddy," Devon says.

"He won't come!"

"Yes, he will." She wraps soaked towels around her sister's head and body, then tends to herself. She leaves the tap open. She has noticed that the water is starting to run warm, and that the flow is dwindling. "He will."

And now Michael Florio's black Porsche screams to a halt in the street in front of the grand old house. Here is the master. The servants hurry to him, babbling.

"Where are the girls?" he yells at them.

"They're sleeping in the guest wing," Mrs. de Castro tells him. "But the staircase is cut off. Nobody can get up there."

Florio runs around the house. He cuts a strange figure. He is in evening dress, snowy tie and snowy carnation immaculate. The gate is locked, but Florio climbs over it, looking like James Bond, except that he is a lot clumsier; he loses his carnation, tears his hands open on spikes, and rips his eight-hundred-dollar jacket across the shoulders. When he gets around the house he sees that the rear section is burning furiously. The ground floor, where Barbara sleeps, is incandescent. Barbara's goose is cooked. The flames are streaming up to the floor above, where the girls are. For a moment, he is blinded with tears of sheer despair.

"Devon!" he screams like a banshee. "Therese!"

There is no sign from the upstairs windows, some of which are starting to glow red, like malevolent eyes awakening. He keeps screaming. His own fire alarm drowns out his voice. He is a security expert. The computerized alarm system, which he himself has planned and installed, is designed to ring the local fire station and police station. It also rings all his personal telephone numbers, and gives a coded message of tones, according to the emergency. The chip has called him on his cell phone in the middle of an award ceremony, and he has made a great stir by rushing out, leaving his lovely partner stranded at their table. He has arrived ahead of the police, ahead of the fire department. The only people in the garden are neighbors, mostly elderly, who are crowding around him, bleating advice.

He picks up the biggest rock he can find—he is a very strong man in his forties—and hurls it at one of the back windows. The double glass is hard to break, and the rock bounces back. He has to fling the thing twice more before the glass explodes, giving him a jagged passage into the house.

It is not a house any longer, but a realm of fire. He staggers to the hallway and looks up. The second-floor landing is starting to collapse. The fire has consumed its strength in an astonishingly short space of time. As he flinches back, shielding his face, the balustrade sags out of the flaming woodwork and crashes with a fountain of sparks onto the marble tiles below. For a short while the flames are blotted out by a column of choking black smoke. Then, steadily, the fire bursts into life around the wood, and reaches up again.

Maybe he can get up alive, but it is unlikely he can get back down. He thinks for a moment. He is trained to think coldly, even in the most hellish situations. He makes his decision, and runs forward.

He takes the stairs four at a time, leaping on the yielding timbers, somehow reaching the top of the stairs. He is choking on the smoke. It claws at his lungs, hurting unbelievably.

Down the corridor, smoke and flame whirl in a funnel. He throws open the guest bedroom. The two beds are empty, the coverlets flung back. He shuts the door again. They must be in the bathroom, at the end of the corridor, where the red blossom glows brightest. There is a cupboard halfway down, and in that cupboard is an extinguisher. Hauling his jacket over his head, he staggers down the corridor.

The extinguisher is there, though he is almost blinded by the time he reaches it. The cylinder is heavy. He knows it is charged; he takes care of such things himself, though he no longer lives in this house. He gropes for the retaining pin and jerks it out. Then he blunders toward the last door. He squeezes the trigger. The nozzle bucks and a white bloom of foam explodes outward. It disappears into the smoke with a hiss. The heat recedes infinitesimally, giving him just enough time to shoulder the bathroom door open.

And there he finds his daughters, huddled in the bath, terrified faces turning to him.

"Daddy!" both scream at once. "Daddy! Daddy!"

They clutch at him, and he clutches at them, his hands groping at them to see if they are hurt. He sees their feet are bare. He wraps their wet towels tightly around their bodies. He does not bother looking at the window. The burglar guards are tempered steel.

"Hurry" is all he says to them.

The three of them stumble out into the corridor. It is now a billowing darkness of acrid smoke. Florio points the nozzle of the extinguisher at the center of the smoke, and presses the trigger. He sprays the white foam in a constant stream until it dwindles and runs out. Then he throws it aside and grabs a daughter in each hand. *Forward.* Both girls stumble, their knees buckling. He jerks them to their feet savagely, and hauls them into the smoke. The terrible heat envelops them, sucking the air from their lungs, tearing at their flesh. The children are numb, beyond fear. But Michael Florio is not. He tries to run, dragging them with him. They are in the heart of the fire, where nothing can live.

They burst through a wall of flames, into a flickering world, lit by the dull radiance of its own dissolution. Nothing is real. No furniture, no architecture exists here. Florio has lost his bearings. He no longer knows which way to go.

But suddenly, here is a denizen of this world, walking slowly toward them. A bulky creature with a shining, wrinkled skin and a monstrous head. In the head is a glass panel, from which a human face stares anxiously.

The fireman peers at Florio and the children for a moment, then lifts the hose he is carrying, and jerks the metal lever to one side. A spray of water envelops them, hissing and sizzling. The girls hunch away from the needles that hit them.

The fireman points with a gauntleted hand toward the gaping hole where he himself has gained access: a window that he has smashed with his ax. Their father thrusts the girls forward. He and the firefighter manhandle the children onto the ledge. Blessed oxygen, flavored with soot, rushes into their lungs. A monstrous fire truck is down there, motor roaring. Its ladder reaches up to the window. Standing in the cradle, his arms outstretched to receive them, is another firefighter.

Therese goes first, retching and sobbing, more dead than alive. Devon follows, her head lolling in semiconsciousness, eyes brown slits in a dusky mask. Then comes Florio, a smoking and blackened thing with a face that is no longer human. Fear and fire have given it a Gorgon look to frighten any stranger.

The cradle swings up for a moment, away from the house. They are lifted high. It is all spread out around them, the glorious sight of a house on fire, the dozens of vehicles, the blue lights whirling, the milling crowds. There is something to exult in here, something to send the spirit soaring. The night air is hot. The sky is stained with smoke, and no stars are visible. Florio clings to his daughters as the ladder swings them down, down, down.

KATHMANDU

"You have fractured the femur and the patella. You have also torn several of the medial and lateral ligaments in your knee. You're a doctor, so I'm sure you know what all that means?"

It meant a lot of pain, but she smiled tiredly up at the man. He was a tall, pleasantly ugly fellow with gentle eyes. He was patting the thick white tube that encased her left leg and kept it extended. It was attached to a weight that was going to imprison her in this bed for weeks.

She nodded. "A plaster cast and traction."

The Nepalese doctor smiled back at her. She knew now that his name was Mohan Singh, and that he was chief of orthopedics. "You are becoming yourself again. I am so glad. The traction will be necessary for at least three weeks. We don't want your leg flying to pieces, do we?"

"No," she said dutifully, a docile intern following some eminent professor doing the rounds. She could feel the medication working on the dark ache of the injury.

"You are also suffering from some minor frostbite." He sat beside her, checking his watch. Singh took her wrist and lifted her hand in front of her eyes. She was wearing white mittens. He pulled one off.

She considered her blackened fingers. They looked as though she had grasped fire with them. Her other hand was the same. "I see."

"You were lucky. That is a great blessing. We doctors cannot work without our fingers, can we?"

"No."

He saw her sniff the odd-smelling grease that had been smeared on her fingers. "As you can see, we're treating it with a special ointment. It's made with Tibetan yak butter. You won't find it in any Western pharmacopoeia," he added with a chuckle. "But we believe in Nepalese treatments for Nepalese problems."

"You're the doctor," Rebecca said. "You're giving me excellent care. I want to thank you for everything you've done."

Under the man's dark skin, she saw him flush with pleasure. "We will do our best for you," he said solemnly. He put the mittens back on her hands and touched her face. "There is a degree of frostbite around the mouth and nose. There will be a lot of peeling, and then you should be as comely as you ever were."

She did not smile at that archaic *comely*. The man was evidently enjoying practicing his excellent English. "Good."

He cleared his throat delicately. "Yesterday you were asking for your baby. That was a hallucination produced by trauma and drugs, yes?"

"It was a memory," she said quietly. "I had a baby, once. That was the last time I was in a hospital as a patient."

He looked embarrassed. "Oh, I see. But now you know why you are here? You can tell me the date, and that sort of thing?"

"I know why I'm here." She nodded.

"There was no organic trauma to the brain," he said. "No concussion, nothing like that. We checked very carefully. But of course, we do not have the equipment we would like to have."

She was suddenly icy-cold, and had started shivering violently. Singh pulled the blankets up around her shoulders and tucked her in like a concerned parent. "You are still in shock, Dr. Carey. Your body temperature drops suddenly from time to time. Would you like me to ask the nurse to bring you a hot cup of tea and an extra blanket?"

"Thanks, I'd love that."

"Your friend, Mr. Warren, is back on his feet. He asked me whether he could come and see you. Do you feel strong enough?"

She was silent for a while. She didn't feel ready to see Robert, yet. She was too angry with him. But there was no point in delaying the interview; Robert would probably be eager to leave Kathmandu.

"Yes," Rebecca said at last. "Tell him he can come."

"Excellent," Singh said cheerfully. He rose and left the ward.

She had warmed to Singh; he was doing everything in his power to make her comfortable. The hospital was modest, to put it charitably, by the standards Rebecca was used to. Its equipment was outdated, the structure flaking and dilapidated. On the wall in front of her, a crude, dog-eared poster in Nepali exhorted hygiene.

There were five other beds in this ward, all of them occupied. Dingy curtains separated the most seriously ill patients from the others. There was a large window in front of her bed. Conifers dripped heavily outside the window. She could see the tiered roofs of the Nyatapola temple rising above the town, the low mist clinging to the hills beyond. Somewhere in the scattered villages, something was burning; the plume of dun-colored smoke made a smear against the purity of the mist. Beyond that, the Himalayas rose, pitiless and stark.

The cast had been competently done. It was a basic, old-fashioned orthopedic procedure, well within the capabilities of this hospital. The X ray of her knee was still clipped to the board at the foot of her bed. She thought of the sweeping corridors of her own hospital in America, of the millions of dollars' worth of machinery, the tests they would have run on her.

The nurse came, bearing her tea. It was the color of blood and scaldingly hot. The brackish tannin taste seared her tongue, but she held the cup in both mittened hands and sipped obediently, wondering what Robert could find to say to her. All that needed to be said had already been said, up there on the mountain. But of course, Robert had the hide of an elephant.

"Rebecca?"

She looked up. Robert was shuffling into the ward, leaning on an aluminum crutch. His bandaged feet had been stuffed into Nepalese sandals.

He lowered himself gingerly into the chair that Singh had vacated and blew out his breath with an audible puff. His dark blue eyes met hers very briefly. His face had suffered from the wind. The tip of his nose was raw, his cheeks burned dark. His blistered lips moved in a rueful smile. "How's the knee?"

"Okay," she said shortly.

He lifted one bandaged foot. "I lost a couple of toe joints. Gonna take me some time to get my balance."

"That's too bad."

He waggled his foot proudly. "Something to show the grandchildren, huh?"

That was the way he saw things. To have come close to death was a matter of pride. She knew he had prepared something to say to her, but she was damned if she would make it easy for him. She kept silent.

"We both lucked out, didn't we?" he said.

"Is that what you think? You took pretty good care of yourself. *I* lucked out, considering you left me there to die."

He leaned forward. "No way did I leave you to die! We would never have made it, roped together. In a situation like that, each person has to move at their own pace. I unclipped the rope, because you kept falling, and you were endangering me. Then I led the way down."

"Oh, is that what you did? You 'led the way down'?"

He grimaced at her sulfuric tone. "Unclipping the rope gave you the motivation to make it back," he said sharply. "You've got me to thank for that."

"Oh, bullshit, Robert! You decided to save your own skin. I can understand that perfectly. But don't try to dress it up as some kind of noble deed. It was not."

"Would you rather we'd died together on the mountain? Would that have been better than making it back alive, separately?"

Black anger was boiling inside her. "I came to Nepal at *your* invitation. You're by far the more experienced mountaineer. You should have stayed with me. You cut the rope and ran, Robert. The only thing I don't understand is what you're doing here at my bedside, trying to rewrite history. You can't."

"When I was a kid," he said, in a different tone, "I was the smallest of three brothers. They taught me to swim by throwing me in the lake. Every time I made it to the shore, they'd throw me back in again. Until I learned not to drown."

"You've told me that story, Robert."

"They taught me to climb the same way," he went on. "They taught me everything the same way. We all do what's bred in the bone, Rebecca."

She no longer wanted to hear his voice, or look at him. She turned her face away from him. "You'd better go, Robert."

She heard him pull himself to his feet, heard his grunt of pain. "I'm sorry it turned out like this," he said at last. "Good-bye, Rebecca."

She listened to him shuffle away from her bed, his footsteps fading into the silence. Now she was on her own.

SAN FRANCISCO

"She didn't make it out of bed," Kendall commented.

"No, she didn't." Louise Steiglitz took a photograph of the site. The bed itself had been mostly made of nonflammable materials, and had only half collapsed. What lay on it was pathetic and familiar.

When Dr. Evan Brockman had thought of Louise Steiglitz, a year earlier, as a Valkyrie, he was doing her an injustice. She was a tawny blonde in her mid-thirties, and her figure was excellent, though more muscular than he liked. Strength was a useful attribute in her work.

This was the third time she had been called out to the Florio home.

The first time had been two years back, when a live-in member of the staff had been seriously burned in her bed, the result of falling asleep with a lit cigarette in her fingers. The disfigured woman had denied any guilt and had unsuccessfully tried to sue the family. Right now, Steiglitz was wondering about that cigarette.

The second time had been about a year ago, when one of the children had tried to incinerate her doll collection with a couple of gallons of gasoline. That had not resulted in any prosecution either, though it had been a strange case, with some unexplained anomalies.

This time, the fire had been more deadly. The modern back extension of the house was badly damaged, though the main Victorian structure was intact. A surgical fire, one might call it, which had accomplished its purpose swiftly and efficiently, without too much collateral mess.

All the other occupants of the house had been accounted for. The live-in staff had their own quarters in the other wing of the house. The two children, now heavily sedated and in the care of their father, had been sleeping in a guest bedroom. The reason was that their own bedroom was being redecorated. One of those weird coincidences that save or destroy lives, Steiglitz reflected; if they'd been in their own beds in the nursery at the back of the house, both would now be dead.

Steiglitz had already interviewed the two painters, and both had sworn blind that they had not been using blowtorches or hot-air guns to peel paint, nor a gas stove to melt gunk of any kind, nor left anything electrical plugged in when they went home at five. Earlier that day, the dog handler had combed through the wreckage with Alex, the specially trained black Labrador, who had sniffed in vain for traces of any accelerants like gasoline.

Judging by burn patterns and the wind, Steiglitz was prepared to bet the blaze had started somewhere right here, in what had been Barbara Florio's bedroom.

Steiglitz and her forensic assistant, David Kendall, had been crawling through the wreckage, taking photographs, occasionally slipping some minuscule bit of ash into a bag. There would be hundreds of such bags by the end of the investigation; but the real evidence, if there was any, would be found where the fire had started: somewhere like a crawl space, a closet, or under the floorboards.

She crouched beside the pathetic corpse. The winch had been used to lift heavy wreckage that had collapsed from the bathroom above. She had, Steiglitz was guessing, been dead before the flames had reached her flesh. Barbara Florio's body was intact, though heavily charred. A skilled autopsy would confirm that. It was difficult to tell exactly what position she had been in when she had died. As the ferocious heat had shriveled muscles and tendons, her limbs had flexed in that way characteristic of badly burned cadavers, and the body had writhed.

Louise Steiglitz peered at the face. She had seen too many such faces to be greatly horrified. But, as always, she felt pity. She remembered Mrs. Florio clearly from her last visit to this unlucky house: a handsome blonde who had overdosed right after the fire, and had to be taken to the hospital along with her daughters. Absolute identification was going to be by dental records. Nobody could be called in to recognize any human feature here.

She turned her attention to the hands. There were a couple of rings, which would also help. She made notes and took photographs. Then she looked closer, and felt a sudden cold wind touch her skin under the stifling asbestos coveralls.

The stick arms were raised in a praying-mantis position that was typical. But here they clutched something to the black washboard of a chest. Something that had been cremated along with Barbara Florio, but not completely destroyed, because part of it was made of ceramic.

"What the hell is this?" she muttered.

From the other end of the bed, David Kendall looked up. "Find something, Louise?"

Steiglitz used the end of her pencil to delicately probe the object. She teased aside leaves of incinerated material. Barbara Florio's clawed hands were brittle as twigs, and she took great care not to break them.

Then she saw what it was the burned woman clutched.

"Jesus," she said. "Come take a look at *this*."

KATHMANDU

"Dr. Carey? Are you awake?"

She had been dozing lightly. She lifted her head. The man was a Westerner, his slouch hat and parka dripping wet. It was raining heavily outside. "Hello?"

The man took off his hat, revealing gray hair and a weatherbeaten, red face with a dripping gray mustache.

"My name is Franklyn Barber. I'm with the U.S. Embassy here in Kathmandu. How are you doing?"

He held out a cold, wet hand, which she squeezed briefly. "I'm doing okay, thanks."

"That's great." Barber sat by her side. He put a plastic bag on Rebecca's bedside table. It contained some American magazines. "I thought you might like some reading material."

"That's very kind."

Yet another storm was gathering. It was swiftly becoming dark in the ward. The neon tube in the ceiling flickered on, washing out the colors of things. Rain slashed at the window. Thunder rumbled around the hospital. Her visitor waved his dripping hat at the plaster cast. "Comfortable?"

"If you like sleeping with a cannon in your bed." She smiled. "It's bearable."

"Good. I've been speaking to Dr. Singh. You're going to be staying in Kathmandu for maybe a month."

"I know that."

"It was bad luck and bad weather," Barber went on. "Summer blizzards materialize so fast. Every year people are lost."

Rebecca nodded again. "I was lucky."

"You sure were. Your parents have been in contact with my office. They're very concerned about you. Your father sent this for you in the diplomatic pouch this morning."

"Thank you." The bulky envelope felt heavy. She laid it on her bedside table.

Franklyn Barber studied her. Senator Carey's reach was a long one. He did not make a habit of visiting every injured American tourist in Kathmandu. "What we'd like to propose," he said, "is to transfer you to the International Clinic in Naxal today or tomorrow."

"I'm happy with the treatment I'm getting here," she said.

He looked surprised. "You'd have American doctors there. Much better facilities. This hospital is somewhat primitive. And you'd at least be with other Western patients. With this bad weather, the wards are full of climbers with frostbite, climbers with broken bones, climbers with hypothermia."

To Rebecca, it did not sound as appetizing a prospect as Barber obviously thought it was. She had no desire to be cooped up with the kind of rich socialites who bought ascents of Annapurna and Everest out of catalogs. "I'll think about it," she said. "Thanks."

"Our own medical officer took a look at you the day you were brought in. You probably don't remember. He tells me Singh is doing most of the right things."

"Dr. Singh is a good doctor," she said, disliking that *most*.

There was a glare of lightning. Simultaneously, the lights went out, leaving them all in the gloom. A shattering clap of thunder made the windows rattle. In the dark, Rebecca heard Barber's voice.

"I'd like to be able to send a message to your father today, Dr. Carey. Can I tell him you're doing fine? That you're happy with the medical treatment?"

It was so typical of her father to avoid direct contact, to use embassy staff to check on her. "Yes," she said. "You can tell him that. Thank you for coming to see me."

"No problem." Barber rose. He groped for her hand in the dark and said his good-byes.

SAN FRANCISCO

Michael Florio's immobility was so profound it denoted either total relaxation or electric tension. The trouble was, Detective Bianchi couldn't decide which.

There were contradictory signs. His tall, lean body was dressed in deep black, and she couldn't make up her mind whether that was mourning (according to friends, Florio was a devout Catholic) or some kind of decadent hip (according to enemies, the man had been heavily into drugs, alcohol, and depravity during at least some stages of his life). She had not yet seen him take off his Ray-Bans. Was that to hide eyes puffed with crying, or to help him lie? Either way, the black lenses never left the faces of the detectives who were interviewing him.

Carla Bianchi leaned next to the window, her back to the light. Her partner, Al Reagan, sat behind a cluttered desk. Florio was accompanied by legal counsel in the form of his attorney, Paul Philippi, who had a good, if sharp, reputation. The four people made the small interview room claustrophobic.

While Reagan held the floor, Bianchi was thinking that she would withhold judgment about whether Florio was the most interesting man she had ever seen until he took his shades off. It would be a sharp disappointment if the eyes revealed were mean or weak. The rest of his face was very strong, with a curving nose and a wonderfully cruel mouth. It was the sort of face that made you want to take it all on—the decadence and the devoutness, the malice and the compassion. This was a complex man, no question. He had an aura of authority that made him very different from the kind of interviewee she and her partner usually had in this room. He was neither cowed nor hostile. He had answered all their questions in a calm manner, although his prickly little lawyer had made a lot of objections.

"Mr. Florio," Al Reagan was saying, "our crime lab has been analyzing the burn patterns, and they're certain that the fire began in your wife's closet. A team has been examining every shred of evidence. The best answer we can come up with is that her clothing somehow caught fire on the hangers. Logically, it had to have been arson."

"Why is that logical, Detective Reagan?" the lawyer asked briskly.

"When a fire kills somebody, counselor, we label it suspicious right away. Unless we find evidence to the contrary. Like a short circuit, or a lightbulb too close to a shade. We found nothing like that here."

"But you haven't found any *positive* evidence?" Philippi asked.

Reagan shook his head. "Not yet."

"No device?"

"No."

"No traces of any accelerant, like gasoline?"

"Not yet. But fires can't start themselves." He turned back to Florio. "How come there have been so many fires in your family, Mr. Florio?"

"I wasn't aware that there had been." Florio had a deep, slightly husky voice.

"Well, let's take a look at the fire department records. They got a call-out last year, when your younger daughter set fire to her dolls, and burned down a garden shed. You recall that?"

"Oh, yes," Florio said. "The dolls." He seemed to be smiling faintly, dismissing the whole thing.

"A couple of months previous to that, she had been involved in another fire, hadn't she? Some cooking oil caught fire and there was nearly a nasty situation. You recall that?"

"Therese should never have been allowed to work in the kitchen unsupervised."

"Right. The year before, one of your staff, Carmen Pruneda, was badly burned when her bed caught fire. She sued you over that, didn't she?"

"Carmen Pruneda was a heavy smoker," Philippi cut in. "She fell asleep with a lit cigarette. Happens to thousands every year."

"She claimed she had given them up."

"Well, she wouldn't admit liability, would she?" Philippi said with a thin smile.

"And there was at least one previous fire that we know about. A family car burned out in the street in October three years back. A brand-new Mercedes. That makes five serious fires, Mr. Florio. One bad injury, one death, and a lot of destruction. Wouldn't you call that unusual?"

"You don't have to answer that, Michael," Philippi said.

Florio took his lawyer's advice and kept silent. His head was set at an arrogant tilt, and the deeply carved mouth still held that faint, ironic smile.

Bianchi saw him turn his wrist so that he could check his watch, some kind of ultrathin platinum contraption.

"The point we're making," Bianchi said quietly, "is that we have a background that would lead us to think arson now. This was a killer fire for three reasons. One, because it took hold in the early hours of the morning, when nobody was around. Two, because it spread fast. And three, because the victim was drugged."

"Drugged?" Philippi demanded sharply.

"You haven't seen the blood-analysis report?" Bianchi asked, feigning surprise.

"No," Philippi said curtly.

"It was sent out to you Thursday," Reagan lied easily. "Maybe it got held up in the mail."

"Held up?" Philippi glanced warily from one to the other. Both police officers were large, solid people. Carla Bianchi was happily married, a fundamentally caring person who saw her role as propping up a crumbling society. Al Reagan was acrimoniously divorced and fundamentally mean. He wasn't interested in propping up anything, just in arrests and convictions.

"Here." Bianchi rooted out copies of the lab report and passed them to Florio and his lawyer. Both men studied the photostat sheets. "We already knew that death was caused by smoke inhalation. Mrs. Florio was dead before the flames got to her. She didn't make it out of bed. She probably wouldn't have been able to. As you can see, these lab tests show a high blood-alcohol level, and high levels of . . ." She read carefully so as not to stumble over the names. "Amitriptyline, cyclobenzaprine, lorazepam, and diazepam. Do you recognize any of those names, Mr. Florio?"

"These all look like tranquilizers or antidepressants," Florio said, looking up from the sheet. "My wife was addicted to both."

"Uh-huh. The highest level is for cyclobenzaprine. See? Now, that's basically a muscle relaxant. We spoke with your wife's physician, Dr. Brockman, and that particular drug wasn't prescribed by him."

"My wife had a mix-and-match approach to drugs," Florio said. His hair had gotten singed in his rescue attempt, and he'd had to have a very short haircut as a consequence. It suited him. He wore several bandages on his hands. Beneath his black shirt and pants, Bianchi could see his body was constructed with the same dangerous, lean grace as his face. "People who do that develop an uncanny resistance to drugs. I know. I've been there."

She couldn't help pausing at the admission. "You've had a drug problem?"

"You could say that."

"Mind telling us which drugs?" Reagan asked.

"Amphetamines, alcohol, cocaine, heroin," Florio said easily. "You name it. I came back from Vietnam with a big monkey on my back."

"And a dozen medals on his chest," Philippi put in quickly. "This isn't relevant. Can we move on?"

"Just a moment," Reagan growled. "How long were you an addict, Mr. Florio?"

"I'm still an addict," Florio said silkily.

Reagan sat up sharply. "You still take drugs?"

"No. I kicked drugs years ago. But an addict is always an addict, Detective." He paused. "Just as an alcoholic is always an alcoholic."

Reagan, who had a drinking problem, looked sour at that. "How did you kick heroin, as a matter of interest?"

"I asked for help, and I got it."

"Are you talking religion or rehab?"

"Is there a difference?" There was dry amusement in the deep voice. Bianchi realized the interview had been derailed, and she tried to get it back on track.

"Your wife may have been resistant to drugs, Mr. Florio, but the effect of cyclobenzaprine at such a high dosage would have been hard to shrug off. It would have made her very sluggish. On top of the alcohol that was found in her blood, she probably couldn't move. Even if she wanted to. But she may have been aware of what was happening to her."

"That's terribly, terribly sad," Florio said. The husky voice had darkened impressively, like an actor's. Yet even as she felt gooseflesh prickle her arms, Bianchi was assessing the shadow of mockery in his tone. Was he playing with them, and letting them know it?

"There's an odd detail," she went on. She selected an eight-by-ten close-up from the postmortem file and walked forward. She held it out for Florio and his lawyer to see. "This shows an object we found clutched in Mrs. Florio's arms. Do you see what it is?"

She watched Philippi and Florio study the shot. Philippi turned his head on one side to get a better look.

"It looks like a doll," he said.

"That's right, Mr. Philippi, it *is* a doll. Do you recognize it, Mr. Florio?"

Florio seemed unmoved. "I don't believe I do."

"The head and limbs are made out of porcelain. The ceramic survived the blaze, though of course it's badly discolored, and the hair and clothes burned up. The whole thing was fused onto the rib cage by the intense heat." Bianchi used the tip of a pencil to indicate a detail. "This survived, too. It's a little medallion around the neck. It's inscribed."

At last, Florio reached up and took off his shades. His eyes were neither mean nor weak. They were black, arrogant, and disturbing. He was an incredibly handsome man. The hooded lids lifted slightly, so his gaze met hers. She felt her heart shift pace, despite herself. She held the photo closer to his face. "Maybe you can read it?"

Florio's eyes stayed on hers. It was Philippi who read it out. " 'Daddy to Therese, Innsbruck 1996.' You recognize this, Michael?"

"Now I do," Florio said, leaning back. "I bought it for my daughter during a vacation in Austria."

"Do you know where this doll was usually kept?" Bianchi asked.

"It was at my apartment. It was one of the few dolls that didn't get destroyed when . . ."

Reagan spoke. "When she burned the others?"

Florio turned his head. Now that the dark glasses were off, Bianchi saw that one of his cheekbones had been seared, high up. It was red and swollen. "Yes."

"Did you notice it was gone from its usual place?"

"No, I didn't. It was kept in a drawer."

"So why would your wife be clutching this when she died?"

"I have no idea."

"Maybe someone put it there? Some kind of sick joke?"

The attorney laid his hand on his client's arm to stop him from answering. "You don't need to reply, Michael."

Florio just shook his head. The faint smile was gone now. He toyed idly with his shades.

Al Reagan was getting irritated, and Bianchi could sense it. "You adopted Therese when she was a baby, right?"

"She was a week old."

"And you adopted your second daughter, Devon, later?"

"Yes."

"And she was older."

"She was a few months short of her sixth birthday." Florio's black eyes were fixed on Reagan. "Where is this leading?"

"It's just an inquiry, Mr. Florio. How long had you and your wife been separated?"

"Thirty-one months."

Bianchi noted the precision of the answer. "When were you planning to divorce?" she asked.

"When Therese and Devon were a little older."

"I would have thought a separation was just as difficult as a divorce for a child," she said.

"A divorce is a rather more permanent arrangement," he replied.

And death is the most permanent arrangement of all, she thought. "Were your daughters upset by the separation?"

Florio was silent for a while. "They both knew we didn't get along," he said at last.

"You fought with your wife?" she asked easily.

"We found it easier to separate," he said.

Her eyes were locked on Florio's. Al Reagan was watching intently. The little, dark lawyer was on the edge of his seat, obviously ready to cut in when his client put a foot wrong. "We've been questioning your wife's household staff, Mr. Florio. Their answers indicate that your wife had an unusual number of sexual partners after your separation. Were you aware of your wife's relationships with other men?"

"Yes," he said.

"Did that upset you?"

"No."

"Why not?"

"Why should it?"

"You might have been concerned for your daughters."

"They are my chief concern," he said, inclining his head.

"And do you think Devon and Therese were aware of their mother's relationships with other men?"

"Barbara was as open with our daughters as was appropriate with their understanding. I doubt whether her affairs hurt the girls."

"Did they hurt you?"

"I was not jealous," he said brusquely. But his dark eyebrows were brooding over the deep-set eyes now. The laid-back look was giving way to something more intense. She needed to keep up the pressure.

"You didn't mind who she slept with?"

"I made no effort to control her," he said, even more stiffly.

"Did she have affairs with any other men while you were still living together, Mr. Florio?"

"No."

"How can you be sure of that?"

Arrogance and anger tightened his face. "Our problems were not sexual, Detective. She didn't need to go looking for gratification elsewhere."

She smiled slightly, thinking, *You kept the little woman satisfied, huh? She didn't need lovers because you kept her purring.* Aloud, she asked, "If your problems weren't sexual, what were they?"

"They had to do with personal development."

"You developed, and she didn't?" she asked sweetly.

"We developed in different ways." There was a rasp in his voice. "We grew apart. There was never any strong antagonism between us."

"Nevertheless, you couldn't live together?"

"We decided to have separate households," he replied. "We still had a great deal in common."

"You still loved her, Mr. Florio?"

"I loved her, yes," he said deliberately. "And we both loved our daughters."

"I'm still not getting a good feel for why you separated," she said, giving him the smile again. "A three-year separation would suggest some serious incompatibility, wouldn't it?"

"Incompatibility, not hostility." He was glaring at her, a flush spreading across his cheeks. The burn was livid; the infusion of blood must be hurting like hell. "There was no anger on either side."

"Oh, come on, Mr. Florio. If you'll forgive me, that's most unusual."

"By your terms, perhaps. Not by mine."

The lawyer shook his slick head. "Detective Bianchi, I'm appalled at the way you and your partner are badgering my client," he said sadly. "It's heavy-handed and crude. Is it really necessary?"

Bianchi shrugged. This was no more than a discussion at present, with little legal weight. "These separate households you refer to: How did that work?"

"Barbara kept our family home in Pacific Heights. I moved out to an apartment in the city."

"And your daughters visited you there?"

"I had them most weekends. I also saw them almost every day. Devon and Therese attend a convent school in the city. I got away from work so we could meet for lunch every day at noon."

"Were they happy with that arrangement?" Bianchi asked.

"They accepted it. They're both very practical girls."

"In the event of your divorce, who would get final custody of your daughters?"

"We would probably have continued the same arrangement."

"If a divorce was in the cards, Mr. Florio, how would that leave you financially?"

Florio's patience was clearly running thin. "I don't understand."

"Don't you? Your wife was a very rich woman when you married her. She owned property worth tens of millions of dollars. I assume she helped you set up your business. So," she said in a honeyed voice, "I think it's a fair question. How would the divorce leave your personal finances?"

"There would be a fair division," Philippi broke in, forestalling his client. "You have no right to ask Mr. Florio to speculate on any of those issues. Don't answer, Michael."

Pompous little prick, Bianchi thought. She was forced to nod amiably. "We'll leave that issue. For the time being." She let the threat hang in the air. Philippi seemed unimpressed. He checked his heavy gold watch.

"Officers, Mr. Florio is still shocked and grieving. Can we bring this to a close?"

"You know all about sabotage, don't you, Mr. Florio?" Reagan said suddenly.

The lawyer grabbed his client's arm to keep him from answering, but Michael Florio jerked his arm hard, so that the lawyer's hand fell away. "Yes, I have some knowledge of sabotage. But that knowledge is over twenty years old."

"Mr. Philippi here says you were decorated in Vietnam."

"Yes, I was decorated," Florio said flatly.

"How many times, may I ask?"

"I don't recall."

"Your assignments involved unusual tasks, am I right?"

"There's very little that is unusual in a war," Florio said in a grim voice.

"Maybe I should have said *specialist* tasks."

"That would be a better description."

"What I'm talking about," Reagan pressed, "is sabotage, booby traps, that kind of thing. You did that?"

"Sometimes."

"Ever burn down somebody's house with your Zippo?"

"Wait, hold it," the attorney said quickly, half rising, as if in court. "Michael, don't respond to that outrageous remark!"

"It's okay," Michael Florio said. "No, I did not burn down anybody's house with a Zippo. I saw it done by others. What's your next question, Detective? Would you like to know whether I would have been capable of setting a fire that left no traces?"

Reagan's eyes narrowed. "Yes, I would like to know that. If you'd care to tell us."

"The answer is yes. Setting fires is not difficult. With one proviso."

"What's the proviso?"

"You would need to be capable of burning an innocent human being to death."

"You killed in Vietnam, Mr. Florio."

"So did tens of thousands of other young Americans." Florio was drumming on his thigh with lean fingers. His hands were beautiful, strong and precise. "I provide security for business premises, Detective Reagan. In some ways, my civilian work is a continuation of my military experience. I employ people who are trained and armed, *direct* people who are trained and armed."

"Detectives," Philippi said pompously, "I have to register my strongest objection to the content of your last few questions, and I'm not too happy about the tone, either. I'd like to draw to a close, now."

"One more question," Reagan said. "Mr. Florio, have you been talking to the press?"

"No."

"You've given no interviews?"

"None."

"Issued any statements?"

"No," Florio said flatly.

"I take it you've seen the tabloids yesterday and today?" Reagan growled.

"I never read the tabloids."

"But you must be aware of their content?"

Florio nodded slowly, his face hard.

Carla Bianchi glanced at her watch. She did not believe that Reagan was getting anywhere, and Philippi would soon insist on getting his wealthy client out of here. "We'd like to thank you for coming to see us today, Mr. Florio," she said briskly. "There's one last matter. We'd like your permission to speak to your daughters. In your presence, of course, and in the presence of any professional person you'd like to call in."

Florio's eyes met hers. Their impact was almost physical. She had a sense of an alien, unfathomable personality, of a man who might be capable of many things to get his own way. "Not a chance," he said flatly.

She showed no disappointment. "That's your privilege. But in that case, we'd like to suggest that both girls talk to a psychiatrist, Dr. Helen Brancepeth. She's an associate clinical professor of medical psychology at the university. She advises both this department and the fire department, and she's also very experienced with adolescents. Both girls are traumatized by what happened. They need to talk about it to a professional, and Dr. Brancepeth will be able to help them start coming to terms with it."

The attorney held up his hand. "Hold it, Michael. Detectives, I want a moment in private with my client, before he answers."

"Sure."

The two detectives switched off the desk tape recorder and left the room, closing the door behind them. They walked down the corridor together to the atrium, Bianchi carrying her briefcase.

"What do you think?" Reagan asked at the ice-water dispenser.

His partner lifted the cold paper cone to her lips. "He was shaken by the doll thing."

"You think so? I think he was faking it."

"I don't know. Did you see the way he balled his hands up when you asked about Therese's mental state?"

"That was faking. He and Philippi had the whole scene planned. They were way ahead of us."

"So what do *you* think?" she asked warily.

"Barbara Florio had all the money. He knew he was in for a rough ride when they divorced. Without her financial backing, who knows? Maybe she was going to leave him high and dry. She was also going to get the kids. When she died, he got back his manhood, kept his kids, and got to keep all the money. Not bad for one flick of a Zippo, huh?"

"So what are you saying?"

"I think he set some kind of device," Reagan replied, "knowing we would put the blame on his daughter. I think he deliberately fed all those stories to the tabloids yesterday."

Bianchi dug in her briefcase and pulled out two tabloid newspapers. Both had pictures of Therese on the front page. "You really think he'd let his thirteen-year-old take the rap for this?"

"Oh, sure. He thinks we wouldn't even bring an investigation against Therese. He's betting we'll just shut the case, rather than face indicting a kid. And if she does have to take the rap, and winds up in psychiatric care for the rest of her life—hey, she's only adopted."

"Florio strikes me as tough, but not a monster."

"You and me have seen a lot of monsters who look just like plain folks, Carla." Reagan took the newspapers from her, and studied the headlines, which screamed that Therese Florio had burned her mother to death. He wiped his mouth with a handkerchief. "You're telling me you'd rather believe a thirteen-year-old girl deliberately torched her mother?"

"No," she said reluctantly. "But I could believe in an accident, a wild prank that went wrong. Maybe she didn't know her mother was so stoned. She's already had a couple of goes at burning down the family. Not to mention torching a brand-new Merc."

"Exactly." Reagan took out a pack of Camels and offered her a cigarette, but she shook her head. "What better smoke screen could he have?" he asked, exhaling. "He has two daughters. One's doing great. The other one's crazy. He kills his wife and dumps the crazy one. It makes sense, Carla. I know it and you know it."

"Florio's been separated from his wife for nearly three years."

"O.J. Simpson was separated from Nicole for two years before she was killed."

"O.J. was acquitted."

He gave her a dry look. "Don't remind me." They both knew the lab team was working intensively, but neither had much hope the forensic evidence would amount to much. And even if it did, recent history had shown how easily an eloquent legal team could derail a forensic case.

"He says he loved his wife."

"Yeah, he was crying his eyes out, back there."

"He's certainly very calm."

"That's one way of putting it. How about 'callous'?"

"Maybe he's psychotic," she mused, still trying to assess that dark, un-fathomable personality. "If he's kicked multiple-drug addiction, he's im-pressively self-controlled."

"And maybe he hasn't kicked it, and maybe he's stoned out of his head behind those Ray-Bans."

"Finish your cigarette," she said dryly.

The atrium was the only place in the building where smoking was permitted. Reagan took several hungry drags on his Camel before pushing it into an ashtray. They walked back up the corridor and waited near the interview room. The door opened at last and the swarthy attorney invited them in.

As they entered the interview room, Bianchi saw that Florio's striking good looks were somewhat marred by a blur of tiredness. There were shad-ows under his eyes, and harsher lines around the mouth. He was touching the raw, red burn on his cheek, as though it was hurting him.

She settled herself behind the desk, opposite Florio, and switched the tape recorder back on. "Mr. Florio, I'm repeating our request that you allow your daughters to be interviewed by Dr. Helen Brancepeth. Have you made your mind up?"

She was absolutely convinced the man would refuse, so she was startled when he nodded. "Yes. I agree."

"Thank you," she said, showing no triumph. "When could they be available? Is Thursday afternoon too soon?"

"Thursday afternoon is acceptable."

"The interviews must take place at Mr. Florio's home," Philippi put in briskly. "He insists on being present. And so do I. We'd also like to bring a psychiatrist of our own."

Bianchi leaned back in her chair. "That's not an interview, it's a sym-posium. With all due respect, I'd like to request that Dr. Brancepeth be allowed to speak to your daughters alone, individually, for no more than forty minutes each. The interviews could take place at your home, and you could be in the house—but not in the same room. I promise you, that will be a lot less traumatic for your girls than some kind of group meeting."

Florio considered. Philippi was obviously itching to put in his two cents' worth, but Florio did not consult the attorney. At length, he nodded. "Very well. I'll tell the girls to be ready."

Bianchi smiled. The man's best and worst responses were all connected with his daughters. *Whatever you did*, she thought, *you did for them, didn't you?* "That's great." She rose, extending her hand to him. "Good-bye, and thank you." His hand gripped her own with unexpected force, almost as though he were telling her something, though she did not know what. As he turned away, his grasp left her fingers tingling.

KATHMANDU

Mohan Singh came to see her early the next morning. The nurses had already checked her blood pressure and heart rate, but he repeated the checks himself.

It was breakfast time, and most of the visitors had brought pots of food for their relations. Smells of asafetida, cumin, and coriander wafted from other beds. "Are you not hungry?" he asked.

"There is kind of a rumbling down there." She smiled.

"The custom in Nepal," he said apologetically, "is for patients' families to bring in food for them. You have no one to bring you food, I suppose?"

"No."

"We have only a very basic catering service, I'm afraid. If you were to transfer to one of the Western clinics, you would be brought food three times a day."

"I'm content to stay here."

"If you like," he suggested, "I could arrange for an outside caterer to prepare food for you. It would not be very expensive. They would, of course, be Nepali-style meals."

"That's very kind of you. Yes, I'd be happy with that."

"Any questions?"

She could not help wondering whether she had already been infected with one of the strains of hepatitis that were endemic in Nepal. Like all the others, she had taken a gamma-globulin shot, along with vaccinations against polio, cholera, typhus, and paratyphoid, before coming to Nepal. But that gave only limited protection, and any one of the medical procedures she had been through in this hospital might have infected her.

"Yes?" he prompted gently.

"I'm a little concerned about hepatitis," she said.

He looked shocked. "Not in my hospital," he said firmly. "We have no hepatitis here, Dr. Carey. All our staff are regularly screened, and our procedures are par-*tic*-ularly diligent. Please believe me."

She smiled, believing him. "Thank you."

"Thank *you*," he said briskly, evidently piqued. "Now I will see about your food." He hurried off.

She had tried not to assume patronizing Western attitudes. But she knew that Nepal had no more than a thousand doctors in all, less than five thousand hospital beds. It was one of the poorest countries in the world, rich only in mountains, which drew people from every quarter of the globe to crawl up that indifferent vastness, and touch the face of God. Or die.

As he hurried away from her bed, Mohan Singh was thinking about Rebecca. She was an intriguing curiosity: not just a fellow doctor, but a woman. And not just a woman, but a fascinating woman.

Mohan Singh was no great judge of Western beauty—at least, not of the Hollywood kind, which favored blue eyes, blond hair, and yellow skin, all of which he found off-puttingly artificial. However, this woman had soft, dark hair, and her eyes were a gentle, deep gray. She looked inward, and considered her own soul, and that was a quality he found rare in Westerners. Her mouth was full, not merely full in form, and generous to kiss or smile, but full of emotion. It was shaped like a leaf, calm, yet waiting to unfold with feeling.

She was thirty years old. He had seen the muscles that lay beneath the fine skin. The thighs, the back, and the stomach were smooth and strong. Her hands were strong, too, with tapering fingers and short nails, hands he at once had recognized as a doctor's hands. They were hands made for healing, like his own.

And despite all her strength, there was a softness to make a man's senses swim, a curve of breast and hip, a deep dip of the navel, a fullness of the dark nipples.

Rebecca was not sure why she had not jumped at Barber's offer to transfer her to a Western clinic. Perhaps the reason was something to do with Singh himself. The things he said touched her. *Nepalese treatments for Nepalese problems.* That had made sense to her. She would stay here for the time being, at any rate.

The lights had not come on again last night before she had fallen asleep, and she hadn't opened the package Barber had brought her. She reached out now, and opened it. It contained a drugstore package with Tylenol, antidiarrhea pills, antiseptic cream, and a whole slew of other medicines appropriate for foreign parts. Her father's share of the care package. From her stepmother, there were two pop-psychology paperbacks about how to feel better than well. There was no letter. She and her parents rarely communicated with words these days. A bottle of Tylenol was much less controversial.

She repacked all the unwanted medicines. Dr. Singh might find some of them useful. She reached for the copy of *Time* Barber had brought, and flicked it open, seeking distraction.

She read idly for a few pages, not much interested in last week's news. And then she saw a face and a headline that sent her heart surging into overdrive.

Rebecca tried to sit up, her eyes raking the first sentences of the brief article. Her eyes flicked back, reading them again and again, as though she could not get any further. She felt something was crushing her chest, stopping her from breathing.

"Oh, my God," she whispered. *"Oh, my God."*

SAN FRANCISCO

Dr. Helen Brancepeth took a scoop of chamomile tea from a little wicker contraption like a tiny cage, and dipped it in her painted Japanese mug of boiled water.

"I'm finding this case interesting," she told the two detectives. "Mr. Florio is aggressive in defense of his daughters. Which is perhaps natural, but not very helpful. He walked into the room at exactly the forty-minute point. He wouldn't hear of the encounters being extended. And he made it a precondition that no video or tape recording take place."

"Whatever the truth is, he doesn't want us to find it," Reagan said.

"Maybe not," Dr. Helen agreed, examining her chamomile tea with a critical eye. Unlike many of her colleagues, she had always disliked the title "Professor," which she thought sounded too remote. She preferred to be called Dr. Helen. She not only advised the San Francisco Fire Department and sheriff's department, she had headed a prestigious ATF arson-profiler program in the wake of the huge fires that had ravaged Southern California in recent years. But her real interest lay in the children, adolescents, and young people who so often set fires, rather than in the crime itself. And when she approached those patients, it didn't help to be called Professor Brancepeth. Dr. Helen was a lot easier.

The meeting was taking place in her office. Dr. Helen, a spry and yogic fifty-five-year-old, favored large brown corduroy beanbags, rather than chairs. Bianchi didn't mind too much, but Reagan found them uncomfortable and somehow demeaning. He sprawled awkwardly. His partner nestled slightly more happily into her own sack of beans. Only Dr. Helen looked relaxed as she went down into an enviably effortless lotus position.

"So you got somewhere in your meetings with the girls?" Bianchi asked hopefully. They had heard rumors that the interviews had been dramatic in some way, and she was eager for news.

Dr. Helen gave a little secret smile, which made Bianchi's spirits rise. "Well, both the Florio girls are traumatized by their mother's death," she told them. "Which meant it was difficult to push the pace. And I have to admit I took little relish in probing. But there were results." She reached for her notebook. "Shall we get under way?"

"Go ahead."

"Let me start by giving you my initial take on the two girls." Dr. Helen flipped a page. "I talked to Devon first, then to Therese. There's a very noticeable difference in affect between the two. Devon is fifteen, and physically almost an adult. Yet there's something rather endearingly girlish about her. She struck me as a very balanced young person, in no great hurry to grow up. She's enjoying her teenage years, not a very common thing, as you'll probably agree."

Al Reagan grunted, thinking of his own teenage children, now strangers to him. "I'll say."

"Devon is not hankering after an adulthood that is beyond her reach. She's content to be where she is. She knows adulthood brings responsibility and pain, and she's in no hurry to reach it. She's very poised, far more so than her sister. She's articulate, friendly, open. We were able to discuss almost all the aspects of her mother's death. She did her level best to answer my questions, and talk about what had happened, but now and then broke down in tears, despite herself.

"In many ways, Therese is the reverse of Devon. A dark mirror image, if you like. The grieving was quite different. Devon was horrified by the loss of a beloved parent, but there was no rage. Therese Florio reacted with anger or bitterness to almost all of my approaches. There's a fierce quality to her grief that's very distinctive. She is almost overwhelmed with rage about what has happened."

"Rage against who?" Reagan demanded.

"I was coming to that. Therese is a clever girl, but she's a poor communicator. I think of such children as 'blocked.' For one reason or another, normal means of expressing themselves are blocked off to them. So they choose other means, occasionally very violent means. They hurt themselves and others in the process. Therese expresses herself so badly, and her anger gets so much in the way of communication, that it's hard to understand her. Both girls were adopted, as you know. Therese was adopted first, as a newborn baby. Her mother was a single teenager who didn't want the child, and the adoption was handled by a reputable agency. Devon is older by two years. She was adopted later, when Therese was already four. Devon's mother was also single, but she had cared for Devon until she succumbed to cancer. A form of leukemia. She died when Devon was almost six, and there was nobody in the family prepared to look after her. Her legal guardian, an aunt, put Devon up for adoption, and the Florios took her right away. So we have Devon, aged six, joining the family when Therese is four. Clear?"

"Right," Bianchi said.

"Devon, of course, has always known that she is an adopted child. She retains some strong memories of her real mother. Therese first confronted the issue when Devon came into the family. It was then that the Florios began to explain to her, in simple terms, that she was not their biological child. This was a severe shock for Therese. She had to face the whole issue of adoption at the same time as accepting the arrival of a sibling. And not a baby sibling: an older, more developed, dominant sibling. Therese may have already been suffering from what we call attachment disorder, a deep sense of rejection that may even start in the womb. Such children often believe that, if they were given up once, they can be given up again. Therese, at four, certainly showed a lot of indicators. She threw sharp objects around. She spent the nights roaming inside and even outside the house. She broke things. This is a pattern we know can lead to extremely violent, uncontrollable adults. Okay, so far?"

"Sure." Bianchi nodded. Reagan was not bothering to take notes. He was apparently studying Dr. Helen's collection of snarling African masks.

"Therese's rage has multiple targets. She's been angry with Barbara Florio for a long time, probably since Devon arrived. Now she's angrier than ever. She feels her mother brought her death on herself."

"Did she say that in those words?" Reagan asked.

"She is angry with her mother because she blames her drug and alcohol abuse for what she calls the accident. She says her mother's lifestyle killed her. She also claims that her mother has been intermittently abusive for years."

"Abusive in what way, exactly?" Reagan wanted to know.

"She referred to punishments that she thought had been exaggerated, even cruel. She claims their mother beat both girls savagely during drug or alcohol binges. With a belt, shoes, whatever came to hand. I asked Devon about that, but Devon said it was more bark than bite, and that their mother never physically harmed either of them."

"So which one is lying?"

"Maybe neither of them. This issue of abuse is a two-edged sword. Violent children often have to be restrained violently. It starts being hard to see who is abusing whom. Excuse me."

Dr. Helen rose from her beanbag to refill her Japanese mug at her desk. She was so slim that she barely made a bulge in her Levi's or cotton shirt, a sparrow-light woman who seemed about to take flight at any moment. She drifted back down onto her beanbag.

"Okay," she continued. "Therese is also angry with her father, though in a different way. In part, she seems to feel that her father's absence was an additional cause for her mother's death. In other words, her mother would still be alive if her father had been there to prevent the accident. In general, she blames most of her own misconduct on her father's leaving home. Therese prefers to think her delinquency dates from then, though there's clear evidence she's always been difficult. She feels her father prefers Devon because Devon is a high achiever, articulate, and never gets in trouble. And she recognizes that she has been very destructive."

"You mean, she feels guilt?" Reagan asked.

"She certainly feels guilty about things she's done in the past. We talked about the previous fires, especially the time she burned her doll collection. She got very agitated. I asked her directly why she had done that, and she responded in the most interesting way." Dr. Helen showed them her secret smile. "Her head shot back, as though she were in a hangman's noose. Her eyes rolled back till only the whites showed. Her teeth were clenched tight. Her whole body went into a state of rigid shock, her arms flexed, her fingers clawed."

Bianchi had a harrowing flashback to Barbara Florio's charred corpse. "How long did that last?"

"About a minute or two," Dr. Helen replied.

"Does this mean Therese is mentally ill?"

"It's certainly a disorder," Dr. Helen agreed. "How serious depends on many factors. Therese's obsession with dolls is interesting. Children use dolls for many reasons, especially to act out role-play. For many children who feel threatened and helpless in a world they cannot control, dolls become actors in a psychic theater, a world in which they can make things happen the way they want them to happen. Therese may have burned her doll collection as a response to her parents' separating."

"Would you say Therese Florio was expressing murderous aggression when she did that?" Reagan asked.

"Let me go on a little way, please. This fit took place around thirty minutes into the interview, which meant I only had ten minutes left. And as I said at the outset, I took little relish in subjecting these children to any unnecessary stress. But I knew I had very little time, and that the father would probably not be sympathetic to a further interview. So in that time, I approached the issue of the mother's death. Again Therese grew very agitated, crying and raging, but without losing consciousness. The key question seemed to relate to the doll that was found in the corpse's arms. I asked her directly if she knew how that doll had come to be there."

"And she threw another fit, right?" Reagan asked, his face intent.

Dr. Helen smiled thinly, not pleased at having her thunder stolen. "This spasm was more violent. The head went back as before, with rolling eyes and the tendons of the neck strained. The hands curled into claws, and the whole body twisted sideways, so that she slid out of the chair onto the floor."

Bianchi pictured the scene, feeling sicker and sadder than ever. "Did she come out of it, like before?"

"It was more intense and longer-lasting. When she clenched her teeth, she bit her tongue rather badly. There was quite a lot of blood. I had no option but to try and make the girl comfortable, and then call the father. He came into the room with Devon."

"I bet he was in a great mood," Reagan said.

"He was very angry," Dr. Helen replied. "He was also frightened. He and Devon took Therese in their arms and nurtured her, kissing her and murmuring to her. He told me she'd been having seizures like this since her mother's death. After a while, Therese relaxed and started to sob, clinging to her sister. I prepared to leave." Dr. Helen studied her notebook carefully. "But there was a final, arresting development. Therese started to shout. Much of what she was saying was incoherent. But several phrases were quite distinct. One was 'I thought she would wake up.' That was repeated at least three times."

"Jesus," Bianchi said quietly.

The psychiatrist was reading her notes. "She also said 'I didn't mean it,' several times. Then she pulled away from her sister, and grabbed her father by the arms. She spoke very fast, almost screaming. What she said was, 'I thought she'd wake up. I didn't mean to kill her.' She repeated several of those phrases, or variations of them."

There was a prolonged silence. "What did Florio do?" Bianchi asked at last.

"He was badly shaken," Dr. Helen replied. "He turned on me with a great show of anger, and asked me to leave. But I think he was covering up his own dismay."

"Could he have been acting?" Reagan suggested.

"Of course."

Bianchi spoke quietly. "Doctor, would you say that Therese admitted her guilt?"

Dr. Helen studied the faint dregs of her chamomile tea. "Yes, I think so. As I said, what I really need is a great deal more time with both girls. I think it would help if we could get both of them away from their father for a week or ten days. He is a big obstacle to communication. We need to put them in some tranquil environment and just let me talk to them. Dig deep enough to get at the truth. Is that possible?"

"We could ask Social Services to intervene," Bianchi said. "The girls could certainly be considered as being in serious danger."

"We gotta get this rolling," Reagan added grimly, "get a motion to compel Florio to give the girls up. With what we have so far, I don't think there'll be any problem."

Reluctantly, Bianchi nodded agreement.

•   •   •

When the two detectives got back to their office, an hour and a half later, they found Joshua Wong, one of the sheriff's department investigators, awaiting them.

"Florio sure spun you a load of crap," he said without preamble.

"What do you mean?" Reagan demanded.

"Practically every statement on that tape is a lie," Wong said. "Michael Florio and his wife had an adversarial relationship that spilled over into violence on more than one occasion. They fought bitterly over the daughters. By the way, did you know they were both adopted?"

"Yes," Carla Bianchi said. "Go on."

Wong was pulling a finger out of his closed fist to count off each lie Michael Florio had told them. He moved on to the next finger. "Florio behaved violently to at least one of his wife's friends after they separated. A Catholic priest named Father Timothy Dean."

"A priest?"

"Father Dean filed a complaint against Florio last year, trying to get a restraining order stopping Florio from coming near him. He accused Florio of threatening him."

"With a weapon?"

"He threatened to break the priest's back over his knee."

"Go on."

"Mrs. Florio was planning on making a very large donation to the church, through Dean. Dean claimed Florio was trying to scare him off. Florio said in judge's chambers he didn't care what his wife gave away."

"Did Mrs. Florio testify?"

"No," Wong said. "Florio made a statement, voluntarily agreeing not to go near Father Dean. The judge was satisfied by that. He ruled that Dean was in no danger from Florio. But Florio had no control over what his wife gave away, in any case. Mrs. Florio was getting ready to file for divorce in the last couple of months before her death. Her lawyer is prepared to discuss some of the details, but not all. Financially speaking, Florio was a cipher in the marriage. Practically everything belonged to her, either because it was hers before the marriage, or by prenuptial contract." Wong smiled cynically. "The prenuptial contract looks like *Webster's Encyclopedia,* by the way. All the property was hers, all the investments, the vehicles, the boat, you name it. Even his business premises were in her name, because it was her money that allowed him to start the company. Florio would have gotten nothing. Zilch. He'd have been cleaned out. In spite of the fact that his company is apparently very successful."

"What'd I tell you?" Reagan gloated to Bianchi.

"And get this," Wong said. Another finger. "That drug they found in the victim? The muscle relaxer?"

"Yeah?"

"It was never prescribed for Mrs. Florio. But Florio goes to a sports doc at his club, a man named Ian MacIver. Dr. MacIver says he prescribed a course of the stuff for Florio two months ago, to treat a sports injury. We checked: Florio had his pharmacist fill the prescription, fifty tablets. More than enough to account for the levels in the deceased."

Bianchi and Reagan looked at each other. "Well, I'll be," Reagan said.

"Yes." Bianchi nodded. "But all he needs to say is that he took the whole course. Period."

"Ah, but here's the thing," Wong said with relish. "According to MacIver, Florio hates taking drugs. He has a kind of fetish about it. MacIver specifically asked Florio, 'If I prescribe these, will you take them?' and Florio said yes. So he went ahead and gave Florio the prescription. Florio said he would take them. But MacIver remembers being skeptical."

"Florio's a former addict," Reagan said. "He wouldn't take psychoactive drugs lightly."

"I hate this kind of thing," Bianchi said. "It doesn't cut much ice with juries, and it gives defense lawyers a field day."

But Reagan was grinning like a hound dog. "He would have kept those pills at his apartment, right? So we need to know if he still has them. If he doesn't, then he probably ground them up in his wife's bedtime brandy." He turned to Bianchi, surly face triumphant. "What about that? You still think little Therese did it? Looks like Daddy was the bogeyman all along, doesn't it?"

"Maybe." Bianchi sighed. "I still have problems with that."

"Why, for Christ's sake? What kind of illusions do you have about this guy?"

She thought. "Well, for one thing, the way he got his kids out of that fire was pretty heroic, Al. If he cared about them enough to put his life on the line saving them, would he have put them in such danger to start with? And if he gave her the overdose, he could have just left her to die in her sleep, choke on her vomit, whatever. We wouldn't even be investigating right now. Burning a house down is a crazy way to kill someone."

"Arson's a favorite tool, Carla. You know that. It's the only crime that destroys its own evidence. And it's very cute timing that he arrived just in time to save the kids, but not his wife. He had that alarm rigged so he would be the first to know if there was a burglary or a fire. How do we know it didn't call him just fifteen minutes before it called the fire department? How do we know he didn't have the whole thing planned like a military engagement? He was a soldier, a saboteur."

Carla Bianchi nodded slowly. "We need to nail down the motive, Al. All we've got is a mishmash of ill feeling."

"We'll get him," Reagan vowed. "We'll get him."

"When will you question Florio again?" Wong asked.

"Day after tomorrow," Reagan said brightly. "The coroner released her body yesterday. The funeral's tomorrow. We see him the next day."

KATHMANDU

"There is no possible way the treatment can be speeded up," Dr. Mohan Singh said firmly. "The cast has to stay on. You're a doctor, you know that as well as I do. As for your making the journey back to America in this condition, it's out of the question. You might destroy your knee, and have to walk with a stick the rest of your life." Mohan Singh had polished his

English in conversation with Rebecca, and was proud of his fluency. They were on first-name terms already, and he felt they were becoming friends. Her present agitation upset him. "What on earth is the problem? Do you not have faith in the treatment?"

"It's not that."

"Why, then, are you so anxious to get back to America?"

She was silent for a moment. "Mohan, thirteen years ago, I had a child. I was just seventeen. I felt I couldn't keep her, so I put her up for adoption. Now, something terrible has happened to her, and I must go to her."

Singh sat. "You were married?" he asked.

"No. I married later on. Not the father of my child; I married another man, a surgeon, and it didn't last long. But when I had my baby, I wasn't even an adult."

"And what has happened to your child?"

"Her adoptive mother has been killed. In a fire."

Singh's almond eyes were grave. "That is very bad."

"It's horrible. Worse than you can imagine." Rebecca lifted the copy of *Time* and held it out. "There have been other fires." Her hand was shaking, and her voice was unsteady. "Serious fires. The tabloids are saying my daughter is a pyromaniac. They're saying she killed her mother." She couldn't speak anymore, her throat was too tight.

Singh took the magazine and read the article slowly. When he had finished, he took off his glasses and looked at her somberly. "What are you going to do?"

"I have to go to her."

"But what can you possibly achieve?"

"I can comfort her," Rebecca said. Despite her self-control, her gray eyes were swimming with tears.

"Do you think they will give her back to you?"

"No, I don't think that. I just think she needs me *now*. She has no mother, and they're going to crucify her."

Singh's heart was heavy. He had hoped she might remain in Kathmandu for at least part of her physiotherapy. He hoped that his understanding of her, limited as it was by doctor-patient etiquette, could grow and deepen.

Now he feared that his dreams were empty. Now he knew that there would be no convalescence in Nepal, no tender romance in the autumn. She would rush back home, on crutches if need be, as soon as the cast was taken off. "Your arrival at the present juncture might do more harm than good."

"It might. But I believe I can help."

"Does this girl know who you are?"

"I don't know," Rebecca said. "I doubt it. Arrangements were made to cut me out of the picture. I'm legally prevented from ever approaching her without the adoptive parents' permission."

"In that case, how are you going to make your approach?"

"I don't know. I'll work that out."

"And if the child *is* responsible for this terrible crime?" he asked. "Are you going to her so you can shoulder some of her guilt?"

Her face became grim, in a way he had never seen before. "Guilt?" she repeated harshly. "Mohan, if a thirteen-year-old girl does something like this, it's because she has been systematically traumatized for years. Not because of some genetic, inborn *taint*."

Singh moved his head in a way that might signify either agreement or disagreement. "You imply that your child might have been abused in some way. But if this Mr. and Mrs. Florio wanted children enough to adopt, one can assume they would be good parents."

She made a slight movement with her shoulders. "Maybe they wanted children for darker reasons. Abnormal reasons."

He was lost in thought. "Did your family make you put her up for adoption?"

"No. The decision was mine alone. I made it long before she was born. I wanted to be a doctor. I had ambitions for my life. I didn't want those ambitions thwarted."

"And the child's father?"

"He felt the same way."

"Did you love him?" Singh asked.

"Oh, yes. Ryan is a wonderful person. He was very unhappy about the decision. We both were. But what happened was an accident, in all senses. He didn't want to get married any more than I did. Not then. He was even more ambitious than I was. When I got pregnant, we both knew that neither of us wanted marriage or children for a long, long time. The decision to put the baby up for adoption was mutual."

"Do you still see him?"

Rebecca paused. "I haven't seen him in years. He went into pediatrics. He got married some years ago, about the same time I did. I don't know if they had any children."

"He chose the same field as you?"

She smiled painfully. "Maybe his mind worked the same way mine did. Who knows?"

"Don't you think you should talk to him?" Singh asked delicately.

"To Ryan?"

"He is the girl's father. And you say you once loved him."

Rebecca shook her head without answering. Ryan had written to her, a long and passionate letter, some years earlier. He had married and divorced, and was now working in a children's hospital in Monterrey, Mexico. He had wanted to see her again. Between the lines of his letter, she had read the continuing depth of his feelings for her. He had spoken of the terrible mistakes they had made, of their need to repair the wounds of the past.

But that letter had arrived practically on the eve of her own marriage to Malcolm Burns. She had written back to him, in neutral terms, unwilling to revisit that painful territory again. She had wanted to give him the message that she was trying to find happiness and rebuild her life, with another man. She knew she had succeeded in passing on that message. She had not heard from him since.

Singh had been studying her. Her eyes were clear now; she was neither self-pitying nor sentimental. "Did you meet the adoptive parents, this Mr. and Mrs. Florio?" he asked.

"I only met the woman."

"Not the husband?"

"No."

"So you knew next to nothing about them?"

"The agency people had checked them out very carefully. They vouched for the Florios. It was a reputable agency. Ryan and I searched long and hard to find one that we could really trust."

"And you never saw your child again?"

"No."

"That would be abnormal in our society. We are open about such things. There are many, many adopted children in Nepal. Such children are always told who their biological parents are. In most cases, they see them every day, and know all about them."

Rebecca grimaced slightly. "That's very commendable, Mohan. Our society is a little different. We cover the whole thing with a veil. It's called confidentiality."

He was clearly repelled. "What good does that do? There is no shame in such things."

"To us, there is. Besides, this was thirteen years ago, and confidentiality was the norm. The agency took legal steps to make it hard for me or Ryan to reappear in the child's life. We signed a document agreeing that we would have no access to the child. We also agreed that we would never approach the child without their prior consent. They didn't even want us to know who the new parents were, but I insisted on meeting the mother. I wanted to know whom Therese was going to. The original birth records were sealed. Only a court order can open them. New records were issued, telling the world that our child was born to the Florios. A lot of other things were done to cut off the way back."

"Were you given counseling at the time?"

"Nobody mentioned it," she said dryly. "Basically, Ryan and I counseled each other. Which meant we cried a lot. The focus was on the adoptive couple. The agency people always spoke of them as their *clients*. Ryan and I weren't clients. We were simply a means of production, and our baby was the product."

"That was very destructive." Singh's pager was beeping insistently. He was normally very proud of this device, but now he switched it off impatiently as he rose. "We'll talk later." He leveled a stern finger at her. "No getting up, Rebecca. Your knee will not stand the strain. Possess your soul in patience."

She watched him walk away, her mind still locked in the past. Therese had been eight days old when she and Ryan Foster had given her away.

What Rebecca now knew was that she and Ryan had signed away rights they should have kept. They had condemned themselves to an emotional limbo, assuming that they would forget their child, when in fact they would be haunted by the memory of that child for the rest of their lives.

If she had insisted on some access to her child, it would have been infinitely better for all of them. Instead, she had buried a bomb in her own heart, and in the heart of her child. Had that bomb finally exploded in San Francisco? She had been unable to confess that awful fear, even to kindly Mohan Singh.

For years she had seen her child in dreams. In those dreams, the child cried out to her in grief and anger, accusing Rebecca of having stolen her identity. The pain of that was unbearable.

Rebecca had studied to become a pediatrician. Her wide reading told her that her child had a very good chance of finding out the truth, even if the adoptive parents made it a secret, and that such a discovery could be very destructive. It might produce, at the least, an unresolved question that would haunt her all her life. At worst, she might face emotional chaos and emptiness that could lead her to an act of desperation. Was that what had happened in San Francisco?

Suddenly, she did want to speak to Ryan, very badly. She wanted his wisdom, his sensitivity, his kindness. But Ryan was oceans away in space and time. They had once belonged to each other, but since then, they had become the property of too many successors.

Exhausted by her emotions, she closed her eyes and let sleep approach.

Rebecca's afternoon meal arrived in two bowls, one containing a relatively mild vegetarian curry, the other a stew of domed black mushrooms pungently flavored with asafetida. Both, though Rebecca did not know it, came from Mohan Singh's house, where they had been prepared by his relatives for the poor lonely American woman with no family to look after her. She was indifferent to the food, or to the pains that had been taken over it. She was too obsessed with her thoughts. She ate a few mouthfuls from each bowl, then picked at the *chapatti* bread.

When she had taken the edge off her hunger, she pushed the tray away from her chest. The movement strained her leg and a vicious bolt of pain shot through her knee.

Rebecca had been thinking of Barbara Florio. She had not liked Barbara particularly. The agency had wanted to shield the identity of the adopting parents as much as possible. Rebecca knew they were trying to seal off any avenue by which she could later on, uninvited and unwanted, make her way back to Therese. But Rebecca had flatly insisted on meeting the mother, at least, threatening that there would be no deal otherwise. And so, with some reluctance, two meetings had been set up.

During their brief contacts, Barbara Florio had been eager to impress Rebecca with the wonderful life that awaited the about-to-be-born baby. The talk had been of wealth and privilege. Barbara Florio had made the assumption, which was natural, Rebecca supposed, that the teenage mother had come from a background of drab poverty. It had not occurred to her that Rebecca might herself have come from a world of rank and money.

During their second meeting, Barbara Florio had begun pressing money on Rebecca, offering to pay all her bills, "with some pocket money for you, dear." Rebecca, proud and in pain, had cut the interview short at that point, and had not asked to meet her again. Though she had understood that the catalog of possessions had been intended as reassurance, not as barnyard crowing, she had been offended at the materialistic crassness the woman had shown. She had almost changed her mind about the Florios. Only later had it occurred to her that Barbara Florio had been desperate to show herself in a favorable light, but had just not known how to go about it. It had been the agency people who had told her of Mrs. Florio's endless treatments to try and allow her to have a child of her own, of her desperation to be a mother.

And now she had died, dreadfully, burning in a fire.

It was the worst of all deaths. The most frightening, the most painful. It was a vision that sickened and haunted her. The media were evidently reveling in the suggestion that Therese Florio, a troubled thirteen-year-old who burned things for fun, had set the fire that had killed her adoptive mother. That anybody could find such a suggestion titillating nauseated Rebecca, but evidently a lot of people did.

She closed her eyes, tormented by that fiery vision. Flames reflected in a child's eyes. A child's fingers, striking a match. A child's scream.

San Francisco

Barbara Florio's grave, discreetly covered with a green cloth, was magnificently sited, on one of the highest promontories of the cemetery. It commanded sweeping views down to the city and the bays beyond. In the midmorning sunshine, the towers of the Golden Gate Bridge gleamed brightly. But today it was not a gate of gold, but a gate of cloud. A strong northeast wind had lashed the sea until masses of icy water had welled up from the deep ocean floor. The cold flood, driving the bathers shivering to shore, had also chilled the warm Pacific air, condensing it to a thick, creamy fume, which now rolled steadily inland, drenching the valleys.

The cortege was arriving. Bianchi and Reagan, who had arrived early, watched the black limousines gliding up the hill. Reagan took a last drag on his Camel and flicked it away, buttoning his own jacket closed.

"Here we go," he said.

A straggling procession emerged from the limousines and progressed toward the plot. One or two of the older women already had handkerchiefs to their faces, having evidently cried through the mass. A lone child of five or six frolicked in the rear until a nanny or parent hurried up to take her in tow. The arrivals studiously ignored the police officers, recognizing them for what they were, and not wishing to be reminded of the gruesome and inelegant way Barbara Florio had died.

"Here come the troops," Reagan said. A dark red Saturn had arrived. It parked, and Louise Steiglitz and David Kendall got out, accompanied by Leonard Moore, the head of the arson detail. Bianchi and Reagan went to meet them. They exchanged discreet handshakes.

Moore was casting his eyes around. "Well, well. The great and good of the city are here today. A genuine society funeral."

"Have you spoken with Florio this morning?" Reagan asked Moore.

"Not yet. We have a meeting tomorrow. We're applying for a court order to take both girls into care for questioning. The judge will ask for an interim psychiatric report. If Therese pulls her little stunt again, there's no way the judge will refuse. Then we can get both girls to a retreat where Brancepeth can dig as long and as deep as she wants."

"Great. Where are the girls?"

"They've been staying with their father at his apartment. The family doctor prescribed some sedatives last week, because they're both sleeping badly. They spent last night at the Pacific Heights house."

"Where their mother died? Was that a good idea?"

"Apparently that's what they wanted."

The graveside was now crowded, and there was a carefully muted drone of conversation. Over a hundred people had turned out to see Barbara Florio buried.

The hearse had parked under the spreading branches of a huge cedar. The police officers fell silent, watching as the coffin was lifted out and carried to the grave, a young Catholic priest leading the way. There was no sign of Michael Florio. Bianchi was aware of butterflies in her stomach.

"Where's Florio?" she asked. "I don't see him."

"I don't either," Reagan said. "Maybe he's somewhere in back."

She hunted among the dark-clad crowds, but could not see Florio's tall figure. Nor could she see the girls. She glanced at Reagan. Their eyes met for a moment. Then she was hurrying around the graveside, making her way through the mourners toward the priest. She reached him before he got to the grave and touched his sleeve.

"Father," she said in a low voice, "Michael Florio and his daughters aren't here yet."

He looked up, shocked rather than angered at the interruption. "Who are you?"

She showed him her badge. "My name is Detective Carla Bianchi. I'm assigned to Mrs. Florio's case."

"Then you ought to know that Mr. Florio and his daughters aren't attending the funeral. Now please—"

"Why not?"

He shuffled through the pages of his prayer book agitatedly. "*Please.* I have to start the service in a moment."

"Why not?" she demanded.

A red flush filled the priest's smooth cheeks. "They did not want to come."

"Did they attend the mass?" she asked.

The priest shook his head, almost speechless with anger. His voice was choked. "They did not wish to."

"When did they tell you they weren't coming?"

"Last night. Now, would you please let me continue with the service—"

"What time last night?"

"Around ten. Really, I must insist. You have no right."

"I'm sorry," she said, and walked away quickly.

The priest stationed himself at the covered grave, his prayer book open. Silence fell. Clearing his throat, the priest began the service in a high voice, backed by a muttered amen from the mourners. Curious eyes followed Bianchi over black shoulders and from beneath black veils as she left.

She was grim-faced as she headed back to the group of police officers. "He's not here," she said shortly. "Neither is Therese or Devon. He called the priest at ten last night to say he wasn't coming. You spoke to him this morning, didn't you, Al?"

"On the phone. I called him to check on the funeral arrangements. He didn't say anything about not coming."

"You called him on his cell phone?" Bianchi asked.

There was a silence. "Call him again," Moore commanded.

Reagan took a phone out of his pocket and punched in a number. Eyes from the congregation were fixed on them, in outrage or interest, and the responses had become faltering. Reagan tried several numbers, muttering a few words each time, then shook his head. "He's not answering any of his numbers now. I've asked Wong to check the house."

The priest was holding a vessel filled with holy water. He was intoning in Latin now, which would no doubt have had a solemn effect but for the distraction of the five police officers. As it was, his voice was still shaking, · · and he sounded halfhearted about the whole thing.

The ceremony was nearly over. The distant clang of a cable car drifted up to them through the still air. Somewhere, a mower began to purr, manicuring more acres of emerald lawn. The fog was still rolling in from the Pacific. It had all but swamped the Golden Gate Bridge. Only the tops of the towers emerged from the creamy sea of vapor.

The coffin began lowering into the grave. The priest, pronouncing the final phrases in Latin, sprinkled holy water on the bronze casket as it went.

The warble of the cell phone cut through the moment like a knife. Reagan pulled the device hastily from his pocket and spoke into it briefly. He turned to the others.

"Wong says Florio's gone," he said. "So are the girls. They're not in the house."

"Is his car there?"

"It's still parked outside. They left sometime in the night. He must have taken Devon and Therese with him."

"Do we panic now, or later?" Carla Bianchi asked ironically.

"How did he get past the cops?" Reagan demanded forcefully. "You could put out an APB right now."

"Let's get down to the house and take a look before we do anything hasty," Moore said.

Barbara Florio's casket had now been lowered into its final resting place, and a grim old man in an English-cut suit moved forward to toss a handful of earth after it.

Leonard Moore crossed himself, then jerked his head at the others.

"Let's go."

The burned section of the house had been shut off with a tarpaulin, and the builders had evidently already been busy. It was such a big house that part of it could burn down while still leaving plenty of room for life to go on. A maid let them in the front door and led them to a reception room. In the center of the room, a long table had been set with an array of dainty refreshments for the mourners, with cut-glass sherry decanters and a display of cream lilies. It looked beautiful, but if you sniffed, you could still smell smoke.

The housekeeper, Mrs. de Castro, had been at the funeral, and had evidently hurried back at the same speed as the police, in order to host the mourners. She received the police officers with a mixture of defiance and pride. Her eyes were heavy-lidded with crying, but her face was expressionless. She was dressed in impenetrable black. A maid, also South American–looking, also heavy-lidded with weeping, stood behind her with tightly folded arms, wearing a pinafore starched to the impregnability of a suit of armor. In the background, a man who was evidently a gardener-handyman hovered in case he was needed.

"What time did they leave?" Leonard Moore asked Mrs. de Castro.

"I can't be sure of that. I went to my room at eight-thirty and watched television until I fell asleep. That must have been around ten-thirty. When I got up at seven, they was gone."

"You didn't hear any movement?"

"I had the television loud," she replied. "I got a little deafness in one ear."

"Mr. Florio didn't mention to you that he wasn't planning on attending his wife's funeral?"

"No."

"Do you know whether they packed anything?"

"Mr. Florio brought a bag when he came from his apartment. Just a small one. He must have took it with him when he went."

"What about Devon and Therese?"

There was a gleam in the dark eyes. "I haven't had time to check on their things. I can't say."

"Maybe we could check for ourselves?"

"You got a search warrant?" Mrs. de Castro asked, bristling like a glossy porcupine.

"Mrs. de Castro, we're just trying to find out what might have happened to Therese and Devon. We're concerned about them."

"If Therese and Devon is with they father, they okay," Mrs. de Castro said briefly. "You ain't gonna go tramping all round the house, specially not right now."

"Could you ask someone to check?" Bianchi requested gently. She added her sweet smile.

Mrs. de Castro's manner eased infinitesimally. She spoke briefly in Spanish over her shoulder to the starched maid, who slipped away. "She going to check. Maybe you ladies and men would like to wait in Mrs. Florio's study?"

"Sure," Moore said. "We don't want to intrude more than is necessary."

The hall had started to fill with mourners. They followed Mrs. de Castro's majestic back. It was manifest to Bianchi that behind her reticence, Mrs. de Castro had been a willing accomplice in getting Michael Florio and his daughters out of the house unobserved, despite the not-so-discreetly parked police car in the street outside.

Mrs. Florio's "study" was a feminine den, filled with pretty fripperies. She had done her work at burr-walnut desks and dainty bureaus. The flock-papered walls were hung with pastel portraits of the family, signed by Barbara Florio herself. The quality of the work was high. The pictures included a handsome sketch of Michael Florio. She had evidently intended to give her husband a Heathcliff-like romanticism, but the shading was thundery and imprecise, and the overall impression was darkly frightening. Through large windows, elaborately swagged in beige silk, the room overlooked a sweep of lawn extending to a big, lush back garden.

"They just walked right out the back door," Moore said.

"That's exactly what they did," Reagan said, joining Carla Bianchi and Louise Steiglitz at the window. "Back of the garden is a lane that goes all the way down to Divisadero. He probably had another vehicle parked there."

"If he got going early yesterday evening," Moore said, "he's already had eighteen hours to get clear."

The starched maid named Emilia came into the study. "None of The-rese or Devon's things are missing," she said.

"Not even a toothbrush?"

"Nothing, ma'am."

"Thank you," Bianchi said. "They had more stuff over at their father's apartment, didn't they?"

The maid nodded. "Yes, ma'am."

"Thank you."

"Mr. Montrose wants a word, please, sir."

"Ranolph P. Montrose the Third is Mrs. Florio's father," Moore mut-tered to the others.

"What's he like?"

"Rich, conservative, influential."

"Great."

The door of the study opened, and two men came in. One was the grim old man who had been first to throw earth in the grave; the other looked enough like him to be obviously a son. Both were pale and gaunt-faced.

The elder Montrose didn't bother with formalities. "I take it he didn't inform you in advance?" he asked Joshua Wong in a thin, harsh voice.

"That he wouldn't be here today? No, sir. Did he say anything to you?"

"Of course not. The first we heard was at the church." Ranolph P. Montrose III glared at them with red-rimmed eyes. "Well? This about settles it, doesn't it?"

"What exactly do you mean?" Wong asked cautiously.

"Don't play the fool with me," the old man said with startling energy. "His fleeing like this is tantamount to an admission of guilt. Goddamn it, he has my granddaughters with him. Are you going to get an arrest warrant issued?"

"I'll decide that in the course of the day, Mr. Montrose. If you—"

"In the course of the day?" the son said in a bitter, nasal tone. "He'll be in Brazil by tonight."

"We can't be certain that Mr. Florio intends to abscond," Wong said, trying to be firm and polite at the same time.

"Is it normal for a man to creep out of his house, unseen, during the hours of darkness?" Montrose demanded. "Is it normal for a man not to attend his wife's funeral, and to prevent his daughters from attending? Is any of this normal, while police are still investigating her death?"

"No, sir," Moore admitted.

"He has Therese and Devon with him," the old man repeated. He lifted trembling fingers to his mouth, the only sign he had given so far that there was grief beneath his anger. "Those poor children. He'll kill them, too."

"Why do you say that, Mr. Montrose?" Bianchi asked.

Ranolph Montrose turned to her sharply, reminding her of some elderly bird of prey. "He's already murdered my daughter," Montrose said. "Isn't killing Therese and Devon the logical next step in his insanity?"

"You believe he is insane?" she asked.

"He's a very dangerous man," the son cut in. "You know his Vietnam record? He's practically a war criminal."

"Did he ever make threats against your daughter?" she asked. "Did he ever tell you he intended to harm her or the girls?"

"He didn't need to," Montrose said grimly. He lifted a bony hand and snapped his fingers against his thumb. "He could wipe them out like *that.* We knew it. He knew we knew it. To a trained assassin who lived for weeks at a time in that festering jungle, killing and maiming, you think it would be any problem to wipe out a woman and a couple of girls?"

"Are you saying the threat was implicit in anything he said or did?" she pressed.

"A man like that," the son said grimly, "has no need to make threats. What he *is* constitutes a threat to anyone who angers him."

"And he was angry with Mrs. Florio?"

The elder Montrose turned his aquiline face back to Bianchi. "You better do some homework, Detective," he said bleakly. "I don't intend to use this occasion as a briefing for your benefit. I have just buried my only daughter." He turned to Moore. "Get an arrest warrant issued without delay, and hunt him down. Good day."

With the barest of nods, Ranolph P. Montrose III and his son left the room. He had obviously given an imperial command.

"Are you gonna issue a warrant?" Al Reagan asked Moore.

"I'll speak to the judge at lunchtime. Until we get some solid evidence, I doubt he'll be enthusiastic. Or that it would do any good."

Reagan glowered. "He's a fugitive from justice, as far as I'm concerned, and he's probably armed and dangerous."

"Keep your shirt on, Al."

"We'll have to think about it," Bianchi said, cutting off whatever intemperate reply her partner was planning. "There's some way to go before we can show anything to a grand jury yet."

The muted sounds of the post-funeral reunion at the front of the house drifted into the study as a door opened, then closed again. Moore sighed heavily. "I think we've been dismissed."

KATHMANDU

"You have the pernicious Western habit of thinking more than is good for you," Mohan Singh said.

"What else should I do?" she panted, gripping the exercise bar over her bed. "Go stir-crazy?"

"I do not mean that you should not use your mind, Rebecca," he said. "I mean that you use your mind in the wrong way. You should think less, meditate more."

"Is that right?"

Singh studied her with a smile as she sweated. He had personally supervised her daily exercise and breathing routines. Nevertheless, she had lost weight in these three weeks, at least fifteen pounds. That splendid body was thinner, her skin too pale. For an active woman, the confinement must have been purgatory.

He had tried to teach her to meditate, hoping it would help her to endure her imprisonment better. She had never caught the trick; instead, the lessons had sparked some (to him) delightfully lively arguments about Western versus Eastern thought. But today she was not interested in debate. She was restless, her gray eyes constantly searching for the window, pulling away from him.

"Your meditation doesn't help me, Mohan," Rebecca said, panting. "Your meditation is about resignation. Acceptance. I've tried that. I thought I'd taught myself to be resigned. But it hasn't worked. It was a terrible mistake. This time, I need to do what my heart tells me to do."

"I wish I understood you, Rebecca," he said with a sigh.

"You wouldn't like me very much if you did understand me."

"I think I would feel even more—" He bit back the perilous words that trembled on his tongue. "Even more respect. Keep going. I'll be back in five minutes."

Rebecca saw the flush on his cheeks as he turned and hurried away. It had not escaped her that the gentle Nepalese doctor had grown very fond of her, had perhaps even fallen in love with her to an extent. She knew he was grieving at the thought of her departure. But now, of all times, romance was very far from her thoughts.

She had had little luck with her men. She'd never pretended to love Robert Warren, though they had been friends and sexual partners. She hated the term *sexual partners,* but it was the only one that fit; the word *lovers* was one she had always avoided, as though she were afraid of it. Her marriage to Malcolm Burns had been so short as to be an embarrassment: Within five months of their wedding, they had already been living apart. She hardly thought of Malcolm these days. But she had never blamed him for wanting to escape from the arid badlands of their marriage. He had been right in all his accusations. She *had* been cold and ungiving. She *had* been unable to commit herself.

Looking back over the past thirty years, it sometimes seemed to Rebecca that the only time she had been truly happy had been, briefly, with Ryan Foster. That period still glowed in her mind with a hot radiance. They'd been no more than two unhappy teenagers, entering their adulthood. But their time together had been wonderful. Perhaps it had just been their youth. One of those glimpses of nirvana that life gives you before the steel trap slams shut. In any case, the arrival of Therese had destroyed all that. Giving up their child had left each too wounded to keep going.

They had been so determined that they could not keep her. But what if they'd been wrong? What if they'd kept her, married, struggled together? Might their lives have attained that glimpsed nirvana? Might they all have avoided the grief and tragedy that had followed?

Thirteen years after giving away her baby, Rebecca Carey was an experienced pediatric specialist. She worked in a big Los Angeles hospital. She was poised and admired. She thought of herself as a good doctor, dedicated to her patients, eager to learn, a valued member of a first-rate team.

Yet each day, in the faces of the sick children she worked with, she saw the face of her own child. Each night, when she went home from the hospital, she was left empty. Up to the age of thirty, she had been unable to love anyone.

Had it been the same for Ryan? Was that why he, like she, had found no happiness in his own marriage?

There was no point in such speculations. Ryan was too far away, in every sense. She had to do this on her own.

Therese was now not so very far from the age Rebecca had been when she had become pregnant. The terrible fire that had destroyed her adoptive mother had come just when the girl's thoughts would be engaged with the mysteries of womanhood: of sex, motherhood, the cycle of life. Now, if ever, she would be thinking about her own origins. Now, if ever, she would be reaching out for truth.

And now, Rebecca could not fail her again.

But what if the child rejected her? What if the girl was bitter, contemptuous—indifferent? Could she deal with that pain?

What if the child was truly disturbed—violent, a killer? What if she had to face having passed on some inherent evil?

Could she deal with *that*?

The weights on the traction had been diminishing every few days. Mohan Singh took the last weight down and cut the plaster from her thigh with an electric saw. Fretful about hurting her skin, he worked intently, his dark cheeks flushed.

"There!" With a final explosion of dust, he reached the end of the cast. The nurse, who had been easing aside the cords that had been attached to the weight, prepared to help Singh separate the two halves of the binding.

"It's like some kind of weird cocoon," Rebecca said, looking down at the thing that had encased her leg for weeks. "I wonder what's going to hatch?"

"We will see. This may hurt."

Rebecca could not help gasping as the adhesive bandages were stripped off her flesh. With a rip, they came away, one by one. Rebecca's leg was revealed.

She had always been proud of her strong and elegant legs. This white, blotchy thing belonged to someone else. Singh, on the other hand, was beaming with delight as he palpated her knee.

"My word! What a perfect job, if I do say so myself."

"You think so?" she asked.

"Look how well it has healed!" he exclaimed. He rolled her thigh from side to side. "Any pain?"

"None." But his touch on the long-encased flesh felt weird.

"There is no distortion or contraction. We'll take you up to X ray this afternoon and get a good look at it."

She knew that if the X ray was not promising, she might be splinted up all over again. "Help me stand up," she commanded.

"You cannot just jump out of bed," he said, laughing. "The leg will not support your weight."

"I want to get up," she insisted. "For one minute." Her skin was crawling with desperation to be out of this bed, off her back. She clutched at Mohan Singh's lean shoulders for support. "Please, Mohan. Get me out of here. Let me just get to the window! Please!"

He was reminded of the desperate way she had begged for her baby when she had first been admitted. He nodded at the nurse. Together, they helped Rebecca sit upright on the edge of her bed.

"My head is spinning," she said.

"Breathe deeply," he commanded.

She obeyed. They lifted her to her feet. It felt like soaring into outer space, an impossible height. "How wonderful," she said, half laughing. "Oh, my God!"

Singh and the nurse helped her upright between them. She could feel her heart, used to pumping blood in an undemanding horizontal plane, start to pound wildly. "Oh, my blood pressure!"

" 'Oh, my God, oh, my blood pressure,' " Mohan Singh echoed with gentle mockery. "There speaks the secular Western doctor. Can you put one foot in front of the other?"

With an effort, she could drag her left foot forward. Despite her disappointment at finding just how weak she was, she was elated and dizzy. Half shuffling, half hopping, she made it between them to the window.

"Let me go for a moment," she begged. They stepped away. She supported the weight of her upper body by bracing her arms on the windowsill and resting her forehead against the cold glass. The mountains blazed white in the distance. But a whole new world had also opened up: The city of Kathmandu spread out before her, shabby and wonderfully romantic. Below her lay the hospital yard, with a huge pipal tree spreading its branches. A lone cow had wandered in, unchallenged.

The relief of getting out of that bed was wonderful. From here, it was but a step to going home and finding her child.

"A shower," she begged. "Please, Mohan."

He was reluctant. "If you slip and fall?"

"I've given up falling. Please."

"Very well. The nurse will help you."

"Then can I put my own clothes on?" she asked. For weeks she had worn faded green hospital shifts, which were not even modest, let alone flattering.

"Your own clothes?" he asked. His heart was heavy. Already, she was fluttering in his arms. In a few days she would spread her wings, this beautiful bird, and soar away over the mountains, leaving him bereft. "I see no reason why not," he said, pretending cheerfulness.

She hobbled on crutches to the shower. The chipped white tiles and

plain iron pipe-work looked like Versailles to her. The nurse brought her
a plastic stool to sit on and a bar of transparent, disinfectant-smelling soap.

"I'll be all right on my own," she insisted, so the nurse drew the plastic
curtain and left her with the shower running.

Both legs felt like ropes of spaghetti. She struggled to her feet and
propped herself under the steaming jet. To be washing her own body,
standing on her own feet, was heaven. She plunged her head under the
spray, soaking her hair, working up a thick lather with the soap. It felt as
though pounds of grime were sluicing off her.

The daily exercise and deep-breathing routines had helped only a little.
She had lost pounds. Her breasts were small, weightless; her stomach was
a hollow beneath ribs that stuck out hungrily. She had always eaten carefully, worked out strenuously. Rebecca had been proud of her strength
and stamina, of her strong limbs and taut lines. Now she felt pared to the
bone.

She turned off the shower and stepped out. There was a mirror over
the sink. She wiped a patch clear of mist and peered at herself. Wet, dark
strands of hair clung to a pale oval with a pale mouth. She was thirty, and
she looked sixteen.

Her trembling legs could not support her any longer. She called for the
nurse, who came in with a towel. When she was more or less dry, she
asked for her knapsack and opened it. The huge pack was the only luggage
she had brought to Nepal; she and Robert had each left another bag in
storage at their hotel in Bangkok, on the way here. Until she got back to
Bangkok, she would have only her trekking gear to wear. But anything
was better than the horrible hospital shift, which opened at unanticipated
moments to expose her backside. She groped through the crumpled clothing and found some blessed underwear. She pulled out jeans, a T-shirt,
and a sweater, the things that had best survived being scrunched up for a
month. Dressed for the first time in weeks, she hopped back to her bed,
assisted by the nurse, feeling as exhausted as though she had just climbed
Annapurna. She lay back against the pillows and fell at once into a shallow
sleep.

•   •   •

Lowering clouds and mist swept down from the mountains into the valley of Kathmandu. It rained heavily. The sound of falling water was incessant, sometimes light, sometimes a thunderous downpour that would last for hours at a time. It cascaded from the eaves into the streets, turning the busy thoroughfares into red rivers of mud. The cold was intense.

The tourists had all gone home. Peace settled on Kathmandu. Rebecca found her way down to the courtyard, leaning on her crutch, and huddled in the doorway, looking at the rain.

My child, my child, she thought. Here, on the roof of the world, she had reached a decision of profound importance. Her heart fluttered in her breast like a bird eager to soar out of this rainy valley. Shivering in the doorway, Rebecca watched the rain give way to sleet, and then snow. The pipal tree grew gray, then white. The snow blew into her face and eyes, each tiny pinpoint burning for a moment before melting on her skin. Rebecca felt something shift inside her, like the engaging of gears. She was ready to go. She turned, and limped back into the hospital to find Mohan Singh.

He was in his tiny, bare office, sitting at his desk, staring at his clasped fingers.

"I'll never forget you, Mohan," she said quietly.

He looked up. With an effort, he got to his feet and smiled brightly. "So. You're ready to leave us?"

She patted the crutch she was leaning on. "Yep. Me an' my ol' faithful burro here, we're ready to go."

"Let me see you walk," he commanded.

She hobbled down the corridor, swinging on her crutch. Singh's eyes followed the straight line of her back, the poise of her head. There was no reason for her to stay here. He could do nothing more for her. He caught up with her and laid his hand gently on her shoulder.

"Go in peace, my beautiful bird," he said to her in Nepali. "Learn to fly again."

She looked at him, her misty eyes interrogative. "What does that mean?"

He shook his head, smiling. "Nothing."

She leaned forward and kissed him on both cheeks. "Thank you for what you did for me. You're a very good doctor."

"Of course." He tried to sound cheerful. "Good luck with your quest."

"Thanks. I have a feeling I'm going to need it."

Their eyes met for a moment. She did not want to cry, but she did.

"No, no," Singh said in agitation, groping for a handkerchief for her, "that is not the way."

"I mean it, Mohan. I'll never forget you. Maybe I'll be back someday."

"If we don't meet then, we will meet in some other life. Just as we met in this one, and no doubt in lives before this one. Go now."

He watched her go. She reached the end of the corridor and opened the door. For a moment she looked back at him. Then the door swung to, and she was gone.

High over Mongolia, after too many hours without sleep, her mind finally slipped into a neutral gear. The galloping horses slowed. She dreamed of Ryan, haunting dreams from a time before grief, before the loss of innocence. She dreamed of the way Ryan's arms had felt, of the safety that enveloped her, the sound of his laughter. She dreamed of things they had done together, things they had never done.

Then she dreamed of their final parting, of the way she had sunk into hopelessness when he had gone, a little deeper each day, a little more remote and silent. She dreamed of the remainder of her life, without Ryan, of the long gray procession of days that held no color, no joy. She dreamed of her own tears, and awoke feeling wretched.

She slept dreamlessly for several hours after that, but when she woke again the earlier part of her dream was fresh in her mind, sweet as youth, sweet as Ryan's lips on her own. Then the present, with all its doubts, rushed in. She opened her eyes, her heart pounding.

She glanced at her watch, the gold-and-steel Rolex she had bought herself shortly after her marriage had broken up. Three A.M. Los Angeles time. The hour when hope died. She lifted the window shade. The sky outside the aircraft was lightening, stars beginning to fade. Far below, a sheet of gray cloud stretched endlessly, a country made of lead.

Where was she heading? To defeat or victory? To healing or yet more grief?

Two

EARTH

URBINO, ITALY

Signora Fiorentini had reason to be grateful to Rebecca.

She was different from the usual run of students and ten-dollar-a-day travelers Signora Fiorentini accommodated in the little upstairs room. She was so quiet, so gentle, so helpful around the house. Signora Fiorentini had taken to calling her *la smarrita*, the lost one, the waif.

She had come to Umbria to be a nanny to the children of a wealthy American couple. But the couple had quarreled, and had gone back to America. So Rebecca had found her way to the Fiorentini farmhouse, looking for cheap lodgings.

The waif spoke halfway decent Spanish, which gave her a good start into Italian. Within a week or so, she was making herself understood. From the beginning, she had voluntarily done odd jobs around the house, and had proved herself so useful that Signora Fiorentini had offered to reduce the already small rent almost to nothing in exchange for the household work. And so Rebecca had become less like a lodger, and more like one of the numerous, quarrelsome, affectionate Fiorentini family.

And, dramatically, the waif had saved Arturo's life. Arturo was the youngest child, a clumsy boy, always the one who choked himself on his food or—as on this occasion—gashed himself on his tools.

The gash had been appalling, a great hole in his wrist, from which the blood sprayed, drawing patterns of horror all over the ancient clay tiles of the kitchen. Signora Fiorentini had all but passed out cold, and the rest of them had screamed and milled around the fainting boy. But you never saw anything like the way Rebecca had calmly taken Arturo's arm in her hands. She had known exactly where to dig in her thumb so that the spouting dribbled to a close. She had lifted his arm over her shoulder, had briskly demanded what she needed to bandage the wound and make a tourniquet. When the doctor had finally arrived, he had said nobody could have done it better. Rebecca had shrugged it off, but it had taken the doctor almost an hour to get to the farmhouse, and Fiorentini knew what she knew, and would take no more rent from Rebecca. She could stay as long as she pleased.

Breakfast was noisy. The male members of the clan had made a pet of the waif in their own way, which meant what in any other country might well be called sexual harassment.

This morning, as on most mornings, Rebecca endured the chaff with her usual tranquil smile, her nose buried in a tattered guidebook, her gray eyes distant from the hubbub around her. She was huddled in jeans and a quilted anorak; despite the domed, wood-burning oven, which dominated the kitchen, it was autumn in the Marche, and the house was cold.

The male Fiorentinis set off one by one for their work in the cooperative, each leaving a smoldering compliment for Rebecca, which she serenely ignored. The female Fiorentinis went a few minutes later, heading toward town jobs in shops. Fiorentini and Rebecca cleared the kitchen, now silent, but still resonating with the noisy joy of the family breakfast.

"Why do you limp, *cara?*" she asked Rebecca at the sink.

Rebecca turned her luminous eyes on the older woman for a moment. "I fell and broke my leg," she said, in her half-Italian, half-Spanish argot.

"How did you fall?"

"Climbing a mountain."

"Which mountain?"

Rebecca smiled her sweet smile. "A mountain far away."

Which was the kind of answer Rebecca usually gave to inquiries about her past. "It's not permanent then?"

"The limp? No. I hope it will go away as the muscles get stronger."

"Good," Fiorentini said.

"I'll go to the market this morning, and do the shopping," Rebecca announced.

While they were finishing, Marchetta the hairdresser arrived in her van. She bustled into the kitchen, carrying her suitcase. She did the rounds of all the farms around here, and did Fiorentini's hair every Tuesday. Fiorentini was a round little woman with a proud chin and a beak of a nose, but she had once been very handsome, and she still prided herself on her chestnut curls—even if the chestnut owed more to Marchetta's suitcase than to nature these days.

"I'll go," Rebecca said, starting to slip out of the room.

But the hairdresser stopped her from leaving. "Look, child." She held a magazine open for Rebecca to see. "That style is perfect for you. It would show off the shape of your face. You have sensational cheekbones."

"Eh, *cara?*" Fiorentini coaxed, interested. "What do you think?"

Rebecca looked at the photograph. The model's face stared boldly back from confections of glossy hair. "Thanks," she said, "but not right now."

Fiorentini was excited. "Your hair is in a mess, *cara.* And you're such a pretty girl. Isn't she, Marchetta?"

"No," the hairdresser replied, tilting her head to one side to study Rebecca. "She's not pretty. She is beautiful."

"I'll pay," Fiorentini pressed. "A little gift, to say thank you for Arturo."

"You're so sweet, but no, thanks."

Marchetta tapped the magazine with a scarlet fingernail. "You see this model? She has nothing you don't have. After I've done your hair, I'll show you how to do your face."

"No, thanks." Rebecca laughed, evading them. "But you're a very kind and dear person, Signora Fiorentini." With that swiftness she had, of a wild thing, she leaned forward and kissed Fiorentini's ruddy cheek, then flew out of the room. Fiorentini lifted both fat hands to the heavens in irritation.

The nasal buzz of a scooter started up in the courtyard. Fiorentini went to the window, and was just in time to see Rebecca leaving. Under the stone arch, the girl stopped her Vespa to check for traffic on the farm road. With some animal's sixth sense, she turned and looked back at the house. Fiorentini saw the white teeth flash in a brief smile, the dark hair blowing around the oval face. Like everyone else around here, Rebecca went helmetless. Her Vespa was made ungainly by two huge baskets, slung mulewise across the backseat. She waved, then was gone.

The road into Urbino was already rutted and muddied by autumn rains. It would be spring before the tractors would come and grade it. In the meantime, Rebecca had to put up with the mud and the bone-rattling potholes. It was bitterly cold on the Vespa, chilling her hands and legs to the bone. When she got to Urbino, she would buy herself something hot.

She smiled to herself, thinking of Fiorentini's eagerness to get her smartened up. Fiorentini couldn't know that she was trying very hard to cultivate scruffiness.

She had been treated with great kindness by the Fiorentini clan. It did not occur to Rebecca that in saving Arturo a pint or so of blood she had done anything extraordinary. But she knew she would find it hard to leave Fiorentini and her brawling family.

Most of the journey was uphill, and the Vespa struggled like an angry bumblebee in the mud. Ryan had taught her to ride a motorbike. She had learned on his heavy, powerful Harley-Davidson, and had gotten her license on it. She'd done it to get closer to him, to enter his world, rather than because she really enjoyed motorcycling. But right now that skill was coming in very handy.

The town of Urbino was snuggled into the folds of the mountain, its gold and bronze tints melting into the dark green of the woodland around it. She had come to love this city. It was miraculously unspoiled, its ancient palaces intact, its way of life tranquil. But it was no museum. The students of the university filled the ancient piazzas with color. Wherever she went, young people bustled and argued. She loved to slip into the flow, to blend into the conversations. It reminded her of her own student days, long ago and far away.

She parked the Vespa in a blind alley behind the cathedral and unhitched the baskets. The journey back to the farmhouse, laden with shopping, was often hazardous. More than once, she had misjudged the slippery roads, and had gone sprawling, with all her vegetables and cans rolling around her. That was how she had first conceived her plan.

She had promised herself a cup of hot coffee. She headed toward the coffee bar near the market, conscious of her limp. Her knee hated the cold, and was punishing her with a vicious throbbing. In the noisy, smoke-filled interior, she bought a cappuccino from rat-faced Alfredo the barman, and edged toward the window, where she found a seat. She sipped at the boiling froth, cupping her hands gratefully around the mug.

The market filled the square and spilled over into several side streets. As she searched the crowds with attentive eyes, she had an odd thought: Therese had been the one unpredictable event in her life, the only wild card in the deck. Since then, she had been on track, fulfilling the stern expectations she had set for herself. Now, years later, she was off the rails again. Here, at least temporarily, she had escaped from the master plan.

The window of the coffee shop misted over with a spatter of rain. Her knee still hurt like hell. She watched a group of Little Sisters moving between the stalls. With their small funds and collegiate mentality, nuns made terrific hagglers. It was a pleasure to watch them, and learn.

And then, suddenly, she saw Michael Florio.

He was alone. He wore a sheepskin jacket, the fleecy collar pulled up around his neck.

She had watched him from a simple bivouac in the shelter of an old ruin that overlooked the millhouse where he was holed up. He was a formidable man, alert and active. Once or twice he had seemed to sense her presence and had stared hard at the woods where she had lain. She had felt as though his eyes were meeting her own, and had shrunk into the bracken like a deer.

He was making his way through the stone arch at the far end of the piazza. He was such a tall man that he ought to have been conspicuous, but he had a way of gliding through the crowd that disguised his size. It was almost an animal movement. *Here he comes,* she thought, holding her breath.

She was afraid of him.

He did nothing without first studying the field. Even something as mundane as coming into town to shop had to be prepared for, planned, executed only when his instincts told him it was safe. He was a self-controlled and physically very powerful man, who left nothing to chance.

Another cat's-paw of rain dabbed at the window of the coffee shop. Rebecca gathered her baskets, as though drawing her courage around her, and went out into the cold.

She approached him, both her baskets looped over one arm, her purse clutched in her free hand. He paused at the stall owned by the di Sirolo brothers, two old men who grew the best tomatoes in the area. The tomatoes were glowing with autumn brilliance, almost the last crop of the year. Rebecca edged toward the stall beside the di Sirolos, until she was only a few yards away from him.

"How much are the *melanzane?*" she asked. "I want to make some preserves."

"A thousand lire the kilo."

"That's way too much," she told the young man earnestly. She started negotiating, stumbling over the words, but nevertheless bargaining hard. She sensed that Florio was watching her. "And I'll want some zucchini, if they're cheap."

"Six kilos at six-fifty," the boy said.

"Okay." She gave him a ravishing smile.

"How is Signora Fiorentini?" the boy asked, holding out his hand for her basket.

"Fine," she told him. Florio never bargained. He simply paid whatever they asked, and so they robbed him blind. She watched the boy fill her basket with the glossy purple vegetables, talking to him idly about the Fiorentini clan. She bought some zucchini, then deliberately turned her back on Florio and walked the other way. She felt, or thought she felt, his dark gaze on her. Despite the cold, she was sweating.

For the next twenty minutes, she circumnavigated the piazza, keeping him in her line of sight. Her baskets got heavier, creaking under the weight of the produce, straining at her arms. She did not need to accentuate her limp; her knee was sore, and the wet cobbles were treacherous.

Her moment came suddenly. Their paths crossed in front of a butcher shop, where an ancient gutter made a perfect trap for unwary feet. His eyes met hers for an instant. They were black, intense. At that moment, almost as though she had not wanted it to happen, her boot slid into the gutter. Her ankle turned, and a horrible pain shot up her bad leg. She tried to bite back the cry of anguish, but it burst out of her. She let go of both baskets. They crashed to the ground, overturning. The contents exploded in all directions. Even if he had intended to prowl on by, he was forced to stop, to avoid treading on the riot of colorful vegetables that scurried across the cobbles around his feet.

Rebecca sank down onto the sidewalk, clutching her knee in both hands. "Oh, *shit*," she said, gritting her teeth. She had really hurt herself.

Then a shadow fell over her world. He squatted in front of her. "Are you okay?" he asked in a husky voice.

"It's my stupid knee," she said, babbling. "I broke it earlier this year. It's still weak. Sometimes it just gives way. I'll be okay."

Without a word, his fingers pried hers away from her knee. She gasped in an explosion of worse pain as his thumbs expertly probed the half-healed ligament, found the red-hot heart of the pain. "Is that where it hurts?"

"Aaah," she quavered. "*Yes.*"

"You've torn the ligaments. You should be in a plaster cast."

Rebecca tried to laugh. "I wouldn't be much use in a cast. I'll live."

Through her wet lashes, she saw he was studying her intently. In any other circumstances, he would have been an incredibly handsome man. But the coal-black eyes were dangerous. Set under forbidding brows, they seemed to envelop her, reach deep into her. Surely it would not be possible to fool those eyes? She groped for her baskets. "All my things!"

"Don't move." He started gathering her scattered vegetables and putting them back in the baskets. She sat, watching him, massaging her knee. It hurt like fury now, and the cold, wet cobbles were soaking the seat of her blue jeans, but she felt a hot glow in her belly. It had all happened so naturally that she could hardly believe she had succeeded. "It's okay," she called to him. "I'll get all that stuff as soon as I can move." Then she wondered whether she was laying the wounded-waif routine on too thickly. "Thank you," she added.

He was scrupulous in locating the last lemon, the farthest-flung orange. He set the filled baskets at her side and looked down at her. "Your tomatoes will never be the same again."

"I'll make *ragú* for the pasta. Thank you so much."

"You're American," he said.

"Los Angeles," she said, nodding. "And you?"

"San Francisco. Want to get up?"

"I could try," she said. He reached down to her. She gave him her hand. His fingers closed around her wrist. He was frighteningly strong. He lifted her to her feet with easy, careful power. When she was upright, he let her go. The bad leg was still weak. She staggered, and he steadied her, his arm closing around her shoulders.

"Can you stand?"

"Just about." Her heart was starting to beat wildly. She had to pant a little to compensate for the tachycardia. Her body shrank from the arm around her shoulders. Though she knew she should look grateful, she could not keep herself from twisting away. "I'm okay. Thank you." He released her, and she took a hopping step away from him. She stooped and rubbed her knee with both hands. Her untidy mop of hair fell around her face, covering her burning cheeks. "Wow. That really *hurts*."

He considered her, one fist on his hip. Despite the cold, he wore only a cotton shirt under his sheepskin coat. At the V of his throat, the muscular flesh was deeply tanned. "Where's your car?"

"I haven't got a car," Rebecca replied. "I came in on my Vespa."

He tilted an eyebrow. "You carry all that stuff on a Vespa?"

"It's an acquired art," she admitted. She looked at him with bright eyes, her face still flushed. "Kind of like crossing Niagara on a tightrope."

"Where are you staying?"

"In a farmhouse, about ten kilometers out of town."

"Ten kilometers on a Vespa, loaded with groceries?" There was unmistakable suspicion in the brooding gaze.

"I enjoy it. I just need to sit awhile before I get going." She swallowed. "Thank you for picking up all my stuff. Look, let me buy you a cup of coffee. Or a beer." She tried desperately not to sound too anxious, to make the invitation almost reluctant.

"My favorite bar is right over there."

The market whirled around them, noisy color orbiting their moment of stillness and silence. It was all a pageant, she thought in some remote corner of her mind, a flamboyant festival that had as its real meaning this chance encounter between two foreigners.

"You can buy me a beer," he said. He lifted her baskets with easy strength, and walked toward the bar she had indicated. She stood still, watching his broad back.

Enter the dragon, she thought. Her gossamer net had fallen around the beast. Would it somehow, miraculously, hold fast, and immobilize him long enough for her to snatch the princess from his grasp, and run with her, run far away?

The smoky bar was less crowded than it had been an hour earlier; most of the students had left for their morning classes. He chose a table at the back, well out of the doorway's line of sight. She sat gratefully while he went to the bar, rubbing her knee. The mock fall had been a painful exercise.

Her mind was racing, almost too fast for her to isolate the thoughts. This was her opportunity, and fear or eagerness must not let her spoil it.

Florio seemed to be taking his time ordering the drinks. He and Alfredo the barman were engaged in a conversation, but their voices were too low for Rebecca to hear any of it. She caught Alfredo's smile. He had probably seen that little byplay in the piazza, and had guessed something of her game. She prayed he wouldn't make any clever remarks and alert Florio.

He returned with the drinks and sat opposite her, seeming to hem her into the corner with his broad shoulders. For an instant she caught a tang of woodsmoke from him, the primitive smell of a man who lived a primitive life. "How is the leg?"

"Oh, it's improving, thanks."

"How did you break it?"

"In a climbing accident this summer."

"Maybe you should keep your weight off it. I've seen you hiking across the countryside. You get around."

There was a note in his voice that gave her a chill. She shrugged. "They told me to walk. I walk a lot."

"And sometimes you fall?"

"Sometimes I fall," she agreed.

"You appear to be looking for something out there," he said calmly, drinking. "I wonder what that might be."

So much for her notion that she had been prudent. She swallowed. "I'm interested in archaeology. I—I find all sorts of things."

"I'll bet you do," he said without inflection. "You're not a student, are you?"

"Oh, no."

"I didn't think so. You're older than you look."

"Am I?"

"You dress like them," he said. "But that's just a pose, isn't it?"

"I don't know what you mean by a pose," she said warily.

His mouth seemed to hold a mocking smile, but no warmth came into his eyes. "You look twenty, but you must be ten years older. That's what your eyes say."

"My eyes?"

"I don't mean you have crow's-feet."

Rebecca held his gaze for a second longer, then let her own slide past him. "I'm not a student. Just a poor working girl."

"A poor working girl," he repeated. He sat very still, she noticed, his body immobile but for the silent drumming of his fingers on his thigh. "Why are you stalking me, working girl?"

She felt the color fill her cheeks, partly from shock. "I don't have any idea what you're talking about."

He swung his big body so he could look under the table. "You always wear those boots. They have a distinctive yellow patch on the side. They also have a distinctive tread. You've been prowling around my place. Three days ago, I heard something in the trees up above the house. I went up there. I found where you'd been lying."

"Me?" she said, her voice catching in her throat.

"You must have been there a couple of hours to have flattened the underbrush like that," he said. He took a drink of his beer, watching her all the while. "I knew it was you because I found your tracks. Your limp made it a certainty. I followed your trail down to the road. I found where you'd parked your Vespa. Now, today, you throw your groceries under my feet."

Her mouth was dry. "That's crazy. I don't even know who you are."

"Let's not jerk each other around, working girl," he said, suddenly very menacing. "What's your story?"

Rebecca was silent, her mind whirling. If she lied badly now, she would blow it all. She did not know how much he had guessed about her, but she would have to concede some of the truth just to stay in the game. "Okay," she heard herself say in a still voice. "I did come to your place."

"Why?" he asked.

"To see if it was true you had kids."

Florio's dark brows came down swiftly. "Now what the hell would my kids have to do with you?" he demanded harshly.

Her hands were shaking. She gripped the glass and forced herself to look into his face. "I need a job," she said baldly. "I've been looking after two kids for an American couple, but now they've gone back to the U.S. I badly want to stay on, but I don't have any more money. Somebody told me there was an American man living alone with his children. So I went to take a look." She moistened her lips. "I love children. Looking after them is what I do best. And I'm not expensive."

"You're asking me for a job?" he said quietly. "Is that what this charade is all about?"

"Yes."

He glared at her as though he would like to wring the truth out of her with two hands around her throat. But more than her physical fear was her terror that she would fail Therese yet again.

"You know my name?" he asked.

"I heard you were called Florio."

"Do you have a name?" he asked.

"Rebecca Burns," she replied, giving him her married name, knowing it was at best a flimsy shield for her real identity.

"Rebecca? It was lucky for you that you weren't there when I came looking for you three days ago, Rebecca," he said with silky quietness. "If I'd found you, you would have regretted it."

She sat up straighter. "Don't threaten me, please."

He studied her in silence. Again, she had the sense that his gaze was piercing her thin disguise, digging into her soul. Her greatest danger was that he would guess who she was, either by some physical resemblance to Therese, or through some resonance of her name. She did not like to imagine how he would react if he guessed her identity, but she had images of being dredged out of the bottom of a lake. However, instinctively, she felt that if he had to guess her identity right now, the last person on earth he would think her to be was Therese's mother.

"What makes you think I want a stranger taking care of my children? What makes you think I can't take care of them myself?"

"Nothing," she replied. "I'm just hoping that you could do with a little cheap, reliable help. Look, Mr. Florio, I'm a pediatric nurse. I've worked with children all my life. I'm trustworthy, believe me. I'm a hard worker. I could even teach a little."

"Teach?" he repeated.

"As in schoolwork."

He grunted. "These people you worked for. What are their names?"

She had the answer ready. "The Algers." It was a name she had taken from the locked gate of an untenanted villa on the Scheggia road. She had looked hard to find a suitable place, a big house, as this one was, with children's swings and slides visible from the road. If he checked, there would at least be a vague corroboration for her story.

"If you're a nurse, why don't you get a job in an Italian hospital?" he asked.

"I've tried. There are about a thousand applicants for every medical job in Italy, and a foreigner doesn't have much chance. Especially when my Italian is really half Spanish."

"Spanish?"

"My last job was in a children's hospital in Los Angeles. Most days I spoke more Spanish than English."

"I see," he said, never taking his eyes off her. Was he swallowing her story?

She went on. "I took a climbing vacation in the summer, but everything went wrong. I broke my leg. Other things broke up, too. I came to Italy to get away from all that. It seemed to feel right here. I'm happy here. I love the people, the country, the history. I don't want to go crawling back home with my tail between my legs." She swallowed, wondering how sincere she sounded. She was whipping truth and fiction up into a plausible froth. "All I want is somewhere to stay and enough money to live on."

"Spying and laying traps is a strange way of getting my trust."

"I didn't think of it as spying and laying traps. It would have been a lot better if it had worked out the way I planned it. Which was, I would innocently tell you all about myself, and you would say, Hey, I have a job for you. But I guess I put my size-seven boots in it, didn't I?"

The dark eyes stayed on hers, the fingers drumming silently on the taut thigh. "One of my kids . . . needs help."

"What kind of help?" she asked, her heart pounding suddenly.

"She has special problems. Special needs."

"How old is she?"

"Thirteen."

"And your other child?"

"She's fifteen."

She leaned forward. "What do you mean by special needs?"

Florio seemed to hesitate. For the first time, his eyes were looking inward, instead of boring into her. "Therese is an unusual child. She's very intelligent. She's also very vulnerable. This is a difficult time for her. Her mother died earlier this year."

He said it with no sign of grief. "Died?" she could not help repeating.

"There was a bad fire in San Francisco."

"Oh, how horrible. I'm so sorry."

"The girls were in the house. They weren't physically hurt, not seriously, but they were emotionally traumatized. Especially Therese."

"Then isn't her place at home, among her friends, and where she could have access to professional care? Keeping your daughters buried in the woods in a foreign country can't do any good." She had not meant the note of authority to enter her voice, but it had done so anyway.

"It can keep them from harm," he said brusquely.

Rebecca nodded slowly. "Listen, Mr. Florio. Don't write me off because I tried to be too clever. I really do need a job, and maybe you need me. If . . ." She swallowed before she could pronounce the name. ". . . if Therese is ill, or lonely, or disturbed, I can help. I mean it."

He drained his glass. She hated him because she held him responsible for what had been done to Therese, not just over the past months, but over the years. She also feared him. But right now she had to look at him like an earnest puppy dog begging for a biscuit.

"Also," she went on, "I could help out with the chores, the way I do at Signora Fiorentini's, where I'm staying. I can share the cooking and washing. And you certainly need someone to do your shopping for you. You pay whatever they ask, so they're all robbing you blind."

"What is autism?" he asked abruptly.

Rebecca's blood seemed to freeze in her veins. "What makes you ask?"

"Just answer the question."

"Autism is a clinical disease similar to childhood schizophrenia. It's primarily a communication disorder. Characteristics would be deep withdrawal, failure to develop speech, obsessive behavior, repetitive movements like rocking or jumping. Does either of your children show any of those patterns?"

The silence was like a dark chasm. "No," he said at last. "They don't."

She stared at him, feeling the blood start flowing through her veins again, realizing it had been some kind of test.

Florio took a pen out of his pocket and pushed a paper napkin toward her. "Give me a number where I can reach you."

Her hand shook so badly, the pen ripped the soft paper. There was a gleam of hope, but she had run her luck as far as it could go. Any further, and she would wreck it all. She had to get away from him now. As soon as she had finished writing, she rose to her feet and picked up her baskets. "I have to get back. It was nice meeting you. And I'm sorry I was so clumsy."

He rose. "I'll take you home."

She shook her head vigorously. "Oh, no, thanks. Somebody would have to come back and pick up my Vespa. It's okay, really. The knee's much better."

Despite her protests, he insisted on helping her carry her baskets to her scooter. Neither of them said a word to the other. Under the shadow of the cathedral, in the alley that smelled of cats and Italian cooking, he helped her load up. The baskets swayed wildly on either side of the scooter.

"There's one thing you could do," she said, steadying the vehicle.

"Yes?"

"Kick-start my scooter? Could you?"

He put a booted foot on the pedal and kicked down twice. The Vespa popped into life. She gave him a wobbly smile. "Thanks! See you— maybe." She clambered on and shot off down the cobbled alley, leaving him standing there, without looking back.

•   •   •

A fine drizzle washed the misty landscape as she rode home. Awkwardly balancing the loaded baskets, her knee throbbing, Rebecca felt chilled and shaky. All her schemes had come to a head. She had gambled, and still did not know if she had won or lost.

When she'd first heard of Michael Florio's flight from San Francisco, her instantaneous thought was for Therese. How traumatized was she? What inner strength did she have to defend her psyche against such a dreadful situation? Rebecca had dealt with too many traumatized children not to dread the psychological consequences.

Conventional wisdom had it that Florio's escape had been a public admission of guilt, the kind of flight from justice that ended in either a permanent exile abroad—or a bloody shoot-out in some seedy motel. But whose guilt? His or Therese's?

Rebecca had at once realized that all that mattered to her was her child's welfare. Questions of guilt came after that.

In San Francisco it had looked as if she had no hope of ever seeing Therese again. Yet there had been a spark of light in the darkness, a chance remark Barbara Florio had made, thirteen years ago, and which had remained in Rebecca's unconscious all these years.

The conversation, which had been intended to set Rebecca's mind at rest about her child's future, had been mainly about possessions. Barbara Florio had spoken proudly of the many homes they had: the ranch up in the hills of Marin County, the skiing chalet in Austria, the cottage in Ireland.

And when Michael really wants to get away from everyone and everything, she had said with a deprecatory laugh, *he has this old millhouse hidden in the woods near Urbino. That's where his family came from, back in the old days. It's the one place nobody ever gets invited to, and believe me, nobody in their right mind would come. It's not even properly restored, and I loathe the place, but it's his sanctuary, and he loves to hole up there. He makes sure nobody knows about it.*

Rebecca could still remember the indulgent smile on Barbara Florio's face. More than that, she recalled with clarity the way the woman's voice had dropped as she said the words, sharing not only a male absurdity, but also a secret of some kind.

That handful of sentences about Urbino had sunk to the bottom of her memory. But the words had risen again. And when she had been told that Michael Florio had fled San Francisco on the day of his wife's funeral, taking Therese and her sister with him, she had seen the indulgent smile on the glossy lips, had heard the name *Urbino* in her ears.

That had been Barbara's gift to her. She had taken Rebecca's child, but in exchange, she had given Rebecca the clue to finding Therese again.

Nobody else had any idea where Florio might be. She had debated whether or not she should tell the police. But right from the start, she had realized that her objectives were different from theirs. Even if Florio, and not Therese, was the guilty one, Therese would be taken into institutional care. As the girl's biological mother, who had given her away at birth, Rebecca would never be given access.

She had flown out to Rome, riding on her instincts, banking on her hope that Urbino was a small enough place for her to have a realistic chance of locating Michael Florio's millhouse. She had reached Urbino in the black hours of a Monday midnight, and had sat awake in the bus station until the sun rose, and she could continue her search.

Michael Florio's millhouse was even more remote than his wife had suggested. It did not have a telephone, and nobody seemed to have heard of it. It took her days to find the small local post office that knew of it, and the postman's wife who told her how to get there.

On her very first expedition there, she had glimpsed the mud-spattered Jeep hidden in a barn, and had known that Barbara's legacy had been solid gold. Lying in the bracken, she had wept with relief. But how could she get into that fortress? The only way was to let him find her, and voluntarily bring her into the house. She reasoned he would need help in looking after two teenage daughters. That same day, her plan had been born.

It had been developing in her mind for some time, but lying there in the bracken, it had taken its final shape. She had known exactly what she was going to do.

She was going to take Therese away from him.

She knew it would be kidnapping, but Florio had forfeited all right to the child. Whatever the truth was, Therese must not be made to suffer the terrible price that would have to be paid.

She would get next to Therese, win her confidence, win her heart. Then, when the time was right, she would tell Therese the truth. And she would take Therese away, far away, to the sun and the fresh air of some better place. She had enough money to make a new start in Australia or New Zealand, somewhere clean, somewhere nobody knew about the horrors of the past.

And there, starting afresh, she would heal Therese. Together they would solve it, whatever it was, the dark shadow that had loomed over the child's life.

If she had found the Urbino house, others would follow. Her time was limited. All that mattered was getting Therese out of that trap. When the dogs closed in on Michael Florio, she had to be long gone. She would take Therese and run farther and faster than her adoptive father had been able to do. Whatever Therese had done, she would never let go of her daughter again.

Rebecca lifted her face to the sky and squinted into the cold drizzle. The mist was thick, enveloping the wooded hills. She had been too anxious to play it safe, too desperately drawn to her unknown child. Had it worked?

All she could do now was wait. Wait, and pray he would come after her.

Rebecca did not go into Urbino the next day, or the next. She spent the days in the Fiorentini farmhouse, relentlessly cleaning every surface she could get her hands on, as if taking refuge in the hard manual work. Perhaps sensing her need for isolation, Signora Fiorentini left her in peace.

Two days of fruitless waiting later, and there were flutterings of panic inside her. She had made getting Therese back the focus of her life. What if Florio did another disappearing act, and went somewhere else, even more inaccessible? She longed to ride out to the millhouse and take a look, but she knew that would ruin everything.

She was starting to realize that she had given herself an ultimatum. If Florio did not fall for her scheme, she would have no option but to tell the police where he was.

She needed exercise or she would go crazy. Despite the cold, she told Fiorentini she was going to get some cabbages. She mounted the Vespa and rode down the muddy lane to the big cabbage field beyond the hill. It was a misty, freezing, not very fragrant place, but it was good to feel cold air on her face and see the sky. She took a brisk walk around the field to warm up before starting work.

The cabbages they grew here were the Lombardy variety, a favorite dish in these parts, massive and heavy as stones. The first frosts had already scorched the weighty vegetables on the outside. She was stripping away blackened outer leaves when she heard the roar of a big engine, and turned. Michael Florio's Jeep was pulling up in the lane.

Her heart contracted painfully in her chest as she saw the dark figure get out. She was suddenly regretting having come to this ghostly place, where he could do anything he chose to her. But she stood her ground, waiting for him.

"Your landlady told me you were up here," he greeted her. He was wearing his heavy sheepskin coat. His face and hair were wet with the mist. "What's the matter? You look like a scared rabbit."

"I'm just cold."

Florio moved his head slightly. "My car is over there. Let's go."

"What for?" she demanded, and this time she could not keep the apprehension out of her voice.

"You started this conversation," he replied. "Let's finish it."

Rebecca's heart felt like lead in her breast. Had he already raked through her flimsy cover, and found it full of holes? He was waiting for her. Heavily, she walked in the direction of the big Jeep.

He held the passenger door open for her. She got in and looked around the neat, clean interior. He got in beside her and slammed the door shut.

In such close proximity, he was frighteningly big, looming over her. She pressed her back against the door, feeling for the handle, wondering how fast she would be able to get out, if she had to. But she kept her chin up, meeting his eyes defiantly. "Well?" she demanded.

He contemplated her for a moment. "If you think I'm some kind of reclusive millionaire, forget it."

"I'm sorry?" she said, genuinely nonplussed.

"If I did take you on, it would be room and board, plus fifty bucks a week. That's it."

Not quite believing what she was hearing, Rebecca felt her pulse give a sudden leap. "Fifty dollars a week?"

"You told me all you wanted was somewhere to stay, plus a little extra money."

"I meant it."

"Fifty bucks is all I can pay. You'll be able to save ninety percent of that. We don't have any frills."

"I'm used to doing without frills." She took a deep breath, still unable to quite believe it. "Are you offering me the job?"

"I'm offering you a week's trial," he said. "If you don't shape up, you're out."

"Oh, I'll shape up," she assured him quietly. "I will. Don't worry."

His fingers were drumming on the steering wheel as he assessed her reaction. "The offer is subject to a lot of things," he said. "The most important is that you get along with the girls. I discussed you with them. They're willing to meet you. Tomorrow morning. Before eleven. Come to the house. I don't need to tell you how to get there."

"No, you don't," she said. "I'll be there."

"I've just been treated to an hour-long testimonial about you from your landlady."

"Signora Fiorentini?" Rebecca smiled. "We get along."

"She thinks you're wonderful. It seems you even saved her son's life."

"He cut his hand, is all."

"I made some other inquiries about you," he went on in his quiet, slightly husky voice. "Nobody has a bad word to say about you. Everybody thinks you're wonderful." He paused. "But nobody has ever seen any real evidence that you are who you say you are."

"Why shouldn't I be who I say I am?"

"I think you're a liar," he replied calmly. "But who isn't, these days? You have a right to your little secrets, however sordid they may be. I don't really give a damn what's in your past. My children's welfare is all that really interests me. If you can help them, you're in." His voice dropped a notch, grew harsh. "But if you ever harm them, in any way, then I will harm you in return."

"I have never yet harmed a child, Mr. Florio," she said tightly.

He nodded slightly. The expression in his eyes told her he meant exactly what he said—he saw in her a tool he might be able to use, a tool he would snap and discard if it proved troublesome. "We're going to be living in close proximity," he said. "Here's the deal. Do your job, and don't ask any questions about us. In return, we won't ask any questions about you. When it's over, we turn our backs on one another and walk away. Is that acceptable?"

She forced herself to smile. "Perfectly acceptable."

It had started to rain. The drops drummed on the roof of the Jeep, in time to his fingers drumming on the wheel.

"Two other things. One: The children's safety is paramount. Everything you do comes second to that. You understand?"

Rebecca nodded.

"Two: While you're in my employ, I expect you to do as I tell you. Implicitly. I don't expect to be disobeyed in the slightest thing. We live by set routines. Once you've learned what those routines are, you will follow them unequivocally. No exceptions. No bright ideas or improvisations. It all goes by the book. You understand me?"

"You want a lot for your fifty bucks," she said.

"That's why I'm telling you this in advance. If it isn't acceptable, then let's stop wasting each other's time right now."

"I didn't say it was unacceptable," she said, forced into swallowing her anger. "I've worked in hospitals. I know how to follow a routine. Just that, the way you're talking, you want a slave, not a nanny."

"You're not going to be working any harder than you have been at the Fiorentini place," he retorted. "You won't have any expenses, and you'll have money in your pocket. That is not slavery."

Rebecca nodded. "You're right." She had to be conciliatory with this controlling, paranoid personality. If she didn't fit right into his dark projections, she had no chance of reaching Therese. "Very well. I accept those conditions."

His eyes were fixed on her mouth, as though trying to read her commitment or otherwise on her lips. "Good," he said, with no change of tone. Florio reached past her and pushed her door open. A blast of cold, wet air swept in. "Tomorrow, at the mill. Before eleven."

She climbed out of the Jeep. He did not wait for her to close the door—he slammed it shut. The engine roared to life, and the big vehicle lumbered down the road. She caught a glimpse of his dark shape through the foggy windows. Then there was just the fading roar of the motor in the mist.

You have a right to your little secrets, however sordid they may be. What did he think she was? Some kind of petty criminal, some kind of drug abuser? The thought of working under those contemptuous black eyes was like swallowing a jagged rock. It sat in her gullet, choking her.

Then it suddenly dawned on her that she had successfully presented an image that he had been fooled by. She thought of Therese, and remembered that she had just achieved a great victory. She was winning, not Michael Florio. She was in control, not he. He just didn't know it. She was going to meet her child tomorrow. She could hardly believe it.

It occurred to her that Florio must be violating all his instincts, all his rules of survival, by inviting her into his life. He must be seriously concerned about Therese to have taken such a chance. Now all she wanted was to be with her daughter.

She was singing as she negotiated the slippery road, and exhilaration carried her along as if on wings.

•   •   •

During the journey to the millhouse, Rebecca wondered once or twice whether she could go through with this.

She had been unable to eat a morsel of breakfast, her stomach a hard ball that could accept no food. She had told the concerned Fiorentini family a lie about having eaten unwisely at a *trattoria* in Urbino the day before. The sensation of nervous queasiness remained. Now that it was at hand, the thing she had desired so much terrified her.

The mill was a hard place to reach, accessible only along a maze of dirt roads. Without directions, you would never find it. And the house dominated almost all approaches. There was no way of getting a vehicle there unobserved.

Florio must have chosen this house years ago. Like some primitive warlord, he had ensured himself a last refuge. Had he always known that one day he would need this secret place? Had he anticipated that something would drive him to this?

She parked in front of the mill and paused for a moment. The house was bigger than she had thought, built in an L shape that enclosed a paved courtyard. It was a handsome structure, its gray stones sprinkled with orange lichen, heavy oak beams framing the doors and windows.

It was quarter to ten, and very quiet. Rebecca walked to the door and watched, as if in a dream, her own hand reach for the heavy iron ring and rap on the wood. After an interminable pause, the door swung open, and Michael Florio stood framed in the doorway.

"Hi," she heard herself say brightly. "I'm not too early, am I?"

"No," he said. "Come in."

She forced herself to smile at him, and stepped inside.

Her first impression of the interior was of silent bareness. The house smelled of wax, woodsmoke, and linseed oil, a mixture of scents she found hauntingly familiar. The only piece of furniture was a huge eighteenth-century cupboard, which stood in the hall, a thick bronze key stuck in its lock.

"We're in the kitchen," Florio said, leading the way. The walls were bare stone. As with so many Tuscan farmhouses, the ground floor had been originally designed to keep stores and animals. The high, vaulted ceilings were hung with wrought-iron candelabra. The sockets held candles, she noticed, not electric lightbulbs. A couple were lit, providing a flickering light.

"You don't have electricity?" she asked.

"Not yet," he replied. "Maybe by the end of the month." He was wearing a checked shirt and faded denims, sneakers on his feet. Without the heavy sheepskin coat, his frame was not as bulky as she had supposed. He was lean, moving with a smooth grace that was different from the hulking presence he acquired from the coat. From behind, she saw that his thick, dark hair fell over his collar.

He led her up a long flight of stairs that emerged into a family kitchen, a large, bright room with big windows. As in the Fiorentini house, a domed wood oven dominated the kitchen, spreading comfort around it. In the center of the room was a round pine table. And sitting at the table, with an array of books open before her, was a girl.

Rebecca went blank, like an actor who had been fed the wrong line and was helplessly lost.

The girl looked up. Her hair was glossy, blondish. She was very pretty, almost a woman. Her eyes, a deep brown, met Rebecca's. "Hi," she said. "I'm Devon."

Devon. The older daughter. Where was Therese? Rebecca managed a stab at a smile. "What are you working on?" she asked, with a breeziness that sounded artificial, even to her own ears. "That looks like algebra to me."

Devon turned the exercise book around so Rebecca could see the lines of algebraic formulas. "Differential calculus. I just started this week."

"Really? Looks like you're doing pretty well," Rebecca said, looking at the neat rows of numbers and symbols.

"I'm having a few problems." The girl shrugged. "It's not really that hard. It's mainly logic."

"You must be good at math, if you can teach yourself calculus," she said brightly. "That's wonderful."

She saw Florio's expression curdle at her banal dialogue. He was leaning against one of the pine cupboards, arms folded across his broad chest. "Any chance you could give her some help?" he asked.

"With the calculus?" Rebecca picked up Devon's work and tried to focus on it. "My strong points were biology and chemistry. I was never brilliant at math. We'll take a look at it later on, if you like. Okay?"

Devon brightened. "Sure." Devon was very poised, Rebecca thought; she had Florio's ability to be herself without squirming.

"Devvy," Florio said, "why don't you offer our guest something to drink?"

"Would you like some juice?" Devon asked gravely.

"I'd love some," Rebecca replied.

"Where's Therese?" Florio asked Devon.

"Still in bed," the girl said, intent on her work.

Florio glanced at his watch. "At this time of day?"

"She had a bad night. She's tired."

Rebecca thought she caught some tiny, meaningful glance between them. Florio straightened. "I'll go up and see her, leave you two to get acquainted for a while."

"Okay."

"Call if you need me," he said, ruffling Devon's glossy hair as he passed.

Rebecca watched Devon squeeze the fruit. She studied the clean profile, the lips slightly compressed in concentration. The girl wore tight jeans and a black Red Hot Chili Peppers T-shirt. Her fine hands were almost a woman's, and the swell of breast and hips showed that puberty had already been and gone. Rebecca was sick with anticipation to see Therese.

"You have a lovely place here."

"It's kind of isolated," Devon replied. "But it's pretty, isn't it?"

"It's beautiful." Inside, she was thinking what a desperately lonely place this must be for two teenage girls.

"My father made all this," Devon said, waving briefly at the kitchen.

Rebecca glanced around. The kitchen had been expertly fitted in gorgeous figured pine. There was a gas stove, but there were only gaping holes and empty sockets where the electrical appliances should have been.

No fridge. No machines to wash dishes or clothes. Life must be hard here. "Who does the cooking?" she asked.

"We take turns."

"All three of you?"

"Well, me and Dad. Therese—that's my sister—hates cooking and cleaning and all that stuff."

"Really? Are you a good cook?"

The girl had made two glasses of juice. She wiped her hands on a cloth. "When we left San Francisco, I took a Chinese cookbook with me. I love dim sum. You like dim sum?"

"Sure, though I've never made it."

"It's my favorite food in all the world. Dad used to take us to a dim sum place every week. I thought I would learn how to make it. Do you have any idea how difficult it is to make dim sum?"

"It looks difficult," Rebecca said, smiling.

"It's a lot more difficult than calculus." She set a glass of juice in front of Rebecca and seated herself. "I should have chosen something a lot simpler."

"So, in the absence of dim sum, what do you eat?"

"When it's my turn, I make tuna and salad. My father does salad and tuna."

Rebecca laughed. "I can't make dim sum, but I can make more than tuna and salad."

"That's good. But you have to be careful. Therese is allergic to a whole lot of things."

Rebecca couldn't help looking over her shoulder, as if to see whether Therese was coming in. "You know why your father asked me to come here this morning, Devon?"

The brown eyes met hers. "We don't need a nanny," she said calmly.

"How about a friend?"

There was a silence. "Were you really good at biology and chemistry," Devon asked, "or were you just saying that?"

"No, I wasn't just saying that."

"It's important," the girl continued. "I have to do well in those subjects. I want to go to medical school."

"You want to be a doctor?"

"Yes."

"Can I ask why?"

Devon shrugged. "That's what I want," she replied.

"Well, I trained as a nurse. I'm sure I could coach you through your science subjects, even if you're on your own as far as differential calculus is concerned. But you'll be back at school soon, won't you? I mean, this is just a vacation, isn't it?"

"Not exactly."

"Oh? What is it, then?"

"It's a retreat," the girl said.

"A retreat?"

"Yes."

"Okay. I think I get your point. You need a tutor more than you need a nanny. Am I right?"

"My father says you're very bright," Devon said.

"Is that what he said? I'm flattered."

"You want to take a look at my syllabus?" Devon offered.

Rebecca nodded. At fifteen, Devon Florio seemed to have picked up something of her adoptive father's commanding manner. The girl passed Rebecca some printed sheets. Rebecca leafed through the syllabus. From somewhere at the back of the house, she heard what sounded like a child crying. Her heart seemed to stop. She forced herself to look calm. "And your sister, Therese? Does she study as hard as you do?"

"When she feels like it," Devon replied, "which isn't exactly every day. She's not very disciplined. On the other hand, she's probably twenty points ahead of me on the IQ scale." Devon smiled. "One day she'll be picking up a Nobel prize or something while I'm taking out tonsils."

Rebecca kept her expression neutral. "Well, I think I can help you with all this. Studying at home is very different from studying at school. You can do a lot more, if you have the intelligence. But it's very easy to go down pointless side alleys, to get bogged down in details you don't need. Maybe the biggest danger is of tiring yourself out. Do you know what I'm talking about?"

Devon nodded. "I think so."

"I'd suggest you do no more than two hours in the morning and two in the afternoon. I can be around to help you during those periods, if you need me. That way, you should be well up to speed by the time your— retreat—is over. How does that sound?"

Devon was looking happy, as if responding to the brisk tone in Rebecca's voice. "We could try that out."

"Good. But I meant what I said just now, too. I can be your friend as well as your tutor. I hope that happens."

"Me, too," Devon agreed with more warmth. "Do you want to go upstairs? Therese ought to be out of bed by now, so you can meet her. And I'll show you the room you'll be using."

"Fine."

Walking up the stairs behind Devon, Rebecca could see that the girl was developing an excellent figure. Yet she felt Devon was in no rush to grow up. Her face was innocent of makeup. She didn't pluck her eyebrows or paint her nails, and she'd made no great effort to emphasize her figure with her choice of clothes. There was something comforting in knowing that Therese had this balanced, studious girl as an elder sister.

They reached the landing. "That's my father's room," Devon said, pointing to big double doors at the end of the corridor. "My room is next door. And you'll be in here." She pushed the door open, and stepped aside to let Rebecca go in first.

The room was pretty. A bathroom with a shower led off it. It had built-in closets, a small writing desk, and a comfortable-looking bed, all evidently made by Florio himself out of the same figured pine. The window looked out over the millpond, the view bisected by the steel burglar bars that had been set solidly into the stone.

Devon followed her glance. "My father runs a security agency," she said. "He's fanatical about things like that. It wouldn't be easy to break in here."

Or out, Rebecca reflected. She thought of the word Devon had used to describe their presence here. *Retreat.* Had she meant it in the sense of running away from a victorious enemy, or in the sense of a withdrawal from the world? Perhaps she had meant it in both senses. "It's a pretty room," she said aloud.

"Do you think you'll like it?"

"I've stayed in a lot worse places."

"Really?" Devon's cool eyes surveyed her.

Rebecca wondered just how Michael Florio had described her to the girls. She didn't want to come across as some kind of hippie. "I meant, when I was a student. I shared some pretty seedy digs."

"Didn't you stay in a nurses' dorm?"

"For a while."

"What hospital did you train at?"

"As a matter of fact, I trained at several different hospitals. General, psychiatric, children's. All in L.A." She edged away from the topic quickly. "This room is just fine. The view is lovely."

"Would you like to see my room?"

"Yes, please."

Devon took her down the corridor. Her own room was big, with two windows. Both were protected with heavy steel bars. Florio had done the woodwork in this room, too, but here the work was more than workman-like. He had taken pains to embellish the fittings. The bed was finely carved with flowers and leaves. Rebecca looked around the neat room. There were fluffy stuffed animals, collections of glass animals and sea-shells, and several big posters showing the same handsome young man flexing his muscles and his pout.

A large bookcase was filled. Not one book was out of place. In fact, not a teddy bear or a glass snail was out of line. The woodwork was as glossy as Devon's hair, and the quilted bedspread was immaculate. There was a boot-camp neatness about the room. Rebecca had a sudden, strong flash of herself at fifteen. She'd had the same self-discipline, the same funda-mental seriousness, the same determination to be a doctor. "You certainly keep your things neat."

"Thanks. We'll go see Therese now, okay?"

"Sure."

Devon paused. "Look, my sister isn't always easy to get along with."

"Oh? Why's that?"

"Well, I guess you'll find out for yourself. I don't want to frighten you or anything, but she can get pretty crazy."

" 'Crazy'?"

"She can be frightening sometimes." The big brown eyes were solemn. "If you treat her the way Dad and I tell you, nothing will happen. But if you make her angry, she can be . . . dangerous."

Rebecca recoiled slightly. "In what way?"

"She can hurt people," Devon said calmly. "Let's go and see if she's surfaced." And she led Rebecca to the room next door.

This room was smaller. It was also dark. The curtain was still drawn, only chinks of light escaping from around the heavy drapes. There were no posters on the walls and no shelves of toys, but there was plenty of stuff on the floor. In the dim light, Rebecca could see that dirty clothes were scattered everywhere. A plate of half-eaten, congealed food was partly hidden under a shirt; ketchup had soaked into the cotton. There were dozens of books strewn around, almost all of them open and facedown. Rebecca remembered how her own stepmother had detested that habit. Michael Florio was sitting on the bed. Huddled under a blanket next to him was a girl.

Rebecca's first impression was of a thicket of dark, tangled hair, from which two gray eyes stared out like a wary animal's. Rebecca could see little of the rest of her face. The girl was hugging her shins under the blanket, her chin pressed to her knees, almost in a fetal curl. Rebecca's heart was pounding violently, so loudly that she felt sure they must be able to hear it. If she gave herself away now, all was lost. Transfixed by those gray eyes, Rebecca forced herself to smile. Her lips were dry as bone.

"Hello, Therese. I'm Rebecca."

There was no response. "Say hello, Therese," Florio murmured.

The girl lifted a hand and fiddled with her bangs, her fingers short-nailed and dirty. She had evidently not washed them for some time. At last she said, "Hi," in a quiet little voice, and stuck her mouth back behind her knees again. She did not take her eyes away from Rebecca.

Rebecca had to tell herself that her instinct to comfort and kiss the child was insanely inappropriate. The swimming sensation in her head was so turbulent that without being invited, she sat on Therese's bed. She would have fallen otherwise. "I think I took those stairs a little too fast," she said, and tried to laugh. The three of them were staring at her, and she guessed she must have gone as white as a sheet. *Don't blow it*, she pleaded with herself desperately.

"Are you okay?" Florio asked her curiously.

"I'm fine."

"It's your knee, isn't it?"

"Just a little food poisoning," she babbled. "I had a bad night. Pay no attention." She could not tear her eyes away from Therese. "I hear you had a bad night, too."

"She didn't sleep too well," Devon said, when Therese failed to respond. "I had to come in and give her a glass of water. Didn't I, Tree?"

Therese nodded slightly. "I had some horrible dreams," she said.

"What about?" Rebecca asked.

Therese lifted her face over the protective embankment of her knees, and rested her chin on her forearms. Rebecca could see she had been crying recently; there was a moist track down one cheek. The face was pale and thin. The mouth, wide and shockingly like Ryan's, turned down at the corners. "About Mommy," she said.

"Oh, I'm sorry," Rebecca replied. She knew her daughter was thirteen, yet her instinct was to treat her like a child three or four years younger. "Everything seems horrible at night, doesn't it? But it's bright sunshine outside now. If you got up, you might feel better."

"I guess," Therese said without conviction.

Devon had stooped to pick up the dirty plate. "Tree, it's awfully messy in here." She sighed. "It smells like a zoo."

Florio put his hand on Devon's shoulder. "We'll leave you two to get acquainted," he said. "When you're ready, why not bring Rebecca out to see the mill, Therese?"

"Okay," Therese said in a small voice.

He and Devon left the room. Rebecca rose, hating the darkness and sorrow that hung over this room. She went to the curtains and drew them back. Sunshine flooded the room, surprising Therese, who buried her face in the blanket.

"Looks like you need some fresh clothes," Rebecca said. She started to gather the scattered things. She was looking busy but feeling, if anything, even less in command of herself. The sunlight she had let into the room had made the chaos more visible. It was depressingly like a chimpanzee's cage in here.

The blurred picture of Therese printed in the magazines and newspapers had told Rebecca little about what her daughter looked like. There had been vague similarities to her own childhood face. But this child was so neglected-looking that it was hard to make out anything about her. She felt desperately sorry for this subdued, unkempt girl. *I'll get you out of this,* she vowed silently. *We'll break free.*

She was feeling a dreamlike quality wash over her in reaction to the adrenaline rush she had just experienced. She was physically weak and drained. So this was the end of her quest? Then she realized that her quest was only just beginning. There was an eternity yet to cross.

As she picked up clothes, Rebecca glanced at the titles of the books that lay on the floor. To her surprise, almost all of them were heavyweight Victorian novels—Dickens, Trollope, Thackeray. She could not believe this was typical reading for a thirteen-year-old, but Therese seemed to be halfway through all of them.

She had gathered an armful of Therese's clothes. "Have you got a basket or something for the laundry?"

"I'll get it." She swung her legs out of the bed, pushing the tangle out of her eyes. Now Rebecca could see she was already dressed. She wore jeans and a loose gray shirt, which had not been pressed, and which crumpled unflatteringly around her slim shoulders. Her bare feet were dirty. She pushed them into loafers that were shabby and torn. This was not California laid-backness; it was just plain neglect. Rebecca felt angry.

They should not have let her get like this, no matter how difficult she might be.

Therese got a wicker basket and held it out for the clothes. Rebecca dropped the dank bundle into the basket. They were face-to-face for a moment. Therese's tangled mop of hair was a rich brunette color, not unlike Rebecca's own. She could not stop herself from wanting to find more than that, to find traces of her own features in Therese's face, but so far she could detect none. But Therese was very like Ryan, especially in the full, obstinate mouth. That had been a shock from which she was still reeling. The girl's eyes were her best feature, big and fringed with long lashes.

Rebecca stared into them, wondering, *Did you set that fire? Did you mean to hurt her, even kill her? Was it all a terrible mistake? I can help!*

But she could not say the words, not yet, and Therese turned away and manhandled the laundry basket into the corridor. She turned to face Rebecca, clawing the hair out of her eyes in what was evidently a habitual gesture. "Are you going to be staying with us?"

"Well, if you and Devon want me to."

"You mean, we get to decide?"

"Actually, I suppose your father will decide. But I doubt he would insist if you and your sister thought I was awful."

Therese considered. "You're not awful."

"Well, thank you."

"You're welcome."

The girl was half turned away, but she was studying Rebecca with a sidelong glance from under her bangs. "You're a nurse, right?"

"Yes, that's right."

"Have you got anything to do with psychiatrists?"

"Not much. I'm a pediatric nurse on a medical ward. My patients are all sick in their bodies." She paused. "Why do you ask? Don't you like psychiatrists?"

She saw the mouth, too big for the thin face, pull into a bitter expression. "No."

"Well, I promise not to make you look at any inkblots."

She had meant that as a feeble joke, but it fell flat. "Inkblots?"

"Oh, that was just a test that used to be common when I was a kid. I don't even know if they do it anymore."

"It must be one they haven't tried on me yet," Therese said dryly.

"Have they tried many?"

"Plenty," Therese said shortly.

Rebecca decided to skip the subject for the time being. "Sure you don't want any breakfast? I saw some luscious fruit in the kitchen."

"I'm not hungry," Therese replied. "I don't eat breakfast."

"You shouldn't skip it. It gives you a good start to the day."

"I'm not anorexic," Therese replied coolly.

"I didn't think you were. It's just something my stepmother always said. I guess I had it drummed into me."

Therese cocked her head. "Your stepmother?"

"My real mother died when I was ten. My father remarried a year later."

"That's gross," Therese said in disgust.

"Well, it happens."

"Men are disgusting."

Rebecca smiled. "Oh, I think he did it partly for me. Maybe he thought I needed a mother."

"You needed your own mother. Not a prosthetic one."

Prosthetic? Not bad for a thirteen-year-old. Rebecca remembered Devon's comment about her sister's intelligence. "No, actually, I needed any kind of mother."

The girl leaned against the door, her lean figure taking on a slouch that reminded Rebecca of a thousand adolescent rebels. The neck of her loose gray shirt drooped, and Rebecca saw she wore a thin gold chain on which hung a tiny gold key. "So, did you like her?"

"My stepmother? As a matter of fact, we detested each other."

"Why?"

"I was rude and she was cold."

"And now? Do you get along?"

"No, I'm still rude and she's still cold. But we keep smiling." She demonstrated the death's-head grin she reserved for her stepmother, and was rewarded by seeing Therese's eyes gleam with amusement for a moment. "But I feel sorry for her now. It can't be easy starting out with a job description like *stepmother*. It goes together with *wicked*, doesn't it? Right away you're thinking poison apples and ugly sisters."

"She should have been more understanding."

"It's not easy to understand what losing a mother is like. Until it happens to you."

Therese's eyes seemed to shimmer with an inrush of tears. She turned away, as if angry.

"Hey, I'm sorry." She ached to take Therese in her arms and hold her close. For a moment she considered blurting out the truth here and now, confronting Therese with her identity. The words almost burst out of her. Swallowing hard, she managed to fight down the crazy instinct. "Let's get rid of this basket. Where do you do your washing and ironing?"

Therese kept her back turned. "We take everything into the Laundromat in Urbino."

"Don't you wash anything here?"

"We've got a stone sink, if you like scrubbing by hand," Therese said. "We'll have a washing machine soon. When Daddy gets the wheel running."

"Wheel?" Rebecca asked.

Therese nodded. "Do you know what my father's doing back there?" she asked.

"I have no idea."

"I'll show you. It's neat."

Rebecca didn't want to go anywhere. She wanted to stay here, close to Therese, drinking her in. But she agreed.

Therese shrugged on a heavy wool sweater. She took a white Giants baseball cap off the back of the door—the only garment, Rebecca noticed, that she had bothered to hang up—and pulled it on her head. She pulled it down hard, so the peak hid her eyes from the world, showing only that wide, sullen mouth and pointed chin.

Rebecca followed Therese out. The child was tall and slender. Under her deeply unflattering clothes, there were slight signs of budding woman-hood, enough to tell Rebecca that puberty was under way. Her mind and body would be full of questions, full of urgent confusion. Rebecca re-membered her own motherless adolescence, and her heart went out to Therese. If only the child would let her close, there was so much she could do for her!

So far, she reflected with some surprise, it was going okay. She felt as if someone had been jumping up and down on her stomach, but she had behaved with aplomb. Or so she flattered herself. And Therese had been like any of the teenage patients she treated every day. She was not drooling or feral. She hadn't tried to disembowel Rebecca with a switchblade. The crazed delinquent depicted by Devon had not materialized, just a rather pathetic girl in a dirty Giants cap. She was almost starting to wonder what all the fuss had been about.

"I said I would help your sister with her schoolwork," she ventured. "Maybe I could help you, too?" She had seen no sign of study in Therese's room. "Have you got any schoolbooks?"

"Some," Therese said with no show of enthusiasm.

"We could do an hour or two a day, if you like."

"Maybe."

They went out the back door. There was an enclosed courtyard behind the house, where a clothesline had been erected, and where there were more signs of building work in progress. A Honda gasoline generator was chugging outside a big stone barn, its power lines snaking into the open doorway. Therese led Rebecca into the barn.

The interior was dark and cool, and filled with the sound of roaring water. Michael Florio was sawing planks of lumber with a circular saw, and the smell of freshly cut wood was strong. Behind him, a tall wooden wheel was propped against the wall. At the far end of the barn, a waterfall thundered down a vertical drop of fifteen or twenty feet. The water rushed into a chute, then through a wide, deep channel, dark and turbulent, in the center of the barn.

"This is the millrace," Therese said, lifting her voice above the rush of the water and the whine of the saw, and Rebecca realized that the waterfall and the channel directed the river itself, pouring from the dam through an arch, and hurtling out through another arch at the other end of the structure. "The wheel used to turn a millstone down in that cellar, for grinding wheat and corn. Daddy's converting it to make power for the house."

Rebecca stared around. In the corner was a boxy apparatus labeled TRANSFORMER: DANGER—HIGH VOLTAGE, bearing a skull and crossbones. By the side of the mill wheel was an industrial-specification electric generator, still covered in grease. Rebecca took it all in, seeing the new machinery, understanding the project intuitively. Florio was restoring the mill wheel to run a compact electric plant. She was awed by the scale of the work and by Michael Florio's evident mastery of technique and material. The mill wheel was evidently a few decades old, the multitude of fresh patches in the old wood showing where Florio had reinforced and altered the original mechanism.

"Wow," she said.

"I told you it was neat."

Florio heard their voices. He cut off the saw and turned to them. His face and hair were spattered with sawdust. "Hello." He looked surprised to see Therese. "You managed to get the sleeper out of bed, I see. What's your secret?"

"I just pulled the curtain open," Rebecca replied, smiling at Therese.

"You just pulled the curtain open?" Florio said. "You're lucky to be alive. How's it going?" he asked Therese.

"Okay," Therese replied indifferently.

"How have you two been getting along?"

Therese just shrugged, her face hidden beneath the peak of her cap. So Rebecca said, "We've been getting along just fine," in a firm tone.

Florio looked from one to the other, his dark eyes serious. He dusted shavings from his big hands. "Let's go talk in the kitchen with Devon. Will you wait?" he asked Rebecca.

"Of course," she said. "I'll just take a stroll."

Feeling a little like a stray dog waiting to get a string tied around its neck, Rebecca wandered around Florio's turbine. When he completed his work, the house would have its own electricity supply, free, eternal, and impossible to tamper with. The house would be completely self-sufficient. A terrific setup for a paranoid.

She walked outside, into the crisp winter morning. The dark millpond spread out beside the house. After hurtling through the millrace, the stream plunged into deep undergrowth and was lost to sight, though it could be heard running swiftly down rocks.

It felt very strange to stand here and know her daughter was discussing her with her adopted family, discussing whether to take her on as a servant. *Remember*, she told herself urgently, *you're here as an employee, not a guest*. Rebecca had always been cursed by too much pride. Even as a child, she had been proud, too proud for her own good. She knew that about herself. And she also knew that doctors tended to slip into thinking they were gods. The power of life and death, the pleading eyes of patients and their families: It was heady food for the ego. She would have to suppress that ego firmly.

At last, she heard a footstep behind her, and turned. Michael Florio came up, tall and dark. "What are you looking at?" he demanded as he joined her.

"The view." She shrugged. "It must be pretty in the summer."

He shrugged slightly, as though implying she wouldn't be here to see it. "Well, are you ready to start?"

Her shoulders sagged. "Does that mean I get the job?"

"If you want it."

"I want it."

"When can you start?"

"Tomorrow," she said succinctly.

"Shall we discuss hours, what you will and won't be expected to do?"

"We can work out the details as we go along. I promised Devon I would help with her schoolwork. With my medical background, I can help her with her most important subjects. I'll also take a look at Therese's work, when she's ready."

"She agreed to that?" Florio asked in obvious surprise.

"Well, she said maybe. I'll share the shopping, the cleaning, and the cooking. I won't work before eight A.M. or past eight P.M. And I'd like Sundays off to do my own thing. Those are my terms."

She had never before used that tone to Florio. He had seen her only as the timid waif. He was very still, and for a moment, she thought he would be angry. Then he nodded. "That seems acceptable. Just remember, we do things my way around here."

"I won't forget," she said dryly.

"I hope this works out," he said, half to himself. With a fluid movement, he hauled his checked shirt over his head, and shook sawdust into the water. His long, naked torso was lean. His stomach was muscled, his chest and shoulders deep, his arms powerful. *My goodness*, Rebecca thought, something changing inside her. She was suddenly remembering what it was like to gape at a muscular male body. He caught her staring at him, and she felt the hot blood rise into her face.

She turned away. Her own blush embarrassed her so much that she was angry with herself. "I'll get back to Urbino," she said stiffly. "See you tomorrow."

"Bye," he replied briefly, pulling his shirt back on. She walked around the house, back to her Vespa. As she passed the kitchen window, she looked in. The girls were sitting at the table. Rebecca caught a glimpse of Therese's pale face, shadowed under the baseball cap. She waved. Therese did not respond, but the dark gaze followed her as she walked away.

SAN FRANCISCO

Detectives Al Reagan and Carla Bianchi had waited patiently for their audience with Ranolph P. Montrose III. They had been dumped in the waiting room of the great man's office, and left to sit there for an hour. The presence of an elderly secretary, who apparently had little to do, made discussion impossible. Both were thoroughly bored with looking at the old-fashioned furniture, the leather-bound books, and the marine oil paintings by the time a device buzzed on the secretary's desk, and she ushered them into the inner sanctum.

Montrose was waiting for them, his large knuckles clasped on a gleaming, bare mahogany desk. His eyes had lost their red rims since the police officers had last seen him, but he still looked to Bianchi like some kind of predatory bird as he rose and gave them each a bony handshake.

"I hope you have some positive news to relate," he said ominously, as he signaled them to chairs. "I am expecting nothing less, I warn you."

This was not a progress report for Montrose's benefit, and Reagan scowled. But Bianchi smiled blandly at the old man.

"We're making headway, Mr. Montrose," she told him, "and I promise we'll have some news for you very soon. This morning we're hoping you can fill in a few gaps for us."

"Gaps?" he snapped. "Where is Florio? That's the biggest gap I can see, Detective."

"We're working on it," she said patiently.

"Does that mean you have any idea where he and my granddaughters are?"

"No," she admitted, "it doesn't."

"So when you speak of 'making headway,'" the old man rasped, "that is a lie, is it not?"

Bianchi swallowed the insult. Montrose had already exerted pressure at high levels in the police department, and that pressure had made its way down to their own office. The man had powerful cronies, and offending him was not going to help. "We believe Mr. Florio and the girls flew to Canada on the day of the funeral," she said evenly. "We think they then flew on to a second destination in Europe, using forged passports. Right now, the Canadians are checking through the airline computer records, trying to track down where they might have gone. It looks like Mr. Florio planned his departure carefully, and that means tracing him is going to take a little time. But we will do it, Mr. Montrose. You have my word. And as soon as we have information, we'll notify you."

"I was expecting something better than that," Montrose said coldly. "I intend to lodge a complaint about this heel-dragging."

"That's your privilege, sir," she replied.

"Could we talk about the money arrangements in your daughter's marriage?" Reagan demanded, unimpressed by Montrose's threat. "We spoke to your daughter's lawyers, but they referred us to you."

"Of course they did. I left instructions to that effect," Montrose said, his tone sharp. "As far as I am aware, my late daughter is not the one under suspicion. I see no reason why her affairs should be pried into."

"This is a police investigation," Reagan said irritably. "We're not a couple of busybodies here."

"Nobody is trying to throw any suspicion on Mrs. Florio," Bianchi said soothingly. "This information is very important to us, Mr. Montrose."

"To establish a motive for murder, you mean?" Montrose rapped. "My son-in-law didn't bring a penny into the marriage. Everything he had, he milked out of her. When she divorced him, he was going to be flushed back into the sewer he crawled out of. How's that as a motive for murder?"

The old man's energy was venomous. Bianchi glanced quickly at her partner. "Could you be a little more specific?" she asked.

Montrose glared at her for a moment longer, then swung his chair to face the wall. A row of gloomy oil portraits of Victorian males stared back at him from tarnished gold-leaf frames.

"He was never interested in anything but her money," Montrose began abruptly. "He didn't have a cent. Her mother and I begged her to reconsider, but she was under his spell. Hypnotized. He sank his teeth into her like a piranha, and nothing would make him let her go. Nothing."

Bianchi wondered if that meant Montrose had tried to pay Florio off before the marriage, and had failed. "You felt he didn't really care for your daughter?" she asked.

Montrose was glaring at his ancestors; that all these ugly old men were past Montroses was born out by the beaky noses and frowning eyes, and the fact that the long-vanished Montrose factory was featured in the backgrounds of several of the paintings. "He was trash," Montrose said at last. "He claimed to be Italian, but God knows what he really was, with those eyes, that skin. Whatever he was, he came from the gutter."

As far as Bianchi knew, Florio's parents had been hardworking, decent people, who had arrived from Italy after the war. Michael Florio had several brothers and sisters, all of whom were doing well. Whatever his faults, it could not have been easy for Florio to have a virulent bigot like Ranolph Montrose III as a father-in-law. She cleared her throat. "You make it clear you didn't like your son-in-law," she said. "The feeling was mutual, I guess?"

"He despised me. He despised us all. *That* much was mutual."

"You said that Mr. Florio brought no money into the marriage. So his success was based on your daughter's money?" Bianchi asked.

"His success?" Montrose snorted. "Let me show you how hard we tried with Florio. After the wedding, we tried to bury the hatchet. We wanted, above all, for Barbara to be happy. We offered Florio a position in the business. Tantamount to a place on the board. A fat salary, a car, and nothing much to do to get it. He threw it back in our faces. Told us he wanted to make his own way. You know what that meant? Using the Montrose name to chisel every kind of loan he could, legal and illegal. He borrowed a fortune against property that belonged to my daughter, and he plowed it all into his protection racket. He wanted *our name* to veneer that ugly, violent business of his."

"I thought Florio's business was a cash cow," Reagan put in.

"It's easy to make an income when you have someone else's name and someone else's fortune behind you," Montrose said contemptuously. "But Florio still owes a lot of money in this city, Detective. How do you think he was going to pay it back after Barbara kicked him out?"

"Are you referring to the South of Market plot, which your daughter was planning to donate to the Catholic Church?" Bianchi asked carefully.

Montrose swung to face her. "That was chief among the Montrose assets he attempted to mortgage."

"Your daughter must have encouraged him to raise money on that property," Reagan said. "In fact, she must have given her consent. Are you saying she subsequently took it away?"

"Most of the loans were arranged through a private bank over which my family has a measure of control," Montrose said. His eyes gleamed. "Barbara allowed the plot to be used as security for the biggest loan, retaining the proviso that she could dispose of it at any time, and in any way that she wanted to. She decided, with my full approval, I might add, to donate that plot to the church."

"Donate," Reagan said thoughtfully, "not sell. Right?"

Montrose inclined his head.

"In that way, the plot went out of the family, but no money came in. Meaning there was no longer any security for Mr. Florio's loan. No land, no cash, nothing." Reagan leaned back, staring at the old man. "Isn't that like encouraging a man to climb on a bucket and put a noose around his neck—and then kicking the bucket away?"

Ranolph Montrose's face darkened. For a moment, Bianchi anticipated a furious outburst. Then the livid color faded from the old man's thin cheeks. He actually smiled, showing yellowed teeth. "In my family, Detective, we believe in insurance. That was a policy I took out early in my daughter's marriage. For her protection. You understand me? I knew the time would come when we would need that insurance, even if she didn't."

Bianchi cleared her throat. "So without Montrose support, Mr. Florio's ownership of his own business was at risk?"

"Unless he could drum up several million dollars from investors in a hurry," Montrose said.

"Do you know whether he tried?"

"I neither know nor care. But I doubt it. Florio was not the sort of man who would want somebody else owning his business. He was much too arrogant. Much too conceited."

"I take it your daughter never got to make that bequest she was planning?" Bianchi asked.

Montrose shook his head. "No. She died on the eve of making it legal."

"So the plot of land . . . ?"

"All of Barbara's property goes to the children under the terms of a trust."

"Including the South of Market plot?"

"Yes."

"And they inherit fully . . . when?"

"When they are twenty-five."

"Which gives Mr. Florio another ten years' grace, right?"

"Why else do you think he killed her?" Montrose sneered. "As their legal guardian, he keeps control of the estate for another decade. And longer, if he can pervert their innocent minds still further in that time."

"I'm going to ask you to let us see the details of these loans," Bianchi said.

"I'll have a consent typed up today," Montrose said. "You'll have it tomorrow. My bankers will show you everything."

"You had his nuts in your pocket right from the start," Reagan said, with a harsh laugh. "When the time came, you just told your daughter how to slice 'em off, right?"

Montrose's lip curled in disdain, but he did not deny Reagan's crude comment. Bianchi wondered whether it had ever occurred to Ranolph Montrose that, in attempting to castrate Michael Florio in this way, he had possibly sentenced his own daughter to a terrible death. "I have always done what was needed to protect my children."

"Perhaps Mr. Florio also felt that he was doing what was needed to protect *his* children?" she suggested, flattening her voice to cover her dislike of Montrose.

"When?"

"When he took Therese and Devon away from San Francisco."

Montrose's voice darkened. "I hope you no longer cleave to the ludicrous theory that Therese was in some way responsible for her mother's death. You must surely see that would be impossible."

"When we locate Mr. Florio and the girls, we'll need to speak to all of them," Bianchi said neutrally.

Montrose leaned forward. "You cannot take anything that Therese says seriously," he said sharply. "Even if she gave you a written confession to the murder, it would be meaningless. The poor child is crazed."

" 'Crazed'?" Reagan repeated.

Montrose realized he had chosen the wrong word. "Disturbed. She is not in control of what she says or does."

"Then how do you know she didn't have a hand in the fire?" Bianchi asked. "She set other fires, didn't she?"

A look of intense pain crossed Montrose's face. He drew back. "That is not something I wish to go into."

Bianchi started to speak, but he raised his hand to stop her. "I am not going to discuss this issue any further with you," Montrose said. He took a vial from his pocket and fumbled two white pills out of it. He slipped the pills under his tongue and closed his lips. He took out a handkerchief and mopped his mouth, hooded eyelids closing for a moment.

Reagan was bursting to speak, but Bianchi shook her head briefly at her partner. The two detectives waited while Montrose absorbed his medication. The blue tinge left his lips after a while.

"Are you feeling all right?" Bianchi asked.

The old man shook his head, his eyes opening. She saw now that the irises were ringed with gray. That arctic color was partly what gave his stare that haughty, bird-of-prey look. But in reality, it was a sign of disease. He laid a hand on his breast. "Get my babies back," he whispered.

He must have touched some kind of buzzer under his desk, because the door opened, and the elderly secretary came in to escort them out.

Bianchi's mood, as they emerged from the Montrose headquarters, was both depressed and frustrated. Reagan, by contrast, was excited.

"What'd I tell you?" he asked, lighting up a Camel in the street. "I told you we had a strong motive. Florio was going to lose his business."

"I'm happy with the financial angle, Al," she told him. "But remember—Barbara Florio was no saint. And Montrose is a vicious old man. It's clear he loved keeping Florio in his place."

Bianchi had an ominous sense that the truth was slowly falling into place, a dark and sinister truth. "Those poor kids," she said softly. "They may be in terrible danger, Al."

"They were always in danger," Al Reagan replied, opening the door of their car. "From the moment they entered that family, they were in danger. Anyone who crosses Michael Florio's path is in danger. Let's go."

URBINO

Devon was studying in the kitchen, which was apparently her headquarters, when Rebecca arrived the next afternoon. She helped carry Rebecca's things upstairs. There was no sign of Therese. Her door was shut, and presumably she was in her room.

It didn't take long to hang her clothes and put her toothbrush in the glass. She stored her bag of medicines under the bed. She traveled with enough junk to treat twenty different ailments, but she could not bear to be parted from the tools of her trade. She went back down to the kitchen, and set to making the evening meal, her first task in the Florio household.

"Anything I can do to help?" Devon asked.

"No, thanks, this won't take a minute," Rebecca promised, pulling open doors. "I have a technique in a new kitchen. I leave every cupboard wide open, so I can see what's inside."

"Don't knock your teeth out," Devon warned, looking at the multitude of pine doors that Rebecca had swung open. She sat quietly at the table, poring over her work while Rebecca prospected and delved.

She found garlic, laurel, and basil in one of the cupboards. With them, she made tomato sauce, using some of Signora Fiorentini's sun-dried tomatoes, which her landlady had pressed on her that morning. She threw chunks of smoked sausage into the fragrant sauce, then poured it into a square earthenware dish she had found at the back of a cupboard. It was strong and heavy, and she earmarked it to supply many a family meal from now on. She mixed the dry macaroni straight into the same dish. The pasta would absorb its moisture directly from the tomato sauce as it baked, making a *pasta al forno* solid enough to be sliced like a pie, and hearty enough to stick to the ribs in this bitter weather. If nothing else, she had learned to cook Tuscan farmhouse food at Fiorentini's place.

By now, Devon was watching her intently, chewing on the end of her pencil. "Wow, that smells wonderful."

"It's the easiest dish in the world to make."

"What's *that* stuff?"

"This?" Rebecca held up the fat glass jar. "It's mozzarella cheese, the stuff you see melted on the top of your pizza."

"I never knew it came like that," Devon said dubiously.

"It has to be kept underwater or it dries out." She fished out several of the soft white balls and recapped the jar. "It's made from water-buffalo milk."

"You're kidding. Are there water buffaloes in Italy?"

"Up in the Po Valley there are plenty. There are rice paddies, too."

Devon's brown eyes were wide. "Cool. We know hardly anything about this country."

"Hasn't your father brought you here before?" she asked casually.

"This is the first time. We've come to Europe lots of times before, but it was usually to Austria for skiing, or to Ireland. We've got houses in both places. But Dad kept this place as his own private sanctuary until now."

"Sanctuary?"

Devon smiled. "You know, the fox's lair, the eagle's nest, that kind of thing. He came here some after he and Mom separated."

Rebecca was slicing the mozzarella onto the pasta mixture, sprinkling the cheese with more oregano. "That must have been tough on you—the separation."

"It was the only thing they could do," Devon said. "All they did was fight all the time."

"That can't have been easy, either."

"It wasn't. But it's over now."

Rebecca heard something in the girl's voice, and turned. Devon's eyes were wet with tears. "Oh, I'm so sorry," Rebecca said remorsefully. "I didn't mean to upset you."

"It's okay." She blew her nose, and turned back to her work. But Rebecca could see her eyes were blurred, and her full lower lip was trembling. Not knowing how to comfort her, Rebecca heaved the ponderous dish into the wood-fired oven and pushed it right to the back, among the glowing embers.

The delicious smell of the baking pasta soon filled the house. It was a spectacular meal, and one she hoped would appeal to Therese. It was for Therese that she was doing this, on the theory that the way to a child's heart was through her stomach.

Michael Florio came in from his work, covered in sawdust. He sniffed. "This place smells like a five-star restaurant."

"It just smells like a home, Dad," Devon said, in the light, dry way she sometimes said things. Rebecca could have hugged her for that little remark.

Florio looked into the oven and grunted. "Looks better than tuna salad, at any rate."

"I'll go and call Tree," Devon said. She cleared her schoolwork off the table and went upstairs.

Florio opened a straw-wrapped flask of Chianti while Rebecca set the table. "How're you doing?" he asked her.

"I'm groping my way along. I haven't seen Therese yet."

"She likes her room," Florio said flatly.

"Has she been in her room all day?" Rebecca asked, eyebrows lifting.

"Just about."

"That's a lonely way for a girl to be."

"The best thing is to get used to it," Florio replied. "Don't try to get too close."

The advice jarred on Rebecca's nerves. It sounded like a recipe for rejection and neglect. But she said nothing. She got the earthenware dish out of the oven. The pasta had baked perfectly. The cheese was bubbling and golden, and it smelled spectacularly good.

Devon came back down alone. "Therese doesn't want any dinner," she reported.

In some dismay, Rebecca glanced at Florio, waiting for him to insist that his youngest daughter come down. But he just shook his head slightly. "Okay. Let's eat."

"Has she had any breakfast?" Rebecca asked.

"She hasn't even gotten out of bed," Devon said. "She's reading."

"She really reads those tomes?" Rebecca asked. "Dickens and Trollope?"

"They both read that stuff," Florio said.

"The difference is that Therese reads them six and seven at a time," Devon said. "She runs a couple of hundred megahertz faster than the rest of us."

Rebecca was painfully disappointed that Therese was not here to enjoy her first meal. "But if she's had no breakfast, and no lunch, she'll be starving."

"She'll sneak down when nobody's looking," Florio said, "and scarf half that dish, cold. Don't worry about her."

"It's true," Devon said. "We call her Miss Rat." She rose, pulling out a chair for Rebecca. "Why don't you sit down, Rebecca?"

Rebecca was repelled by the idea of Therese scavenging in their wake, like some kind of outcast. In silence, she heaped plates for Devon and Florio. Then she made a third helping and put it on a tray with a glass of water and a piece of bread.

"Where are you going with that?" Florio asked, dark eyes settling on her.

"I'll take it up to her room. At least she can enjoy it hot."

"Forget it."

"It's no bother," Rebecca said firmly, hefting the tray.

"Rebecca, lay off," he said. "If she doesn't want to eat with us, then she won't eat with us."

"Then she can have this in her room," Rebecca said lightly. She walked out.

Going up the stairs, she was in a quiet rage. It hadn't taken her long to find out how Therese had ended up in such an abandoned state. She was a pariah in her own family. Nobody cared whether she got out of bed in the morning, whether she was decently clean, whether she kept up with her schoolwork, not even whether she ate enough to keep body and soul together. Any guilt she had been experiencing about her plan to kidnap Therese was evaporating fast. Disciplined, high-achieving Florio and his disciplined, high-achieving elder daughter were tight together, while little Therese was an irrelevance. A delinquent and a firebug. *We call her Miss Rat.*

Her teeth clenched tight with anger, Rebecca reached Therese's door and knocked. There was no reply. She knocked harder, and heard Therese's voice.

"What?"

"I've brought you some food. It's Rebecca."

"I don't want any food."

"I made it specially for you."

There was no answer, so she opened the door and went in. The curtains were drawn and the room was dark, as it had been the first time she had come in here. The zoo smell and mess were as before, and Rebecca wondered how the girl had possibly managed to get so many clothes dirty and on the floor in so short a time.

Therese was crouched in her bed, books all over the crumpled blankets. She had a thick volume in her hands, held right up to her face so she could see the print in the poor light. She looked at Rebecca in outrage. "I told you I didn't *want* any food," she said coldly.

"You haven't even tried it." Rebecca put the tray down on the bed and went to the window. She pulled the curtains aside, as she had done before. The wintry light burst into the room. Therese plunged her face into the blankets with a little cry.

Rebecca went to her, touching her shoulder. She felt the girl's muscles taut and quivering. "You don't have to come down if you don't want to. Just eat the food hot. It won't taste good cold."

Therese swung around in the bed. Rebecca had a brief impression of the speed of some wild creature. The heavy book flew past her ear with a ripple of pages.

"Get *away* from me!" Therese snarled in a voice unlike anything Rebecca had heard her use before. "How dare you come in my room without being asked?"

Startled, Rebecca took a couple of paces backward. She looked at the book Therese had thrown at her. It was a bulky hardcover. "Therese, that could have hurt me. Please don't throw anything at me again."

The girl drew back, like a cobra poised to strike. The wide mouth was stretched taut. "Don't tell me what to do!" she said shakily. "Get out of here!"

"Now, look—" Rebecca was walking back to the bed, reaching out, when Therese seemed to rise out of the bed. She snatched up the tray, and with explosive strength hurled it at Rebecca. It crashed into her chest, splattering her with hot food, the glass splintering on the floor.

Deeply shocked by the violence, and by the pain of the assault, Rebecca looked down at herself. Melted cheese hung on her, burning her through her clothes. If any of it had hit her face, it would have been disastrous.

Therese was quivering on the edge of her bed, panting. Her white face was twisted in rage.

"Now get out," she hissed. "*Get out.*"

Rebecca had worked with children for years, and had never seen behavior like this. The children she was used to—sick children—behaved with extraordinary courage and self-possession, patiently enduring pain and boredom without end. She had never been so offended and angered before. It was all she could do to stop herself from slapping the girl's face.

She hauled off her scorching sweater and shirt. Wearing only her bra, she confronted Therese. "Get out of that bed and clean up this mess," she said quietly.

Therese's eyes glittered. "Screw *you.*"

"Come on. Now." She grasped Therese's slim arm and hauled her upright. "You broke this stuff. You clean it up."

"No!"

"Yes." Therese was resisting with surprising strength, dragging away, panting through her nose. But Rebecca was determined not to be intimidated by a tantrum. She dragged Therese off the bed. The girl wore only a T-shirt, her slim, pale legs bare. She spat a string of obscenities through her gritted teeth. Rebecca grabbed her other arm and shook her. "Stop that," she said sharply. "You're not a baby anymore."

Now Therese was struggling with almost frightening violence, lashing at Rebecca with her hands. Her clenched teeth were bared, her eyes and nostrils flaring. She was no longer spitting swearwords, but Rebecca could hardly hold her back. It was starting to dawn on Rebecca, as real alarm overtook her anger, that she had bitten off more than she could chew. She was barely able to keep Therese's fingers away from her face. If she let go, the child might claw her eyes out. She staggered back, wanting to shout for Florio and Devon, yet appalled that they should see what was happening.

For a few black, frightening seconds, the silent struggle continued.

Then Therese's clawing movements changed, became less purposeful. Rebecca saw the cords standing out on the girl's neck, her eyes no longer glaring, but starting to roll back in her head.

"Therese!" she said urgently.

The flailing became an aimless, repetitive flapping. Rebecca tried to get Therese back to the bed. But before she could get there, Therese's spine arched and her head went back. She slid to the floor. The spasm had turned her torso as rigid as a bow, while her limbs kept jerking. Her breath came in gasps that spluttered through her teeth. Rebecca saw blood and froth on her lips: Therese must have bitten her tongue, but she could not get the girl to open her mouth. What in God's name was this? Grand mal? She managed to thrust her fingers between Therese's clenched teeth and got her tongue out of the way. She was desperately trying to remember everything she knew about epilepsy. Therese's bare legs were wet: Her bladder had emptied.

By now Florio and Devon had come running up from the kitchen. "Help me get her onto the bed," she panted.

Together, they lifted Therese onto her bed. Rebecca put her on her side in the recovery position. She lifted Therese's lids. Her eyes were still rolled back.

"What did you do to her?" Devon demanded.

"I opened her curtains," Rebecca said, taking Therese's pulse. "She flew into a tantrum and threw the tray at me. I tried to get her to clean it up and she attacked me. Then this happened."

"I told you to leave her alone," Florio said harshly.

She looked up at him, taut with anger and fright. "How long has she been having these seizures?"

"A couple of years."

"She's sick. She needs a doctor."

"She's been to a dozen doctors," Florio retorted. "There's nothing organically wrong with her. She just needs to be left to do things her own way. I told you, but you damned well wouldn't listen." He sat down on the bed and lifted Therese's head onto his lap. He stroked the girl's tangled hair with his big hands. "Are you hurt?" he asked Rebecca.

"Just burned a little," she replied, becoming aware that she was half-undressed. "You might have warned me."

Devon was picking up broken crockery. "Therese can be dangerous," she said. "I told you, too. I *warned* you."

Therese's shuddering was easing as her father soothed her. Rebecca closed her eyes for a moment. What a god-awful shambles. Her first day in the house. And here she was, half-naked and shaking, with everything in ruins around her.

"You agreed to do things my way," Florio said grimly. "Why did you lie to me?"

You bastard, she almost spat at him. Reaction had set in. Rebecca's skin was bumpy with gooseflesh. "She can't spend her life in a darkened room, reading Dickens."

"You are not the one to decide that," Florio said, his voice like a rasp. She saw him look at her breasts. Her rigid nipples were making exclamation points in her light bra, and she felt exposed, nauseated. She was afraid he would tell her to go, now, tell her to get out of their lives.

She folded her arms, covering herself. "I'm sorry," she said, getting the words out with difficulty. "I didn't mean this to happen."

Florio rose, and Devon took his place, hugging her sister and pressing her cheek to Therese's, whispering endearments. Under Devon's touch, Therese started to relax. Her panting turned into tired crying. She put her arms around Devon and clung to her.

"Get out of here," Florio commanded quietly. "Just leave us alone."

Rebecca, very close to tears, went straight to her own room. In the mirror she caught sight of her own face. She wore the same expression she had seen on accident victims.

She pulled out her medical supplies and rifled through them. She had a bottle of tranquilizers, which were standard treatment for this kind of thing. But she did not want to give them to Therese now. They might be useful at some later stage.

Would Florio fire her tomorrow, tell her to get out of their lives? She lay on her bed, covering her eyes with her arms.

. . .

The next morning Rebecca rose early. The house was silent and still. She went down to the kitchen. There were only embers left of the fire, so she piled more wood in the oven, and it started to crackle happily. It was even colder out than yesterday. She could see a heavy white frost on the trees and grass.

She thought back over the events of yesterday, feeling a heavy dread as she wondered what today held in store. She started making focaccia, a lengthy slab of pizza dough made with olive oil and home-ground flour. At the Fiorentinis' she had learned how to make it crusty and light, with shavings of ham and chunks of cheese. There was even a typical long, flat baker's paddle hanging alongside the oven. She guessed the Florios thought of it as a quaint decoration, but it was a useful tool. She used it to slide the focaccia into the oven, after which she filled the percolator with freshly ground coffee. Then she sat down and wondered just what the hell she had gotten herself into.

Formulating her grand plans, she'd imagined herself swiftly striking up a rapport with Therese, getting her confidence, telling her who she was, then spiriting her away. But why on earth had she thought it would be easy to get Therese's confidence? Just because she was the girl's biological mother? That was stupid. And if Therese had been seen by the best specialists available, how was she going to heal her with her limited experience of mental illness? She would have given anything to have had access to a couple of good psychiatry textbooks, but that was impossible.

She heard a footstep and looked up. It was Therese. She was wearing a denim dress with black wool leggings and a black long-sleeved shirt. The white Giants cap was pulled down over her eyes, hiding most of her face, except for that unhappy mouth. She carried a book under one arm.

Rebecca tried to sound casual. "Hi. Sleep well?"

"Okay," Therese said in a small voice. She pushed her hands in her pockets and peered in the oven.

"It's a focaccia," Rebecca said. "Your basic farmhouse breakfast in this neck of the woods."

"What is it?"

"Well, it's a kind of pizza with no topping."

Therese lifted her head slightly, so one wary gray eye could glance from beneath the cap. She didn't look directly at Rebecca, but past her. "What's the point of a pizza with no topping?"

"For one thing, it's not so rich at breakfast time. You might like it."

Therese turned her back on Rebecca without comment and stared out the window at the frost. She was tugging at the fine chain around her neck, fiddling with the little gold key that hung there. The tension between them was painful. Rebecca felt it was almost tragic.

The bright sound of Devon's laughter drifted down from upstairs. Florio's deep voice said something, then there was a happy shriek, and more laughter from Devon. Rebecca glanced at Therese. The girl had not moved, but was it her imagination, or had the lean shoulders tightened as if in pain? She wanted to go to the child and touch her, but knew it would be stupid. She stood there, listening to the footsteps of Florio and his other daughter approaching, hearing their happy banter.

Just before they came in, Therese half turned her head, showing no more than a cheekbone. "I didn't mean to hurt you yesterday," she said, in such a quiet voice that Rebecca sensed the words, rather than heard them.

"Oh, Therese," she replied, "and I didn't mean to upset you. Can we call a truce?"

She saw the peak of the cap dip infinitesimally. Then Devon came in, still trailing laughter at something her father had said or done. "Hi," she called to Rebecca, then saw her sister. "Therese! You're up and dressed!" She gave her a kiss on the cheek. "Hey, something smells terrific!"

Michael Florio came in, his dark hair still tousled from his shower. He nodded an unsmiling hello to Rebecca. Then he, too, put his arm around Therese's shoulders. "How's my little girl?" he asked gently.

"Okay," Therese said. Rebecca could see no reaction from Therese to her father's hug. She just stood there with her hands in her pockets, looking out at the frost. Florio lifted the cap, kissed her temple, then pulled the cap back down again. He did not seem troubled by her blank response.

Breakfast took some time, partly because nobody except Therese could resist second and third helpings of the focaccia. And even Therese ate a few mouthfuls and drank half a glass of orange juice, sitting silently reading her book—George Eliot's *Middlemarch*. Rebecca wondered how a girl her age could be so engrossed in such a demanding book, but Therese turned the pages as though inhaling the words.

Ryan had read like that, she remembered suddenly. He had devoured books so fast, she'd accused him of skimming, then he would quote whole chunks verbatim. Perhaps that formidably hungry intellect had come from him.

Devon, Rebecca thought, was the kind of daughter parents dreamed of—studious, balanced, mature. It occurred to her to wonder how Therese's life might have turned out if Barbara and Michael had not also adopted the older girl. As it was, insofar as Rebecca could tell, Therese was no more than the shadow to Devon's brightness. It made her very sad.

After breakfast, the girls went out of the kitchen, leaving Rebecca alone with Florio. She took a deep breath. "If you wanted to fire me, you'd be justified," she said quietly. "I was stupid. I just want you to believe my intentions were good."

"Yeah." He pushed the percolator toward her, and she refilled her cup. "The jury's out on both those questions."

She tried to relax her muscles. "How often does that happen?"

"Sometimes months go by. Then she'll do it three, four times in a short period."

"Is she confused afterward? Drowsy?"

Florio shook his head. "No. She's not epileptic. It's hysteria, according to most of the doctors, though one thought it might be a form of autism."

Rebecca recalled the hissing rage, the furious onslaught, the sudden lapse into spasm. She shivered. "It's not autism. Is she always aggressive beforehand?"

"No. She can be very aggressive without going into a fit. And she can go into a fit almost without warning."

"Did she ever show anything like this before her mother's death?"

"Once or twice. When her mother and I started to break up."

She took another gulp of coffee. "Was this one of the reasons you wanted to get her away from San Francisco?"

His expression changed. "You've just finished apologizing. Don't ask too many questions, Rebecca." He rose and went out, leaving her to clear the kitchen.

The next day was market day in Urbino, so Rebecca offered to do the shopping. Florio took her to the garage and showed her how to open the cantilevered door. The Jeep hulked inside, next to a motorbike.

"The Jeep's an automatic," he told her. "Be sure to lock the gas cap after you fill up. If you get bogged down in mud or gravel, this is how you engage full four-wheel drive."

When he'd shown her the levers, he took a sheaf of Italian money out of his back pocket. "This is fifty dollars' worth. Is that enough?"

"More than enough," she said, with an attempt at being pleasant. "I told you, I'm a good shopper."

"See you later then," he said. He did not give her a smile as he walked away.

She started up the Jeep and took off down the road. Winter had set in hard by now. The sky was dark, and frost had made a hoary lacework of the hedgerows. The Jeep felt heavy but competent, its big wheels churning up the icy mud. She reached the gate of the property and stopped the car to open it. She got out and unlocked the chain. She was about to get back in the car when she heard a faint call.

She looked back. A figure was running down the track behind her. She recognized the white baseball cap, and felt a mixture of dismay and pleasure seize her heart.

Therese came up, panting. She wore denim overalls over a striped pullover, muddied sneakers on her feet. "What are you doing?" Rebecca asked.

"I want to come," Therese replied.

"Does your father know you're here?"

"Sure," Therese replied.

Rebecca reached out and lifted the baseball cap. Therese's face was pinched-looking with cold. "Really?"

"Of course," Therese said irritably. "I wouldn't sneak out without telling him."

Rebecca considered, torn. She did not believe Therese. On the other hand, this was a unique opportunity to be alone with her. "If you're not telling me the truth, we're both in for the firing squad when we get back."

"I'm telling you the truth."

On impulse, Rebecca decided to face the consequences, whatever they might be. "Okay." She smiled. "Hop aboard."

She made Therese buckle her seat belt, and they set off. She glanced at her companion, who was staring out the window. "It's odd to see you without a book in your hands. Won't you get withdrawal symptoms?"

Therese did not smile. "I just finished *Middlemarch*."

"How long did it take you to read it?"

"A couple of days."

"Wow. I remember it took me weeks when I was a student. It's not exactly fast reading."

"I've read it twice before," Therese said flatly. "I'm on some of my books for the fourth time."

Rebecca blinked. "You're telling me you're reading those books again and again and again?"

"Until I can get some new ones," Therese replied.

Rebecca was both impressed and troubled. "You have an exceptional brain, Therese. But don't you think you should do something else now and then?"

"Like what?"

"Go for a walk. Get some air."

"Back home, my dad takes me to Giants games."

"You like baseball?"

"No," Therese said.

"So why do you go?"

"He thinks I'm having a great time. And Devon hates baseball."

"I see," Rebecca said slowly. So that explained the affection for the

Giants cap. Baseball games were the one place Therese could have her father all to herself.

There was something she wanted really badly to do, and that was to take Therese's cap off, pull her tangled hair back, and just drink in her face. Since meeting her daughter, all she'd seen of her had been fleeting glimpses. Therese was there, and yet not there, like some forest creature that managed to camouflage itself against any available cover. Her hair was truly awful: It was a ready-made thicket for her to hide behind.

"You know what? Today's the day the hairdresser comes to cut Signora Fiorentini's hair. That's my old landlady. The house is practically on our way, and we have plenty of time. What do you say we stop by and see if she'll give you a wash and trim?"

"No" came the flat reply.

Rebecca thought for a moment. "Listen to me, Therese. Your father is going to skin me alive when we get back. You know that. Do me this one favor and I won't feel so bad when he gets out the cat-o'-nine-tails." She glanced across at Therese, who was drawing something on the window with her finger. There was no response, but there was no refusal, either. "Signora Fiorentini's very nice. I think you'll like her." She took the next fork toward the Fiorentini house.

Marchetta's van was parked outside the old house. Signora Fiorentini, wrapped in a plastic sheet in the kitchen, was delighted to see Rebecca, making as much fuss as if Rebecca had been gone weeks instead of days. Rebecca introduced the silent Therese as one of her new charges, and explained what she wanted. Marchetta was quite willing. She finished Signora Fiorentini's hair and blew it dry. Then she beckoned to Therese.

"Go on," Rebecca urged with a smile as Therese hesitated. Looking tense and miserable, Therese allowed Marchetta to take off her cap.

"Is she normal?" Fiorentini asked Rebecca in Italian, watching dubiously.

"She's a lonely, strange little girl," Rebecca replied. "But I don't think there's anything wrong with her." She did not mention the possibility that Therese had set a fire that had killed her adoptive mother.

Marchetta made Therese bend over the sink, and shampooed her hair thoroughly, clicking her tongue at the knots. Rebecca saw Therese's knuckles turn white as bone as she clutched the sink. *Don't let there be a scene*, Rebecca prayed. The last thing in the world she wanted was for Therese to have one of her fits here. When her hair was clean, Marchetta wrapped Therese in the sheet and sat her in the chair.

Rebecca chatted to Fiorentini as Marchetta's scissors clicked, but her attention was on Therese, not on the small talk. Covertly, she studied the child's face. She was nowhere near as pretty as Devon, but hers was a more interesting face than Devon's conventional prettiness. The nose was long and straight, with delicately arched nostrils. She had fine eyes, big and level, when she bothered to look at you, but the top lids were that pale blue that Rebecca associated with exhaustion, and there were shadows beneath the lower lids. Her most expressive feature was that wide, mobile mouth. If only once she could get it to smile instead of sagging so sadly, she knew the resemblance to Ryan would be even stronger, painfully so. Therese was gripping the arms of the chair with the same desperation that she'd gripped the sink. Rebecca felt a rush of pity. Life seemed to be one long sequence of ordeals for this girl.

"Do they treat you well?" Fiorentini asked solicitously.

"The man is a bit of a tyrant, but the other girl is very sweet. I play it as it goes."

"If things don't work out, you can always come back here," Fiorentini assured her. "Nobody's going to take that room in the middle of winter. And even if someone does come, we can always squeeze you in somewhere."

"I appreciate that, Signora Fiorentini," Rebecca said.

Fiorentini, gleaming after Marchetta's ministrations, tucked her clasped hands under her big bosom. "And if that man lays a finger on you, just say the word, and my boys will make him wish he'd never been born."

Rebecca could see Therese literally gritting her teeth through the haircut. Marchetta chattered to her nonstop, oblivious to the girl's lack of comprehension. But when she had finished and was drying the new cut, the results were exciting.

"You look wonderful," Rebecca said in delight. "You're so pretty, Therese. Take a look!"

Therese studied her reflection briefly in the mirror that Rebecca held up for her. She looked unimpressed by the transformation, but to Rebecca it was deeply gratifying. The wild tangle had become a mop of softly shining curls. Cutting the dirty tousle away from her cheeks and neck seemed to have altered the whole shape of her face. Her cheekbones were revealed as broad, losing the narrow, ferrety look, and her neck was long and slender. She looked lovely.

Marchetta got out the can of hair spray, but Rebecca shook her head. "She's perfect just the way she is, Marchetta. Thank you so much."

"She could be your daughter," Fiorentini said, laughing. The chance remark made Rebecca flinch, and she was glad that it had sailed past Therese. Whatever indignation she was in for when she got back to the millhouse, nobody could possibly object to this constructive change in Therese's appearance.

She paid Marchetta, said good-bye to Fiorentini, and set off with Therese in the Jeep.

"I used to do this journey on my Vespa," she told Therese, happy with what she had achieved. "It's a lot more fun in your father's Jeep."

Therese was sitting with her cap in her lap, watching the road ahead. She looked so different, as though the haircut had freed her from something. The poise of the slender neck was vulnerable yet somehow brave.

"You fit right in with those people," Therese said.

"Well, they're very kind people."

"Yes, but they're nothing to you, are they? You're a stranger to them. I could never be relaxed like that with people I didn't know."

"You have to give a little," Rebecca said. "If you make the first move, people usually respond."

Therese turned to her, her eyes sad. "You make it sound so easy. I wish I was like you."

Rebecca made no response to that, not trusting herself. "Maybe we should go back home now. Did you really tell your father you were coming with me?"

"I left him a note," Therese said.

"Promise?"

"I promise," Therese said firmly. "We don't have to go home. Let's go shopping, like you were planning."

"Okay."

They reached Urbino, and managed to find a parking place in the ancient streets, squeezed in between a church door and a marble fountain carved with entwined dolphins. Therese got out, staring around her with wide eyes.

"Can you carry one of the baskets?" Rebecca asked her.

Therese took the basket as though it were some kind of unknown animal. Rebecca led her along the steep, cobbled streets, pointing out interesting things. Therese was staring around her, pale-faced. Rebecca saw that she was fascinated by the most disparate things: a nun striding along in her black-and-white habit, a shop window full of bread, even the funny little Fiat Cinquecentos, which were the perfect vehicles for these narrow streets.

"What does this say?" Therese asked, stopping in front of a stone inscription on a church wall.

"It's in Latin," Rebecca said. "Something about a building project by a pontiff called Innocent. That's one of the popes."

Therese deciphered the Latin date. "That's 1468, isn't it?"

"Yes."

"Five hundred and thirty years ago."

"Amazing, isn't it? I love this town," Rebecca said cheerfully. "Isn't it beautiful?"

"Everything's so *old*," Therese said doubtfully.

"Well, you seem to prefer to live somewhere around 1860, so you should enjoy it."

They reached the bustle of the market. Even in this dreary weather, the mountains of fruit and vegetables on display made a tumult of color. Everything conceivable was for sale—Gypsy-looking men selling suspect Walkmans and even more suspect compact discs; boisterous Senegalese hawkers selling African beads and peculiar secondhand clothing; refugees from Bosnia and Macedonia selling vivid carpets that came from God knew where.

Therese seemed to shrink back from the tumult, but Rebecca took her hand firmly. "Come on." She laughed. "Into the fray."

The market was a thriving, haggling hubbub, where, if you understood the best places to shop and how to bargain, you could get anything at a fraction of supermarket prices, or where, if you understood neither, you could get magnificently ripped off. She tried to show Therese how much of a game it was, though Therese seemed slightly overwhelmed by it all. She tried to teach Therese that in these town markets, shopping had not yet evolved into a distant war between consumers and organizations. Here it was hand-to-hand combat, a duel from which one side or the other emerged breathless and triumphant. Rebecca had learned to love it, and she hoped Therese was absorbing some of the fun.

Florio had given Rebecca more than enough money for what she needed. Weighed down by baskets of fruit and vegetables, she stopped in front of the flower-seller's stall, sorely tempted by the bunches of white winter lilies. The millhouse was handsome, but somehow bare; a vase of flowers would do so much to lighten the atmosphere.

"What do you think?" she asked Therese.

Therese lifted her shoulders. "My dad never buys flowers, but Devon would like them."

Rebecca made an impulsive decision. "Okay, let's blow ten thousand lire."

She bought a big bunch of the lilies, whose faint smell of honey was poignant. Therese pushed her face into the flowers, inhaling their scent. The stamens left powdery yellow marks on her chin. The flower seller selected a single rose, and held it out to them with a smile.

"For your pretty daughter," he said to Rebecca.

Therese took the rose with little more than a nod, but Rebecca was glowing inside. As they made their way through the stalls back toward the Jeep, she was experiencing something she'd never known before, the special pleasure of receiving a compliment about her child. She'd thought she'd known what she was missing all these years. Today, she was starting to realize just how vast a stretch thirteen years was in the life of a child. But even that dark thought could not dampen her happiness. It had been a wonderful morning.

As they drove back home, Therese was as silent as ever. Rebecca felt that the morning had been a terrific success, but she was not so stupid as to expect any kind of confirmation from Therese. "What are you going to read next?" she asked.

"I'm starting the Palliser novels again."

"That's Trollope, isn't it?" Rebecca asked. Therese nodded. "How many are there?"

"There are six of them. They're all about the same family."

"And how long will it take you to read all that?"

"It depends. I try to make them last as long as possible."

"But you're absolutely immersed in them, aren't you?" Rebecca said.

"Trollope's wonderful," Therese said, with more enthusiasm than Rebecca had seen her show for anything yet. "He makes the people come alive. I mean, really *alive*."

"Really? I always liked Dickens better than Trollope."

"So did I, when I was younger," Therese said, unaware of saying anything crushing. "When Trollope invents a character, he goes into that person's very heart. He'll spend three or four pages describing an old lady, and when you've finished reading it, it's like, *wow*. She's really there. You want to go back and read the whole thing all over again."

"Well, that's great," Rebecca said flatly. She was struck by the pathos of a thirteen-year-old girl finding the characters in a hundred-year-old novel more alive than anything in the real world. "You'll have to show me."

Therese looked up, her eyes brightening. "You want me to show you a couple of good passages to read?"

"Yes, I'd like that."

"Okay. When we get home." The suggestion seemed to have cheered

Therese even further. "I talk about my books with Devvy, but we think so much alike that we hardly even need to say anything. Devvy's ordered me a whole lot of new novels from a bookshop in Oxford, England. They should be here soon."

"You and Devon think alike?" Rebecca asked. Her tone was neutral, but she was wondering how someone as introverted as Therese could compare herself to someone as poised as Devon.

"Sure. We're not real sisters, you know." She glanced at Rebecca. "We're both adopted."

Rebecca cleared her throat. "Your father didn't tell me that."

"But we're very close. It doesn't matter about the biological stuff, does it? I mean, what really matters is who brings you up. Who you grow up with." She was still watching Rebecca with her clear gray eyes. "Don't you think?"

"Yes," Rebecca said stiffly, "I suppose you're right. Who brings you up is probably the most important thing in forming your character. But what you call the biological stuff is also important."

"I don't ever want to meet my biological mother," Therese said brusquely, turning away.

"Don't you?" Rebecca asked, feeling a fist close on her heart.

"Not ever," the girl said stonily. "Devon can't meet her real parents, because they're both dead. Mine are alive, but I never want to meet them. Why should I? They didn't want me when I was born. They couldn't wait to get rid of me. So why should I care about them?"

Rebecca's mouth was dry. "Maybe it wasn't as simple as that," she began, but Therese cut through with the steel-edged logic of thirteen.

"I was eight days old when my mother gave me away. Eight *days*. Like I said, they couldn't wait. When you know that, it's going to hurt you the rest of your life. You can't forgive it."

There was a tight silence in the Jeep. Rebecca kept driving, with no expression. But it was as if she were on automatic pilot, numbed. Had Barbara Florio encouraged this kind of thinking in Therese? "Well, I guess that's logical," she said at last, and her voice sounded empty. "How do you know your real parents are still alive?"

"My father told me a couple of years ago. He offered to try and put me in touch with them. But I wasn't interested."

"Why would he want to do that?" she asked.

"It was when I started to do crazy things. He thought it might help."

"Didn't *you* think it might . . . help?"

"It would just have made me crazier. Mom met my biological mother before I was born. She said she just wasn't interested in me. It was like she didn't even want to admit she was pregnant at all. She just wanted to get on with her own life."

"Did your mom say how old this woman was?" Rebecca asked quietly.

"She was old enough to have a baby," Therese said. "If you're old enough to have children, you're old enough to know what you're doing."

"That doesn't necessarily follow," Rebecca said.

"Sure it does. She should never have had me at all."

"Well, the alternative is abortion, and that's a very, very difficult question."

"I'm pro-choice," Therese said in a hard voice. "Are you a pro-lifer?"

"I don't think labels help much when it's such a complex issue. But I'm a health-care worker, and we're sworn to protect life."

"Even when someone's life is just agony?" Therese retorted. "Even when you're forcing mothers to have babies they'll hate? Doctors should let a woman abort a child instead of forcing her to have it when it isn't wanted."

"In that case, you wouldn't be here right now, Therese."

"That's what I'm talking about," Therese said in a small, cold voice.

Rebecca was shocked. "You mean you'd rather never have been born? All this *you*, all this intelligence, all this life and brightness—you're telling me you'd rather it hadn't happened?"

"You don't understand," Therese said in the same tight little voice. She was jerking at the gold key that hung around her neck. Rebecca felt empty, drained. She had heavily underestimated the difficulty of getting close to Therese and winning her confidence.

After another long silence, she said, "Therese, you're a special, precious, wonderful creation. It would have been a poorer world if you hadn't been born. You'll enrich the lives of countless people. Maybe you'll be a teacher who shows students how to appreciate great literature. Or maybe you'll make beautiful movies, or compose wonderful music, or write superb books. Maybe you'll be the kind of loving mother your biological mother couldn't be, and that's the greatest work of all. But don't wish you'd never been born. That's wishing darkness instead of light."

But Therese was jerking at the gold key even harder, so the chain cut into her pale neck. Rebecca wondered if she had been listening at all, whether anything could break into that darkness. She wanted to pour out eloquence, but now was not the time, and she did not have the words. She doubted whether she would ever have the words.

They pulled up in front of the house and started to unload the groceries. Rebecca was beginning to feel somewhat nervous about facing Florio, but the first person they encountered was Devon. She came hurrying down from the kitchen to meet them in the hall.

"Tree! What happened to you?"

"Nothing happened to me," Therese replied. "I went shopping with Rebecca."

"How can you be so irresponsible?" Devon gasped. "Don't you know what Dad has been going through?"

"I left him a note saying what I was doing," Therese said, lugging the basket past her sister. "He knew where I was."

"You must be crazy," Devon said. She stared at Therese's hair. "What happened to your *hair*?"

"I took her to Signora Fiorentini's for a wash and trim," Rebecca said. "Where is your father?"

"He's out looking for you on the motorbike," Devon said.

Rebecca's heart sank. "That really wasn't necessary."

Devon was twisting her fingers nervously. "I wish you hadn't done this, Rebecca," she said unhappily. "I imagine Therese sucked you in, right?"

Rebecca glanced at Therese, who was arranging the fruit and vegetables in bowls, apparently enjoying the composition. "Nobody needed to suck anybody in," she said coolly. "It was a simple shopping trip. Therese was a great help to me."

Devon shook her head. "You don't understand," she said.

"So everyone keeps telling me," Rebecca said, forcing a smile.

Within a few minutes they heard the roar of the dirt bike pulling up outside, followed by the sound of boots ringing on the stairs. Michael Florio, spattered with mud, came in. Rebecca had the sensation of a thunderstorm descending. Ignoring her, he went straight to Therese.

"Are you all right?" he asked quietly.

"I'm fine," Therese said. Her tone was casual, but Rebecca caught the edge in her voice.

"What did you do to your hair?"

"Rebecca took me to this friend of hers. There was a hairdresser there." Therese's face twisted at the look in her father's eyes. "Nothing *happened*, Dad. I left you a note, didn't I?"

Florio stared at his daughter in silence for a moment. "Go to your room. I'll talk to you later."

"If you're going to be angry with Rebecca, you needn't bother, Dad. The whole thing was my fault."

"I don't see why there should be a question of fault on anybody's side," Rebecca said, walking forward. "It was a perfectly harmless expedition."

Florio did not even look at her. "Please go to your room, Therese. You, too, Devon."

Therese glanced at Rebecca, then shrugged, picked up her book, and left. Devon followed her, her normally bright face pale with anxiety. When they were gone, Florio turned to Rebecca. His eyes were so flinty that she felt chilled.

"Sit down."

"I'd rather stand," she replied stiffly.

He reached for the flap of his leather jacket and jerked it open. The rip of the zipper made an ugly sound. "You've been here two days, and you've already fucked up twice," he said savagely, his eyes glittering.

"Don't swear at me," she retorted. "Therese had a fun morning. Nothing happened. Nothing went wrong. You have no right to take that tone."

"No right?" he asked, his voice thickening. "Who the hell do you think you are? Do you think you make the rules around here?"

"I know who makes the rules," she said. "Going shopping is a normal activity, out in the real world."

"She is not a normal child," he said tightly. "Normal things are shut off to her."

"She can't go out?" Rebecca asked incredulously. "Not ever?"

"Not without my permission. Never without telling me. Don't ever do this again, Rebecca. Don't take her out of the house. Don't cut her hair. Don't try and manipulate her in any way. It was stupid, irresponsible, and negligent beyond belief."

"*Manipulate* her? Now, hold on. I didn't ask her to come. I left the house alone, and she must have been waiting for me. She came running up to me at the gate."

"Then you should have brought her straight back."

"Straight back to prison, right?" She had spoken in anger, but it had been a mistake. He moved forward as if he wanted to hurt her in some way. She lifted her chin. "You've already cursed me. Are you going to hit me, too?"

"You presumptuous, arrogant little nobody," he said softly.

"I don't have to take this," she said, turning on her heel.

"No, you don't," she heard him say. "And you don't have to stay here, either."

She stopped, and turned slowly to face him. His jaw was hard with anger. "All right," she said. "I guessed you'd be upset. I should have refused to take her. The truth is, I felt very sorry for her. I thought it was a positive sign that she wanted to come out with me."

"Positive?"

"She's locked into a dark little world, Michael. Her wanting to get some fresh air could only be a good sign."

"And what if she'd had more on her mind than a little fresh air? What if you'd turned around from buying eggplants and found she'd disappeared, run away, vanished into thin air?"

"She wouldn't do that!" Rebecca said, eyes widening.

"For a pediatric nurse, you're very innocent," he replied dryly.

"Well, she didn't do anything crazy, did she?" Rebecca challenged. "And I thought you'd be pleased about her haircut. It makes her look so much better. I can't believe any father would wish his daughter to look so . . . *neglected.*"

"Your beliefs are irrelevant," he said contemptuously.

There was a silence. "Do you want me to go?" she asked quietly at last.

"I just want you to do as I tell you," he said, as though talking to an imbecile. "Can you understand that?"

"I'm doing my best to help, Michael. I think you're overreacting."

"I told you not to try and get too close to her," he replied. "You'll get hurt and she'll get hurt, I promise you that. Stay in the background, Rebecca. If you can't do that," he said quietly, but with force, "then you may as well leave right now."

"Let me just say one more thing," she replied. "Therese spends twenty-three hours out of the twenty-four in a darkened room, devouring nineteenth-century novels. As a nurse, I can promise you that is not a healthy life for any child, let alone a disturbed one. She needs distractions. She needs to be taken out of herself, even if it's no more than a shopping trip to the nearest town!"

"You're not a doctor, and she's not your patient."

He turned on his heel and left her. A foreboding silence settled over the house. There was no sound from upstairs. Fighting down tears, Rebecca put the things away, and made lunch. It was to have been a celebratory meal, linguini with clams, shrimps, and olives. Her stomach felt as if it already held a granite boulder.

Devon came into the kitchen, still looking pale. "Rebecca, don't be upset with him," she said. "He's doing his best for her. We all are."

"I'm not upset," Rebecca said, not caring that that was a patent lie.

"You have to understand that we took Therese away from San Francisco to protect her. Daddy just wants her to be as sheltered as possible while she's here. He doesn't want her exposed to any dangers."

"Dangers? In Urbino?"

"You don't understand," Devon said, shaking her blond head.

"Well, explain it to me then," Rebecca said, taking a deep breath to quell her anger. "Tell me what happened in San Francisco."

"You don't want to know." Devon walked out again.

Rebecca felt like someone who had tried to wade across a river, and was finding with every step that the water was deeper and the current stronger than before.

It was going to be long and slow, and possibly very messy. But having waded so far into the river, she could have no thought of going back now, or the current would sweep her to destruction.

She went up to Therese's room. Therese was lying on her bed with the curtains drawn as usual, books piled haphazardly around her.

"When you came to town with me," Rebecca demanded, "were you planning any kind of escapade?"

Therese did not look up from her book. "I don't know what you're talking about."

"Your father thinks you were planning to go AWOL."

Therese looked up. Her face was sullen, but she looked a hundred times better after Marchetta's haircut. "Did he yell at you?"

"He wasn't very pleasant," Rebecca said shortly.

"He's doing his best."

"Therese, you put me in a bad position. I don't enjoy having my butt kicked. If I thought I could trust you, I would do a lot for you. But if I thought you were fooling me, I'd start treating you the way everyone else does."

"And how's that?"

"Like someone who can't be given the slightest responsibility."

She'd never heard Therese laugh before. It was a still, mirthless laugh. "I don't want any responsibility, thanks all the same."

"You mean you want to live in a prison the rest of your life?"

Therese's body tightened swiftly. Rebecca had a chilling memory of the way the girl had attacked her on her first day in this house. "What do you mean by that?"

"This house is a prison," Rebecca said. "Your father and your sister think you have to be kept locked up. I find that horrible. I can't believe you benefit from it."

Therese's eyes were wary. "I'd rather have my family do it than some jerk in a white coat."

Rebecca sat on her bed. "People in white coats can help." She saw Therese's face tighten even further, but she pressed on. "Running away from your problems never solves them. They always catch up, bigger and meaner than ever. At some point they have to be faced."

Therese drew up her knees under the quilt, and hugged them tight with her slim arms. Her expression was fierce. "My father will never let them lock me away."

"You read too much Dickens. They don't lock children away anymore," Rebecca said gently.

"You need a reality check," Therese said bitterly. "Why do you think we came here?"

"I have no idea."

"I killed my mother."

It took Rebecca's breath away. She laid her hand on the girl's arm. "Oh, Therese," she gasped. "I can't believe that!"

"Plenty of other people do."

"Who?"

"The police and the social workers and the psychiatrists and the judges and all the other people who think they know everything. They say please and thank you and have flowery wallpaper and fluffy animals, but they mean to rip open your mind and fish out whatever dark little secrets you have in there." Therese was speaking fast, almost incoherently, her body shaking. Rebecca was braced for her to go into another seizure.

"Therese, listen to me," she said urgently. "Do you *remember* killing your mother? Or is that just something other people have put into your head?"

"I don't know." Therese was trembling, her fingers digging into her shins. "If I knew, I'd be sane, right? But I don't. So that makes me crazy."

"It doesn't make you any such thing," Rebecca said, grieving passionately for the child. "If you did nothing wrong, then you don't need to be afraid of anybody. And if you feel you did do something wrong, then you need help. Facing the problem is the only answer."

"Are you one of them?" Therese asked in a low voice. She was staring intently at Rebecca.

"You mean someone who wants to lock you up? No, Therese, I'm not one of them."

"You told Dad things about yourself that weren't true. Devon says you might be an undercover cop."

Therese's eyes were very hard to lie to. Rebecca managed a little laugh. "I'm nothing like that. As a matter of fact, I'm not so very different from you. I'm also someone with a problem I've been running away from."

"That's what Dad said."

"Your father is perceptive."

"What problem?"

"I can't tell you yet, but one day I promise I will."

"What *kind* of problem then?"

She reached out and touched Therese's cheek with her fingertips. The girl's skin was as smooth as a rose petal. "A big problem. Half the things that have gone wrong in my life went wrong because I wouldn't face it. I made a terrible mistake a long time ago. Now I'm trying to get together the courage to make things right. But it ain't gonna be easy."

"Nothing ever is," Therese said wearily. Slowly, her body was relaxing. Seeing that the girl had calmed somewhat, Rebecca leaned forward and kissed her lightly on the forehead.

"It's okay, Therese," she said. "I'll never do anything to hurt you, I swear it. I came in here to ask you to trust me, that's all."

"I can't trust myself. So I'm not very good at trusting anybody else."

"Okay," Rebecca said after a pause. "I'm glad we could talk." She got up to leave, afraid that she had already said too much to Therese.

Rebecca went downstairs to the laundry. She hated the physical labor of washing by hand. The house had been fully wired, with plugs everywhere and smart halogen lights set in all the ceilings, but without power, life was primitive, and the electrical equipment just a mockery.

Florio himself had been working intently on his turbine, evidently wanting to finish the work before the first heavy frosts came. The only signs of his presence were the rumble of the concrete mixer or the whine of power tools.

She hadn't bothered to arrange the big bunch of lilies she'd bought at the market. She'd just thrust them into a bucket of water and left them there. She gathered the moist blooms now and arranged them in a big vase. She carried the vase into the sitting room and put it on a table well away from the big fireplace, in which Florio stoked up a blaze every evening. She was arranging the lilies when she heard a footstep in the doorway. She glanced briefly over her shoulder and saw Michael Florio. She did not turn around again as he walked up behind her.

"They're lovely," he said quietly.

Rebecca's anger and hurt were like a nagging bruise inside. She made no answer, but her back felt rigid.

"Rebecca, I was very worried." His voice was husky. There was no anger in it anymore. "I didn't know what had happened to Therese, and I tend to think the worst these days."

Again, she made no response, putting some final touches to the flower arrangement.

"I spoke harshly to you. I didn't mean to wound you."

"You didn't," she replied in a clipped voice, still without turning.

He hesitated. "In the short time I've known you, I've come to respect you. So have the girls. We all feel you're special. I'm just asking you to trust that I know what's best for Therese."

His presence behind her was making her spine tingle. If she had been a cat, her coat would have bushed out like a brush by now. Suddenly, she had the fleeting thought that he was going to step forward and put his arms around her waist, that she would feel his body press up against her back, that she would feel his lips touch her neck.

As if afraid that thinking it would make it happen, she turned sharply and met his brooding gaze. "Are you getting around to an apology?"

That seemed to stick in his craw. "I meant the things I said. But I will admit I probably said them in an inappropriate way."

"Well, I sure as hell thought so," she replied briskly. "But that's irrelevant. You told me what was on your mind, and I agreed to do as I was ordered. Let's not go over it all again."

"I don't want to go over it again. I'd just like us to get back to normal."

"When have we ever been normal?" She smiled, the kind of glacial grimace she gave her stepmother. "It's okay. Your non-apology is accepted."

He looked down at her, dark-eyed. "You look tired," he said softly. "Is this all too much for you?"

"Of course not," she retorted, tilting her chin.

"I told you Therese could be difficult."

"Therese is not the difficult one," she replied, without thinking. Then, flushing at her own words, she turned back to the lilies and straightened the stems busily.

After a silence, Florio said, "Buy flowers anytime you want to. This house needs things like that."

Ain't that the truth, she thought as he walked away.

Therese's prediction, that more books were on their way from England, came true the next day. The postman made a rare visit to the house, with a slip addressed to Devon, telling her to collect a parcel at the main post office in Urbino. Devon asked Rebecca to take her, so they went in the Jeep together.

Devon was a different sort of companion from her sister, chatty and bubbling with observations. It had snowed lightly the past couple of days, and the landscape was dusted with white. The streets of Urbino were bustling with activity.

"Was Dad rough on you the other day?" Devon asked artlessly as they walked toward the post office.

Rebecca shrugged. "We had words, as my stepmother would say."

"I told him to apologize. I hope he did."

Rebecca said nothing, though it jarred on her somewhat to learn that Michael had only come to her on Devon's prompting.

"Therese can be really wild," Devon went on. "Even if you think she's responding to you, it usually doesn't last. Suddenly, all hell breaks loose again. You never know what she'll do next." Devon glanced at Rebecca. "I told you she could be dangerous. I meant it. Mom found out, the hard way."

Rebecca told herself to stay calm. "What do you mean?"

"The police think Therese did it. Killed Mom. That's why Dad took us away from San Francisco. She told you, right?" Rebecca asked.

"Yes. Why would they think Therese would do such a terrible thing?"

"Because she's set a lot of fires. And because Mom was abusive."

"And you, Devon? What do *you* believe?"

Devon smiled. "It doesn't really matter what I think, does it? I've never been afraid of Therese. She's never hurt me. She never will."

"Don't the police suspect your father?"

"Why should they?" Devon said sharply. Then she laughed, tossing her blond hair. "Maybe you're right. Dad could kill. What he couldn't do is kill Mom. Our mother could be very violent, especially when she was drunk, but he never lifted a finger to her. He loved her, right up to the end, when she'd turned into another person completely. You would have to know my dad to understand he would never do something as devious as setting a fire. He's the most honest, direct person on earth. When he wants to say something to you, he just comes right out and says it. Most security firms try and be sneaky, you know? They save money by sticking little cameras everywhere and having a couple of guys keep track of a hundred monitors. Dad's idea of security is to have real, live, trained, armed guards patrolling. He trains them himself. That's why he's the best. He just does what needs to be done." She turned her face to Rebecca. "Do you know what I mean? A person who sets a fire to kill someone is creepy. And Dad is not creepy."

"Is Therese creepy?"

Devon's eyes grew cold. She looked away from Rebecca. "Hey, there's my package."

The package was bulky and very heavy. It bore a sticker from Blackwell's bookshop in Oxford.

"What's in there?" Rebecca asked. "A complete set of Dickens?"

"She's already got that," Devon said. "This is mostly Trollope. She can't get enough Trollope. He wrote over fifty books, and they're nearly all huge, thank God."

"But you haven't read all these books, have you?"

"It would take me a lifetime to read what Therese reads in six months. But I know what she likes. I just make sure she doesn't run out of fodder." Devon's cheeks were flushed with the cold and the exertion of carrying the books. Her hair tumbled out of her cap charmingly.

They stopped for cappuccinos and toasted sandwiches at Alfredo's bar. The place was filled with students, as always. Huddled into greatcoats, muffled in college scarves, they crowded around nearly every table, arguing and drinking Cokes until it was time for their classes to begin. Devon seemed to inhale the atmosphere as if it were heady perfume.

"I can't wait to get to college." She sighed.

"Do you have a boyfriend?" Rebecca asked.

Devon's eyes were bright. "I have this really great fantasy about Brad Pitt. You want to hear it?"

"If I have to."

"He comes for me on this huge, throbbing motorbike. He picks me up and races me to the beach. We tear our clothes off. He has this tub of melting caramel fudge ice cream. He smears it all over my body, and then licks it off. Then he gets on me, and we make wild, crazy love while the waves pound over our bodies. What do you think?"

"Sounds interesting," Rebecca said flatly. But she was startled by the explicitness of Devon's erotic imagination.

"What about you?" Devon asked. "Does anyone rub caramel fudge ice cream on you and lick it off?"

"Now and then." She smiled.

"Anyone special?"

"Not right now."

"How come?"

"I don't think I'm in the market for a heavy relationship right now. Devon, can I ask you a question that might be intrusive and dumb?"

"Go ahead."

"Has Therese ever said anything to you about the fire? Has she actually admitted that she was responsible?"

Devon's smile faded fast. "Boy, you're kind of obsessed with her, aren't you?"

"Not obsessed. Just concerned."

"Why?"

There was a hardness in Devon's brown eyes that Rebecca had not seen before. She remembered Therese saying, *Devon says you might be an undercover cop.* "I have no dark motives, Devon. But if your sister feels that she killed her mother, that's a crushing burden for a thirteen-year-old to have to bear."

"Yeah," Devon said shortly.

There was an unmistakable coldness in the atmosphere. Rebecca tried to ease it with a smile. "I told you I might be intrusive and dumb," she apologized. "Forget it."

"We'd better be getting home," Devon said with no return of warmth.

Before going back to the house, Rebecca, mindful of Michael's request, bought some more flowers, this time yellow and red lilies. She also bought a bag of chestnuts to roast at the fire at home, and one of the big almond cakes that were traditional here. Might as well try and work up a little Yuletide cheer, she thought dryly.

SAN FRANCISCO

Father Timothy Dean's name was slotted in the number 6 position of the squash ladder at his club. He was an excellent player, and only the pressure of his ecclesiastical duties prevented him from rising higher on the ladder. As it was, nowadays he seldom challenged those above him on the oak-and-brass frame, being content to field contenders from the ranks below him. That kept him quite busy enough.

This morning, he was playing the number 7, a lean and skillful young insurance broker who was putting up a good struggle, but who had underestimated the task at hand. Father Tim was sweating, but he had been in control of the game from the start, and there was space in his mind for reflection, as he bounced on rubber soles.

He was thinking about Barbara Florio, whose last rites he had performed with his own hands, and whom he had buried with genuine grief.

It was true he had flirted with her. It was also true that she had enjoyed his flirtation, even though she had known that what he had renounced when he made his vows had not been the solace of soft female bodies like hers, but of athletic male bodies like his own—or that of the swarthy insurance broker who now lunged vainly after a neat crosscourt ball, crashing onto the wooden deck with a grunt.

"You okay?" Father Tim grinned as the broker picked himself off the floor, dusting off reddened knees.

"Sure," said the man, panting as he crouched for Father Tim's next service.

Father Tim popped the ball at the back wall, moving after it smoothly. Barbara's death had left him with a feeling of deep anger. He had liked the woman. She had been an alcoholic and a pill popper. There had been a streak of venom in her, as there was in all the Montroses. He had no doubt that she had been a difficult wife, a nightmare mother. But he knew how hard she had tried to conquer her demons, how desperately she had wanted to lavish her love. It was not altogether her fault that she had failed. And she had certainly not deserved to die, her body tortured by flame.

He swung the racket hard enough to blitz the ball past his startled opponent, who lunged a yard too short for the rebound. Father Tim picked up the ball, checking it for damage.

Feeling eyes on his back, he half turned. The two police officers had arrived. They were sitting on the deserted benches, watching him stolidly through the glass wall. He waved his racket to them in brief acknowledgment, then turned back to the game. He was poised for victory now, and he cleared his mind momentarily of other thoughts.

Five minutes later, he emerged from the court, a towel wrapped around his flushed neck. He greeted Reagan and Bianchi courteously.

"Give me a moment to shower, and I'll be right with you," he told them. "Why not take a seat on the terrace? I'll join you there."

Under the stinging needles of the shower, Father Tim thought of Barbara Florio's fiery martyrdom. His own religious upbringing had been relatively free of stock terrors. But from childhood, he had had a horror of death by fire. To feel the lipids beneath one's skin actually melt and ignite, to splatter and blaze like a steak on a barbecue, to feel one's nerves burning, one's flesh burning, eyeballs boiling, organs roasting. . . .

Barbara Florio had not been a saint. But in his mind, she was a martyr. He had no doubts about that. She had been burned alive by a pagan tyrant, exactly as those early martyrs had been, for her faith.

The detectives were waiting for him on the terrace. He shook hands with both of them. He remembered the woman well, a Latin-looking brunette who had interrupted him at the funeral. She had a pleasant face and manner. Her partner, a fortyish male, had neither.

"Sorry to keep you waiting," he said apologetically, adjusting the white dog collar at his neck.

"That's okay," Carla Bianchi replied easily. "We were early, anyhow."

He sat, laying his cell phone and his car keys on the table, together with his electronic diary and his dark glasses. He caught Reagan eyeing the pile sourly. The man probably hadn't been to church in twenty years, Father Tim guessed, but would be full of preconceptions about how a priest ought to dress and behave. He smiled at them. "How may I help you?" he asked.

Carla Bianchi opened a thick notebook. Father Tim saw the neat, dense script covering page after page. A methodical, orderly mind, he decided. "We want to ask you some questions about the trouble between you and Michael Florio just before Mrs. Florio's death," Bianchi said.

Straight to the point, the crux of the issue. Father Tim's approval deepened.

"Sure," he said. "Go ahead."

"At that time, Mrs. Florio was planning to give a large plot of land to the Catholic Church?"

"That's right."

"She wanted to build a church on the land, am I right?"

"That was her hope," Father Tim agreed. "Barbara and I discussed the possibilities in some detail."

"Uh-huh. Were you aware that the property had been used to secure a large bank loan to Mrs. Florio's husband?"

"Not at that time," Father Tim replied. "Barbara didn't mention it. I was told that later."

"Who told you?" Reagan put in, hard eyes watching the priest.

Father Tim laughed briefly. "As a matter of fact, Michael Florio himself gave me the information."

"This was when he threatened your life?" Reagan demanded.

Father Tim laughed some more. He signaled the waiter. "Yes. That was when he threatened my life."

The two detectives waited while he ordered a glass of fresh grapefruit juice. Both declined the offer of refreshment.

"You felt obliged to seek a court order against Florio," Reagan went on.

"For my own protection. Yes."

"We took a look at the court records. Seems like Mr. Florio blamed you for his troubles."

"That's right. Mr. Florio blamed me."

"Maybe you could understand his reaction?" Bianchi put in.

Father Tim had his own understanding about men who threatened the lives of priests. "Anger and evil are not hard to understand, in my experience," he said shortly. "They may be hard for decent people to accept. But there is no mystery as to their origin or development."

Bianchi nodded seriously. "Could you tell us exactly what happened between you?"

"It took place right here at the club," the priest said, looking around.

"That's partly why I asked you to meet me here. The memories are freshest here." He paused while the waiter brought his fruit juice. He took a sip of the bittersweet liquid, then went on. "He found me in the gym, working out on the machines. He came over to me, very intense, very angry. He accused me of trying to destroy him. I had no idea what he was talking about at first. Michael Florio is a nominal Catholic," he told them, "but in all the time I knew the family, he never bothered to hide his own atheism—or to make it clear that he despised his wife's faith. But this was something new. I was at a disadvantage, and when he told me that his wife's bequest was going to make financial trouble for him, I was reluctant to discuss the matter any further. Not there and then, in any case. I told him to come by my office. He became enraged. That's when he threatened to kill me."

Reagan's brutal face wore a faint smile, though Father Tim could not for the life of him think why. "You claimed in judge's chambers that he assaulted you."

Father Tim sipped his grapefruit juice, remembering. "I tried to push past him, to get to the locker room. He grabbed me quite suddenly. He bent me backward over a piece of apparatus." He transferred his gaze from Reagan's flinty face to Bianchi's concerned one. "I'm a fit man. I think of myself as physically powerful, and I don't have any moral reservations about a priest defending himself from an unjust assault, though I would not of course strike back. But there was nothing I could do. Michael Florio is exceptionally strong. And he has something else." He traced a pattern on the beaded glass with his fingertip. "Do you know W. B. Yeats, the Irish poet?"

Bianchi tapped her pad with her pen. "Rings a bell."

"In one of his poems about evil, he says, 'The best lack all conviction, while the worst/ Are full of passionate intensity.' That's the quality Michael Florio has. The passionate intensity of evil."

"Uh-huh," Bianchi said politely. Reagan looked bored.

"Michael put his mouth close to my ear, and said, 'I'll break your back, priest.' I believed he would do it. I was in fear of my life."

"Were there any witnesses?" Reagan demanded.

"There were other people in the gymnasium. But it all happened very fast. And in any case, Michael Florio would physically intimidate most people. You know about his war record?"

"Yes."

"When he released me, I stumbled away to get dressed. I felt . . . *naked*. By the time I was dressed, he had gone."

"You went straight to your lawyer?" Reagan asked.

"I went to my bishop first. We agreed that I needed protection."

"The judge wasn't too impressed, it seems," Reagan said.

The priest read the expressions on their faces. Stabbings and shootings were daily fare to them. Perhaps they were not impressed by his account. He did not want to be thought of as a wimp. "I could hear the vertebrae in my spine cracking," he said softly. "It felt like my brain was exploding. My legs had gone numb. For several days after the attack, I had severe headaches, and difficulty walking."

"Father Dean," Bianchi said gently, "we don't doubt for one minute that the attack was serious. Did you speak to Mrs. Florio about the incident?"

"Briefly," he replied. "She was furious, but I didn't want her to be involved in any of the ugliness. I did say one thing, though."

"What was that?" Reagan asked.

"I warned her that her life might be in danger from her husband." His hands were shaking, and he was forced to put the glass down to avoid spilling any juice. "I've never stopped reproaching myself since then that I didn't make the point more strongly, that I didn't . . ." He had to stop, his eyes and throat too full of tears to continue.

This time, even Reagan seemed impressed by his distress. "Take it easy, Father," he said. "You aren't to blame for any of this mess."

The priest mastered his emotions. "I should have seen it coming," he said. "It was a tragic household. There was an imbalance of power that could never be resolved. I believe that Barbara and Michael truly loved each other once. And they wanted to be good parents to the girls. But Barbara held the financial whip hand, and Michael held the emotional whip hand. Neither would give up an inch of power. Michael spent his life clawing after money, and Barbara spent hers clawing after emotional

fulfillment. Neither got what they wanted. They just succeeded in destroying each other."

"It was a tense household?"

"Terribly tense. Even after the separation, the unhappiness there was
palpable. Therese being so difficult didn't help."

"She was something of a problem child, wasn't she?"

"That's putting it mildly," Father Tim said ruefully.

"Lying, arson—those aren't signs of a happy childhood, are they?"

"No. Therese was not having a happy childhood." He met Reagan's
eyes. "I know you people think Therese set fire to her mother's bed."

"Do we?" Reagan said impassively.

"You think her other acts of arson were trial runs. But I beg you to
consider that a child setting fire to a car, or a pile of dolls, is very different
from a child killing a parent."

"Uh-huh," Bianchi said. "There's been some suggestion that the girls
might be in danger from Mr. Florio. That they're all that stands between
him and a great deal of money."

Father Tim paused. "Michael is a greedy man. He saw money as a way
of validating his own importance, and he pursued it relentlessly. That's
partly why he came to neglect and then despise Barbara. But as a
father . . ." He shook his head. "Raising two such complicated children in
such an unhealthy household was terribly, terribly difficult. He was actually a better parent than Barbara. A far better parent. I even urged Barbara
to let him have much more access to the children, maybe even to let him
have custody."

"You did? Even though he was hostile to the church?"

"They were at a convent school. They were getting a sound religious
education. But they desperately wanted to be with their father, not with
Barbara. She was struggling with the heavy burden of alcohol and drug
dependency, and she was frankly a disaster as a mother, as far as I could
see. But she always refused to consider it." He shook his head. "And he
could be a loving, thoughtful father. He would do anything for those girls.
Anything."

"And maybe they would do anything for him?" Bianchi suggested quietly.

It took Father Tim a moment to see what she was hinting at. When he did so, he winced. "If Therese was in any way responsible, which I cannot in my heart accept, then it was either an accident, or a prank that went horribly wrong."

"You just said their parents were at war, Father. This generous gift of Mrs. Florio's to the church—it was the strategic nuclear weapon, right? It was going to destroy Michael Florio. That's what the donation was all about, wasn't it?"

"That is *not* what it was all about, Detective Bianchi," Father Tim said firmly. "I said just now there was a tragic imbalance in that family. The root of the problem was that Barbara worshiped God, and Michael worshiped money. God and mammon cannot exist under one roof. That is why Barbara had to die. She would not give up her church, and Michael would not give up his money. When you call the gift a weapon, you're thinking like Michael Florio."

"I'm trying to think like all of the parties involved, Father."

"He martyred her," the priest said obstinately.

"She was about to martyr him, wasn't she?"

Father Tim was upset. "Detective, you're distorting vitally important words. Michael would probably have suffered an economic setback. Maybe even lost control of his business. Barbara was burned alive, for the crime of clinging to her church. *That* is martyrdom."

Reagan was looking bored again. He cleared his throat to get his partner's attention, and raised an eyebrow. Bianchi sighed. Trendy as his external appearance was, Father Tim saw things only in shades of dogma: black and white. She was convinced the truth lay somewhere in the murky gray area that covered most of human behavior. "You've been very frank, and we're grateful. I think we have all we want, don't we?"

"For now," Reagan said. The detectives rose, and said cordial goodbyes to Father Tim. He watched them leave, feeling his heart heavy with the dark memories the interview had unleashed.

At the exit, the woman suddenly turned, and came back toward Father Tim. He rose politely to meet her. She was uncapping her pen.

"Sorry," she said. "One last thing. That phrase you used. The something something of evil?"

"Passionate intensity," he said.

" 'The passionate intensity of evil,' " Bianchi repeated, jotting it down. "Thanks. I like that. I want to remember it." She smiled at Father Tim, and left.

URBINO

Rebecca awoke in the night, thinking she could hear crying. Sitting up, she listened, trying to clear her mind of the confused dreams she'd been having. Something like a faint sob drifted through the thick stone walls. She groped for the matches at her bedside and lit the candle. Its yellow light turned the blackness into a thousand undulating shadows. She clambered out of bed and padded on bare feet across the icy floor into the corridor.

At night this was the darkest house she had ever known. Once all the candles and lamps had been extinguished, the darkness was total. No pilots glowed, no night-lights lit the way. It was also the most silent house she'd ever been in at night, not even the hum of a refrigerator breaking the stillness. She stopped outside Therese's door and listened. Nobody in the house seemed to be stirring. Then she caught the sound of Therese's voice, whimpering something incoherently. She pushed the door open softly and went in.

Therese was sprawled on the floor beside her bed, moaning quietly, her head arched back. At first Rebecca thought she was having a seizure, but then she saw the languid way her arms were moving, and realized she must have fallen out of bed while dreaming. She knelt quietly beside her and stroked Therese's forehead.

"Are you okay, honey?"

Therese's eyes opened. "Mom?" She muttered something, angry or afraid.

"It's all right," Rebecca murmured. "It's only a bad dream. I'm here."

She heard a sound behind her, and turned. Michael Florio's tall figure was looming over her. She gasped.

"Oh," she whispered, "you frightened me!"

Michael's face was shadowed. "What's going on?"

"I heard her crying. She must have fallen out of bed. She was having a nightmare, but she's peaceful now."

He knelt beside her, stroking Therese's hair gently. "Are you all right, sweetheart?" he murmured.

Therese nodded. Michael lifted her in his arms with easy strength and put her back on the bed. Rebecca's heart was still pounding from shock.

"Can I have a glass of milk?" Therese asked.

"Of course," Michael said. "I'll go get it. Rebecca will stay with you."

Rebecca sat by the girl while he went for the milk. Therese had been sweating, and her skin was clammy. In the soft candlelight, the child's face was angelic. Her eyes were closed. Sleep had smoothed away all her usual frowns and grimaces. Now her face was like a troubled pool that had grown still. It was transparent, and you could see down to the depths. Rebecca leaned over her, drinking in her image. Strange shadows chased across the girl's face, likenesses of other people. Now that she was at peace, Rebecca could see traces of her own mother's face in Therese's, traces of Ryan's face—and traces of her own. The likeness was there, stronger than she had realized before. But genetics had lengthened a line here, filled a curve there, made something that was like, and yet unlike. She wondered whether Michael or Devon would ever see that likeness, and guess who she was. Rebecca leaned forward and touched her lips to Therese's cheek. *My daughter, but not my child*, she thought.

Michael came back with a glass of warm milk. He helped Therese sit up while she drank it. Then she rolled on her side, bringing her fist up to her mouth in a movement left over from infantile thumb-sucking. Rebecca covered her with the quilt. Therese's lids fluttered as some new dream drifted through her mind, and she stirred uneasily for a moment, before she drifted back into tranquillity.

For a moment Rebecca and Michael stood side by side, looking down at the candlelit face on the pillow. Almost like real parents, she thought. The way it should have been.

Michael turned to her. "I made warm milk for us, too. Come down and get it."

"Thanks, but I don't like warm milk."

The candlelight glimmered in his dark eyes. "You'll like this. It's all ready."

The offer was not welcome, and she would have preferred to refuse. She sighed. "I'll just go and get a robe."

She went to her room and put on her slippers and robe. She caught sight of her reflection in the mirror, her face a luminous oval framed in a dark blur of hair. Her heart was still beating fast.

Michael was in the kitchen, pouring something that smelled alcoholic. He wore a dark red robe that made him look rather majestic in the light of the kerosene lamp.

"What's that?" she asked.

"Rum and milk."

"Some nightcap."

"It's what I make when I think I'm not going to sleep."

"Haven't you been to bed yet?" she asked.

He shook his head. "I was working on some calculations. I want to try the turbine out in a couple of days. It's hard to calculate the flow of these old mills. The column of water varies so much."

"I wouldn't even know where to begin."

"I need twenty horsepower to make ten kilowatts. Calculating the horsepower means multiplying the height of the waterfall in feet by the flow in cubic feet per second. Then you multiply that figure by 62.4 and divide by 550. That gives you the crude theoretical output in horsepower. To get horsepower to kilowatts, you divide by 0.746. Let me know when your eyes glaze over."

"They're glazing fast," she admitted. "Is it going to work?"

"We'll soon find out," he said succinctly. He held a glass out to her. "Careful, it's hot."

She took it gingerly, clinked her glass against his, and sipped. "Wow."

"You like it?"

"It gives a whole new dimension to insomnia."

"Let's go sit by the fire. It's still warm in there."

They carried the lamp through to the sitting room, flowing shadows hurrying beside them. As Michael had said, there was still a warm glow in the fireplace. She curled up with her hot rum in an armchair while he tossed another log on the embers.

"How long have you been planning this turbine thing?" she asked.

"Years," he said. "One of the reasons this place fell into ruins was because it was too far away from the power lines. Connection would have cost a fortune. Nobody seems to have thought that here was a perfect setup to generate your own free, clean power."

"So you got the place cheap?"

"Dirt cheap. Once we have power, all the rest follows. A proper communications setup, lights, heat, energy, Western civilization."

"Electrified fences?" she suggested.

He glanced at her. "You've convinced yourself I'm some kind of crackpot, haven't you?"

"I didn't say that. Just that you're talking as though this is going to be your permanent hideout. And I wonder whether it's the best setting for two girls to grow up in."

"We're not planning to stay here forever, Rebecca."

"How long then? When will it be safe to leave? What has to happen to make it safe?"

"You've been talking to the kids. You know why we're here. You know how complicated things are."

"I know there's one question you desperately need to answer," she said. "And that's whether Therese set that fire or not."

He glanced at her sharply. "Of course she didn't set that fire," he said, his voice deepening.

"Then you must have done it." Rebecca felt the rum making her pugnacious, and knew it was unwise.

But Michael seemed amused. "You think so?"

"I think you're capable," she said.

"You're wrong," he replied.

"So why are you on the run?"

"Because the police and their tame psychiatrists were planning to take Therese to pieces like a cheap watch."

" 'They mean to rip open your mind and fish out whatever dark little secrets you have in there,' " she quoted.

"What?"

"That's how Therese put it. It's violent language to describe psychiatric care."

"Your experience is probably different from ours," he said dryly. "A shrink you pay for is a comforting figure. A shrink the police bring in to interrogate your child is something else altogether."

"I suppose that's true," she said neutrally.

He was watching her. "You still haven't forgiven me for yelling at you the other day," he said. "Have you?"

"You said some shitty things," she replied evenly.

"I took a big chance with you," he said. "After all those lies you told, only a crazy man would have taken you on. But I'm a crazy man. I responded to you in a way I don't normally respond to people. I'm a suspicious, careful man. But with you . . . I thought you were special right from the first moment. When you took off with Therese, I was afraid I'd made the biggest mistake of my life. I was very angry and very scared."

She sat tight, clutching her glass, not knowing what to think.

"The girls think you're special, too. You see Therese as a problem child. But neither Devon nor I have seen her as relaxed around anyone for years. Even the day you took her to Urbino would have been a wonderful thing, except for the way you did it, which freaked everybody out."

"Michael," Rebecca said, "I regret those stupid lies I told. And I do want you to have confidence in me."

"Do you have confidence in me?" he countered.

The words stuck in her throat. "You scare me," she said at last.

"In what way?"

She felt dizzy, devoutly wishing she hadn't drunk the hot milk and truth drug. "I can't make up my mind about you. Whether you're a good person or a bad person."

The fire crackled softly in the silence. "There's good and evil in all of us," he said at last. "Two sides that struggle with each other for as long as we're alive. Sometimes the dark side is up. Sometimes it's down. There's no simple answer."

"With most people there is. Most people are good."

"Only because they've never faced real necessity or real temptation to be evil," he retorted.

"And which of your two sides is uppermost right now?" she asked.

She caught the shadow of a smile. "Let's say my character is a house of many rooms," he replied. "You've got a little secret of your own, haven't you? Something you want to hide?"

"It's nothing illegal or dangerous."

"Why can't you tell me what it is?"

"Because it involves . . . other people."

"I make my living taking care of other people's problems. I know a lot of ways to set things right. Maybe I could help you."

"I doubt it."

He was watching her from beneath lowered lids. "The day I met you I felt I'd met you before. Right now, sitting here, I'm getting that feeling stronger than ever. Do you ever get feelings like that?"

"I don't know," she replied uneasily. "I've taken to the girls enormously."

"And me?"

She had no answer to that.

"My whole life has been based on distrusting people, Rebecca. But it can't go on forever. One day you meet someone you simply have to trust." He smiled slightly. "That's usually when the bullet comes thudding into your blind side." Michael turned to the fire, which was flaring brightly in the grate. He picked up a stick and pushed the burning log back. "I haven't made love to a woman for a long time," he said in a dreamy voice. "Not since things got so crazy." The firelight caressed the side of his face, leaving one side in darkness. "But I want to make love to you, Rebecca."

Shaken, Rebecca touched her dry lips with the tip of her tongue. "That would be insane, for both of us, Michael."

"Is that a yes?"

Rebecca felt her head swimming. The blood was throbbing at her pulses. She had not been with a man in a long time. Her voice was almost inaudible. "No. It's a no."

He glanced at her, eyes reflecting the flames. " 'No' for always? Or 'no' just this time?"

"I don't know," she said, her voice tight. "I'd guess 'no' for always."

"Because you think I killed my wife? Is that it?"

"I don't have to go into my reasons, Michael."

"If you think I burned Barbara to death, you're crazy, Rebecca. I'm not capable."

"Boy, you have a big ego," she said grimly. "Doesn't it occur to you that I just might not find you attractive?"

"No," he replied, smiling. "That hadn't occurred to me. Because I know you do find me attractive. Trouble is, you've concocted a fantasy in your head, and you've cast me as the monster." Michael reached out and touched her hand. She felt shivers rise up her arm. "We'd be very good together," he said softly.

She rose, knowing if she did not escape now, she would never do so. "Thanks for the offer, but no thanks. I'm going to bed, Michael. See you in the morning."

As she walked away from him, she was half afraid he would reach out and stop her. But he did not. He just watched her leave, his face half fire, half darkness.

THREE

WATER

URBINO

She slept little after that, and what sleep she got was haunted by disturbing dreams. She fled from Michael along the dark corridors of the house, not knowing whether he wanted to kill her or make love to her. The dreams woke her, gasping, time after time, until she fell into a doze around seven-thirty. The family's voices downstairs woke her within an hour, and she rose, feeling fragile.

Dressed in jeans and a bulky sweater, Rebecca went down to the kitchen to find all three of them there already. Michael, wearing an apron, was frying eggs and bacon on the gas stove. He turned to smile at her as she came in. That smile went straight to her heart, making her catch her breath. He was so very handsome, and when he did not have that dark, brooding expression, he seemed to light up the room. She wondered what might have happened had he propositioned her in some sunlit room—

instead of in the darkness, lit by the ominous red glow of the fire, where everything that was frightening about him was emphasized.

Therese was sitting with a cup halfway to her mouth. She gave Rebecca a shy smile. "Look outside."

Rebecca glanced out the window and saw that snow, real snow, had fallen thickly, turning the world white. "Hey. When did *that* happen?"

Michael dished out the breakfast and they ate. Both girls seemed to be happy, excited about the snow. Therese had even brushed her hair, unless Devon had done that for her, and was wearing a pistachio-green jersey that made her brunette coloring glow.

"We're going into town today," Michael announced. "I need to pick up a couple of things."

The girls jumped up to clear the table. Rebecca rose to help. She could feel Michael's dark eyes on her. She avoided his gaze as best she could, remembering last night, feeling the heat in her body. If she met his eyes, she feared she would blush and look like a fool.

Urbino was beautiful. There was an atmosphere of enchantment in the old town, compounded of the snow, the bustle, the smell of roasting chestnuts. The streets were crowded and noisy. The shop windows that lined the winding, cobbled lanes were filled with the kind of tempting goodies Italians seemed to do best.

Rebecca found herself alone with Therese, looking at the sumptuous display of a women's clothing shop. "Look at that dress." She sighed hungrily. "Italy's amazing. Even in a small shop in a small town like this, you get Valentino, Armani, Versace."

"Yeah, they're beautiful." Therese huddled in against Rebecca. Without thinking, she slipped her arm around the girl's shoulders, and drew her close to her side. "Thanks for coming to me last night," Therese said.

"That's okay. You must have been having a bad dream."

"I dreamed we were all dead, and people in black clothes were coming to take us away."

"That sounds horrible," Rebecca said compassionately.

Therese was staring at the display with serious eyes. "I have a lot of dreams like that." Somewhere in the crowd, they heard Devon's squeal of laughter. "Dad's in a good mood this morning," Therese commented.

"Yes, he is, isn't he?" Rebecca said neutrally.

"What did you and Dad do after I went back to sleep last night?"

"We just talked awhile, then went to bed. Separately," Rebecca added without thinking, then felt like a fool.

"You like each other, don't you?" Therese asked, still staring at the clothes.

Rebecca felt herself grow cold, then hot. "He's my employer, Therese. There's nothing beyond that."

"Don't you feel anything?"

"I'm very fond of *you*, if that's what you mean."

For a quiet moment, Therese rested her head on Rebecca's shoulder. It felt feather-light. "You're so controlled," Therese said, her voice quiet. "I wish I was like you."

Rebecca thought. "I usually plan my life very meticulously," she said at last. "But lately, things have been happening to me in a way I can't control."

"Are you afraid of your feelings?" Therese asked.

"Sometimes."

"Even when they're good feelings?"

"I'm uptight and screwed down, most of the time. When my emotions catch me by surprise, I start to panic."

"You have to learn to let go sometimes," Therese said seriously.

Rebecca laughed, kissing Therese's temple. The girl's hair smelled good, a spicy smell. "You're right. I have to learn to let go."

It had started to snow again, small twinkling flakes that spun in the air, almost too light to settle. Michael and Devon came up to them, carrying parcels. "You two make an interesting couple," Michael said to Rebecca. "You could practically be mother and daughter."

Rebecca felt her heart twist. She had always seen him as a grim man, with brooding eyes that missed nothing. Now that he was relaxed and happy for a change, he was quite different. He held something out to her. "I got this for you."

She took the soft parcel awkwardly. "Oh. Thank you."

"Open it," he commanded.

Feeling her cheeks grow warm, Rebecca opened the pretty paper. Inside was a cashmere scarf in a deep shade of autumn gold. "Oh, Michael! This is beautiful."

He smiled at her. "Put it on."

She wound it around her neck. The buttery softness was like a lover's caress. "You shouldn't have bought this, Michael. It was expensive."

"No old fogy should be seen in public without a muffler," he said. "Okay, *famiglia* Florio. Let's go." He glanced at Rebecca on the way out of Urbino. "Have a nice time?"

"Great, thanks," she replied, touching the cloudy softness of the scarf around her neck.

"The snow has put roses in your cheeks."

The expression in his eyes was unmistakable. Michael reached out and took her hand. For a moment, she felt the warmth of his palm. Then she pushed his hand firmly and quickly away.

As the millhouse came into sight, big and comforting, Rebecca found herself wondering whether there was a middle way, a God-sent solution that could emerge here. Could it be as miraculously, wonderfully simple as that?

No, she thought reluctantly. It couldn't. Not until she knew for certain that Michael was not a killer.

Over the next days, Therese seemed to undergo a change. She spent less time locked in her room with her books. She appeared to like being around Rebecca, and would come quietly up to help her with some chore. She dressed herself with much more thought. She even gathered all her things off the floor, and put them neatly on shelves. She was a flower ready to open.

Joyful excitement filled Rebecca. She finally felt she was getting somewhere—past the aggression and the confusion that cloaked her daughter, and closer to the sweet nature of the child within—intelligent, gentle, vulnerable.

She even got Therese to talk about her mother on one occasion, as they sat together in her room.

"We weren't supposed to know anything about why they separated," Therese said, "in case we were scarred, or whatever. But basically, we knew she accused him of having an affair with another woman. We never knew who it was. Maybe he did have an affair. Devon and I didn't care about that."

"Maybe your mother felt differently about it," Rebecca suggested.

"Well, he wanted to take us, but Mom wouldn't let us go. She got satisfaction from keeping us apart. She got the lawyers to threaten Dad with all kinds of things. He didn't want to drag it all through the courts. He said it would get very ugly. So he just had to take what she dished out, because he was terrified of losing us, and because he was a lot smarter than she was. He knew he'd work out a way. And he did. She didn't know we saw him every day. We were supposed to eat at the school dining hall, but Dad seduced the teachers, even though most of them are nuns. He's good at that."

"I can imagine," Rebecca said dryly.

"He used to take us to lunch every day. Sometimes we ate at his apartment. Or he would take us to great restaurants he knew." She was smiling faintly at the memories.

"Weren't you happy, living with your mother?" she asked.

"We wanted to be with Dad."

"Because your mother was mean to you?"

"She was sick," Therese replied.

"What kind of sick?"

"Drink-and-drugs sick. She just wanted to hurt people, at the end."

"Did she hurt you?" Rebecca asked, very quietly.

"She hurt everybody."

"Physically?"

"With whatever came to hand. If she was sober, she'd use words. If she was too stoned for words, she'd get violent. She beat Devon with the cord of a lamp once. She still has marks on her back. She wanted to destroy Dad."

"Destroy him?"

"Wreck his business. Make him lose all his money."

"Divorces can get very ugly. I'm sorry."

"Dad would never hurt us. Ever. You think he's cold and ruthless, don't you?"

"I wouldn't use those negative words," Rebecca said reluctantly. "He's a forbidding man. I guess I got on the wrong side of him at first. I like him a lot better lately."

"He's a wonderful father. He'll protect me, no matter what. He's the only person in the world I feel completely safe around. Sometimes I'd like to just crawl in his pocket and stay there." She lifted her clouded eyes to Rebecca. "I'm sick, Rebecca. But I want to be better."

"You will be better," Rebecca promised.

The wide, sad mouth moved into a wry quirk. Unexpectedly, Therese held up her arms to Rebecca. "Oh, Therese," she whispered, and hugged the girl. She could feel Therese clinging to her, like a weak swimmer being tugged by a strong current. "I'm here for you," she whispered. "Always."

The next day, as more snow fell, the two girls went to choose a Christmas tree after breakfast. They went out, muffled to the eyeballs, carrying a ribbon that they would tie around the chosen tree. Rebecca could hear them laughing.

Michael, who was finishing off his coffee, said, "That's your doing, Rebecca."

"What is?"

"Those kids. You're a miracle."

"No, I'm not. Just because the girls are happy doesn't mean your problems are over. How can they be? Until you've gotten to the bottom of what's in Therese's mind, how can they ever be over, here in the middle of nowhere?"

He frowned. "You're starting to sound like the kind of people I had to get Therese away from."

"Those people were only trying to help," she said.

"Their help means pressure. Therese can only take so much pressure before she'll break, Rebecca. As her father, I see it as my duty to protect her from any and all pressure that could hurt her. *That's* why we're here in the middle of nowhere. I'm just giving Therese some space and silence in which to heal herself."

"How can she heal herself?"

"Only Therese can heal herself. Nobody else can do it for her. All we can do is create the environment in which it can happen."

"Michael, when you rejected their help, you took on the responsibility of helping her yourself."

"I took on that responsibility the day I adopted her," Michael retorted.

Rebecca nodded slowly. "Can I ask you why you and your wife decided to adopt?"

"Barbara had had several miscarriages," he replied. "Each one did more damage to her body, until they finally told us she could never have children."

"I didn't mean to pry into that," Rebecca replied. "I know your wife desperately wanted children. But did you want them as badly? Or did you just go along with her wishes?"

He glanced at her with dark eyes. "You think I don't love my kids?"

"I'm not saying that."

"I love them more than you can imagine," he said harshly. He clenched his fist and pressed it to his chest. "They're part of me, Rebecca. Like my heart is part of me. I couldn't survive without them."

She was impressed, even a little intimidated, by his obvious passion. "That's a normal parental feeling."

He seemed to relax slightly. "People have all kinds of misconceptions about adoptive parents. They think we're not the real thing, you know what I mean? We don't feel quite what 'real' parents feel. Well, that's bullshit. When Therese was little, I told her she was adopted. She asked what that meant. I told her it meant she was luckier than other children, because her daddy had wanted her so much that he'd done something very special to get her. Something more than other daddies do. And I believe that, Rebecca."

"I guess you had to tell her," Rebecca said slowly, "when Devon came along. That must have been a big shock for Therese."

"It was a shock," he agreed evenly. "But every time a sibling arrives, it's a shock for an only child, isn't it?"

"Maybe a little more than usual in this case."

"Maybe. But we wanted other children. And we wanted Therese to have a brother or a sister." His gaze seemed to turn inward. "I never met Therese's mother. Barbara did. She said she was a serious, intelligent, beautiful kid. She was impressed by her. For a long time, while Therese was a baby, we discussed an idea we had—of asking her to give us another baby. With me as the father this time."

Rebecca felt the blood come flaming hotly into her face. He was not looking at her, so he did not see her reaction. "That's a bizarre idea," she said in a choked voice.

"Not so bizarre," he said, obviously still staring into the past. "She'd made a beautiful child in Therese. Together, we could have made another."

"Surely she would never have agreed," Rebecca said, turning away so that he couldn't see her face.

"We thought about offering her money."

"Why didn't you approach her?"

He was silent for a while. "Barbara couldn't handle it in the end," he said at last. "She developed this fantasy that I would fall in love with the girl, and go off with her and the children. She knew it would all have been very clinical. Donor insemination. No emotions involved. We didn't even have to meet. But Barbara had a deep fear of losing me. She couldn't face it."

"But she drove you away in the end," Rebecca pointed out.

"You know very little about our lives. It'll take time for you to learn. But, believe me, Barbara was a bad person. Not at first, but she grew to be bad. She was deluded and cruel. She made fantastic accusations against me. Her delight was to say things that cut us all to the bone. She tortured both Devon and Therese for years. We're all free of her at last, though nobody would ever have wished her dead. Now Therese has a chance to make herself better."

"She still has Barbara's picture at her bedside," Rebecca said in a small voice.

"Barbara was a loving wife and mother once. Long ago." Michael rose and walked over to her. "What's the matter? You look upset."

"I'm not upset."

"You look upset. What is it, Rebecca?" He reached out as if to take her in his arms, but she backed off quickly. "Rebecca, I don't think you understand how I feel about you," he said quietly, his eyes warm.

"You were just telling me how responsible you feel for Therese," she retorted. "Well, you can't let her down now to pursue some stupid flirtation."

"Wait a minute," he said. "In the first place, I never stop thinking about Therese. If I didn't think you were good for her, I would never have looked at you. And in the second place, what I feel for you is something very different from a flirtation." Rebecca felt her heart lurch as he took her in his arms. This time she did not resist. He drew her tight against his warm body, burying his mouth in the lush curls of her chestnut hair. "You smell wonderful," he whispered.

Rebecca wanted to push him away, break free of this embrace she found so desirable and yet so inappropriate. But her body betrayed her. "It can't last forever," she said unsteadily. "Sooner or later, they'll trace you here."

"Then we'll face them. And you'll be with us."

"I can't help you."

"You've already helped enormously. You're helping Therese get strong enough to face her accusers. When that day comes, we'll go back and let them ask any questions they want to. But not until then."

Michael's hands were caressing her tenderly. She looked up at him, her oval face pale and tense. He cupped her cheeks in both hands and brushed his mouth against hers.

"Is that true?" she asked.

"Is what true?"

"That when Therese is better, you'll go back and face them?"

"Yes, of course."

His kiss was barely more than a touch. The warmth of his mouth was against hers for a moment, no more. But she felt her own response sweep through her body in a hot wave, bring gooseflesh to her skin. Michael whispered her name and kissed her again, pulling her tight against him.

This time his kiss was brutally strong. Her lips parted under the onslaught. She felt him take the swell of her lower lip between his teeth, biting almost cruelly, until she twisted and bit back, using her own teeth to defend herself. Immediately, his tongue sought forgiveness, tracing the shape of her mouth, meeting the responsive point of her own tongue.

She felt her resolve melting as though in a furnace. She raised her arms around his neck and pulled his head to her, wanting more, wanting him to hold nothing back.

Michael's hands slid under the soft wool sweater she wore, his palms stroking her ribs. Her skin seemed to heat in response. She was not wearing a bra, and the naked skin of her breasts was tightening unbearably at his approaching caress. She drew back a little and looked dreamily into his eyes. She could not hide her change of expression as his hands cupped the swell of her breasts, stroking the satin-smooth flesh, taking their weight.

"I want you," he said huskily. "Tell me you want me."

She could not say the words. But she pressed her hips forward, rubbing slowly against the hard thrust of his arousal. She saw the expression in his eyes change.

"Rebecca, I've been aching for you since we first met."

Before she had time to answer, the voices of the girls sounded from outside, running back to the house. They parted hastily. Rebecca turned to a cupboard and flung it open, groping inside blindly.

The kitchen door flew open and Therese rushed in. Her cheeks were pink, and her eyes were bright, her brown hair tumbling out of her cap. Rebecca had never seen her look so joyful.

"We found one!" she panted. "The most beautiful Christmas tree in the world. It's just up on that hill. Come on, Dad. Come on!"

Michael's voice was uneven. "Okay," he said. "Let's go and chop down this poor defenseless tree."

The tree the girls had chosen was not huge, but it was perfect. Michael put the trunk in a large bucket, supported by rocks. It was an effective, if not very glamorous, base, but the girls wrapped it in baking foil and hung tinsel around it, disguising its mundane origins. Devon went back to her schoolwork, but Therese spent the afternoon shut in the sitting room with the tree and the decorations, working magic. Even when she had finished, she refused to let any of them see what she had done.

"Not until the lights are working," she said firmly, closing the door.

Lying in her bed, later that night, Rebecca closed her eyes and saw Michael's face. She felt like a woman in a whirlpool. She distrusted, even disliked, the man in so many ways. She desperately wanted to get Therese away from him. But on the purely physical plane, he aroused her. Those few moments that morning had left her shaky. Physically, she had seldom responded to a man the way she responded to Michael.

And even if she could get Therese away from Michael, what would she achieve? She had to admit that she did not have the kind of ruthless strength Michael had shown. When he'd felt his daughter was threatened, he had simply taken her away. He'd left his business, his life, had probably laid himself open to all kinds of criminal charges. He did not care a damn about any of that. As Devon had once said, Michael just did what needed to be done, directly and sometimes brutally. There was a strength about him that she could admire. And woe betide anyone who stood in his way. Rebecca did not like to think what might happen if Michael caught her trying to prize Therese away from him.

·   ·   ·

Rebecca awoke from a deep sleep, feeling someone shake her shoulder. She rolled over in bed and tried in vain to see through the darkness.

"Who is it?" she mumbled.

A quiet voice answered her. "It's me, Therese."

"Therese? What's the matter?"

"Can you help me?" said the small voice.

Rebecca sat up in bed and struck a match. Its flare revealed both their faces, wincing against the light. She lit the candle at her bedside, and peered at Therese. "Tell me what it is."

"I think I got my period," she said, her face twisted uncomfortably.

Rebecca swung her legs out of bed, and went to Therese. She hugged the girl lightly. "I'm so glad you came to me," she whispered. "Got any cramps?"

"Yeah, all over my stomach and up my back."

"That's where I get them, too," Rebecca said. "Want something for the pain?"

"Yes, I think I do, please."

Rebecca got a small bag out from under the bed and gave Therese some aspirin and a glass of water. "Have you got any pads?"

"Devon has. But I don't want to wake her."

"It's okay. I'll give you some." She reached into her bedside cabinet and got out some of her pads for Therese. "Let's go to your bathroom."

They walked quietly to Therese's room. "Congratulations." Rebecca smiled. Therese looked at her, apprehensive. "Are you upset?"

"Well, it's all kind of new to me."

"This can't hurt you in any way. In fact, it's a wonderful thing. I'm sure your mother explained it all to you, didn't she?"

Therese nodded uncertainly. "She told me about the curse."

"I really hate that word," Rebecca said cheerfully. "It's a medieval, superstitious, negative kind of word. And there's nothing negative about having your periods. Not a thing. Except, whatever you do, don't go near any milk, or it'll spoil for sure."

Rebecca was rewarded by a faint smile. "Yeah, right."

"You know how to use these pads?"

"Sure."

Therese was evidently proud of herself, and yet unsure about the whole phenomenon. And Rebecca was not at all certain that either Barbara or Devon had done a good job of explaining the biology in a positive way. "How're the cramps?" Rebecca asked.

"Still there."

"The aspirin will help by and by. Why don't you get back in bed? I'll sit with you."

Therese got in obediently. She looked up at Rebecca, holding the bed-clothes open. "Want to get in with me?" she invited diffidently.

Rebecca had a sudden sense of this girl's deep loneliness. "You bet. It's freezing." She got under the covers with Therese. The bed wasn't really big enough for the two of them, but Therese curled up close against Rebecca. Rebecca felt that her heart was melting inside her. She put her arm around Therese. "You'll be okay."

"Yeah," Therese said. She rested her head on Rebecca's shoulder. "Thanks, Rebecca."

"No problem. It isn't a curse, Therese, because without it, no woman can create life. And very few human achievements come up to that."

"But millions of women have kids. It's no big deal."

"As you get older, you'll realize that the most important things in life are also the most universal things."

"Well, right now I'm not looking forward to another—what? How long will this go on?"

"Maybe forty years."

"Forty years of *this*? Mom was right. It *is* a curse."

Rebecca smiled. "It's a fact of life. You'll get used to it."

"Mom used to get terrible PMS," Therese said. "She'd lash out at anybody and everybody."

"It can be a heavy cross," Rebecca said, stroking Therese's soft hair.

"She couldn't have kids of her own. There was something wrong. That's why they adopted us, you know."

"I know," Rebecca said gently.

"It's funny," Therese said dreamily. "Adoption was such a big secret with Mom. I mean, everybody knew we were adopted. All our friends, the whole family, everybody. It wasn't exactly easy to hide—Devon didn't come along until she was six years old. But Mom never liked to talk about it, not with us, not with anybody. Whenever we made new friends, or met new people, we used to tell them right away we were adopted. It was easier that way, because sometimes people asked awkward questions. But Mom would be angry with us, really furious. She wanted to pretend we were her real, biological children."

"That's a sign that she loved you very much."

"Yeah? If I ever asked about my real parents, the slightest question, she'd go crazy. She'd start abusing them, telling me how they didn't want me, how they couldn't wait to get rid of me. It was the same with Devon, even though her real mother was dead."

Rebecca hugged the girl close, wondering what words she could find, wondering how Barbara Florio could have been so stupid. In her selfishness and her vanity, she had infused this girl with a sense of her own worthlessness. "I told you once before, Therese. Other people's mistakes just don't matter. They're in the past. The point is, *you* are not a mistake. Your life is in your own hands. All you have to do is take it, and make it into something beautiful. You'll see the truth of that, once this trouble has passed away."

The girl pressed her cheek to Rebecca's arm. In a short while, Therese was asleep. Rebecca got out of Therese's bed, careful not to disturb her, and tucked the bedclothes around her. She looked down at the sleeping face. In her mind, she was superimposing the image of that infant she had held in her arms so many years ago. Her breasts seemed to ache still as she remembered nursing that baby. Did Therese still carry, buried in the core of her brain, some blurred image of the mother's face that had hovered over her? Was there some infinitesimal trace of memory, somewhere in the mystery of the mind? She would never know.

She picked up the candle and went back to her own room.

•   •   •

The first thing she faced the next morning was a tense-faced Devon in the hallway.

"Therese says she got her period last night," she began without preliminaries.

"That's right." Rebecca nodded.

"Why didn't you wake me?"

Rebecca smiled. "There wasn't any big emergency, Devon. I gave her some pads, and we talked a little, then she went back to sleep. She was fine."

"*I* had pads for her," Devon said tightly. "*I* would have talked to her. She shouldn't have gone to you."

"But she did come to me," Rebecca said practically. "She said she didn't want to disturb you."

"I don't *believe* this," Devon said. She was pale, and her eyes were wide and fixed. Rebecca was starting to realize that she was really very angry. "This was something *special*. Something *important*."

"Well, I know that, Devon—"

"You had no right to interfere!"

"I didn't interfere," Rebecca said, turning to face the girl. "She asked for help, and I simply responded."

"But you're nothing to Therese," Devon said, and her tone was fierce. "You're not family, you're *nothing*. You're just someone Dad picked up in the street!"

"That's perfectly true," Rebecca said evenly, not wanting to get angry. "But I do care about Therese. And I'm a nurse. I don't think this was a situation beyond my experience or capacities."

"We don't know you're a nurse. We don't know anything about you." Devon's hands were clenched into fists, the knuckles white. "You should have woken me. You had no right to interfere. I've been waiting for this. Can't you understand? I've been *waiting*. I was all ready. I was there for her. And now you've gone and ruined everything!"

There were bright tears, of anger or grief, in Devon's brown eyes. Rebecca was taken aback by the intensity of the onslaught. She kept her

voice gentle. "I don't think I've ruined anything. You can still talk to Therese. Don't worry about her."

"Who'll worry about her if I don't?" Devon retorted bitterly. "You? As
soon as you get sick of this job, you'll drift on to be a parasite in some
other family, somewhere else. You're a temporary nobody. I'm the only
one Therese has left. She *needs* me. And I'll be here when you're long
gone."

"Devon—"

"You had no right to butt in. You should have woken me. Don't ever
do that again. Or—" She broke off, her full mouth quivering.

"Or what?" Rebecca asked.

"Or you'll be out of here so fast, your feet won't touch the ground."

Rebecca could imagine Barbara Florio saying those same words, in just
that icy tone. Devon's body was taut. Rebecca felt that the slightest increase in tension would spark her into violence, and the idea of fending
off a physical attack from a strong girl like Devon was not an attractive
one. "I'm sorry you feel that I've intruded between you and your sister,"
she said quietly. "As for my being a temporary nobody, maybe you're right.
But you're not right to imply I don't care for Therese's welfare, or for
yours. I do care, for both of you."

Her words seemed only to increase Devon's quivering fury. "You can
forget about any smart plans you have of worming your way into this family. You're not getting your hands on my father. I'd kill you first."

The tears spilled over Devon's cheeks as she spat out the last sentences.
She turned on her heel and ran out of the hallway. Rebecca walked into
the kitchen slowly. The house had an ominous stillness to it. Therese was
evidently still in her bedroom, reading or asleep. Rebecca had intended to
go in and see how she was, but she did not want to upset Devon any
further.

The depth and passion of Devon's emotion had shocked her. She'd
had no idea that such a placid character could work up such fury. There
was more of Michael in Devon than Rebecca had guessed.

The verbal barbs Devon had flung at her had been childish and spiteful, but they had hurt nonetheless. She tried not to think of them, but they kept replaying in her head, like a broken record.

She set to work in the kitchen. She was shaken and depressed, and she could not get rid of the thundery darkness that Devon had left behind her.

An hour later, Devon came back. Rebecca tensed, fearing another attack. But Devon's face was calm. She walked up to Rebecca. "I'm all the mother Therese has left," she said without preamble.

"It's okay, Devon," Rebecca said cautiously. "I understand."

Devon looked up into Rebecca's face. "I have to protect her. I have to be there when she needs me."

"You *are* there when she needs you."

"I've been so worried about her getting her period. I was hurt when she came to you instead of me."

"I understand that. I'm sorry you were hurt. But I was doing my best for your sister, that's all."

"Yeah, I know." She smiled brightly, the clear Devon smile. "Are we friends again?"

Devon held up her arms for a hug, and Rebecca was compelled to respond. She kissed Devon's cheek lightly. "Yes, we're friends," she said.

"About you and Dad," Devon said, stepping away from Rebecca. "I was just trying to hurt you. But it's none of my business, and I won't get upset about anything that happens. I promise. It's up to you and Dad."

Rebecca was stuck for a reply. "That's a very adult attitude," she said at last. "I know your father will be honest with you. And I will, too."

Devon seemed to shrug off all her hurt in one huge sigh. "Boy, I'm glad that's over. I *hate* getting mad like that. It makes me feel sick and sore inside."

Rebecca answered the smile as best she could. "Me, too."

Devon turned and glanced at the pots Rebecca had on the stove. "Anything I can do to help?"

"You can set the table, if you like," Rebecca said. It was as though the thunderstorm had passed away suddenly, and the sun was streaming in again. But as they worked together, Rebecca reflected that Devon's reversion to charm was as much like Michael as the sudden, shocking anger had been. And the quarrel, unpleasant as it had been, had increased her respect for Devon Florio considerably.

"What was all the yelling about this morning?" Michael asked Rebecca later in the afternoon.

It was a bright day, but cold enough for snow. They had met in the garden. "I didn't think you'd heard," she said, glancing at him.

"I hear everything. Devon was giving you hell about something, right?"

"She was hurt that Therese called me to help her last night." Rebecca shrugged. "It seems to have blown over now."

He looked down at her with thoughtful eyes. "There's a bench over there. Let's sit and talk a moment."

The seat was in a sunny corner, out of the wind, sheltered by an old, gnarled oak. They sat together, looking out over the dark, still waters of the millpond.

"I want to thank you for what you did for Therese last night. Therese has nobody to guide her through the thorns of adolescence—God knows a father isn't much substitute for a mother at this kind of thing. You did the job beautifully."

"Well, Therese always has Devon."

"Devon can never be a mother to Therese." He stroked Rebecca's cheek, making her flinch. "You're a blessing," he said seriously. "Looking after other people's children is a thankless task. Kids can be brutal users of nannies."

"I don't ever feel they're using me," she said, awkward at his praise of her. "And I want to help. Especially Therese."

He nodded. "Therese is very special. I love them both, but I'm aware that Therese needs so much more than Devon. And all through her life, she's often gotten so much less."

"From you?"

"Yes," he admitted. "But especially from her mother."

"Barbara preferred Devon?"

"Barbara desperately wanted kids. But rearing a baby wasn't the bed of roses she'd imagined it would be. She resented the sheer amount of time she had to spend with Therese. She found a lot of it tedious. When Devon came along, six years old, it was as if Barbara had a new toy."

"You mean Barbara switched her attention over to Devon?" Rebecca asked, feeling cold and angry inside, as she so often did when the subject of Barbara Florio's mothering came up.

"Barbara dropped Therese and concentrated on turning Devon into a princess. She went into a whirlwind of buying Devon clothes and toys, arranging for every kind of lesson you can imagine, and some you can't imagine. Devon's mother had been very sick almost all her life, dying, in fact. She hadn't been able to give Devon anything. When Devon first came to us she was emotionally and intellectually starved. Barbara was eager to mold her."

"Didn't you think that was unfair to Therese?" Rebecca asked in a low voice.

"Of course." He nodded. "But being angry with Barbara didn't help. She herself was a spoiled girl from a rich family. I came up the hard way. I had four brothers and two sisters to share everything with, and there wasn't much to go around. I had family values hammered into me from an early age. I'm basically a family man. But Barbara wasn't like that. So there was no use showing my anger, even though I felt it."

"Therese must have been hurt."

"She was hurt, angry, confused. She couldn't understand why her mommy had lost interest in her like that."

"Didn't you try and compensate?"

He shrugged. "I did what I could. But in my experience, with young children, the mother is the important one."

"Is that when Therese's troubles started? When Devon came into the family?"

"Not exactly. She stayed on an even keel for a long time, right up until things started going bad in the family."

" 'Going bad'?" she echoed.

"Devon was getting her periods, and was very cranky. Barbara had started filling herself with alcohol and drugs. It got to be a big problem, very fast. I managed to get her into drying-out clinics a couple of times, but that set off a kind of delusional paranoia. She thought we were conspiring to have her locked away. She refused to go into any kind of therapy after that. She started making crazy accusations against me. That's when Therese starting having seizures, going off the rails."

"What kind of accusations?" Rebecca cut in.

Michael's face twisted with distaste. "I don't want to go into the details. Her imagination wasn't exactly wholesome. She assembled a battery of lawyers and confronted me with an ultimatum: Either I moved out, and left the girls with her, or she would institute aggressive divorce proceedings based on her accusations. She promised it would get very ugly and very messy, and I knew she meant it. The girls were desperate to come with me, but Barbara was implacable. The alternative of fighting it out through the courts was frightening. I was really afraid she would take the girls away from me forever. So I talked to the girls quietly, and moved out."

"And you made your own arrangements to stay in touch with the girls."

He smiled slightly. "They told you that? Yes, the nuns were very understanding."

"I'm not sure I approve of you suborning teachers, especially nuns."

"I didn't suborn anybody. I didn't have to. Barbara made a mistake. She went to the school with her accusations. The headmistress didn't trust Barbara, and she knew about Barbara's drug and alcohol abuse problem. I went to see her. I confessed all my sins to her, and when she saw they didn't include what Barbara had accused me of, she let me take the girls out to lunch every day. And on weekends we would do something special. Sometimes I'd go with Therese to a Giants game, or with Devon to the science museum. Mostly we just did things together. It was almost like having a real family life."

"Until the fire."

"Until the fire," he agreed, his smile fading.

"You don't really know Therese's dark side, do you? The fires she lit. The crazy things she did. You don't understand all that fully. Or do you, and are you hiding what you know?"

"The police sent a psychiatrist to interview the girls. She provoked Therese into a seizure. You should have seen the triumph in her face, Rebecca. She thought she'd cracked the case. Therese was babbling nonsense as she came around, and this woman took it as an absolute confession of guilt. She rushed off to get a court order to take both girls into custody. Is that what you mean by Therese's dark side?"

"Getting past the fits, and finding out the truth, are vitally important, Michael."

"Do you believe Therese killed her mother?" he asked her, watching her intently for a response.

"I don't know," she replied sadly.

"Well, I was not prepared to let them torture a confession out of her. So I took her away. The truth is that she simply doesn't know whether she set that fire or not."

"She might be blocking off memories in her own mind," Rebecca said heavily.

"Then one day those memories will come back," he replied, still watching her.

"Yes," she agreed. "In one way or another, they'll come back. And they just might wind up driving her crazy."

Michael was silent for a while. "Therese hasn't had any kind of fit since the one she had when you first came to us."

"I'm not a faith healer, Michael," she said softly. "Please don't see me that way. Don't hope that some kind of miracle is going to happen, just because Therese has found a kind of mother figure in me."

"That's exactly what you are," he said. "A mother figure. If only Barbara had been like you . . ."

She stared at him, feeling her emotions turbulent within her. She had been urging Michael to seek the truth, yet she herself was hiding one of the most important truths of all. How long could she keep her identity secret? The longer she did, the more destructive the final revelation might be.

She had, she now admitted to herself, started giving up the scheme of kidnapping Therese. Michael loved the girls and they loved him, and each other. She was going to have to live with that reality. If she was going to confront Therese with the fact that she was the girl's mother, she would have to do that in the context of the family.

In which case, was it not best that she tell the truth, right here and now?

"Michael," she heard herself say, "there's something I have to tell you."

"You're Gemini, and there's no hope for us."

"I'm not kidding, Michael. You'd better brace yourself."

"Okay," he said, half smiling at her serious tone. "I'm braced. Tell me."

"I—"

She hesitated, her voice sticking in her throat as she hunted for the right words to tell him. As his dark eyes looked into hers, she could see the warmth in them—and something deeper than warmth, something she had known was growing between them from the very first moment they met.

Suddenly, she felt utterly naked. She knew she could not tell him, not now. She did not have the courage. She gave him a sketchy smile.

"Some other time," she said lamely.

He watched her for a moment. "It's up to you," he said lightly. "I'm not going to rummage after your secrets. Although I think I may have guessed some of them already."

"What do you mean?" she asked, her voice rising nervously.

"You've been married, but it didn't work out," he said. "Is that an accurate guess?"

She nodded. "How did you know?"

"It's a feeling I get from you. You know what it's like to be in a marriage that's destroying itself."

"Yes," she agreed sadly, "I do."

"Any children?" Michael asked casually.

"No," she said, but she knew her face and eyes had betrayed her. "Well, I—I had a pregnancy."

"But it didn't come to term?" he asked gently.

"I lost the baby," she said, temporizing.

"I'm sorry," he said with genuine compassion. "Did that miscarriage have anything to do with your marriage breaking up?"

"Something like that," she said. Rebecca's face and throat were flaming, and her tongue felt thick in her mouth. She hated telling falsehoods. She could hardly meet his eyes.

"You don't have to talk about it," he said, touching her cheek again. "Want to hear my other guesses about you?"

"You're too accurate for comfort," she said. "But go on."

"You went mountain climbing with someone you liked a lot. But when you fell and broke your knee, he let you down badly. What he did hurt and embittered you."

"Yes," she said simply. "All that is true."

"This next one's more of a shot in the dark. You haven't told me the strict truth about your occupation."

"Haven't I?" she asked apprehensively.

"You say you're a nurse, but I think you're probably a doctor."

"What makes you say I'm a doctor?" she asked, staring at her hands.

"When we met, you were trying to project an image. You wanted to come across as this rootless sort of hippie, wandering around Europe doing odd jobs. You thought if you told us you were a doctor, we'd never take you on. We'd ask uncomfortable questions about why a doctor should be looking for a job as a nanny. So you changed it to nurse. But over these past weeks, you've let the hippie image slip, bit by bit."

"Have I?" She was cursing her carelessness.

"You're used to authority and responsibility. Every professional person takes on tiny mannerisms related to their work. You have a doctor's mannerisms, a doctor's way of looking at things."

She was silent, listening to the thudding of her heart. "It's not a million miles off-base," she said at last.

"I didn't think it was," he said easily. "Judging by your character, and your rather stern idealism, I'd guess you worked in a hospital, rather than some nice, profitable private practice. On track so far?"

"Yes."

"You hate telling lies, so you were probably telling the truth when you said you were in pediatrics. And that you live in L.A. So my guess is a big children's hospital in L.A."

"Yes," she said again, somewhat helplessly.

"Which brings us back to the question you wanted to avoid when you first bumped into me. Why would a doctor be looking for work as a nanny in some remote corner of Italy?"

She forced herself to meet his eyes. Had he long since guessed exactly who she was, and was he playing cat and mouse with her? Her lips felt numb. "Why do you think?"

He reached for her hands, his fingers warm and strong around hers. "I think something went drastically wrong at work. A mistake, a misdiagnosis, a patient who got the wrong treatment. Maybe you got fired or suspended. Maybe there's a malpractice suit hanging over your head. It's hard to believe you'd be guilty of negligence. But everybody knows medicine doesn't always go the way it's meant to. Whatever went wrong, it's the reason you're here."

"Well, uh . . ." She shook her head dumbly, not knowing whether she felt worse or better.

"It doesn't matter," he said softly, lifting her hand to his lips. "I don't care what you did or what you didn't do, Rebecca. Whatever it was has brought you to me, and I can only be grateful for that."

"Oh, Michael." She sighed. She watched him kiss her knuckles. Then he turned her hand over and kissed her palm, an intimate caress that made her flush hotly. She drew her hand away from him.

She rose. "I have things to do."

"You always run away, don't you?" he said, looking up at her. "How long can you keep running, Rebecca?"

"I could ask you the same question," she retorted.

He nodded. "You're right. But one day I'll turn and face everything."

"So will I," she promised. She hurried away from him in the cold sunlight. But she kept his kiss clenched tightly in her palm, like something alive and warm.

Rebecca was sitting next to Devon in the early evening, explaining a biology diagram to her, when Therese came in from outside. She was bright-eyed and gleeful.

"Dad's ready to try out the wheel," she said. "He wants you to go and help him, Rebecca. He says wear a raincoat and rubber boots. And a hat."

"This sounds right up my alley," Rebecca groaned. She put on a raincoat and galoshes and went out to the big stone barn, where the waterwheel was housed.

Michael was waiting for her. "Let me explain it first," he said, taking her arm. He walked her up to the millrace, that deep channel down which the water thundered. "We have to lift the wheel and drop it into that cradle. But first we have to shut off the waterfall."

"How do we do that?" she asked, staring at the foaming brown torrent of water, which looked as though it could punch a hole through the side of a house, and probably out the other side as well.

"There's a lock-gate up here, where the water flows in." He showed her the ancient mechanism, its cogs and wheels oxidized orange with the years. "Winding that wheel shuts this gate."

"Does it still work?" she shouted over the roar.

"Only one way to find out," he yelled back. "I've been oiling it every day for a week. Reckon you can help?"

"I can try."

"If you don't think you can do it, I'll ask Devon. She's as strong as a lion."

"You don't need to call Devon," Rebecca told him. "I'll do it."

His white teeth flashed. "Good." He offered her a pair of thick rawhide gloves, which she pulled on. She hauled the hood of her raincoat over her head.

"Okay, I'm ready."

"Let's go then."

Together, they heaved on the wheel. She could feel his muscular body straining next to hers. The wheel grated, moved an inch or two, then uttered a rusty shriek loud enough to be heard over the thunder of the waterfall.

"Pull," Michael commanded. "It's starting to move."

Panting, Rebecca obeyed, trying to synchronize her exertions with his.

She could see the iron gate starting to slide across the opening. "We're doing it!" she gasped, surprised at their own success.

"Together now. Heave!"

She felt her bad knee click ominously, sending a dagger of pain shooting up her leg. With every ounce of strength she had, she hauled on the wheel. It turned, inch by inch, and inch by inch the iron gate slid across. As it cut into the torrent, water started to spit everywhere, drenching them both. The farther across the gate went, the more the water sprayed outward. The thunder turned into a violent hissing. The spray grew so ferocious that it was blowing Rebecca backward, like a fire hose.

"Don't give up," she heard Michael shout. "Just another foot."

She kept heaving at his side. Water hammered into her face, her chest, her arms. Icy water. *This is going to kill me*, she thought. But she was damned if she would give up and have Devon come here and take her place.

And at last the hammering of the spray seemed to ease. She could lift her head and squint at their handiwork. The gate was almost closed now. Through the last couple of inches, the water spurted violently to one side.

Working like a madman, Michael threw himself on the wheel and, in a final jerk, closed it. Water still spattered and dribbled at all the joints.

Rebecca tried to catch her breath, but Michael had leaped down to the solid cradle he had constructed.

"Help me get this wheel upright."

She squelched across to him, water streaming out of every gap in her clothing. "You didn't tell me it would be like this," she said through chattering teeth.

"If I'd told you, you'd never have come," he pointed out. "Take that end. Now lift!"

She was shuddering with cold, and the only available antidote was physical exertion. She helped him heave the wheel upright. It was poised on two car jacks over the millrace. While she held it upright, Michael wound the jacks down, and the wheel settled slowly into its place. When it was firm, he pulled the jacks away. He, too, was shivering violently with the soaking.

"Just one job left," he said. "The drive-belt."

She sank down onto her haunches, hugging her shuddering body as he hooked the drive-belt over the pinion shaft, connecting the wheel to the dynamo. Then he came to her and put his arms around her. "You were wonderful!"

"Don't tell me," she groaned. "Now we have to open the gate again—right?"

"It should be a lot easier than before," he promised.

"It's the middle of winter, Michael. We're going to get double pneumonia. Why can't you organize these things for the warmer weather?"

Winding the gate open again was somewhat easier. This time, as the water started to spurt out of the chute, it pounded on the vanes of the wheel with a heavy drumming sound. Looking over her shoulder, Rebecca saw the wheel start to turn slowly. As the gate opened, the waterfall hurtled out, exerting greater pressure on the wheel. It was turning faster and faster now, and Rebecca could hear the reluctant moan of the dynamo starting to work. And a miracle was happening. The bare lightbulb that hung from the ceiling suddenly ignited in a red spark. As they laboriously swung the wheel around and around, the spark became a glow, and then a dazzling light.

"It's working!" she yelled.

He nodded his dripping head, laughing. "It's working."

At last the gate was fully open. The wheel was whirling around steadily, and the dynamo was whining happily. The big, square block of the transformer, which stood in the corner covered with HIGH VOLTAGE signs, was emitting an excited buzz. And the barn was filled with light.

"I can't believe it," she gasped. "Michael, you're a genius!"

He took her in his arms, kissing her icy lips. "Come on," he said, dragging her along. "Let's go and see."

As they staggered out of the barn, an incredible sight met Rebecca's eyes. The old house had always been so dark at night. There would be the glow of a candle in one or two windows, perhaps a kerosene lamp hanging by the door if someone was working outside.

But now every window of the house glowed with brilliant light. The path from the barn to the kitchen door was lit by a row of pretty lamps, which glowed on the snow. She was awed; the place was suddenly magnificent, a palace sparkling in the darkness.

Michael hugged her. "Isn't it pretty?"

"It's beautiful. I can't believe how beautiful it is!"

"They're turning on every light in the house. I hope the place doesn't burn down. Come on," he said, glancing at her in concern. "You're shaking like a leaf."

The girls were rushing around the house, switching on every light they could find. Devon came hurtling down the stairs.

"Oh, Daddy!" she exclaimed. "I never dreamed it would work as well as this!"

The house was transformed. Dripping and shivering, Rebecca stared around. The soft darkness was gone. Light flooded every corner. Suddenly, the millhouse was modern, glamorous, a home for a twentieth-century family to live in. Once a refrigerator and freezer and washing machine and dishwasher and all the other machinery of modern life were installed, as they soon surely would be, the medieval atmosphere would depart forever. Yet something had been lost, some ancient romance that had lingered on while lamps and candles were still the only form of illumination.

"Don't switch anything else on until I've checked the output," Michael warned Devon. "It might not be safe. It wasn't meant to happen like this." A blast of music from upstairs interrupted him, the sound of Therese plugging in some kind of stereo system. "Therese!" Michael yelled.

Therese's curly head popped over the railing. "What?"

"Turn that off right now, and don't touch anything else electrical until I say so," Michael commanded urgently. He turned to Rebecca. "Rebecca, you need to get out of those wet clothes quickly. There's plenty of hot water. Devvy, take Rebecca up to my bathroom and show her where everything is."

"Boy, you're honored," Devon said. She took Rebecca's icy hand and hurried her up the stairs.

Though she had been in the house for several weeks, she had only had glimpses of Michael's bedroom. As she might have expected, it was the biggest and grandest room in the house, though it was almost austerely plain. Above the huge bed, an old granite millstone six feet across had been set into the wall, making a stark, spectacular focus. On another wall hung a crossbow, medievally grim, yet efficient-looking. Apart from that, there were no ornaments. Devon led her to the bathroom. It, too, was spacious and simple, tiled in marble, with a half-sunken bath in the middle. Devon gave her an enormous towel, evidently also the master of the house's special perquisite, and opened the taps wide. Steaming water gushed into the tub. Devon shot a generous squirt of green bath foam under the tap.

"Soap and everything are over there," Devon said. "I better go and help Dad. Have fun."

Alone, Rebecca got her sodden clothes off and huddled on the edge of the bath, waiting for it to fill. She was feeling rather sick and sorry for herself. She had been chilled to the bone, and she had always hated being cold and wet.

The bath soon filled with wonderful hot water. Wincing at the change of temperature, she lowered herself into the foamy water, her pale skin flushing. The bath was so big that she was almost floating. She closed her eyes, feeling her muscles relax.

She was almost asleep when she heard the tap on the bathroom door. She opened her eyes languorously to see Michael looking around the door. She submerged herself hastily in the foam.

"Go away!"

He showed her that he was carrying an open bottle of champagne and two glasses. "Champagne in your bath, madame?"

"I'll wait till I get out, thanks," she said. "Now go away!"

"Don't pull the plug on that bath," he warned. "I'm next."

"You want my dirty water?"

"It'll be about as close to sex as we've gotten," he said dryly. "Besides, that's all the hot water we have. I'll wait for you out here."

He left her in peace. The house had a new feel to it, she realized, a new life. She was aware of the tiny purr the halogen lights made in the ceiling, could hear the small noises of the central-heating system slowly coming to life, could almost feel the hum of electric power taking over the house. It was as if, all in one night, the house had entered a new age.

She emerged from the bath, wrapped herself demurely in a towel, and went out. Michael was sitting on the bed, naked to the waist. He looked up with a smile. "All my calculations worked out perfectly."

"No problems?" she said.

"None so far." He poured champagne into the two glasses. "Let's celebrate."

She clinked glasses with him and drank. The champagne was very dry and cold. "Congratulations," she said.

"You were great," he replied. "Thank you, Rebecca." He put down the glass, cupped her moist face in his hands, and kissed her lingeringly on the lips. His body was still cold as ice, while her limbs were hot. The contrast, or perhaps it was the champagne, made Rebecca's senses swim.

"You're very clever," she said in a low voice.

"Mmm-hmm," he agreed, looking down into her face from under heavy lids. "Very. But I'm not clever enough to know who you are."

"Michael, I've lied to you," she said. "All I can do is promise that, when I can, I'll tell you the whole truth about me. Just believe that I can't tell you just yet, I *can't*."

"I believe you." He smiled. He had never, she thought, looked so potent as now. Suddenly, she knew she wanted him too much to resist any longer. Despite all her mistrust, all her uncertainty, now was the moment. He took her in his arms, still studying her with those brooding eyes. Rebecca ran her palms over the powerful muscles of his chest, feeling the hard points of his nipples stiffening under her touch.

"You're a very special man," she said softly.

"You're a very special woman," he whispered.

"I almost hated you once, Michael. I was very blind and very stupid."

"And now?"

"Now . . . now I feel different." She could feel his heart pounding under her palms. He unfastened her towel, and it slid away from her pale breasts. He leaned forward to kiss her, his cold, muscular chest touching her warm nipples. She felt a deep shudder pass through her body. "Michael," she whispered, "the girls . . ."

"The girls are too busy plugging things in," he said. "Besides, I already locked the door."

"You're very sure of yourself."

"Usually. Not with you." He kissed the damp side of her neck. "You smell wonderful," he breathed.

"You're frozen." She shuddered, feeling her skin react to the touch of his cold body.

"Ah, Rebecca . . ." He slid off the bed and knelt before her, arms encircling her waist. "I don't care who you are," he whispered, staring up into her face. "I've been waiting for you for such a long time."

"Michael . . ."

"Once upon a time, I used to crave drugs the way I crave you," he whispered. "But you're more addictive than any drug."

His strong arms stretched around her to caress her flanks. She touched his hair with her fingers. It was wet and cold, curling down his muscular neck. Slowly, she let her hands slide across his shoulders, feeling the thick muscles under the chilled skin.

"I'm so glad you came," he said, hunching his shoulders under her caresses. Her towel slid away from her leg, and he brushed his lips against her thigh. "I want you so much."

Her skin seemed to be burning hot. She closed her eyes as he parted her thighs, his mouth seeking among the curly, secret hair. She felt his cold lips kiss her hot ones. His mouth pressed in hungrily, his tongue probing. He seemed to want to devour her there. But then he found the fiery peak of her arousal and, with an almost brutal expertise, drew a husky moan of pleasure from her. She knelt down beside him on the thick carpet, reaching for him. He took her in his arms, so big, so powerful. She knew he would be a wonderful lover, for all his grimness and outward fierceness. She had a drowning thought of how terrible his anger might be when he learned how she had deceived him.

Her life had been a quicksand lately. Michael was massive, real, the only reality she had anymore. He wanted to prolong things, savor every inch of her. But she needed him with a raw, animal urgency. She wanted him so badly that it hurt all through her body, like a flaming cord that ran down her throat, through her heart and belly, through her loins and the burning place between her thighs. She took his thick hardness fiercely in her hand.

"I can't wait," she said urgently. "Now, Michael."

He mounted her, looming dark against the light. She guided him home, raising herself to take him, panting.

"Please," she gasped.

"Rebecca," he whispered. She was melting wet, and he pushed in easily at first. As he filled her, the tightness seemed to stretch her out, pulling her to the borders of pain.

"Oh, Michael, Michael," she was whimpering.

"Am I hurting you?"

"No. Please, Michael."

He went deep, deep into her, so deep she could almost taste it. It was a penetration so profound that she started to climax as soon as he began making love to her, supporting his weight on his elbows, covering her face with rough kisses. He paused, holding still so that she could writhe beneath him, drinking in that sweet impalement.

"Don't stop, Michael," she commanded fiercely. "Come to me."

He gathered her in his arms, whispering her name, and now he gave himself to her with nothing held back. He was a powerful, big man, and he almost crushed her. She could only cling to him, transfigured by his passion. No man had ever made love to her like this before. This was something beyond her experience. She felt she was floating above herself, her spirit twisting in a sinuous dance to the beat of his love.

They clung together as they quivered into stillness, stroking each other. It was a moment of complete perfection. Sex had seldom been as pure as this, as simple or as meaningful.

And yet, somewhere deep down inside, she could hear a still, small voice telling her that everything she had achieved up until now had just been destroyed.

For one reason or another, she closed her eyes and cried a little. They rolled onto their sides, facing each other, still embracing, and looked into each other's eyes. "You're the most beautiful woman I ever knew," he whispered.

She wiped her wet lids. "I'm sorry I was in such a hurry. I wanted to dispense with all the preliminaries."

"We'll save the preliminaries for next time."

"There can't be a next time, Michael," she replied gently.

"What are you talking about?"

"I'm talking about the girls. With everything they're going through, they can't deal with this. It's not fair to them."

He was silent for a while. "I don't want to think about it now," he said quietly. "I just want to think about how wonderful it is that we've found each other. We can't undo what we just did."

For some reason, the words had a darkly ominous ring in Rebecca's ears. The fiery heat of sex was already fading. She was starting to feel she had done something truly terrible.

"No," she agreed. "But I wish we could."

She saw his face darken. "I'm not looking for a quick fuck, Rebecca. I did this as a commitment."

"I didn't," she was forced to reply. "I did it because I was crazy."

Michael rose on one elbow. He gripped her arm with such force that she felt his fingers bite into her muscles. "Are you going to run?" he demanded fiercely.

"You're hurting me, Michael."

"Just tell me you won't run out on me."

She pried his fingers off her arm, rubbing the sore place. "We have to get up," she said in a dead voice, "before the girls figure out what we've done in here."

"Are you really that cold?" he asked, staring at her. "Jesus Christ, Rebecca, didn't that mean anything to you?"

"It was a mistake" was all she could reply. Her desire slaked, she was filled with remorse at her own lack of responsibility, at the way she had thrown away so much for a few fiery moments. She got off the bed and started pulling on her towel, hating herself and her still-weak body. "Get dressed," she pleaded with him. "For their sake, get dressed, Michael."

His face had hardened into some dark emotion, anger, perhaps even hatred. "I really don't know you, do I?" he asked.

"No," she agreed, meeting his eyes. "You don't know me, Michael."

For a moment, she felt they were looking into each other's souls, neither understanding anything about the other. He was so dark, hiding so much. And she, by necessity, was forced to play so many alien roles. She tore her gaze away from his, unlocked the door, and went out of the room where she had just lost so much.

Rebecca emerged from a profound sleep the next morning with the somber remembrance of her folly. She twisted in bed and checked her bedside clock. It was almost ten. She threw off the bedclothes and went into the shower.

This morning there was a torrent of hot water in place of the usual lukewarm dribble. She emerged from the shower and dressed. The house was warm. During the night, the heating system had been at work, powered by the turbine. The clay tiles, normally icy, were warm beneath her bare feet.

She dressed in jeans and a light pullover, putting on the cashmere scarf Michael had bought her in Urbino. On the way downstairs, she passed Therese's door. She knocked lightly.

"Who is it?" she heard Therese call.

"Rebecca."

"Come in."

She pushed the door open. Therese was curled up in bed with a book, as Rebecca had so often seen her. But there was a difference: The curtains were open to show the blue sky, the room was neat and warm. Therese looked over her book at Rebecca. "Hi."

Rebecca remembered the first time she had set eyes on Therese, and heard that small "Hi."

"Sleep well?"

"Okay."

Rebecca came to sit on Therese's bed and kissed her cheek. She indicated Therese's stomach. "How's it going?"

"Okay," Therese said. She made a face. "It's kind of gross."

"Don't think of it that way. You should be proud of your body, and how well it knows what to do."

"Yeah," Therese said, "I am, but I'd still like it to stop sometime real soon, now."

"It will," Rebecca assured her. "Did your mother explain the whole thing to you? All the details?"

Therese shrugged. "Mom didn't talk to me much about anything. It was Devon she was focused on."

Rebecca felt that flicker of anger. "That must have been very hard on you."

"It was also hard on Devon," Therese said in a matter-of-fact voice. "Mom worked very hard on Devon. She didn't see me as good enough basic material to work with."

"That's a very sad way to put it."

"Not at all," Therese said seriously. "I used to thank God for it. Devon had a terrible time. I had my own life. I worked things out my own way. But Mom put an awful lot of pressure on Devon. When Mom and Dad split up, it was basically about Devon."

"I didn't know that," Rebecca said uneasily. "How come?"

"In the end, Devon chose Dad, instead of Mom. That broke Mom's heart."

Not sure she understood, Rebecca stared at Therese. "Devon *chose* your father?"

"She loved him better than she loved Mom. And Mom found out." Therese shook her head, as if not wanting to think about it anymore. "Would you marry Dad, if he asked you?"

Stunned by the question, Rebecca could only shake her head slowly. "He's not going to ask me, Therese."

"He is," Therese replied. "He is, because you're perfect."

Rebecca got up and walked to the window. Blanketed with snow, the world was exquisitely white. The sky was a pearly blue. But her heart was dark. "I can't talk about that, Therese," she said at last. "There are too many other things in the way."

"You mean me," Therese said in a low voice.

"I guess I do," Rebecca said flatly.

Impulsively, Therese jumped up. "I want you to see something." She crouched and burrowed under her bed. Rebecca watched with bemused eyes, wondering what was coming. Therese emerged with a leather-bound book. She gave it to Rebecca. Rebecca looked at it, and saw it was closed with a clasp and a tiny lock. Therese was unfastening the gold chain that she wore around her neck. She slipped off the little key.

"So *that's* what that key opens." Rebecca smiled.

But Therese's face was deadly serious. She held out the little gold ornament. "This is the real me," she whispered.

Rebecca took the key hesitantly. "You sure you want me to look at this, Therese?"

Therese nodded. "Try and understand," she whispered.

"I will," Rebecca said. "I promise."

"You care about me, don't you?"

"Of course."

"Why? Why do you care about me so much?" she asked.

"Because you're so special."

"It's more than that," Therese said.

"No," Rebecca replied. "That's it."

"There's more. You must have some special reason, some . . . special . . ." Therese faltered into silence. She reached out. Her grip on Rebecca's arm was very tight, almost painful.

"Well, maybe there is a special reason," Rebecca said in a low voice.

"Then *tell* me."

"I will. Soon."

They had skirted the truth so closely that it seemed to vibrate in the air between them, perilous and yet drawing them with terrible force. Therese was biting her lip almost to the point of spilling blood.

When she was back in her own room, Rebecca opened the book, using the tiny key. The flimsy lock was pathetic as a defense for Therese's privacy, but Rebecca knew how important symbols like this could be to adolescents. She had worn that key around her neck religiously, and Rebecca was deeply touched that Therese had given it to her. She held the little trinket tightly in her palm as she opened the book. About half of the pages had been filled with Therese's large, irregular handwriting. Most of it, she saw, was poetry, with sections of prose here and there. She read the first page with a slight chill. In capital letters, Therese had written, "BAPTISM OF FIRE." Beneath that title was a simple drawing of a cup, out of which stylized flames streamed.

She turned the page and read the first poem:

> *I tried to give you my love,*
> *But your religion was hate.*
> *So I baptized you with fire.*
> *I set fire to your imagination,*
> *Mommy,*
> *And watched you burn.*
> *And when the skin was gone,*
> *And the flesh was gone,*
> *And the skull beneath the flesh*
> *Was charred, and crumbled at my touch,*
> *Then I saw what you had inside,*
> *Mommy,*
> *All along:*
> *Maggots crawling among the ashes,*
> *Worms burrowing in the blackness.*

Feeling slightly sick, Rebecca reread the poem, then flipped the page. The next poem was shorter, and Therese had doodled a border of flames around it:

> *I will give you the gift of flame, Mommy,*
> *To burn away the ugliness*

And pare you down to the bare anatomy:
A red heart beating
At the heart of the fire.

Rebecca's skin was like ice. She stared out the window at the pearly blue sky, absorbing the words, and their implications.

When she had read the last pages, she sat for a long time, trying to fight off the leaden depression that had settled over her. For a while, she hardly knew what to do. At last, she picked up the book and went to find Michael, who was out back in the barn. He turned as she came in. His face immediately opened in a smile. He came to her, and put his arm around her. "Rebecca!"

She pushed away. "Let me go, Michael."

"I dreamed of you all night," he said, his mouth close to her temple. "I've been thinking about you all morning."

For a moment she relaxed into him. "Michael, please. We have to talk."

"What's the matter?"

"Therese just gave me this." She thrust the book at him. "Take a look."

Michael wiped his hands and took the book from her. "What's this?" he asked with a smile.

"It's her diary."

"Then should you be showing it to me?"

She did not respond to his teasing tone. "It's too important to stay hidden," she said tersely. "Read it, Michael."

He flipped a couple of pages, and started reading. Rebecca watched his face. His smile faded slowly. His expression grew grim. "Jesus," he said softly, when at last he looked up at her.

"The whole book is full of stuff like that, Michael," she said. "It's tantamount to a confession of guilt. It's more than that. It explains her motives, her feelings, her pain. Everything is in there."

He looked intently into her face. "This is an adolescent diary, Rebecca. You think everything in here means what it seems to mean?"

"I don't know what else it can mean," she said, and she could hear the despair in her own voice.

He was obviously shaken. He turned away from her and leaned against the machinery, staring blankly at the book. "You did the right thing, bringing it to me," he said quietly. "Thank you."

"Do you want to read it before I give it back to Therese?"

Michael nodded. "Tell her I have the book."

"She might see that as a betrayal."

"She won't."

"What are you going to do, Michael?" she asked.

He shook his head. "I don't know," he replied. "Right now, I don't know. Give me time to read the whole book."

She nodded. "I'm sorry, Michael," she said quietly as she turned to go.

The day came to a close, white, cold, and silent. The landscape was so white that even after the sun went down, a pale glow lit the world. From a dense gray sky, snow drifted steadily downward, barely a breath of wind to stir it. It silvered the trees and the buildings, finding every tiny horizontal surface and clinging to it.

The atmosphere in the house was somber that night. Therese did not come down to eat, so Rebecca went up to her room. She found Therese lying on her bed, her eyes closed. But Rebecca knew she was not asleep.

"I read your poems," she said, sitting beside Therese and stroking her hair lightly.

Therese's eyes opened slowly. "And?"

"I promised I would try to understand. I'm trying, darling."

"You don't hate me?"

Rebecca stooped to kiss Therese's brow. "Oh, Therese, I'll never hate you!"

Therese's wide, sad mouth moved into a wry quirk. She put her arms around Rebecca and clung to her.

"I'm here for you," Rebecca whispered. "Always."

Therese whimpered some kind of reply.

Rebecca drew back a little. "But I've done something that might make you hate *me*, Therese. I gave your book to your father." She saw Therese flinch. "I had to, honey," she went on quietly. "He needs to know what's going on inside you. He really does."

Therese nodded slowly. "Maybe it's best," she whispered. She rolled onto her side, her eyes closing again. "I didn't hate her, you know," she said quietly.

"I know."

"I don't think she could ever forget that she wasn't my real mother. I think while we were little, she loved us. But when we grew up, and stopped being her toys, she got bored with us. She almost hated us at the end."

"That's what you say in a lot of your poems."

"It's true. I often think about my real mother."

"Do you?" Rebecca asked.

"I try and imagine what she's like, what she did after she had me. I imagine her pushing me deep down in her mind, doing her best to forget all about me, so she could get on with her life. I think she must have gone on and married some guy, had legitimate children. She probably hasn't told her husband about me. She doesn't want the past to jump out of the grave. But somewhere, at the back of her mind, she thinks about me now and then. She sees a face on the street, and wonders if it's me. She wonders if I ever think about her, whether I'm angry with her for what she did. Whether I could ever understand."

"And could you ever understand?" Rebecca asked huskily.

"Maybe I could, if I ever met her, and she took the trouble to try and explain. But until then, how could I ever understand?"

"Maybe she'll try, one day."

"They did a whole lot of legal stuff so that I could never trace her. The way I figure it, my real mother would never have agreed to any of that if she'd wanted to see me ever again."

"Maybe she was pressured," Rebecca said in a low voice. "Maybe she was very young and very confused. Maybe she'll regret the way it happened for the rest of her life."

There was a long silence. Rebecca heard Therese's breathing grow easier, and felt her body relax slowly. She thought the girl was asleep, until she spoke in a dreamy murmur. "Maybe I had to get Mommy out of my life so I could find my real mother. Maybe that's why . . ."

Rebecca made no answer. There was none she could think of. Things were slipping out of her control. Therese was on the brink of guessing who she was, but what the results would be, when the realization dawned, Rebecca could not begin to predict. The contents of Therese's diary had disturbed her deeply.

At last, Therese was asleep. Feeling emotionally bruised, Rebecca got up. As she tucked Therese in, Rebecca uttered a brief prayer that it would all work out somehow.

Something woke her from a troubled sleep. It was a girl's cry, low and prolonged. She listened. After a while, another low moan floated through the air. Therese must be having another nightmare. She got out of bed, went to Therese's room, and let herself in. Since Therese had started tidying her room, navigating in the darkness was a lot less hazardous. She could hear Therese's regular breathing. She sat quietly on the bed and touched Therese's brow. The girl's skin was cool. She seemed to be profoundly asleep. She barely stirred under Rebecca's touch. Whatever dream had been troubling her now seemed to have left her. Rebecca sat with her for a while, stroking Therese's curls with light fingers.

She kissed Therese's cool brow at last and went quietly out of her room. As she was closing the door, she heard that girl's cry again, this time full of pain, then fading away on a dying note. Rebecca felt her skin rise in goose bumps. It had not been Therese who uttered that moan, but Devon.

She went to Devon's door and hesitated for a long while. She had never been on such comfortable terms with Devon as to go into her room at night, and lately, she had felt almost intimidated by Devon's aloofness toward her. But at last she pushed the door open.

Devon's bedside light was on, softly illuminating the room. But Devon's bed was empty, the bedspread thrown back.

Rebecca stared at the empty bed, puzzled, starting to feel concern. Where had the girl gotten to? Was she crying somewhere downstairs, all alone? She went out of the bedroom into the corridor and stopped to listen. There was no sound in the stillness now, but that last dying cry haunted her with a kind of horror.

Then she heard a door opening. She turned and looked down the corridor. Michael's door was swinging open. Rebecca stood transfixed, somehow knowing, like the tolling of a leaden bell in her heart, what she would see.

Devon was naked. In the dim light of the corridor, her body was that of a woman, high-breasted, a dark triangle at her loins. She paused in the doorway, looking back over her shoulder into Michael's room, one hand on the door handle. Rebecca heard her murmur something. Then she closed the door, turned, and saw Rebecca.

For a frozen moment, they stared at each other down the long stone corridor. Rebecca's heart seemed to have stopped beating, her lungs had stopped sucking in air.

At last, Devon moved. She walked toward Rebecca, slowly, without shame, her head held high. She moved with arrogance, with a young woman's pride in her body, in her elastic strength. A shaft of light flitted across her skin, revealing a swath of golden hair, a smear of wetness on the flat belly.

She stopped in front of Rebecca. There was the faintest of smiles on her full mouth.

"Waiting your turn?" she asked quietly.

"No," Rebecca heard herself say.

Devon had an elastic band stretched across her fingers. She reached up behind her head and pulled her hair back into a ponytail. Her breasts lifted at Rebecca insolently for a moment.

"Well," she said. "Now you know."

"Yes," Rebecca said in a dry whisper. "Now I know."

"If Dad finds out you know, he'll kill you."

"He won't find out from me," she replied tonelessly. "How long has this been going on?"

Devon let go her ponytail and slid her palms down over her own breasts, cupping them. There was no modesty in the gesture, only sensuality. "Since I was nine," she said. "But it just keeps getting better and better."

Rebecca's dry lips formed the words without her volition. "And Therese?"

"Therese?" Devon repeated. She laughed softly. "Oh, you mean, is Therese his lover, too? No. I'm the one. Only me."

"Oh, my God," Rebecca whispered, as the full horror began to sink into her mind.

"Are you shocked?" Devon asked calmly. "Don't be. I tried to warn you. You're a temporary nobody. And I will be here when you're long gone. Just don't get in over your head, and you won't get hurt."

"I'm not the one in over my head," Rebecca said. "You are, Devon. You need help."

Devon lifted her chin determinedly. "It's not incest. We're not blood relations."

"It's a criminal act."

She saw Devon's eyes narrow, saw the strong, naked body tense up. "Nobody will ever take him away from me," she said, very quietly. "I won't let that happen. I like you, Rebecca. You can stay here for the winter. I'll even share him with you for a while. But don't betray me. Or everybody will suffer more than you could imagine."

She pushed past Rebecca into her own room. Rebecca caught the smell of her skin, of the soap she used. Then the door closed, and Rebecca was left in the darkness.

She sagged against the stone wall, hugging herself, as though she could somehow physically keep her heart together. Then surging nausea made it imperative she get to her own room.

She stumbled into her bathroom and retched over the sink. She was empty, and nothing came up. She could not seem to rid herself of the smell of Devon's skin, of the innocent perfume of girls' soap. It clung in her throat, cloyed her nostrils. She sank onto the edge of the bath, cradling her head in her arms.

She had been thinking of Ryan a lot, lately. Suddenly, she wanted very badly to be with him, to look into his eyes, and ask, *Why did we give her away? Why didn't we keep her? Was it so important to follow our careers?*

So much was now clear to her. So many isolated fragments had suddenly assembled to form a jigsaw puzzle, a picture that was dark and evil, and yet banal, as evil so often was. Now she knew why the split between Michael and Barbara had been "basically about Devon." Now she knew what had happened to destroy the Florio marriage. Now she knew why Barbara Florio's personality had crumbled, what trauma had been so agonizing that Barbara had been driven to blot out the pain with alcohol and drugs.

Was Devon lying about Therese? Had Michael seduced Therese as well as Devon? Rebecca could hardly bear to think of that. The pain was too great.

Therese's fits, her delinquency, her deadly flirtation with fire: Did they all stem from the misery of an abused child? Or had her pain been simply that of observing her father become her sister's lover? It was a sickening mess, the charred ruin of what had once been a beautiful structure. All that remained now was ash and blackness. And living danger.

Oh, Ryan, she thought, *we did something terrible thirteen years ago.*

Rebecca walked unsteadily to her bed and lay down, covering her eyes with her folded arms. Her body felt polluted by Michael's touch, as though his lovemaking had left some evil inside her.

Michael had given up the legal battle with Barbara without a struggle. But that had not been because he was such a good father, putting the girls' welfare first, prepared to suffer any humiliation rather than put them through an ugly legal battle. It had been because Barbara could prove that he was having sex with his own adopted daughter, had been enjoying that lithe body since before puberty.

The pain of that must have been unimaginable. Now Rebecca could understand why Barbara had hated Michael so much. But Michael had been too strong, too clever. He must have known he would win. He had found a way of fighting off her legal attacks, or at least keeping them to a stalemate. And he had kept seeing the girls. And Barbara had kept suffering. Suffering and struggling and screaming out her anger and pain.

Until she had been silenced by fire.

Rebecca got up and washed her face. She had herself under tight control now. She went to the window and stared out at the snow. There was a streak of lurid light in the sky, like scratched lead. The day was dawning.

She opened the window with shaking hands, and let the icy air blow in, sweeping across her fevered skin. She stood there, clinging to the sill, as if hoping the cold could protect her from the metaphysical flames that threatened to consume her.

Four

FIRE

SOMEHOW, she slept after that. But it was a turbulent sleep, shot through with cold flames, from which she awoke bathed in sweat and gasping for air.

She went to the bathroom and showered, standing motionless under the hot stream. While her mind had been in that sleep of nightmares and white fire, it had been working. She had awakened with an inner conviction. She knew what she had to do now. She had to face Michael again, and somehow behave normally. But not for long. Just for a short, short while.

She looked at herself in the mirror, and saw a white, taut face. She would need cosmetics to carry off an appearance of relaxation. She groped under her bed for her medicine bag. Scrabbling through the contents, she found a bottle of tranquilizers. Like many doctors, she had taken them on rare occasions to help her sleep when she was overtired. Right now, they might help her bridge the chasm that yawned ahead of her.

Was this how Barbara Florio had started? It was so easy to reach for chemical answers to unbearable emotional pain. She pushed the little yellow pills back in the bottle, ashamed of her own weakness. She sat on the bed and talked to herself forcefully, until she felt courage start to replace her pain.

It was eight-thirty by the time she walked downstairs. The house was at peace. From somewhere, music floated through the air. She was in control of herself now, her emotions flattening out like a rough sea under oil.

She went into the kitchen, which was warm and fragrant with baking. Devon was taking something out of the oven, her back turned to Rebecca. The blond ponytail flopping over Devon's shoulder brought back a potent rush of the sickness Rebecca had felt last night.

Devon turned, holding a tray of perfectly baked muffins in oven-mittened hands. She saw Rebecca, and smiled.

"Hi!" she said happily. "Look! Blueberry muffins."

"Where'd you get the blueberries?" Rebecca heard herself ask inanely.

"There was a can in the cupboard. Sleep well?"

"Oh, fine," Rebecca said. She caught the fresh smell of soap from Devon.

"Sit down," she invited. "I'll make us some coffee. It really is going to be a white Christmas! Isn't it awesome?"

"Yes," Rebecca said flatly. "It's totally awesome."

Devon laughed. "Therese and Dad are still asleep. We could take them breakfast in bed but that would only encourage them to be slugs." She stretched her arms up above her head. "I feel wonderful."

Rebecca felt her mind reel at the incongruity of this cheerful banter, after what had happened in the night. Did Devon really think everything was normal?

She had to get out of here, she thought. She had to get Therese out of here.

She met Michael in the hall. He took her in his arms. "Hello, darling."

"Let me go," she said through clenched teeth.

He laughed softly. "What's the matter?"

"I don't want you to touch me," she said, fighting free.

"That's not what you said a couple of nights ago."

"That should never have happened," she said tautly.

By answer, he took her face in his hands and kissed her lips. His mouth was passionate, masterful. She pulled on his hair fiercely, drawing her mouth away from his. She pushed him away, disgusted. "I said, *no!* Respect my wishes, Michael."

The sharpness of her tone made his eyes narrow. "What the hell is wrong with you?"

"Listen to me, Michael. Sex between us should never have happened. It was bad for me, bad for you, bad for your daughters. We behaved like animals, and I hate myself for what I did. It's never going to happen again."

"Animals?" he repeated slowly, his face growing cold. "What kind of language is that?"

"It's my language," she said in a clipped voice. "No more physical contact between us. Not ever."

He stared at her. The darkness in his eyes was hot, and yet the stare was wintry. She remembered the feel of his skin when they had made love. Then, too, he had been ice with fire beneath. "Who the hell are you?" he asked. "Why did you come here? What do you want from me?"

Her throat felt thick with the urge to tell him, to see his face sag with shock. But the words stuck, refusing to be spoken. All she could do was harden her voice. "I mean it, Michael. The next time you lay a finger on me, I'll pack my bags and leave."

She turned away, but he reached out and grasped her arm, his grip hard enough to make her gasp. When she turned to look at him, his face was almost frightening. "You might regret this little game," he said, in a near whisper. "You might regret this very badly, one day."

His tone was like the rasp of a blade. It made her shudder, her skin turning cold. "Is that a threat?" she demanded, her lips dry.

"It's a warning," he said in the same tone. For a moment, she looked into his eyes and wondered just what he was capable of. Then she pulled her arm free from his grasp. Each finger seemed to have left a dot of fire on her skin. She turned and walked away from him.

SAN FRANCISCO

Paul Philippi's offices, as befitted his status, took up a lot of expensive square feet on the sixteenth floor of a prestigious downtown block. For his own personal lair, he had the corner office, a glass-walled aerie with splendid views across the bay, and a lot of blue sky.

He hadn't cluttered up this beautiful space with much in the way of filing cabinets or bookshelves. There was just his desk, which was made of a slab of basalt poised on glass, so it seemed to hover in the air, and some deeply padded armchairs arranged in a semicircle. The distances between the armchairs and the desk were rather wide, so that Carla Bianchi found herself sitting several feet away from Al Reagan, which she did not like, and both of them were even farther from Philippi, which she liked even less. At this distance, the man's facial expressions were barely visible.

"Can I get you people anything?" Philippi offered. "Coffee, a soda?"

"No, thanks," Bianchi replied. "What can we do for you, counselor?"

"I won't take up much of your time," Philippi said generously. Bianchi and Reagan had noticed that his waiting room was crowded with clients. "How's the investigation coming?"

"Considering we can't speak to any of the main witnesses," Bianchi replied dryly, "it's coming along fine."

Philippi had a glass of plain water on his desk, from which he sipped sparingly. "I hear you've been speaking to all of Michael's enemies."

"You mean his father-in-law and the family priest?" Bianchi asked sweetly.

"Don't let's be naive. They both hate Michael like poison. And I feel bound to say something. Barbara had many faults, and one of them was a vicious tongue. It might interest you to know that Michael Florio refused to stoop to her level, even though we have a folder stuffed full of hard evidence about the abuse Barbara inflicted on the girls—I'm talking medical reports, photographs, witness statements. I'm talking beatings, assaults, mental torture. It doesn't make pretty reading."

"If the girls were here," Bianchi said quietly, "they'd be able to speak for themselves."

"They will speak for themselves," Philippi said. "When the time is right."

"Do you find the girls normal?"

"I'd call Devon Florio super-normal."

"And Therese?"

"Therese has problems." Philippi shrugged.

"Any idea what the root of those problems might be?"

"The difficulty between Michael and Barbara, of course. She only started going off the rails when her home life crumbled."

"But Devon didn't go off the rails, did she?"

"No, Devon is a model of stability," Philippi said.

"So what do you put that down to?"

"Who knows?" Philippi touched his own well-groomed temple lightly. "Both girls were adopted, and there may have been some genetic problem in Therese's family background."

"Is that what you asked us up here to say?" Reagan growled.

"No. I don't want to go into any of this. I want you to be able to speak to Michael and the girls yourselves."

"That's gonna be hard, considering he's disappeared."

"Michael wants to see this thing settled. More than anyone else."

"Then he shouldn't have left town."

"You both know perfectly well why he left town," Philippi said. "You people tried to march into his family with tanks, while they were still grieving over Barbara's death. You were going to take his kids away. You went *way* out of line, and you know it."

"We were eager to speak to all the family," Bianchi said. "We still are, Mr. Philippi."

"Are you in contact with Michael Florio?" Reagan asked grimly.

Philippi glanced at him. "Why? You want to apologize?"

Reagan glowered. "He's a fugitive. You better tell him to come home."

Philippi leaned forward. "Have you got any charges to bring? A warrant?"

"No," Bianchi answered.

"Then Michael Florio is not a fugitive."

"What would you call him?" Bianchi asked.

"I'd call him a father protecting his daughters from unforgivably heavy-handed police harassment," Philippi said briskly.

"Are you trying to cut some kind of deal, counselor?" Bianchi asked.

Philippi smiled and swirled his water. "I don't cut deals, Detective Bianchi."

"Then why are we here?"

"Let's call it an exploratory meeting."

"What are we exploring?" Reagan asked.

"The conditions under which Michael Florio might consider returning to San Francisco."

There was a silence. Outside, a wind had come up. White clouds swept across the blue expanse of California sky. Their shadows darkened and lightened the glassy office in rapid alternation.

"Okay," Bianchi said at last. "Let's hear his conditions."

URBINO

Christmas came in a couple of days, and passed in a dull blur for Rebecca. She endured it all, the kisses, the family breakfast, the opening of the presents. Her self-control kept her emotions on ice, enabling her to act out the part without faltering, though not without effort.

She knew that Michael, too, was trying to cloak dark emotions with an appearance of serenity. He had bought her a wraparound coat in dark blue vicuña, light as a cloud, exquisitely warm. He must have spent a long time in one of the smart boutiques in Urbino, choosing it. She could hardly bear to touch the thing. She forced herself to put it on once, thanking him as best she could. Then she left the coat crumpled on a chair for the rest of the day. She could see the anger in his eyes.

By lunchtime, she felt exhausted. The meal was a heavy ordeal. The champagne and wine they drank didn't help, and she had the sensation of struggling to keep her head above water. She was starting to run out of small talk and bright remarks. She just didn't feel like playing the game anymore.

But somehow, she made it through the day to bedtime. Again, she felt cold fire brushing her skin, making her alternately shiver with cold and sweat with heat. Perhaps she was coming down with something, some kind of virus. She lay there, listening to the thud of her own heart and the rasp of her own lungs. She had to get away soon. She could not keep up this charade much longer without betraying herself. And once she started running, she would have to run as hard and as fast as she had ever done in her life. She had to get herself and Therese as far away in as short a time as was humanly possible.

Rebecca awoke the next morning in a mood of quiet determination. No more weakness, she told herself, no more fear. The time had come to do what she had set out to do in Nepal.

The only shops that would be open today were the bakeries, so on the excuse that she was going to buy some loaves of fresh bread, she took the Jeep and drove into Urbino. She churned her way to the town through snowy roads, almost the only vehicle moving so early on Saint Stephen's Day.

In Urbino, she bought bread, tossed it in the back, then drove to the bus depot below the town. The office was manned by a solitary, weary-looking woman smoking a cigarette. Rebecca bought two tickets to Pésaro and then on to Rimini, for the earliest bus the next day, which the timetable told her left Urbino at five A.M. She folded the tickets carefully into her wallet.

Then she went to the ATM in the foyer of the local bank, where she knew she could get cash. Using her card, she started withdrawing money in lots of two hundred thousand lire. She had a thick fistful of notes by the time the machine's screen told her it could give her no more. She had probably emptied it. She counted her haul: almost seven hundred dollars' worth. Not enough, but it would do for the time being.

Walking back to the Jeep, she looked up at the leaden sky. Only a really heavy snowstorm could stop her now. She prayed briefly for kindly weather to accompany her flight.

Her reasoning had been brutally simple. She calculated that when Michael realized what she had done, he would guess she was headed west, for the airport or the railway station at Florence, and the main routes north. But she would be going in exactly the opposite direction, east toward the Adriatic, an apparently futile escape route.

She would take the Jeep, and would do her best to immobilize the motorbike before she left. Even if he could get a car, and chased after the Florence bus, she and Therese would be hundreds of kilometers away, on the other side of the coast, perhaps at Rimini already.

From Rimini, they would take the ferry across the Adriatic to Pula, in Istria, the Croatian-occupied part of what had once been Yugoslavia. Pula, she knew, had one of the very few safe airports in that war-ravaged country; there was even a pathetic vacation industry struggling to survive there, with charter flights to a handful of European capitals. The planes were running little more than a quarter-full, and she had no doubt that any of them would welcome two extra passengers with open arms.

It was a bold move, and one she doubted Michael would be able to second-guess—at least, not until it was too late. Would anyone in her right mind run to Croatia? By the time he got around to figuring it out, they would be long gone.

From Pula, she and Therese would get the first available flight to any-where—London, Paris, Berlin, anywhere. And from there they would fly on home. Once they were back in Los Angeles, she would be relatively safe from whatever Michael could legally do to her. Even if he dared show his face in America again, with the police hot on his heels, she could counter any charge of kidnapping with the highly destructive counter-accusation that he and Devon were lovers.

If that threat didn't stop him, she could go into hiding with her daughter. She could confront the legal technicalities of what she had done, and find a solution. She would find a way to make Therese legally hers. And if she could not easily do that, she would do what Michael had done: She would go somewhere it didn't matter, somewhere nobody could find them, and heal Therese her own way. In a few years, Therese would be an adult, anyway, and able to choose for herself. The important thing was getting her out of the terrible trap she was in.

But first, there was one last hurdle to leap. Today, she faced the incalculably difficult task of persuading Therese to go with her. Rebecca had no doubt that she could do it, but it was going to be very painful, especially for Therese.

The only way she could mobilize Therese would be to confront her with the absolute truth, and that would be deeply disturbing for the girl. In her pain and helplessness, Therese had turned evading the truth into an art form. As Rebecca drove back toward the mill, the Jeep grinding through the snow, she laid out her approach in her mind.

It would have to be done swiftly and simply, and very near the hour of departure. She must not give Therese too much time to think, to fall back into her old refuge from pain, which was to fold into a fetal ball and shut out the world.

First, she would tell Therese exactly who she was, why she had given her away all those years ago, and what she wanted to do now.

Second, she would force Therese to confront the reality of what was going on between Devon and her father. She would make her see what a thicket of cruel thorns she was trapped in, how bleak the future was for her if she did not get out before it was too late.

Third, she would make Therese understand at least a part of what had happened in San Francisco. Therese would have to confront her own culpability, and know that hiding from it would eventually consume her.

Finally, she would offer Therese a way out, an escape to a new life, free of guilt, free of pain, free of the taint that was poisoning her existence.

She rounded the bend, and the house came into sight.

Rebecca's eyes shot open. She stamped on the brake, sending the Jeep slithering sideways. For a moment, improbable thoughts of escape raced through her mind. Then her shoulders slowly slumped in defeat.

She had seen, but had not fully registered, the way the snow in the driveway was churned up and stained. Now she saw why.

Two police cars were parked in front of the house, a black squad car and a big white four-wheel drive. The squad car had its rooftop dome light revolving. The blue beam turned lazily around, a cold wave that swept over Rebecca's sand castle, dissolving it, flattening it back into sand.

Rebecca parked the Jeep and walked into the house, her heart pounding. She was greeted in the hall by two young Italian carabinieri in winter khaki uniforms. She explained tersely who she was.

"Where are the children?" she demanded.

"In the kitchen."

"And Mr. Florio?"

"Talking to American police officers. You cannot interrupt," one of the carabinieri said sharply as she pushed past them.

"I'm going to the children," she replied flatly. "I'm their nurse."

They did not try and stop her after that. She ran up the stairs to the kitchen. A woman police officer was sitting on a chair at the doorway. Devon and Therese were sitting at the round kitchen table. Both were white-faced. Therese was clutching a thick novel in her hands, while Devon was stabbing at her new calculator with a rigid finger, but neither was doing a very good imitation of calm.

As Rebecca walked in, Devon looked up. Her eyes, cold as icebergs, met Rebecca's with an almost physical impact.

"Did you do this?" she asked with quiet ferocity.

"No," Rebecca replied. She turned to Therese. "Are you all right, Therese?" she asked gently.

Therese's fingers clutched the book so hard that the cover was starting to tear. Her gray eyes were fixed intently on the page, but they were not moving. She made no reply. Rebecca pulled up a chair beside Therese. Therese's slim frame was rigid.

She kissed Therese's temple lightly. "It's all right," she whispered. "I'm here. I promise you that I'll never let anything bad happen to you, Therese. Not ever again." Therese was showing no reaction at all, just gripping her book and staring blindly at it, as though projecting herself into some other world, where everything was safe. Rebecca was desperately worried for her.

"Who's interviewing your father?" she asked Devon.

"A woman named Bianchi and some man."

"From San Francisco?"

Devon leaned back in her chair and tiredly tugged on her ponytail. "Yeah. They're the ones who wanted to take us away from Dad and throw us to the thought police."

"Do they have a warrant?" Rebecca asked.

"I don't know."

"Where are they?"

"Sitting around the Christmas tree," Devon replied, closing her eyes.

In the silence that followed, there was a quiet ripping sound. The book was slowly disintegrating under the pressure of Therese's frantic fingers. Rebecca wondered how long it would take before Therese's frail personality started ripping, too.

"Don't worry," she said quietly. "It'll all work out." She held Therese, concentrating her mind on how to get the girl through whatever ordeal might follow.

It was almost an hour before they heard movement from the sitting room. In that time, Rebecca had felt Therese slowly relax in her arms. The child's grip on the book had slackened, and her head had sagged onto Rebecca's shoulder, her lids drooping.

Therese jerked back into rigidity as they heard Michael's voice, followed by the appearance of a burly, rumpled man and a smartly dressed woman.

"Detectives Bianchi and Reagan from San Francisco," Michael introduced them curtly.

Both police officers shook hands briefly with Rebecca. The woman smiled at the girls. "There's nothing to worry about," she said in a pleasant voice. "All we want to do is help."

"Right," Devon said with unmistakable irony. Therese made no reply at all.

Detective Bianchi touched Therese's shoulder for a moment. Her face was not a soft one, but there was compassion there. "I like your Christmas tree," she said. "It's lovely."

The grim-looking Reagan made no attempt at softening the blow. "Are you going to tell them, Mr. Florio, or do you want me to?"

"I'll tell them." Michael looked bleak. "We're going back home. To San Francisco."

Rebecca felt Therese flinch violently. Devon uttered a gasp and flew into her father's arms. She clung to him, her face buried in his chest. He held her, stroking her hair mechanically. Rebecca waited tautly for him to say something further.

At last, Devon drew away from her father. Her face was wet with tears. "Why, Dad?" she asked.

"It's all over, Devon."

"Is Mr. Florio under arrest?" Rebecca asked the American cops.

"Nobody's under arrest," Bianchi said. "No warrant has been issued."

"Not yet," Reagan said.

"Then why are we going back?" Devon demanded.

"Because they need us to answer questions."

"They can ask their questions here!"

"We want you back home," Reagan said shortly.

"We know what *that* means," Devon said. "We don't have to go, Dad!"

"It would be much better if you did," Bianchi said gently. "This all has to come to an end."

"She's right," Michael replied. "We have to go back and see this thing through. I achieved what I set out to achieve. I got Therese away from them when they were going too far. But I always planned to go back one day. You know that, Devon. So do you, Therese."

"But, Dad, that's crazy," Devon said, tears in her voice. "You can't just give up! You *can't!*"

"I'm not giving up," Michael said. "I have these officers' word they won't try and take either Therese or you away from me again. They recognize they were going too far. They admit they were wrong to try and do that. From now on, any further interviews will be conducted with the three of us together, in the presence of Paul Philippi and any psychologist we choose."

"They're lying!" Devon shouted. "You can't trust them!"

"I have to trust them." Michael turned to Rebecca. His dark eyes met hers. "Rebecca, I want you to come with us. We're going to need you very much over the next months. Will you be there for us?"

Her revulsion for him was so great, she could hardly look at him. "Yes," she said wearily. "Of course I'll come."

"No!"

It was Therese who had whispered the word. Rebecca looked at her in concern. The book slipped from the girl's fingers. She was staring at her father with blind eyes. "No, Dad," she whispered again. *"Please."*

Michael's voice was hard. "We can't stay here forever. It's over."

"No!"

Rebecca tried to soothe Therese, but she rose to her feet, every muscle trembling. She gripped the edge of the table, white-knuckled, and stared at her father wildly.

"You can't, Dad," she said, her voice rising. "You can't let them take me."

"They're not going to take you, Therese," Michael said, coming to Therese and gathering her in his arms.

"They are!" Therese's voice rose toward hysteria. "They'll take me away and lock me up. They'll destroy me."

Rebecca was on her feet now, too, and so was Devon. They were all trying to soothe Therese. But her voice was turning into a scream.

"They'll destroy me. They know I killed Mommy."

"You didn't kill Mommy," Devon said urgently. "It was an accident, Tree."

"I killed her. *I killed her.*"

"Stop," Rebecca called, trying to restrain Therese. But Therese was struggling against them all with the shocking violence Rebecca had known once before. The two police officers tried to intervene, but Rebecca turned to them sharply. "Please. Just stay back. You can only make things worse."

Therese clawed at Rebecca, hissing at her in a fury.

"You brought them here. *You brought them.*"

"I didn't," Rebecca cried in anguish. "I swear I didn't."

"Liar!"

Michael used his strength to pull her hands down by her sides. But she was baring her teeth like a wolf, snarling at Rebecca with flaring eyes and nostrils.

Rebecca thought of the tranquilizers upstairs in her room. One of those might forestall a seizure, if she could get it into Therese in time. But she dared not leave now.

Therese was struggling in gasping silence. Michael drew her against his body and held her tight, murmuring to her. Devon watched helplessly, her face intent.

For a few taut seconds, Rebecca thought Therese might not slip into spasm. But then Therese's struggling took on that characteristic aimlessness, her hands fluttering like a trapped bird's wings. Rebecca saw the tendons tighten in Therese's neck and throat. Her eyes rolled back in her head.

"Oh, Therese!" she said sorrowfully.

The random, repetitive flapping started. Grim-faced, Michael lifted his daughter into his arms. Her spine had arched, pulling her head back. She was like a bow in Michael's arms, her limbs jerking.

Rebecca saw the expression on the faces of the two police officers. Suddenly, she knew the rage Michael had felt, understood the desperation that had driven him to take this terrifyingly vulnerable child out of their reach.

"Take her up to bed, Michael," she commanded. She ran on ahead, heading for her own room. Her heart was pounding heavily in her breast. She found the tranquilizers and shook one out into her hand.

Michael had come upstairs and was lowering Therese onto her bed. She was breathing in spluttering gasps, her teeth clenched. Rebecca pushed her fingers into Therese's mouth and got her tongue out of the way either of being bitten through, or of choking her. She crushed the tablet on the bedside table, then smeared the powder on the back of Therese's tongue, mixing it with her saliva. She felt the reflex swallowing response that sent the drug down into Therese's stomach. It would start working soon.

As before, Therese was wetting herself, but Rebecca did not pay too much attention to that. She was now sure that Therese was not epileptic. She pulled Therese's lids back, seeing the pupils still rolled far back in the skull.

"Is she okay?"

Rebecca turned to find that Detective Bianchi had followed them.

"She'll be fine," Rebecca said. "Now *please* leave."

"We'll be downstairs," the police officer said, turning.

Rebecca listened to Therese's heart and lungs, then looked up at Michael. "She needs help."

"We all do," Michael said in an empty voice.

Therese's panting was becoming the exhausted crying of a small child. Rebecca put her arms around Therese and held her. "Please," she said quietly. "Will you all go away. Therese will be fine."

Devon started arguing, but Michael took her arm and half pushed, half dragged her out of the room. He shut the door.

In the silence, Rebecca rocked Therese, waiting for the crying to stop. It slowed at last, though tears kept rolling from beneath Therese's tightly shut lids. Then she heard Therese give a long-drawn "Ohhh . . . ," and she knew the drug had started to kick in.

She felt intense regret for her plan to escape to Croatia with Therese. What was to become of them all? What would happen to Therese? If they pinned her down and ripped her guilt out of her, what would they then do to her? Prison? A secure hospital? A foster family? She could never lead a normal life again. She would be lost forever.

Why hadn't she seized her chance to escape with Therese long ago? At the very next opportunity, Rebecca vowed grimly, she would grab Therese and run as she had never run before.

She stayed with Therese until she was in a deep sleep. Then she covered her over, drew the curtains, and went downstairs.

The woman detective, Bianchi, was waiting for her. "Mr. Florio says you're a doctor," she said. "Is that right?"

Rebecca nodded reluctantly. "Yes. I'm a doctor."

"What's your exact relationship to the family?"

"I'm a friend."

"Not an employee?"

"That, too."

"Anything else?"

Rebecca glanced at her. The other woman's brown eyes were hard and intelligent. "I'm just trying to do my best for both girls," she replied shortly.

"Uh-huh," the officer said, making the neutral sound into an accusation. "You don't have to come back to the U.S. with the family, Dr. Burns. You don't have to get involved."

"I'm already involved," Rebecca said heavily. She pushed past Bianchi and went up to her own room.

They arrived at the Milan airport escorted by the two American cops.

Rebecca had been through Leonardo da Vinci before, and had always found it disorienting and noisy. They were all worn out by the strain, but she was especially concerned about Therese. The child had been alarmingly unstable over the past day and a half. There had been two more seizures, not so violent as the first, but nonetheless depressing when Rebecca remembered how much better she had been getting before Christmas. And she had barely uttered a word. The few words she did say revealed just how deeply she was dreading her return to San Francisco. She was like a prisoner on death row, Rebecca felt, crushed by a sense of hopelessness.

She had debated whether to put Therese on a light dose of Valium, which might keep the fits at bay, but had finally decided against it.

Instead, she had kept very close to the girl. That had not been easy, because the presence of the two police officers put a strain on everyone. Their hard, watchful eyes belied their assurances that this was not an arrest. Any contact they had with Therese seemed to make her visibly worse, until Rebecca had begged them not to come near her, or even speak to her, if they could possibly help it.

As they sat at a café table, grimly drinking coffee to pass the time until their departure, Rebecca was not looking forward to the long flight to San Francisco. Therese had already shown signs of agitation during the relatively brief flight from Florence to Milan. She was claustrophobic, and had seemed to be gasping for air. If necessary, she would give Therese a Valium once they were on board, which ought to knock her out for at least a part of the flight.

"You okay?" Michael asked.

Rebecca looked up. "Fine."

He nodded. He was normally so dynamic, his good looks sizzling with the energy beneath. The past two days had put a shadow on him. Even the way he held his body, usually proud and upright, seemed to be tighter.

Days after Devon's revelation, Rebecca still could hardly bear to look at him. She felt such repugnance for what he had done that her very skin seemed to crawl when he was near her. As much as she tried to keep her attitudes clinical, medical, her emotions got the better of her. She wanted to cut Michael and Devon out of her consciousness, surgically, as if with a scalpel.

Yet how could she do that, and still protect Therese? She knew things were not that simple. As a pediatrician, she knew that incest and child abuse had deep, far-reaching roots. If Michael had abused Devon, was it really possible he hadn't abused Therese as well?

If it ever emerged that Michael had used her that way, she swore she would do everything in her power to destroy him.

Michael's dark eyes met hers, as though he guessed her thoughts. "Don't worry," he said softly. "It's all working out."

"Working *out*?" she repeated incredulously.

"Trust me."

She lowered her voice to a just-audible pitch. "What did you do with Therese's diary?"

"I destroyed it," he replied in the same tone.

"You're sure?"

"I burned it."

She nodded. Therese was staring into nothingness, her face and her body fixed with that rigidity that told Rebecca she was not far from slipping into a seizure. Rebecca stroked her hair. "You should drink your juice," she said gently. "It'll help keep you from getting dehydrated on the flight."

"Can't you stop pawing her?" Devon snapped. "You never leave her alone!" She knelt next to Therese and gave her a plastic bag. "I brought this, Tree," she said softly. "It might make the flight go a little easier."

Therese groped at the bag with numb fingers, and extracted a bright yellow Walkman with headphones. Devon reached into the bag and pulled out a handful of cassettes.

"I brought these, too. Your favorites. And spare batteries."

Therese's taut expression eased, and a faint smile touched her wide mouth. She shuffled through the cassettes. "Thanks, Devvy," she said in a tiny voice.

Al Reagan glanced at Devon with world-weary eyes, then at Therese. "How's the kid?" he growled to Rebecca.

Rebecca just shook her head, to signify *not very good*. She looked at her watch. In two hours they would be boarding. The darkening sky was stained orange by sodium lights. The future, whatever it was, was dawning.

The first-class seats on the 747—paid for by Michael Florio—were set in pairs, two by two. Bianchi and Reagan sat side by side, conferring inaudibly. Devon was sitting with her father. So Rebecca, to her relief, found herself with Therese. Therese had taken the window seat, and right now was scrunched up like a sick child, her forehead pressed to the window. Rebecca saw that her hands were gripping each other so tightly, the nails were bloodless.

"Why not listen to a cassette?" Rebecca suggested.

Therese nodded. She pulled the headset on and slotted a tape into the Walkman. Rebecca heard the tiny tinkle of music start up in the headphones. Therese resumed her unseeing stare out the window.

Rebecca glanced across the aisle. Devon was lying with her head pil-lowed on her father's chest. Michael's strong arms were around her, his chin resting on her golden head. Rebecca felt the revulsion rise in her gorge. How had it happened? How had a man with so many advantages wanted to sink into a relationship that was so debased?

As a pediatrician, she dealt with the sexual abuse of children on a medical basis. She had never been able to quell her fury toward those who violated their own and other people's children. Now, as she saw Devon's lithe body nestle against her father, her hand outspread on his chest, Re-becca found Devon's sexual arrogance deeply offensive, too. But that was what all child abusers wanted others to believe. *She seduced me.* She had heard abusive fathers utter those very words.

Devon had said their relationship had started when she was nine. No nine-year-old could be a seductress. Devon had learned that ugly sexual arrogance from her father. It was Michael, not genetics, that had turned her into what she was now.

Therese suddenly scrambled over her to get out of the seat.

"What's the matter?" Rebecca asked in concern.

"Gotta go to the bathroom," Therese said, pale-faced, pressing a hand to her lips.

"Want me to come?"

"No. Leave me alone."

Rebecca turned and watched Therese hurry to the lavatories at the back of the cabin. Devon had heard the disturbance. She rose and ran after Therese, catching up with her at the folding door. They exchanged a few words. Then Therese slipped into the toilet and Devon came back. She glared at Rebecca, as though Rebecca were somehow responsible for Therese's airsickness.

It was half an hour before Therese emerged, and Rebecca was starting to get concerned. But Therese just slumped back into her own seat, and resumed her gaze out the window. She had the Walkman cradled in her hands.

Feeling very tired, Rebecca tilted her chair back and allowed herself to slide into sleep.

She slept profoundly. When she awoke she felt ravenously hungry. She checked her watch and saw that she had been asleep for a couple of hours. The seat next to her was empty. She sat upright and looked across at Michael and Devon. Devon was asleep with her head on her father's shoulder, Michael staring out the window. Behind them, the two police officers were each reading paperbacks.

"Where's Therese?" she called softly.

Michael turned, his face empty. "She went to the john."

Rebecca stretched wearily. There were still several hours of the flight left. Much as she dreaded what awaited them in San Francisco, she was starting to look forward to the end of this journey.

She groped in her bag for her own book. The smell of food being reheated wafted down the cabin, making her empty stomach growl. She read on, trying to interest herself in the text, part of her mind awaiting Therese's return.

She heard Bianchi's pleasant voice. "Smells like they're burning our dinner," she said with a smile. But there was uncertainty in her eyes.

Rebecca also turned and looked back. She, too, could now smell something strange, and she saw that other passengers were showing alarm or interest. The only people who seemed unconcerned were Michael and Devon, who slept on.

"Something's gone wrong in the kitchen by the smell of things," she heard an English voice say behind her, the words jocular but the tone nervous. She put down her book and unclipped her seat belt. Where was Therese?

Something caught her eye, something gray that scurried along the floor at her feet. She looked down. It was a neat streamer of smoke, coming from the back of the cabin. As she watched, more surprised than afraid, the ribbon of smoke swirled to the front of the cabin, rose up the bulkhead, and broke into an acrid cloud.

Someone uttered a brief scream. Bianchi, who was still peering over the back of her seat, was now looking concerned. "There's smoke in the air," she said, pressing the buzzer to call a member of the cabin crew.

Rebecca felt her heart pounding. She tried to stay calm. She rose and walked quickly back to the toilets. There was a strong smell of burning in the air as she parted the curtains. One toilet was empty, the other occupied. She banged on the closed door.

"Therese! Are you in there?"

The door folded open and a strange woman peered out. "What's that burning smell?" she asked anxiously.

Starting to feel dread, Rebecca went back to the two police officers. "I can't find Therese," she said tightly.

"She's probably walking the aisles," Michael said, easing Devon's head off his shoulder, and rising. "She does that sometimes on long flights." They all looked down the cabin. The air was definitely smoky now, and passengers were starting to mill around in the beginnings of panic.

"I'll go find her," Reagan said calmly.

Michael stepped out into the aisle. "Let me go."

"Why don't you stay with your other daughter, Mr. Florio," Reagan said insistently. He coughed as smoke caught his throat.

"Therese needs *me*," Michael replied. "She doesn't want to see *your* face, Detective."

Bianchi put her hand on Michael's arm. "Let my partner go with you, Mr. Florio. He can only help."

Reluctantly, his face set, Michael headed off with Reagan close behind him. They pushed through the red curtains. The fasten-seat-belts sign went on with a sudden *ping*. A burly flight attendant in shirtsleeves came hurrying up the aisle. His face wore an expression of studied calm.

"Please take your seats at once," he called. "The captain has turned on the no-smoking signs, so please extinguish any smoking materials. Everybody sit down, please, and fasten your seat belts."

"What's going on?" half a dozen people demanded in various tones of anxiety.

"We have a very minor problem," he replied, physically pushing people into seats. "Nothing at all to worry about. The captain will make an announcement shortly. Now *please* resume your seats."

Rebecca slid into the seat beside Devon and fastened the buckle.

"Where *is* the fire?" someone demanded urgently.

"We don't *know* that there is a fire yet," the steward said smoothly.

"Well, if they're burning our dinner, they're doing a bloody good job of it," the passenger in front of Rebecca said loudly.

The steward made no comment, but started pouring glasses of water for everybody.

Rebecca's pulses were racing now. She felt her lungs catch, and coughed. The air was becoming hard to breathe, and she had the sensation, though it might have been hysteria, that the atmosphere was getting hotter. She prayed Michael would find Therese and bring her back safely.

She glanced at Devon's tranquil face. There was no point in waking her until there was evidence of real danger.

Real danger? She stared past Devon's lolling head out the window. At something like seven miles above the Atlantic, and God knew how many hundreds of miles from the nearest land, this was no place for an aircraft to catch fire. *Therese, Therese,* she thought. *What have you done?*

She could hear a tumult of voices from the next compartment back. People were calling out, children were wailing, there were a few screams. Apprehension clutched at her heart.

The address system cut in at last, and a reassuring male voice began to drawl.

"Hello, everybody. This is your captain speaking. We have a minor problem on board, as some of you may have realized. It poses no risk right now, and we're dealing with it as quickly as we can."

Other people were coughing, some of them violently. The air was increasingly murky, smoke swirling visibly against the light. The elderly seemed to be suffering the most. Rebecca saw a white-haired woman, hunched over and evidently in distress, pressing a handkerchief to her mouth. Instinctively, she got up again and hurried to her.

"Can you get some oxygen?" Rebecca called to the steward, seeing the gray-blue color of the woman's face and lips. The man hurried to get it, sealing the compartment with a folding panel.

"She's asthmatic and has emphysema," the elderly woman's companion told Rebecca.

"I see." It was a bad combination to deal with in the increasingly acrid air.

"Is she going to die?" her companion asked in panic.

"Of course not," Rebecca said firmly. "Does she have her medication with her?"

The woman scrabbled in her handbag for the drugs. Rebecca was a lot less sanguine than she sounded. Fear, more than anything, was killing the old lady right now. She managed to get the woman to take her prescribed pills and suck on her various inhalers.

The steward returned, bringing a small oxygen cylinder with a mask. Rebecca held it to her face, soothing her as best she could. The oxygen began to work, and Rebecca watched the blue start to fade from the woman's fingernails.

Where the hell were Michael and Therese? Except for the captain's brief announcement, there had been no information, and there was real panic among the passengers now. The smoke that was drifting through from behind the cabin had changed color from pale gray to an evil dark brown. It smelled poisonous, and quite probably was. She looked out the window, thinking of the intense irony of all those cubic miles of thin, clean air out there, while they suffocated helplessly inside this hermetically sealed aluminum tube. A rush of claustrophobia made her want to pound her fists on the window, smash it.

Someone grabbed her arm. It was Devon, now awake and looking terrified. "What's going on?" she demanded. "Are we going to crash?"

"No. But there seems to be a fire on board."

"Where's Therese?"

"Somewhere at the back of the plane. Your father's gone to look for her."

"Oh, my God," Devon said, her fingers clawing into Rebecca's arms. "She's doing this!"

"That's impossible," Rebecca said brusquely, though the same thought had been haunting her.

"She's doing it," Devon repeated with utter certainty. "She'll kill us all, rather than go back to San Francisco."

They stared into each other's eyes for a strained moment. Devon burst into hacking coughs as the smoke caught in her lungs. She turned aside, stooped, and peered out the window. "We're over the ocean," she said in a high, quavering voice. "There's nowhere for us to land. We're trapped in here!"

She was stammering, all her adult poise gone. Now she was just a child, helpless and afraid. "Sit back down and buckle up," Rebecca urged her, leaving the elderly woman for a moment and pushing Devon back into her seat. "Look. Soak this napkin in the glass of water, then wring it out. Hold it over your nose and mouth. It'll help. When it dries out, wet it again."

"I don't want to die, Rebecca," Devon said in a small voice, her fingers shaking wildly as she tried to fold the napkin the way Rebecca was showing her.

"You're not going to die. None of us are." She stroked Devon's head. "Close your eyes. That'll stop them from burning."

Apart from dispensing inane reassurances, there was little she could do for anyone. Smoke and fume inhalation were killers, and if things got worse, there would be a lot of very sick people in here. The crude masks made of wet napkins helped only a little.

Devon pressed the mask to her face, squeezing her eyes shut. Rebecca left her and went back to her elderly patient, who was still looking very ill. Her companion, a middle-aged woman who was evidently her daughter, was crying quietly into a handkerchief.

If the fire spread, they would all die, burned or choked at this fearful altitude and speed. Would they all just collapse, and would the plane keep flying on and on until it ran out of fuel, and plummeted? Was there somewhere they could land, some island, some stopping-off point in the ocean? Could a plane like this land on the sea, or would it just smash into a million pieces?

She was coughing harshly as she went to the end of the compartment and pushed the panel aside. Her lungs were starting to feel horribly raw. She did not know how long it would be before she started to lose consciousness. *Where were Michael and Therese?* She and Therese might both die up here without ever acknowledging the fact that they were mother and daughter. That, for some reason, seemed a particularly painful irony.

She groped through the murk to the curtains and pulled them aside. Agonized faces peered desperately through a pall of smoke. Children were screaming, adults trying to console them. Several people were lying on the floor in the aisles, evidently seeking cleaner air. The windows glowed fuzzily in the gloom. The haze was so thick that she could not see to the far end of the section. There was no sign of Michael or Therese.

A red-haired cabin attendant came hurrying up to her, thrusting her back.

"Please go back to your seat right *now!*"

"I'm a doctor," Rebecca cut in. "Is there anybody who needs help?"

"Thank you. If we need you, we'll call you. Now please—"

"I'm looking for my daughter, Therese Florio. She's missing from first class. Her father and another man went looking for her some time ago, and they haven't come back."

"They're back there," the woman said, gesturing. "It's a big plane, ma'am, and I'm sure they're both quite safe. Now *please—*"

A steward suddenly came hurrying up the aisle. "They found it!" he said to the redhead, his voice breaking with the strain. "Burning rags in the air-conditioning ducts, back in compartment three. Get the extinguisher!"

"Jesus," the woman said, thrusting past Rebecca.

Her legs weak at the knees, Rebecca went back to first class. She checked on the elderly woman, who looked very weak. The steward was kneeling beside her, holding the oxygen mask over her mouth and nose.

Devon hurried up to her. "Was it Therese?"

"I don't know. She's still missing."

"Where's Dad?"

"Looking for her."

A *ping* came from the address system. The captain's drawling voice broke in. "Thank you for your patience," he said easily. "My flight engineer tells me we've found the cause of all the rumpus, and the problem is now solved. We're starting to clear the air in the cabin right now. As far as we can tell, there's no damage to the aircraft. However, we're going to make an unscheduled stop somewhere on the East Coast of the United States so we can put you all on another aircraft. As soon as I've decided where, I'll let you know. In the meantime, anyone with urgent problems or needs should contact the cabin staff right away."

Rebecca heard the hiss of the air vents start to increase, and felt a cool current of clean air brush her face. *Where was Therese?*

In the quarter-hour that followed, the elderly woman seemed to be recovering a little. The air grew clear and clean. At last, Michael appeared. Therese was clinging to him, her curly head drooping. Reagan was in the rear, looking very tired, and coughing harshly into a handkerchief. Rebecca rose swiftly and went to them.

"Oh, thank God!"

Her stomach clenching with nerves, Rebecca checked Therese over. The girl seemed only semiconscious, her body limp. She stank of smoke, and Rebecca could hear her lungs laboring. She had inhaled a lot of smoke. Her pulse, at least, was steady, though fast.

"Where was she?" Bianchi asked.

"She said she went to stretch out on some empty seats, so she could sleep," Michael replied. His eyes were swollen and red. He looked haggard. "She was right where the smoke was thickest, and she was practically out cold when I found her. She had some oxygen back there. That's why I've been so long."

"Is she going to be okay?" Reagan asked Rebecca.

"If her breathing gets any worse, I'll give her some more oxygen." She used a wet napkin to mop Therese's face. "You don't look so good yourself," she said to the cop, who was gray-faced and sweaty.

"We all breathed a lot of smoke." His voice was a croak.

"Did you see what started the fire?" she asked.

Reagan glared at Therese. "She must have pushed smoldering cloths up into the overhead ducts," he said grimly.

"You don't know she did it," Rebecca snapped.

"Oh, yeah?" Reagan rasped. "You mean we have two firebugs on board?"

"Where the hell would she get smoldering cloths from? It could have been anyone, a careless maintenance worker, *anyone*. I don't see how Therese could have done it."

"In the toilet," Reagan said without hesitation. "She loosened a panel and shoved in some of her spare clothing, whatever. Lit the bundle with a match. Easy."

"You have no *right* to make that accusation," Rebecca said, almost shedding tears of anger.

"Take it easy, Rebecca," Michael said quietly. His strong hand closed around her shoulder, drawing her away from Reagan.

The captain's voice drawled out of the speakers. "We're going to take in some early sunshine, ladies and gentlemen. The nearest spare aircraft is at Miami, so that's where we'll be stopping. We'll try and get you all on your way again as soon as we can. In a moment you'll feel the aircraft change course, and then I'm going to increase our airspeed by a hundred knots. I'll give you a revised ETA in a few minutes. Now I'd like everyone to resume their seats, please."

There was some weak laughter and even some clapping. Passengers were smiling at each other with the dawning euphoria of people who have passed through danger. At the same time, the plane rolled smoothly. The blue sea swung into view down the right-hand windows.

Therese burst into a fit of coughing. She choked for a moment, then gasped in air.

"Rebecca," she whispered.

"I'm here. How are you feeling?"

"So—sore," Therese gasped, clinging to Rebecca.

"It's all over, now," Rebecca whispered. "All over. We're on our way home."

But she knew it was a long way from over. And that home was a long, long way from here.

The 747 began its descent over Biscayne Bay, late-afternoon sunlight gilding the blue water. The city swam into view beneath them, sprawling and immense, bisected with canals and swaths of tropical greenery. Rebecca had spent the last hour of the flight crouched beside her elderly patient, whose condition was growing perceptibly worse. Her color was bad, an indication that her blood was cyanotic. With little more than a bedside manner in her arsenal, Rebecca felt helpless.

The steward touched her shoulder. "You'll have to take your seat for the landing," he said kindly.

Reluctantly, she rose, and went back beside Therese. The girl had said almost nothing, seeming to have retreated into herself. She would answer no questions. She clung to Rebecca now, but Rebecca had the sense that only the body was clinging: Therese's soul was elsewhere, huddled in a dark inner world where nobody could reach it. Rebecca held her tight as the big plane swept down toward the international airport.

It was a textbook landing, which got a ragged cheer from the passengers. As the plane taxied, and despite all the urgings of the aircrew, passengers got up and scrambled in a panicky manner for their carry-on luggage, opening the overhead bins and stumbling over each other. Suddenly, after a couple of hours of relatively calm self-congratulation, everybody was very eager to get off this aircraft. Therese clutched at Rebecca anxiously. "Are we getting off soon? What's happening?"

"We're in Miami," Rebecca said, soothing her. "We'll be getting off in a moment."

Therese started coughing. "I feel . . . awful."

"Just relax. It's all over." Rebecca stayed huddled next to Therese, staring out at the vista of palm trees and diesel fumes.

The cabin door opened. The mobile stairs rolled up. First onto the plane were a couple of paramedics, who pushed through the crowd to the asthmatic woman and checked her vital signs. Rebecca explained briefly what had happened. The ambulance was already waiting at the bottom of the stairs. The paramedics loaded her onto a stretcher, and started carrying her off.

Reagan turned to Michael. "Anybody need medical help?"

"We're all okay."

"Then we'll go to the first-class lounge and rest up. Let's go."

Michael nodded wearily.

At last, they were all stepping out into the light. The warm, moist air was delicious. Rebecca looked up at the sky, feeling as though she'd just stepped out of a dungeon.

Bianchi shepherded them along. Reagan followed in the rear. He was still coughing heavily, and rubbing his chest. Rebecca saw him watching Therese grimly. Rebecca felt with despair that Therese had almost signed her own death warrant by pulling that dreadful stunt.

She glanced at Therese. She felt the same desperation she had felt with other young patients, presented with life-threatening symptoms and no detectable cause. The terrible fever, the collapse of vital organs, the poisoning of the system: Where did it originate? What tiny virus, what process gone horribly wrong, what hidden locus of infection, was producing all this suffering? Unless the answer could be found in time, the organism died, and the answers could only be sought with the pathologist's knife. She had to find the answer, soon, before it was too late. This terrible disease had to be stopped.

After clearing customs, which was expedited by their police escort, they made their way to the first-class area, following the tall figure of Carla Bianchi. In the calm island of luxury, they commandeered a corner for themselves. They took turns going to the washroom and getting some of the smoke and grime of the flight off. Then they all sprawled wearily in armchairs to await their next flight. Michael brought drinks for them all from the self-service bar. He gave Rebecca a tight smile as he handed her a glass of juice, and sat on the arm of her chair.

"You feeling okay?" His voice had degenerated to a harsh rasp.

"I've felt better," she replied.

"You think that old woman will make it?" he asked.

She knew he was thinking of Therese, and what she might be charged with, if it was proved she had set that fire. "Everything else depends on the treatment she gets. God, Michael, what a mess."

He coughed raggedly. Then, unexpectedly, he gave her a faint smile. "I told you, don't worry. It's all working out."

"I don't know what the hell you mean," she replied wearily.

"Just trust me," he said, even more quietly. "That's all I ask of you, Rebecca. That you trust me to get everything straight."

"Get everything straight?" she echoed dully. "Sure, Michael," she said, in the way she would humor a crazy man. "You'll get everything straight."

He touched her cheek. "You really believe in me?" he asked huskily.

"Sure," she said flatly, trying not to shrink at his touch.

"Thank you, Rebecca," he said emotionally. He stared at her intently with red-rimmed eyes. "I love you."

The words sent a pain through her heart. She looked away, loathing him, yet hurting almost unbearably to hear him say those words. She felt as though she were bleeding inside. He must truly have lost his mind, she thought.

He left her, and went to sit with Devon. She snuggled up to him, her blond head once more pillowed on his chest. Rebecca felt something twist inside her.

Al Reagan was coughing violently now, his face going an ominous shade of purple. Bianchi was pounding him on the back, but that didn't seem to be helping. Rebecca got up wearily and went to him.

"How're you doing, Detective Reagan?"

"Can't breathe," Reagan wheezed, clawing at his collar. "My chest hurts."

Rebecca pressed her ear to his chest, and heard the laboring heart and lungs. She saw Reagan's police badge nestling incongruously on his fat belly under his jacket. She took his pulse. "Any history of angina?"

"Yeah, I get chest pains," Reagan gasped. "But never . . . like this."

Rebecca met Bianchi's eyes. The woman was pale. "He never told me about the angina," she said to Rebecca. "Is he okay?"

Reagan's pulse was poor. He was slumped back in the chair, looking awful. Sweat poured down his cheeks. "How long have you been having this pain?"

"An hour, I guess. Maybe more. It keeps . . . building up. Goes down my arm and up into my jaw."

Rebecca turned aside to Bianchi. "I think he's having a heart attack. He needs to get to a coronary-care unit fast. And in the meantime, try and get oxygen here right away."

"You got it." Bianchi didn't hesitate. Tense-faced, she raced away.

"I'm going to give you some aspirin," she told Reagan, producing the pills from her bag.

"Aspirin?" he said, rolling his bloodshot eyes.

"Do you have an ulcer?"

"Probably," Reagan grunted.

She made him take the pills anyhow. The anticlotting properties of the aspirin might make all the difference to his congested arteries if he was indeed in heart failure.

"What's the matter with him?" Michael asked, joining Rebecca. "He looks bad."

"He's having a heart attack," she said. "His chances aren't good if he doesn't get emergency care soon."

"Thank God this didn't happen three hours ago," Michael said grimly.

Carla Bianchi came hurrying back, carrying a small oxygen cylinder, and accompanied by two members of the airport staff. "A cardiac team will be here in ten minutes," Bianchi panted. She showed Rebecca the oxygen cylinder. "You want to give him this?"

"Thanks." She touched the other woman's shoulder. "And please try and reassure him. Tell him everything's okay. Keeping him calm is half the battle right now. And stand by to help resuscitate if he goes into heart failure."

"Right."

She opened the tap and started giving Reagan the oxygen. By his haggard appearance, Reagan was certainly in the early stages of a myocardial infarction. She touched his brow. It was sweaty and cold. "Help is on its way, Detective. It's going to be all right."

Reagan rolled his eyes at Rebecca. He was clutching at his chest with his left hand. She noticed that Carla Bianchi was holding his other hand tightly. "Yeah, right," he mumbled under the flimsy plastic mask.

"Have you still got chest pain?"

"Feels like . . . someone's standing on my sternum . . . in size twelves."

"The best thing you can do is try to relax, Detective Reagan."

"Sure," Reagan said. He closed his eyes, gripping his partner's hand. Rebecca saw that his lips and fingernails were tinged with blue. She felt his pulse again after a few minutes. It was weak and slightly irregular. She took the oxygen mask away from his mouth to look at his lips. The color had returned a little, but they were still cyanotic. She put the mask back right away. The longer his heart muscles labored without oxygen, the more certainty there was of permanent damage.

Suddenly, Reagan arched back. His arms swung up, knocking the little cylinder from Rebecca's hands. He clutched at his chest with both hands, gurgling. His eyes rolled. His face was going blue.

"He's arresting," Rebecca called. "Help me!"

She and Bianchi struggled to get him onto his back on the floor. He fought them blindly, wildly, his body flailing in the panic of the arrested heart. Then he slipped into unconsciousness. Rebecca felt for a heartbeat. "He's gone," she said tersely. "You take the mouth-to-mouth. I'll massage."

She straddled the man's bulk while Bianchi clamped her mouth expertly over Reagan's. At least there were two of them, both trained. She crossed her hands on Reagan's sternum and pressed down five times in succession, willing the blood to surge through Reagan's lifeless body. She paused while Bianchi blew a lungful of air in, and watched the chest deflate. Then she repeated the heart massage.

She could sense spectators all around them, staring in curiosity or horror. *Therese, what have you done?* she thought, with a remote corner of her mind. She and Bianchi fell into a smooth rhythm. After two minutes or so, she sensed Reagan was trying to breathe on his own. They stopped to check him. A heartbeat had returned, but it was faint and fluttering.

Then, with a crash, the cardiac team had arrived, pushing a wheeled stretcher. The lead man squatted beside Reagan. "Let me see the patient."

"He arrested a couple of minutes ago," Rebecca told them. "We started resuscitation right away, and there's a faint heartbeat. He's been in pain for over an hour."

"Okay, you did great. There's nothing more you can do now. Move away, please."

She stepped back, and watched the cardiac team move in with the high-speed calm of their kind. The leader didn't take much time to make up his mind. Rebecca saw him get out the syringe with the big intracardiac cannula, and prepare to inject adrenaline straight into Al Reagan's heart.

She turned, feeling dizzy. The plush, hushed area was milling with people. Bianchi was intent on her stricken partner. Michael and Devon were on the other side of the crowd. She caught sight of Therese, crouched in a chair, white-faced. Rebecca's own adrenaline was surging through her veins. Her mind was crystal-clear, but running five times faster than normal. The decision was formed before she even had time to debate it with herself.

She picked up her bag and slung it over one shoulder. She went to Therese and pulled on her arm, forcing her to rise. "Don't say a thing," she commanded Therese quietly. "Just come."

Therese stumbled along, confused. Rebecca walked with her toward the exit, fast.

In the thronged concourse, Therese looked up at Rebecca. "Where are we going?"

"We're getting out of here."

Therese stopped in her tracks and tried to draw her hand out of Rebecca's. "You mean leaving Dad and Devon? We can't do that!"

"Keep walking."

"No!"

Rebecca turned and faced her tautly. "You saw what just happened to that cop. And to the old lady. What do you think the penalty for setting fire to an airplane is?"

"But I didn't do it—I didn't!" Therese swallowed, her mouth working. "I—I don't *think* I did!"

"The truth is, you don't know *what* you did, do you?" Rebecca said forcefully.

The girl looked back over her shoulder, desperate and torn. "I can't leave Dad!"

"We'll get in touch with your dad later," she lied.

Therese looked ghastly. "B-but we can't just walk out!"

"You want to spend the rest of your life in a padded cell?" Rebecca asked harshly. She saw terror fill Therese's eyes. "Now, come!" She jerked Therese brutally into motion. "Let's go," she commanded.

This time, Therese kept pace beside Rebecca, her fingers knotted tightly around Rebecca's. They were heading for the main exit. Rebecca looked over her shoulder quickly. The first-class area was choked with people. For the next few minutes, attention was going to be focused exclusively on the drama of Al Reagan and the team who were trying to save his life. Neither Michael nor the remaining cop was coming after them. Yet.

And when Rebecca broke into a run, Therese ran, too.

She was following the signs to the taxi stand. But when they got there, the sidewalk was crowded. A long line was straggling to the pick-up point with luggage. There was no hope of breaking into the line without causing a commotion.

"Oh, *shit*," Rebecca muttered. Fear clutched at her heart. They had to get away from the airport fast. There was no time to rent a car, not here.

"Look," Therese said in a frightened little-girl voice. Rebecca followed her gaze. A couple of hundred yards down, an airport bus was waiting. The sign above the windshield said MIAMI BEACH.

"Come on," Rebecca commanded.

They ran. The winter sun was hot, the air muggy, and Rebecca felt sweat bathe her face and neck. She kept a tight grip on Therese's hand, and when the girl stumbled, she jerked her up again. "Keep going," she panted.

They were still fifty yards from the bus when she heard the pneumatic hiss of the doors closing, and saw it start to pull out. She could almost feel the hands of their pursuers clutching at them, dragging them back. She let go of Therese's hand and jumped into the path of the oncoming bus, her arms raised high.

"Rebecca!" Therese screamed in alarm.

Through the windshield, Rebecca saw the driver's face in a blur, mouth opening to shout something. The bus plunged down on its front suspension as it braked hard. It stopped a few feet from her, hot engine fumes washing over her.

She grabbed Therese's hand and pulled her to the doors. She banged on the glass with her free fist. The doors popped open, and they clambered up the steps.

"What the hell you playing at?" the driver said angrily, evidently shaken. "You wanna kill yourself, go pick another driver. There's a bus every fifteen minutes."

"We want this one," Rebecca replied, clinging to the rail. "How much?"

"Well, where you *going*?"

"To the first stop in Miami Beach."

"Convention Center?"

"Yes."

"One adult, one child, twelve-fifty," the man said, pulling out the tickets. Rebecca groped in her pockets. She suddenly realized all she had was Italian money and her credit cards. There hadn't even been time to get dollars. Her panic was starting to build when Therese spoke up quietly.

"I have twelve-fifty." She produced a little purse and took out a ten and a five.

"Bless you," Rebecca whispered, hugging her.

They made their way down the aisle as the bus pulled away again, followed by the inquisitive stares of the other passengers. At the very back, they found two empty places, and subsided. Rebecca felt weak. It would take very little time, she knew, for their trail to be picked up. They had to disappear, unobtrusively and permanently, in the next hour. Or it was all over.

Therese was huddled against her, silent. As the electrifying power of the adrenaline rush started to fade, Rebecca was facing a grim truth: By dragging Therese away like that, she had added yet another piece of lead to the already overwhelming weight of the girl's guilt. There could be no going back. Not now.

She hugged her child.

•   •   •

All the way down the expressway, then along the two-mile causeway to Miami Beach, she kept expecting to hear police sirens, see the flashing lights closing in. It had long since dawned on her that Miami Beach was exactly the worst place to run to. The island was linked to the mainland by no more than a handful of causeways. If they were traced here, they would be effectively trapped. They had to get back off the island as quickly as possible, and keep going as far and as fast as they could.

The past few hours had been exhausting. She needed to stay alert, for Therese's sake. The girl was rummaging in her backpack.

"What are you looking for?" Rebecca murmured to Therese.

"Something to eat. I'm starving. And thirsty."

"Me, too. We'll grab a bite as soon as we can."

"Where are we going? What are we going to do?"

"We have to get out of the country," she said flatly.

"*Forever?*" Therese said.

"I'm not ever going to lie to you, Therese," Rebecca said, squeezing her fingers. "I don't know whether forever or just for a while. But we have to leave the U.S. as soon as we can. If we don't, the police will pick us up, and I won't be able to help you." The simple statements silenced Therese. "It'll take them a little time to get organized," Rebecca went on, "but not long. They'll figure out we took this bus. They'll know all the possible ways out of Miami, and they'll circulate our descriptions to cops on the beat at the airports, the bus depots, the train stations."

Therese was pale. "Where are we going to go then?"

"We'll go to Mexico," Rebecca said. "We'll rest up there, and make some decisions. From there, we can go anywhere we want."

"Mexico?" Therese looked at Rebecca. "Maybe we should have stayed, Rebecca! It's not too late to turn back!"

"We're not turning back!" Rebecca said fiercely. "I know what I'm doing." She squeezed her temples, wondering if that was true. She was trying to extricate Therese from such a horrible, thorny tangle. There was no way it could be done without tearing the girl's already fragile psyche. "I'm asking you to trust me, Therese," she went on, more quietly. "There's a very important reason why you should—I just can't tell you just yet. But I'm begging you, honey, trust me!"

Therese looked away. She was gnawing on her lip. At last she spoke. "Okay."

"When we get off, I'm going to get all the cash I can out of an ATM. But I'll only be able to do that once. After that, every time I use a cash machine, a credit card, my ID for anything, phones will start ringing. You understand?"

"Yes," Therese said quietly.

"That's why we need to get out of the country."

Therese nodded. Rebecca did not know how much further the child could be driven before she needed rest. She stared out the window at the vast white hotels that packed the island, the jostling crowds of high season. The sun was going down, painting acres of stucco flamingo-pink. The word *Mexico* had come to her mouth almost without her thinking it. Ryan was in Mexico. Did she have the right to make the decision to take Therese to Ryan? Would it be fair to either of them? And yet Ryan was the only person in the wide world who would help them now. She had been running people through her mind for the past ten minutes. Her lawyer. Her ex-husband, Malcolm. Robert. Her father. Not one of them would dream of giving her the kind of unquestioning refuge she needed right now. Not one of them would want to become an accessory to her crime. There was only Ryan.

Maybe she had always planned to take Therese to him, somewhere deep inside. Perhaps it had always been her last hope.

But for now, there was tonight to get through.

They got off the bus at the Convention Center and quickly found an ATM. Rebecca extracted twenty-five hundred dollars in cash, using several different credit cards, before the terminal announced it would give her no more. The operation would be traced in hours, maybe less. Added to the money she had assembled for her aborted plan in Urbino, she had well over three thousand dollars. Now they had to get back off the island, fast. But Therese was drooping with hunger and tiredness. They pushed into a crowded fast-food restaurant, piled a tray with junk calories, and squeezed into a booth.

The hot food was welcome. Rebecca was thinking hard as she watched Therese wolf down a burger and fries, eating as though it were her last meal on earth.

"Have you got your passport, Therese?" she asked.

Therese looked up. "Dad has my real one. I still have the phony one," she said through a full mouth.

"Which phony one?"

"Dad got us fake passports so we could get out of Canada to fly to Italy. I still have that one."

"Let me see," Rebecca commanded.

Therese dug into her backpack and pulled out a U.S. passport. Rebecca took it and opened it. The photo was of Therese, but the name was given as Teresa Forbes, and the other details were false. Rebecca gnawed on her lip. Was this good or bad? If Michael either forgot to tell the police about this passport, or didn't want to reveal its existence, maybe it would get Therese through an immigration check.

Her own passport still bore her maiden name, Rebecca Carey. Michael had known her as Rebecca Burns. With luck, it would take him at least a day to guess who she really was, and give her real name to the cops. That was, if he intended to go to the cops. Somehow, she felt in her heart that when Michael guessed who she was, he would not share that knowledge with the authorities. He would come after her at his own pace, and deal with her in his own way. That thought was like a cold iron hook snagging in her guts. But for now, until that situation arose, she was going to have to return to using her maiden name.

Therese was looking at her. "Rebecca," she said in a shaky voice, "why are you doing this?"

"For you."

"But why? You're not, like, some kind of long-lost relation or . . . or something . . . are you?"

Rebecca paused. Therese's wide, passionate mouth was clenched with emotion. She could see that Therese was trembling violently, holding herself in. They stared into each other's eyes, across the gulf of time and distance. It was a gulf too wide to just step across, too deep to risk. But what choice did she have? The noise and smell of the restaurant swam around them. "Would you like me to be?"

"No!" Therese said in a panicky voice.

"No?"

"I don't know." She covered her eyes with her hands. "I'm sorry. I'm so confused. I just want to know the truth."

Rebecca looked at Therese's messy tray. "Are you done here?"

Therese nodded, her eyes blurred.

"Then let's walk down to the beach and talk. This isn't a good place."

They crossed Collins Avenue and walked between canyons of hotels to the beach. The vast sweep of smooth sand was relatively empty but for couples taking in the sunset. They took off their shoes and walked toward the sea. The setting sun had streaked the waves with red and gold. The immense, clear sweep of the sky, its huge purity, seemed to fill Rebecca with at least a temporary sense of hope. She felt like someone who had been underground too long.

"When I was seventeen," Rebecca began conversationally, "I fell in love with a boy named Ryan Foster. He was nineteen. We were young, but I believed we loved each other very truly. At least, when I look back over my life, I've never loved anyone the way I loved him. I loved him so much that I wanted to make love with him. But we weren't as careful as we should have been, and one day I learned I was pregnant. We both wanted badly to be doctors. We knew if we kept the child, neither of us would be likely to fulfill that ambition. And looking at ourselves honestly, we felt we were much too young to make good parents. So we decided to give the child up for adoption. It wasn't an easy decision, Therese. Looking back, our reasoning was selfish and weak. But at that age, people are sometimes selfish and weak in many things."

They had reached the sea. Rebecca turned to Therese. "Can you understand any of this?"

"I'm trying," Therese said in a small voice.

"Good. Ryan and I looked for an adoption agency to help us. We found one, and set things in motion. In due course, my baby was born. She was a girl. A beautiful little girl. The first thing I did with her, the moment she was born, was put her to my breast. She fell asleep peacefully." Rebecca glanced at Therese. The child was facing the sea, the evening breeze blowing her curly hair back from her high forehead. Her eyes were swimming with tears. "Ryan stayed with me. He would sit with me in the hospital room and watch me nurse the baby. We couldn't find anything to say to each other. It was too sad for words. Sometimes he would take the baby in his arms, and look into her face, and I would feel my heart breaking. We both loved that baby so much, yet we knew we couldn't keep her. You were that baby, Therese."

She heard Therese start to cry. She turned, and took the child in her arms. Rebecca felt the heat behind her own eyes, but she could not give way to tears. Not yet. There was too far to go.

The sea had rustled up, and swirled around their bare feet. "Ryan and I couldn't keep seeing each other after that. He went away, and we only met a few times. We were too hurt. From the moment I gave you up, Therese, I felt I was no longer truly alive. I've been like half a person ever since then. But by the time I really understood what I'd done, it was too late to go back."

"Why didn't you tell me?" Therese whispered.

"You mean, like, 'Hi, I'm your long-lost mom'? It wasn't that easy for me. And it would have been worse for you."

Therese tried to wipe the tears from her cheeks. "Why did you come? Why now?"

"I read about what happened in San Francisco," Rebecca said simply. "I thought I could help. I never anticipated it would turn out like this."

"Does Dad know?"

"Not yet."

"You've got to tell him!"

"I will, I promise."

"Call Dad." Therese grabbed Rebecca's arm. "Call him, Rebecca. Tell him you're my mother. He'll work everything out!"

"It isn't that easy," Rebecca replied. "There are the cops to deal with. If we go back, they'll probably arrest me. And they'll make sure you never get another chance to run. This is your one and only, Therese. We'll find a time to tell your dad, I promise."

She would have to find some way of telling Therese the terrible truth about Michael and Devon. But not now. "We have thirteen years to catch up on, Therese. But right now, we have to keep going. Are you strong enough?"

"Yes," Therese said.

"Will you try to trust me?" she asked, looking searchingly into Therese's eyes. "Will you give me the next few days?"

"Yes," Therese repeated.

Rebecca kissed her forehead. "Come on then. I want to make a phone call."

"Who to?"

"Someone in Mexico. Monterrey."

"My real father?" Therese guessed, with some eerie second sight.

Rebecca hesitated, then nodded. "Yes. Your real father."

She watched Therese take it in. "Does he know—about all this?" she asked slowly.

"No. We haven't communicated in a long time."

"Why is he in Mexico?"

"When we were young, before you came along, we took a trip there together on an old motorcycle. We slept out in the desert, stopped anywhere we wanted. Ryan fell in love with Mexico in some way. It was the kind of trip you only do when you're young and very romantic. We were very happy together. Everything was so beautiful to us. The moon, the desert, the mountains. Anyway, we also saw a lot of human misery. The country got into Ryan's blood. He said he would come back to work there one day. I knew he meant it. Years later, he sent me a card from Monterrey, saying he was working in a pediatric hospital."

"So you're both doctors?"

"Yes."

"Devon wants to be a doctor," Therese said abstractedly. "I don't. Isn't that strange?"

"Being a doctor isn't genetic, Therese."

Therese lifted shaky fingers to her mouth. "I feel like nothing's real anymore," she said in a dazed way. "Like I'm suddenly somebody else, living somebody else's life."

"I hate to do this to you, Therese. To me, it makes perfect sense that I should take you to meet your real father. But maybe you can't face that right now."

Therese sank down onto her haunches, elbows on her knees. "Will he help us?"

"I think he will." She checked her watch. Time was so terribly short. But she could not push Therese too hard or too far.

"I don't know if I can face this right now," Therese said, her voice tearful. "Do I have to meet him?"

"Not if you don't want to," Rebecca said gently. "As a matter of fact, I might be wrong in thinking he'll help us. I don't really know how he'll react, whether he'll even want to speak to me once he learns what's been going on."

The sky was crimson now, the lights of the cars making a diamond dazzle in the twilight. They walked up the beach. There was a phone booth on Collins Avenue. She made Therese sit on the wall outside, and let herself in. She took her diary out of her bag, and looked up Ryan's number in Monterrey. Then she drew in a deep breath to steady herself, and punched in the number.

She heard the crackly ringing at the other end. Someone picked up the phone. A woman's voice spoke.

"Hospital Santa Clara, buenas tardes."

"Quería hablar con el Doctor Foster, por favor."

"De parte de quién?"

"Soy una amiga suya."

"*Momento, por favor.*"

She waited, feeling her heart pound heavily, watching Therese through the glass. Then she heard Ryan's voice come on the line.

"Ryan Foster."

Rebecca opened her mouth to speak, but no words came.

"This is Foster," she heard Ryan repeat impatiently. "Who's calling?"

She was suddenly shaking, her hands sweaty. She felt she could not breathe properly. She lowered the receiver with a click, and leaned back against the wall of the booth, closing her eyes.

Why had she been unable to speak to Ryan? Had she felt it was not emotionally fair to spring it on him like this, not ethically fair to involve him in something illegal and dangerous? Or had it been sheer cowardice, the old cowardice that had made her unwilling to face her own emotions all her life?

She pushed out of the telephone booth, feeling as if she were suffocating. She, like Therese, had suddenly become someone else, living someone else's life. She, who had been so reserved, so controlled, was now gambling everything on a throw of the dice. She, who had been so principled, was now an outlaw, free-falling with her outlaw child. Free-falling, with a long, long way to fall.

"Wasn't he there?"

She swallowed. "Yes, he's there."

"Didn't you speak to him?"

"No."

"How come?"

"I don't know. I guess . . . I guess the timing was wrong." She didn't want Therese to know how she'd backed off from speaking to Ryan. "I'll speak to him later."

There was a long silence. Therese was staring at the sea, looking very frail. The breeze was stirring her tangled hair. Traffic was building up, a river of gleaming steel and halogen. Tens of thousands of lights were coming on across the hotelscape. Bright shop windows enshrined costly goods. Beneath all that, the humid evening air carried ancient scents of swamp and sea, growth and decay. Rebecca wiped her moist forehead. "At least he's there. When we get to Mexico, we can make the decision whether to go to him."

"How are we going to get to Mexico?" Therese asked.

"I just made up my mind," Rebecca said. "We're going to fly."

"You mean go back to the airport?" Therese gasped. "That's crazy! Why don't you rent a car?"

"Renting a car means using my credit card, Therese, and that would leave a red-hot trail. Every cop from here to the border would be looking for that car. And it's a long drive with a lot of stops. Even taking a bus would mean too many people would see us. We have to take a chance on a flight. I'll pay cash for the tickets, and we don't need any ID for a domestic flight. We'll fly out of the other airport."

"There's another airport?"

Rebecca nodded. "Fort Lauderdale. It's only a few miles from here."

"Won't there be a million cops?"

"We'll have to gamble that the cops haven't had enough time to really get organized," Rebecca said, keeping her voice firm. "Our clothes are recognizable, but we'll get some new stuff around here, and a couple of cheap carry-ons. We'll be less conspicuous that way. If we have to wait for any length of time, we'll join up with the nearest group. We'll look like we belong to them. We'll talk to strangers if we have to. We'll be a couple of friendly, talkative people with nothing to feel guilty about. Okay?"

"Okay," Therese said. Her spine seemed to straighten at Rebecca's confident tone. Rebecca hoped Therese didn't begin to guess just how terrified she was feeling under that confident tone. "We'll pay cash for everything. I won't use my credit cards again. Not in Miami, at any rate."

"Okay."

"If there are cops at the airport, we'll just have to be brave, Therese. We'll have to assume they aren't looking for us. It's important for us to *be* who we're pretending to be. Really *believe* it. You understand?"

Therese nodded.

Rebecca drew a deep breath. "Okay. Let's go do some quick shopping."

•   •   •

It was dark by the time they arrived at the Fort Lauderdale airport. She had half expected the streets to be howling with patrol cars on their trail, but the vastness of Miami was indifferent to them.

The taxi dropped them off. They got out, wearing cheap new clothes, and carrying their old things in vinyl carry-ons.

Outside the entrance, two police cars were parked, the cops in a huddle, discussing something.

Rebecca felt her legs turn to water. Had they already been told to watch for the fugitives? She pulled back against the wall, yanking Therese close to her side. The cops were drinking coffee from Styrofoam cups. They glanced idly at passersby. Beyond them, the airport was crowded and busy. Once among all these hundreds of people, they would have a better chance.

"Are they waiting for us?" Therese whispered.

"I don't know," Rebecca said. Some kind of mad courage rose in her. "Only one way of finding out. Come on." Clutching her bag, Rebecca pushed forward, Therese gripping her arm. They were walking straight toward the blue shirts of the four patrolmen up ahead. A middle-aged couple was walking a little way ahead of them. Pulling Therese along, Rebecca caught up with them, pressing close, to look as though they were one large group. She chatted inanely to Therese, hardly knowing what she was saying, keeping a wide smile on her mouth. As they passed the cops, she felt a sudden electric jolt of panic. They were staring right at her. She saw one of them move his hand to something at his waist, a radio or a gun.

She kept walking and gabbling, her mouth dry as a bone. She dared not look back until they were among the crowds within. Then she glanced quickly over her shoulder. Two of the cops had come into the concourse after them, one of them talking into a hand radio.

"Look!" Therese gasped.

"I see them," Rebecca said. "Keep moving." She hustled Therese forward almost brutally. If the police were not following them, there was no point in attracting their attention by behaving erratically. She stared intently at the departures board. There was a flight to Dallas, Texas, in two hours. That was perfect for them. In Dallas they would change planes for San Antonio. But at the far end of the concourse, another pair of cops stood with folded arms, watching the crowd. A sense of nightmare closed in on Rebecca.

"There are some more over there," Therese said shakily. "The place is full of cops, Rebecca!"

"Airports are always full of cops," she replied with icy calm. "They're not paying us special attention. If they really wanted us, they would have stopped us by now."

"Maybe they're waiting for us to try and buy tickets."

"Maybe," Rebecca said. "We'll soon see. Smile at me, Therese."

"Huh?"

They joined the back of the line, and Rebecca touched Therese's shoulder, turning the girl so that she could look into her eyes. "Smile at me," she said gently.

Therese's eyes were haunted with terror. But looking at Rebecca seemed to calm her a little. She managed a fleeting, shaky smile.

"That's great," Rebecca said.

"What happened to that cop who was with us? Did he have a heart attack?"

"That's what it looked like."

"Will he die?"

"The cardiac team was there very fast. Statistically, that means his chances are much better."

"But he could still die, right?" Therese's face was taut. "Then they'd want me for murder!"

"Only if you set that fire," Rebecca said flatly. "And you said you didn't, remember?"

"They would never believe me," Therese said, staring fearfully at the patrolmen.

"Just do me one favor," Rebecca said lightly, "and don't set fire to this next plane, okay?"

Therese grimaced.

They arrived at the counter, and she heard her own voice asking for three tickets to San Antonio, Texas, with a transfer in Dallas. The clerk smiled vaguely at her as she asked where they wanted to sit, but went through the transaction without any further comment. Then they were walking away, and the cops still hadn't come over.

"Why did you buy three tickets?" Therese demanded.

"So that it doesn't look too obvious when they check the records," Rebecca said briefly, "and to give us a little space on the flight." She counted her remaining money. There was just under two thousand dollars left. She wondered if they were going to make it.

"They're looking right at us," Therese said in a high voice.

"Pull yourself together," Rebecca snapped, with such force that she startled both herself and Therese. She lowered her voice. "Try and stay calm, Therese. All we have to do now is concentrate on catching this plane. Okay?"

"Okay," Therese whispered.

"The flight's at ten-thirty. That means we only have an hour before they start boarding. Come on, Therese, you can do this."

"I'm scared," Therese said in a trembling voice.

"Nothing can happen to you while you're with me," Rebecca said.

The flight seemed lightly booked, and they joined the group waiting at the gate. They sat down together on a bench. There were no cops here. Through the plate glass, the vast shapes of airliners glided among a dazzle of lights.

"I think I always knew who you were," Therese said softly, her voice all but drowned out by the noise around them. "Right from that moment you came into my room. I recognized you."

Rebecca pulled her close, so Therese's head rested on her shoulder.

•   •   •

They had spent the night in the Dallas airport, waiting for the first flight to San Antonio the following morning. Once aboard the plane Therese had slept, her head pillowed on Rebecca's shoulder, for most of the way. Rebecca was glad of that. There was still so much ahead for this child to endure.

For the past hour, she had been thinking of Ryan. He had vanished so completely from her life over the past thirteen years that even to bring back memories made her feel strange.

Ryan had been two years older, and he had been very remote from her during her childhood in Southern California. But she had always been aware of him, a thrilling, sinful presence, the bad boy of the neighborhood, forbidden by parents, in trouble with the police, at the edge of what was tolerable.

He came from a broken home. His background had been the first thing to attract Rebecca to him. Her own home had been broken, too, by the early death of her mother. Her father's quick remarriage had only made her unhappier. In Ryan Foster, she had seen a kindred spirit.

But if Ryan felt the same misery and insecurity that she felt, he showed it in different ways. Where Rebecca had been introverted, cool, and studious, he had been the epitome of rebellious youth, indifferent to rules, a wild, unpredictable force. So many tales had circulated about his misdoings that it had been hard to separate the truth from the legend.

Until she was fifteen, he had been no more than an icon to her. She had glimpsed him thundering along the road on beat-up bikes, had half heard scandalized tales of his sins. She had barely met those electric blue eyes more than once or twice. She had admired from afar.

And then Ryan's life had taken an unexpected turn. Somehow, the wild boy who had never been known to willingly open a book had performed amazingly well on the SAT's, and had won a scholarship to Stanford. The leather-jacketed rebel had wanted to be a doctor.

Rebecca's own fierce ambition to become a doctor had been growing since her childhood. Now there was an added reason for her to feel close to Ryan. Now she had looked at him with new eyes. And one day, instead of thundering past her on his motorbike, he had screamed to a stop, turned in the saddle, and looked back at her with those amazing eyes.

And now she was hurtling toward him, after thirteen years, bringing him their misbegotten child.

They were descending toward San Antonio. Rose-colored light was stealing across the plateau, the hills casting mile-long shadows. The city was set in a rippling landscape that looked absolutely lifeless from this height, though she knew that there would be scrub and grassland down below. The rising sun sent a shaft of light glancing from the tilting wing of the aircraft. The blaze seared across Therese's sleeping face, making her moan and twist.

She awoke with a violent start. "Where are we?" she asked, her voice panicky.

"Coming down to San Antonio."

"I dreamed about the night Mom died."

Rebecca stroked her curly hair gently. "What did you dream?"

"I dreamed I was burning her."

Rebecca was silent, holding Therese close. "Did you?" she asked at last. "Did you burn her?"

She felt Therese's slim body tense up and start shivering against hers. "I don't know," Therese said in a tight voice. "It's, like, when I try to think about it, I lose control. I go into my crazy spiral, and I can't get out. I'm terrified to even try."

"If you trust me, I might be able to help."

Rebecca thought of the fire on the 747, seeing the faces stark with terror. The horror of that experience would haunt her for the rest of her life. She could not stop thinking of how catastrophic it might have been. Far worse than the fire that had killed Barbara. Hundreds of human beings might have plummeted in a fireball into the sea. It didn't bear thinking of.

She had taken Therese away from Michael and Devon's sickness, but their ordeal was not over. Not by a long, long way. She held the girl tighter. "Therese, whatever happened in San Francisco, I want you to know that I blame myself for all that you've suffered. I don't think I'll ever be able to forgive myself."

Therese was trembling even harder. "Don't say that. It's all my fault."

Therese had spoken in such a thin, empty voice that Rebecca was chilled. She cupped Therese's chin in her palm, and looked into her face. "We're starting a new life, Therese. That's what matters. Not the past. Don't think about it right now. Look, isn't the view beautiful?"

Therese kept her eyes fixed on Rebecca. "What do I call you now?"

"You could keep on calling me Rebecca, if you want."

"Don't you want me to call you Mom?"

Rebecca smiled crookedly. "If that's what you want. See how it goes."

"Okay," Therese agreed. "I'll see how it goes."

Rebecca was slightly shaky with weariness as they emerged into the concourse. A small group of people awaited the arriving passengers, faces jaded at this early hour. At least there was no posse of police to welcome them.

"What do we do now?" Therese asked urgently. "We ought to get going."

"You're right," Rebecca said, fighting to think clearly through her weariness.

"Well, come *on*, then," Therese said, her voice rising.

Rebecca glanced longingly at the ATM terminals, where lines of people shuffled impatiently. More money would be so useful. But hours had passed since she and Therese had fled the police in Miami. San Antonio was a long way from Miami, but in this wired world, computer talked to distant computer in milliseconds. By now, her card was probably primed to go off like a grenade. They wouldn't make it out of the building before some hotshot cop pounced on them. She forced herself to smile brightly. "Come on. Let's go get a bus into town."

Outside the airport building, the sun was already hot, the desert wind dry as a bone.

When the bus pulled up, they took seats at the back, huddling together. With a lurch and a hiss of pneumatic doors, they were off, leaving the airport behind. Rebecca tried to think clearly. Texas was dazzlingly bright, the blustering wind bowling pink clouds of dust across the road. The sky was huge after the gray intimacy of Umbria. The route into town from the airport cut through sprawling tracts of houses. Beyond, the landscape was arid.

"How are we going to get through immigration?" Therese asked.

"I'll be using a passport that has my own name, Rebecca Carey. You've got the Teresa Forbes passport. That might fool a careless cop, or an unsuspicious one. Maybe we'll get lucky."

" 'Maybe'?" Therese echoed, her voice almost shrill. Over the last couple of hours, Rebecca had sensed Therese's confidence in her ebbing. The girl's mood was changing.

"When I made that trip with Ryan, crossing the border was very easy. They hardly checked us leaving the country. Even if there is an alert, it probably won't be for anyone with the names on the passports we'll be using."

"But won't the guards be looking out for a woman and a girl, under any names?"

"I don't know."

"It's a safe bet, isn't it?" Therese said in an irritable, adult way. For some reason, Rebecca felt she had picked up that tone from Barbara.

"Yes, it's a safe bet," Rebecca said tiredly. "The fact that we'll still have different names might be a problem in itself. We don't have any good reason why we should be traveling together. We need a cover story." She thought for a moment, watched by Therese's doubting eyes. "We'd better say we're aunt and niece," she decided at last. "You're my sister's daughter from San Francisco, and you're vacationing with me while your parents go through a messy divorce. We'll get all the details straightened out before we cross. Okay?"

"Okay," Therese said, shrugging. "So, what's the rest of your great plan?"

Rebecca swiveled in her seat to look at a road sign that read MEXICO 90 MILES. She felt the unreality wash over her again. Ninety miles. No more than a couple of hours by car.

What *was* her great plan? Buy a car from a used-car lot? Some cheap wreck that would just get them into Mexico? But even junkers cost money. The purchase would wipe out their finite resources. And what if they needed to go a long way, farther than a junker would take them?

The bus pulled into a station, and the doors hissed open. She got out with Therese. People milled around them. This was hat-and-boot country. Everybody wore some kind of Western headgear and footwear, men, women, children. The blunt Texas accent was on everything—the drawling voices around them, the hats and embroidered boots, the brash ads on the billboards outside the waiting room. Feeling conspicuous, Rebecca walked up to a large schedule framed behind glass, and stared at it. The fine print blurred before her tired eyes, and she had to squint to concentrate on the destinations. A name caught her eye. *Laredo.* Laredo was on the Mexican border. Once there, they would be on the very doorstep of freedom. She checked her watch. There was a bus to Laredo in half an hour.

"Come on," she told Therese, "we have to buy tickets."

"Where to?"

"Laredo."

"Where the hell is Laredo?"

"Laredo's practically in Mexico," she told Therese. "It's right on the Rio Grande."

"What are we gonna do, swim across?"

"I hope it doesn't come to that," Rebecca said easily, forcing herself to sound cheerful, confident, and in control. She suspected Therese knew her well enough to sense that she was faking it.

"Haven't you heard of the U.S. border patrol? If you haven't got a surefire way of getting us across, we might as well be back in Miami."

"Well, maybe we *will* swim across," Rebecca said, hearing her own voice turn sharp. "One thing at a time, Therese."

She bought tickets, found out where their bus was waiting, and hurried there with Therese. They must have bought the last couple of tickets, because the bus was full. A lot of the passengers talked in swift, voluble Spanish. She and Therese found their way to the back of the bus, and wedged themselves in among a pile of baggage.

Rebecca put her hand on Therese's. "Sorry I snapped at you. How are you feeling?" she asked.

"Tired," Therese said brusquely. She turned her back on Rebecca and hunched against the window, staring out.

They reached Laredo late in the afternoon. A sunset glow was on the town, which was bigger and more modern than Rebecca had anticipated. As the bus passed the city hall, she caught sight of the river, wide and glazed orange by the setting sun. There were islands in the stream. The town beyond was in Mexico.

Somehow, the sight of Mexican soil made Rebecca's flagging spirits soar, and she felt her heart start to beat fast in her breast. Therese, too, sat up and stared at the Rio Grande. Rebecca tried to guess what thoughts were going through her head. She wondered whether Therese really knew what a huge step she was taking. Had she done enough to inform Therese just what it was she was committing herself to? She hadn't wanted to make a big scene out of it. In any case, there hadn't been time so far. But Rebecca knew that while she was getting Therese out of the United States to protect her, she was also making it far more difficult for Therese ever to go back to what she had been before.

Was she, Rebecca asked herself suddenly, any better than those misguided, selfish people who kidnapped their own children from their ex-spouses? She had a sudden vision of herself and Therese, farther down the line, living as vagrants in some forlorn town, forgetting who they were, with no future and no past.

She pulled herself together sharply. It wasn't like that. Therese needed to be protected, from her father and from the police. If either got their hands on the child again, she would be doomed. Come to that, if either got their hands on Rebecca, it would get ugly. She shivered slightly as she thought of Michael's anger. Prison might be preferable to facing *that*.

Across the road from the bus depot was a modern hotel, the Guadalupe. This day was over. They needed comfort, she decided, hot water and clean beds. They went into the lobby. She booked a room with twin beds, giving her name as Rebecca Blake.

The room was large and clean, with a picture window that faced due south, out over the Rio Grande, toward Mexico. In the dying light, Mexico looked alluring, a land of purple and gold, like the cover illustration of a Louis L'Amour novel. The reality, Rebecca knew, was much less romantic.

Therese came to the window beside her and, as if reading her thoughts, said, "Will we ever come back to the U.S.?"

"We haven't left yet," Rebecca said, trying to make light of it.

"You know what I mean."

"You can always come back, if you want to." Rebecca was silent for a moment. "What I've done qualifies as a serious crime. I'd be lucky not to go to jail. I'd be unlikely to work as a doctor again. Not for a long time, anyway." She drew a deep breath, trying to quiet the dizziness in her own head. "I don't think I'll be coming back for a while." She saw that Therese was crying. "What is it?"

Therese wiped her eyes. "Am I ever going to see Dad again?" she asked.

"Oh, Therese. I don't know what the answer to that question is."

"But you *must* have an answer," Therese said in a choked voice. "You told me you knew what you were doing, Rebecca. That's why I came with you. Dad will be going crazy by now. So will Devvy. We've never been apart."

Rebecca struggled to pull her thoughts together. She was trying to frame the words she needed to say to Therese. "None of this is going to be easy. You're at a crossroads. You're very young to have to face decisions like these, but for one reason and another, you're going to have to face them soon. You're going to have to decide. When I hauled you away from that airport in Miami, I wasn't just trying to get you away from the police. I wanted to get you away from your family, too. I think there's a kind of horrible sickness in your family, and I had to get you away from it."

"What kind of sickness?" Therese asked in a still voice.

She hesitated for a long while, wondering how she could broach such a dark subject. "Your father and Devon have a relationship that isn't natural," she said at last. "It goes beyond what a father and a daughter should ever do."

Therese's eyes widened. "You mean sex?" she asked.

"Yes. I mean sex."

"Did Devon tell you that?"

"Yes. Devon told me."

Therese's face flushed. "You don't understand! She's lied about that before, Rebecca. She lied about that to Mom."

Rebecca felt her stomach twist inside her. "What do you mean?"

"She told Mom that Dad had done things to her. But when they called the doctors to look at her, they said it wasn't true. She made up a lie to hurt Mom!"

"When was that?"

"Two years ago."

"I don't think it's a lie anymore," Rebecca said. Up in the sky, fluffy clouds were turning crimson. "And apart from anything else, I was afraid that this relationship between them was going to hurt you. It makes it easier for them to exclude you. Use you. Maybe even lay the blame on you for things they did." She touched Therese's shoulder. "Do you understand?"

"You're wrong! You should have told me all this before we left Miami," Therese said urgently.

"Well, we left in a rush," Rebecca replied. "There wasn't a lot of time for talking."

Therese's hands were snatching at each other now. "I don't believe it," she said, her voice unsteady.

"It's true."

"It's not. You made a mistake, Rebecca. A terrible mistake."

"I don't think I've made a mistake."

"Devon's a liar," Therese said. Tears spilled down her pale cheeks. "You were *crazy* to believe her!"

"You once told me that your parents split up because of Devon. You said Devon chose your father. I think this was the real reason. It's not a lie."

"I want to speak to Dad! I want to hear it from his own lips!"

"I'm so sorry, Therese."

"I thought you were in love with Dad! How could you believe something so awful about him?"

Rebecca hesitated. "I thought I was falling in love with Michael, too. But I no longer trust him. I *can't* trust him. What he's done to Devon is something that I just cannot accept. As a mother, as a doctor, as a human being, I find it sickening. More than I can say. The way I see it, he's had his chance with you. I gave you to him years ago, trusting him. He broke that trust, and now it's over. I never want to see you with him again."

"You've got to go back to Dad," Therese said forcefully, "and straighten this out. For my sake."

"Therese, you can't ask me that."

"You mean I just have to forget all about Dad, all about Devvy?"

Rebecca sighed. "No. You can't forget them. But I believe your best chance lies in making a new start. And that usually means leaving something behind. Even if only temporarily."

"You're wrong about Dad. But that doesn't matter to you. You just want an *excuse*," Therese said. She was suddenly trembling with passion. "You just want to throw Dad in the trash, so you can go on your merry way. Just like you did with me."

"No!"

"You did," Therese said fiercely. "You can't handle commitment. You didn't want the hassle of a baby to look after. So you just threw me away."

Rebecca was aching inside. "I can understand how you would feel that, and I'm terribly, terribly sorry."

"Now you want to throw Dad away. But I'm not going to run anymore," Therese said. "I don't want to be like you."

"Does that mean you're going back to San Francisco?" Rebecca asked huskily.

"I don't know!" Therese said in a thin voice.

The silence stretched tight. Rebecca wanted to hold the girl, but dared not. "Just promise me you'll tell me when you make up your mind. Tell me before you do anything final. Okay?"

Therese nodded silently.

Rebecca held out her hand, but Therese either didn't see it, or ignored it. She went to one of the beds and threw herself on it, full-length.

Leaving Therese staring fixedly at a movie on TV, Rebecca went downstairs and into the lobby. There was a rack of information at the desk, and a bored-looking boy behind a sign advertising a local car-rental company. It would be so deceptively easy to pick up a car for the final dash to Mexico. Could she persuade them to let her pay with cash, telling some story about having lost her credit card? Her heart thudding, Rebecca walked across to the desk. The boy straightened at her approach, rubbing the acne on his chin as if to try and erase it.

"Hi! What can I do for you, ma'am?"

"I want to rent a car," she heard herself tell him.

"Sure thing," he replied cheerfully. He flourished a brochure. "These are our rates."

"I just want a compact," she said, staring at the leaflet. "Something small."

"We have a special offer on these," the boy told her, tapping one of the photographs with the chewed stub of his pen. "It's even better if you take it for longer than a week. But they are small. Depends how far you're going."

"We're taking a short vacation here," Rebecca said, reaching for the leaflet. "My daughter and I. We thought we'd drive into Mexico for a couple of days."

"Uh-oh," the boy said. His thumb clamped on the leaflet, stopping her from taking it. He shook his head. "That's gonna be a problem."

"How come?" she asked, wondering why she'd been so stupid as to mention Mexico.

He laid a red hand on his breast. "We trust you, honest. It's the U.S. border guards. They check the paperwork on all vehicles leaving the U.S. Generally, they won't let you drive into Mexico with a rented car. Not unless it's been rented in Mexico. You have to get a notarized authorization. And you need a special insurance policy. Our insurers won't cover it for compacts. But we will do it for one of these."

He was tapping a picture of a huge recreational vehicle, a house on wheels. Rebecca saw that the rate was over a thousand dollars a week. "I see," she said blankly.

"With one of these, it's much easier," the boy assured her. "But it still takes a little time to set up. My boss has to check you out." He grinned. "Sounds awful, doesn't it? You also need an international driving permit, a credit card, a ninety-day entry visa, and a whole slew of other stuff. We could get you ready in a couple of days."

Finally, he let her take the leaflet. "I'll think about it," she told him. "But this is a lot bigger than we need."

"Maybe one of the bigger companies would help," he offered. "Avis or Hertz. We're a lot smaller."

"Thanks," she said, forcing herself to smile.

"There are lots of buses going down south," he added. "They're real cheap."

As she walked out into the street, she felt hollow. She was cursing herself for her naïveté. She might have guessed that crossing the border would be subject to all kinds of regulations and controls. And she couldn't sit still while some car-rental company "checked her out." Nor did she want to take a bus. Her instinct told her that public transport would be more dangerous than a private vehicle. The thought of sitting hemmed-in in some train or bus, while guards checked her papers, filled her with claustrophobia. She doubted whether her nerves or Therese's would stand up to that test. No, she would feel infinitely better under her own steam.

She glanced up at the window of their room. It was dark. Therese was nearing the end of her tether, and yet they could not sit in this town forever, staring across the river at Mexico. They had to get across, and soon.

She walked toward the border crossing-point. It was evidently a major route into Mexico, and streams of cars were crawling toward the bridge. Cars were one thing, but surely the border guards couldn't be checking each and every one of these thousands of drivers and passengers? Surely an innocent-looking woman and child wouldn't attract attention?

She walked into a bookstore and bought a AAA Travel Guide to Mexico. The first chapter, about immigration requirements, killed any fond dreams of sailing through the border unchecked, the way she and Ryan had done as young lovers. Those laissez-faire days were evidently long gone.

Her stomach was in a knot as she slipped the book into her bag. If she called Ryan, wouldn't he come at once and help them? But again her instincts rebelled. Not yet. She had already turned herself into a criminal and a fugitive, and had possibly wrecked her career in medicine, something she couldn't even bring herself to contemplate fully yet. She couldn't ask Ryan to do that. Not cold, like this. Once she was across the border, she would call him. Some harder instinct also told her it would be better to call Ryan from Mexican soil for other reasons—to present him with a *fait accompli*, not allow him to argue against their leaving the U.S.

She walked fast, thinking hard, nervous energy flowing through her. They would need a vehicle. They couldn't just walk across the bridge. She would have to risk buying a car after all. They had to look like tourists. So they needed a tourist-type vehicle.

It was dark now. Shops were closing, and the torrent of traffic across the bridge was slowing. Maybe the border closed down at night, she didn't know. It was too late to do anything more. Tomorrow, she would make an early start. Walking through the lobby of the hotel, she waved at the pimply boy, praying it would not occur to him to mention her inquiries to anyone else.

She woke very early, with an idea forming in her mind. Why shouldn't history repeat itself?

She sat up, glancing across at Therese's bed in the cool morning light. Therese's curly head was nestled into the pillow. During the night, Rebecca had heard her groaning, sometimes crying out, but for the last few hours, she had slept heavily.

Rebecca got up quietly and showered. She was thinking over her plan. All it had in its favor was audacity. But she had very little else in her armory *except* audacity. Perhaps fortune would favor the bold?

By the time she got out of the shower, Therese was awake. She was sitting up in bed, hugging her knees. The long sleep had ironed some of the tension out of her face, and she smiled at Rebecca shyly.

Rebecca sat beside her, wrapped in her towel. She smoothed Therese's hair back from her eyes. "You look a lot better. I was worried about you yesterday."

"I'm okay. Are we going to cross the border today?"

"Maybe tomorrow. But we're going to get started on some stuff today, if we can." She looked into the gray eyes. "Are you ready for this, Therese? Got any doubts?"

"You're wrong about Dad and Devon," Therese said quietly. "You really are."

Rebecca was silent for a moment. "Maybe I'm wrong about the details," she said at last. "But I don't believe I'm wrong about the overall picture, Therese."

"Dad will tell you the truth one day," Therese said. "You'll hear it from him. Then you'll see."

"Okay," Rebecca said lightly. "The important thing right now is whether you're ready to face the journey to Mexico. It isn't going to be easy, and you'll need to be brave."

"I know I have to leave the U.S. for a while," Therese said in a low voice.

"You're sure?"

Therese nodded.

"Okay," Rebecca said. "We'll get moving."

They dressed, breakfasted, and went out. Rebecca had seen a small tourist-information bureau at the bus station, and they headed there now. There was a plump Latin-looking girl in the booth.

"Could you tell me," Rebecca asked her, "where I could get my motorcycle fixed, dirt cheap?"

"Dirt cheap?" the girl repeated, looking at them doubtfully. "What make is it?"

"A Harley-Davidson."

"Well, there's a Harley-Davidson dealership on Guadalupe," the girl began, but Rebecca cut in.

"It's an old one," Rebecca added emphatically. "Real beat-up. Actually, it belongs to my husband. He can't afford to spend a lot on it. We need someone who can fix it at the lowest possible price. He's in the Hell's Angels."

"The Hell's Angels?"

"It's a motorcycle club," she said in answer to the girl's skeptical expression.

"I know what it is," the girl said disdainfully. She sucked her teeth in distaste, thinking. "You want Jiménez Cycles," she said brusquely. "He fixes all kinds of old motorcycles for people like . . ." She let the sentence trail off.

"Jiménez Cycles sounds great," Rebecca said firmly. "Is it far from here?"

"You can take a bus." She wrote down the address, and the number of the bus, too. Rebecca thanked her, taking the paper.

"What do we want this place for?" Therese asked, as they went to get their bus.

"We're going to buy a bike, if we can," Rebecca told her.

"A *bike*? To go into Mexico?"

"Buying a car is too complicated, too expensive, and involves too much paperwork."

"But we'd stick out like bumps on a log!"

"I don't think so. Thousands of bikers tour Mexico. If we get the look right, I hope nobody will bother us."

"What look?" Therese demanded.

"The look that makes them look at us, yet past us," she replied.

"I don't get it."

"Maybe I don't, either." Rebecca smiled. "We'll see how it goes."

Therese made a face, but Rebecca hugged her lightly. After a long spell of doubt and fear, she was feeling her courage start to return.

Their half-hour bus ride took them to an area just off Interstate 35, the route they'd taken into Laredo yesterday. The neighborhood was run-down, and evidently mainly Mexican, judging by the Spanish signs on all the shops. They got off, and asked directions. On the way through the noisy street, Rebecca caught sight of a pawnshop.

"Wait here," she told Therese.

She went into the pawnshop, leaving Therese standing uneasily on the sidewalk outside. She unclipped her Rolex from her wrist and pushed it across the counter to the hard-faced man on the other side. "How much?" she asked him.

He gave the watch a cursory examination. "Three hundred dollars," he told her flatly.

She winced. "It cost ten times that."

He shrugged. "Take it or leave it."

She knew she was going to have to take it. "Have you got another watch you can throw in, something I can use until I redeem the Rolex?"

He opened a drawer, and pushed a watch across the counter. It was black plastic and not worth more than a dollar or two, but at least it was running. She knew better than to argue further. "Okay," she said, clipping on the plastic watch. "I'll take it."

She signed the form with an illegible scrawl. The only other thing she had of any value was the heavy braided gold chain she carried around with her everywhere, but seldom wore. It had been her mother's, a present bought at Tiffany's by her father. She would save that for the very last ditch.

She walked out, the extra money folded into her jeans pocket. Getting the heavy watch off her wrist gave her no sense of regret—only a greater sense of freedom and courage. "All done," she told Therese cheerfully.

Jiménez Cycles was located in a narrow alley that opened out onto a dirt yard. All kinds of motorbikes were parked in the yard. The shop itself was filthy, and had the depressing smell of rotting machinery that haunted all such places. It was crowded with an assortment of two-wheeled vehicles—children's bicycles, scooters, and motorbikes. All had something in common: dirt and disrepair. Deafeningly loud rock music poured out of a boom box perched on a high shelf.

On the floor, what looked like a trail bike was lying in a dozen pieces. Two men were picking over the carcass. The younger was a dark boy of around eighteen with a long ponytail protruding through the back of his red baseball cap. The elder was a hugely fat man in his fifties. He was squatting beside the engine. The rolls of fat, like tractor inner tubes that strained his overalls, were quaking with laughter at something the younger man must have said. A heavy mustache stretched halfway around his bloated face. Both looked up as Rebecca and Therese came in. The fat man laughed even harder, as though their arrival had been the climax to a wonderful joke.

"Buenos días," Rebecca greeted them, speaking in her most careful Spanish accent. "Are you Señor Jiménez?"

The fat man heaved himself forward. With his hands braced on his vast thighs, he straightened, still chuckling. His twinkling eyes were almost lost in the folds of lard around his cheeks. He reached out and delicately tweaked the volume knob on the boom box, as though selecting a cherry with banana fingers. The noise level dropped. *"Emilio Jiménez, a vuestro servicio,"* he said with mock gallantry. "What can I do for you ladies?"

"We're interested in buying a secondhand motorcycle," she told him.

The fat man's belly heaved, as though he were suppressing more laughter. "Sure thing." He extracted a cigarette from his pocket and lit it. He sucked smoke deep into his lungs, considering them. Rebecca could hear the rasp of laboring bronchi deep within the citadel of fat. He jerked his head to lead them to the back of the shop. There, he had an assortment of step-through scooters. "Take your pick," he said, beaming.

"No," Rebecca said. "I want a real bike. A tourer."

"A tourer?" he repeated, raising heavy eyebrows.

"I don't care if it's old. It just has to run well. And be strong enough to carry me, my daughter, and a couple of knapsacks."

Jiménez looked from Rebecca to Therese, studying the two shabby Anglo females skeptically. "You ever ridden a full-size bike before?"

"I have a license," she said, smiling as charmingly as she could. "And another thing: It has to be cheap."

"How cheap?"

"Less than two thousand bucks."

He grunted derisively. "A touring bike that runs good and costs under two thousand dollars?"

"I told you, I don't care how old it is."

"Bikes only get so old," he said. "Then they turn into vintage machines, you understand me? The price starts going up again." He started chuckling again, loose masses of lard chasing each other around his belly. Rebecca wondered whether the laughter was genuine amusement, or some kind of nervous tic. "Come on out in the yard," he invited them.

They followed him. His weight made every footstep an effort, his feet plodding heavily as they propelled his bulk along. Therese rolled her eyes at Rebecca. Neither the man nor the place inspired confidence.

Jiménez showed them what he had; most of the bikes were 250's or 350's, smallish machines that had led hard lives and were now in unabashedly poor condition. From her experience, Rebecca doubted whether any of these bikes would get very far before developing fatal infirmities.

"Haven't you got something bigger?" she asked. "Something better?"

"What's wrong with these?" Jiménez demanded, his face wreathed in smiles.

"I need something more powerful."

"You want a real bike?"

Rebecca turned. The boy with the ponytail had followed them. He stood, wiping his black fingers on a rag. He was a very handsome young man, with a hard, mocking expression. "I got a bike for sale," he told her. "If you want a real bike."

"How much?" she asked him.

"Take a look first," he said. "Show her, Papá."

Jiménez burst into another fit of chuckles. Therese watched in fascination as the rolls of superfluous flesh wobbled. "It's not for you," he said. "César is joking with you."

"Why not show me?" Rebecca invited.

"Okay," Jiménez agreed. "I'll show you. *Vámonos.*"

César's bike was parked in a shed at the back of the workshop. Jiménez produced a bunch of keys from under the precipice of his abdomen, and unlocked the door. Rebecca peered in. The bike was an old-style Harley chopper, something she had not seen since her girlhood days with Ryan. The tank was painted with a fluttering pattern of flames. The long, chromed forks jutted forward like something out of *Easy Rider*. The handlebars swooped high in the air, old-fashioned ape-hangers that Rebecca had a strong feeling were illegal these days.

"You want a touring bike," César said. "That's a touring bike."

"Holy cow," Therese said.

Rebecca walked slowly around the machine. It had evidently once been a cherished project, but dirt and neglect were now apparent, and there was a small lake of oil underneath the engine. She wondered whether César had made the bike safe, even ridable, before he'd lost interest in it.

"She goes great," César said, as if reading her thoughts. "She's a classic. The motor's off a 1959 Panhead. I rebuilt it with my own hands."

"I need papers," Rebecca said. Jiménez's pebble eyes were half-buried under oily lids. She sought them out with her own gaze, and held them. "I need papers that aren't going to give me problems. Do you understand what I'm saying, Señor Jiménez?"

Jiménez's lips stretched. "Papers are no problem, *muchacha.*"

"I'm hoping you can recommend a good insurance. And I'm hoping you have all the back records of this bike. You know what I mean?"

Jiménez nodded slowly. He was leering. "I know what you mean."

That sounded promising. "Good," she said.

"Try her out."

"I've never ridden a chopper."

"Nothing to it," Jiménez said, giggling. "Fire her up, son."

César wheeled the machine out of the shed.

"You can't be *serious*," Therese whispered urgently to Rebecca. Rebecca just shook her head. César hoisted himself lithely in the air and kicked down on the starter. No electric ignition, Rebecca told herself. The motor exploded into life with a shattering roar, making Therese turn away, sticking her fingers in her ears. César held the throbbing machine, grinning at Rebecca.

"It's not what I want," she said, raising her voice above the rumble.

"You said you wanted a real bike. You scared now?" He jerked his head derisively, inviting her to get on.

Rebecca hesitated. The machine was preposterous, and yet there was something about it that made her scent possibilities. Nobody would imagine that two runaways would choose a flamed chopper to go on the run with. Everyone would be looking at the bike, not at them. Partly in order to answer the sneering expression in César's eyes, she swung her leg over the saddle and grasped the throttle. The engine responded with a healthy blast. She let in the clutch, and rolled the bike forward. The extended front forks made the steering weird and very light—awful around town, but probably okay out on the highway. She rode the bike carefully around the dirt yard, getting used to the strange riding position, with her feet forward and her arms outstretched. The motor and the transmission sounded okay. The solo saddle, though homemade, was bearable. But the clutch was badly worn and starting to slip, and there were serious rattles coming from various bearings and joints. Basically, the chopper was a piece of junk. The interesting question was when it would fall apart.

She rode back to Jiménez and his son, switched off the motor, and pushed out the kickstand. She got off. There was respect in the boy's eyes now. She hadn't stalled, or fallen off, which was what he'd been hoping for. Therese, too, was looking at Rebecca with something like awe.

"The clutch is burned," she said briskly, "and it needs two new tires. All the bearings are shot. Plus, there's oil pouring out of every cover. How much are you asking for this piece of shit?"

Therese blinked at the crude term. César's expression turned sullen. Jiménez started chuckling vastly. "You got *cojones*, I'll say that for you."

"As a matter of fact, I don't," Rebecca said coolly. "How much?"

"Three thousand dollars," César snapped.

"You're kidding me," Rebecca retorted. "Now tell me the real price."

"That price covers papers," Jiménez said, fat hands clasped across his immense gut.

"I don't want photocopies, or anything like that."

"I mean real *good* papers. Good enough to get you across the river. You understand what I'm saying?"

Rebecca glanced at him, thinking fast. "What makes you think I'm going to Mexico?"

Jiménez's clasped hands jiggled as his belly laughed. "Where else would you be going?" He winked. "You wanna have a good time down in La Gloria? You got some business there? Something good you want to bring back for your friends?"

She kept her expression neutral. "I don't know what you're talking about, Mr. Jiménez. All I want is a peaceful vacation. I don't need any problems with the border guards. If I get any, I'll tell them right off exactly where I got the bike and the papers."

Jiménez rolled his eyes drolly. "Don't worry. You won't have any kind of trouble, *muchacha*. You have my word on it."

Rebecca looked at Therese. Therese, slender and frail-looking, was studying the bike with bemused eyes. Rebecca felt the full, awful weight of responsibility descend on her shoulders. She was taking a wild gamble with Therese's whole life. But sometimes, life depended on a gamble. And at that moment, she felt that time and luck were running out. They had to jump into the chasm.

She squared her shoulders and turned back to Jiménez. "Listen to me," she said in a low voice. "I want two decent tires on the bike. I want the flames painted out. I want a new clutch. I want new plugs, new oil, a new filter. I want new brake shoes. I want all the right papers, in my name, including insurance papers. I want it all to show the bike's been my property for five years. You understand me?"

"Sure," Jiménez said. He was still beaming, evidently unfazed by her requests.

"I also want an extra seat for my daughter. I want leather biker jackets for both of us, and a helmet each. The jackets can be old, but the helmets have to be new. Full-face helmets, not shorties. And I want a pair of gloves each."

"*Coño*," César said. He spat on the ground. "Anything else?"

"For that," Rebecca said, keeping her eyes on the fat man, "I will pay two thousand dollars. In cash. I'll give you a two-hundred-and-fifty-dollar deposit now. If I don't like the way you fix the bike, or if I think the papers don't look right, the deal is off. You get to keep the two-fifty, and I'll find a bike somewhere else."

"You're not gonna find anyone can help you better than me," Jiménez said. "Especially not someone who knows how to keep his mouth shut." With that strangely delicate action of his gross fingers, he made a gesture of zipping his lips closed. Then he winked.

She shrugged. "Is it a deal?"

Both of Jiménez's eyes disappeared into creases while he thought it through. At last, he nodded. "Sure," he said. "When you want it?"

"Can I have it tomorrow?"

"You can have it tonight, if you want," Jiménez wheezed.

"Tomorrow is fine."

"*Bueno.*" He held out a hand. Rebecca took it. She could not even feel the bones through the soft fat.

César wheeled the bike around, ready to start work right away. Jiménez started plodding toward the shop. "Come on," he told Rebecca. "We'll go inside. You can gimme the money, and let's get your details written down."

"Are you crazy?" Therese said forlornly to Rebecca behind the fat man's back.

Rebecca put her arm around Therese's shoulders, and hugged her. "Don't worry," she whispered.

They followed Jiménez. He was still chuckling. Why shouldn't he be? Since the bike was worth precisely nothing, all Jiménez would have to pay for was the paperwork. She prayed it would be good paperwork. She didn't care that Jiménez thought she was a drug runner. In fact, she would rather he thought that than guessed what she really was. If he did, he might figure out there was more money to be made by turning her in than by selling her a worthless bike.

.   .   .

From Jiménez's yard, Rebecca led Therese straight back to the pawnshop. She was going to have to part with her mother's Tiffany necklace in order to pay Jiménez and have enough money left over for the trip. But she swore she would come back to Laredo somehow, before the statutory three months were up, and pick it up again. The necklace was one of the few things she had that had belonged to her mother.

Therese waited outside the pawnshop. When Rebecca came out, she asked, "What makes you think Jiménez can get the right papers?"

"I know places like that and people like him."

"How?"

She half smiled. "As a matter of fact, your father sort of ran wild. He used to hang out around places like that all the time. I learned at his knee."

"Yeah?" Therese said nothing more. On the way back to the Guadalupe Hotel, though Rebecca talked eagerly about the trip, Therese showed no more curiosity about the motorcycle, nor even any apprehension about the crossing. Rebecca sensed that, deep inside, Therese had already given up hope, and had resigned herself to being arrested at the border and taken back to San Francisco. After the past couple of days, Rebecca guessed that Therese probably viewed that prospect with something like relief.

But she herself was at the opposite end of the emotional spectrum. For the first time, she felt gung-ho about their chances. Wheeling that motorbike around the yard had filled her with half-forgotten feelings of what it was like to throw caution to the winds, to fight against the current, to do everything she'd studiously avoided doing all her life. Better to die like a lion than live like a lamb, who had said that? It didn't matter. Right now, that motorbike symbolized everything she was straining after: escape, space, emancipation.

Despite her tingling blood, however, she had to make sure that Therese was prepared for any questions she might be asked. She got paper and pencils at a convenience store, and took Therese back to the hotel to start building a convincing cover story.

•   •   •

Before leaving the Guadalupe the next morning, Rebecca checked out and paid the bill. Whatever happened today, she did not want to extend her stay in this hotel any further. If they had to spend more time in Laredo, they would look for somewhere cheaper and more anonymous. But she devoutly hoped they would be out of Laredo before sundown. Could Jiménez be counted on?

They reached Jiménez's filthy shop an hour later. Jiménez was squatting beside a moped, which was being held upright by his son. He heaved up from his place on the floor, like a vast jellyfish surfacing from the ocean deep. He was beaming. "The *muchacha* with the *cojones*," he greeted her. "You're gonna be very happy today."

"Am I?" Rebecca replied.

"Come take a look."

They followed his plodding steps to the shed. He threw the door open with a flourish. The chopper was gleaming. The flamed tank had been painted black, like the fenders. The engine looked clean, and what remained of the chrome had been polished.

"I did everything you asked for," he told them. "New tires, new paint, new clutch, full service. I even put on a pussy pad." He lifted his banana fingers to his lips daintily. "Oops. I mean a *pillion* pad." He giggled.

Rebecca glanced at the shabby little seat Jiménez had fitted on the rear fender. Therese was going to get a sore backside on that thing. The "new" tires had been ripped off some wreck, and had maybe two hundred legal miles left on them. No doubt the rest of the "service" was in the same mold. But at least the bike would now get through a roadside inspection.

"Beautiful, huh?" Jiménez prompted, caressing the tank. "She runs like silk."

"Let me see the papers," Rebecca said.

"They're beautiful, too." Jiménez grinned as he produced a plastic wallet. Rebecca studied the papers as he laid them out on the seat. All were impressive-looking. As she had requested, the papers showed that she had purchased the bike five years earlier. Jiménez had even provided a travel-insurance form from Sanborns, enabling her to cross into Mexico. Her spirits lifted.

"They look okay," she said cautiously. "They look real."

"Look real?" Jiménez chuckled. "They are real, *muchacha*. As real as you are."

"Yeah." She smiled acidly at the pointed joke.

"All you got to do is sign them," Jiménez told her, stroking the papers. "And . . ." He rubbed his finger against his thumb, signifying money.

"What about the jackets and helmets?"

"I got everything ready for you."

They went back to the shop to try on the clothes. César presented them with two leather jackets, used-looking, with worn studs and a fringe hanging from the arms. They wore colored patches on the back from a motorcycle club called Los Coyotes. César held out the larger jacket for Rebecca to try on. Unsuspectingly, she slipped her arms into the sleeves. As she did so, César moved close. She felt his hands cup her breasts quickly. She swung around, furious.

"Nice fit, huh?" César said, eyes mocking.

"Don't play games with me, little boy," she said in a hard voice, and saw the laughter fade from his eyes.

"Bitch," he mouthed, so his father could not hear.

She jerked the other jacket off the counter to stop him from trying the same trick on Therese. Both jackets were large, but they would be wearing sweaters under them. Cleaned up, and stripped of their Coyote patches, they would be respectable. Ignoring the now-sullen César, they tried on the helmets. The helmets were black and new, as she had ordered, though they were the cheapest available. The gloves offered were so dirty that Rebecca decided to buy new ones somewhere else.

"Happy?" Jiménez asked.

"I guess so." Rebecca nodded. She reached into her pocket for the money. As she did so, she grasped her helmet by the chin strap with her other hand. If César tried any other vicious little stunts, she would crack his skull with it. Or wallop him in the nuts, where it would really do some harm. César saw the action, and narrowed his eyes angrily.

Jiménez counted the money, licking his fingertips every few notes. "I'm gonna give you a piece of free advice," he said, pocketing the wad. "Don't drive at night in Mexico. Okay? You never know what you gonna find sleeping on the road." He spread his arms. "Nice doing business with you, *muchacha*. Get the bike out for them, César."

Rebecca put her arm around Therese's shoulders as they walked out into the yard. In their jackets and full-face helmets, neither of them was recognizable, which was what she had wanted.

César pushed the Harley out of the shed. He propped it on its side-stand and stood back. The expression on his face showed he was going to enjoy watching Rebecca try and kick-start the machine. She had learned how to kick-start Ryan's bike, but that had been a long time ago. Well, she would have to start learning again, right now. She switched on the ignition, twisted the throttle to prime the carburetor, and hoisted herself up on the starter. She came down on the pedal with all her weight. She felt the engine turn, and then heard it explode into life the first time.

Grinning in triumph, she settled in the saddle and revved the motor. The heavy roar filled her with a sense of happy excitement. She turned to Therese. "Don't get your legs too close to the exhausts — they can burn. And don't put your feet down when we stop. Okay?"

Therese nodded. She swung a slender leg over the fender, and clasped her arms around Rebecca's waist anxiously. Rebecca nodded to Jiménez, ignoring his son. Then she opened the throttle, let in the clutch, and the bike surged forward.

The afternoon lines at the border were the heaviest, a four-lane stream of cars inching toward the bridge. That was in their favor. She didn't want some bored cop taking too long over them. The motorcycle was hard to manage in the stop-and-go traffic, but at least wrestling with the handle-bars kept Rebecca's mind off the greater dangers ahead.

It was a clear day with a pitiless blue sky overhead. The sun baked down on them, and the fumes from the cars all around them were chok-ing. Therese kept shifting around on the pillion, making the bike wobble.

She was terribly nervous, and once or twice, Rebecca even had the feeling she was going to jump off and run. But she held tight to Rebecca's waist.

Now that the clutch was heating up, it was starting to slip more and more. César had evidently simply monkeyed with the existing worn-out clutch. Rebecca prayed it would not give up before they crossed. As it was, there was a crunch of gears each time she shifted.

The bike was laden down. Earlier, they had bought knapsacks, bedrolls, and sleeping bags at a secondhand store. The gear was part of their disguise, but would also come in useful for emergencies. Rebecca hoped they looked like all the other vacationing bikers.

They crept slowly toward the border. She could not stop the panic from rising in her. Nightmare visions crossed her mind: arrest, herself in jail, Therese hauled into some awful juvenile home, the end of everything. Her body was starting to go rigid with fear. She tried to relax, breathing slowly and deeply.

As they reached the border controls, the lines of traffic started to divide up. Trucks went one way, cars another. There were border guards everywhere, directing the traffic. The sight of their uniforms sent Rebecca's heart racing into overdrive. She found herself bewildered by the huge signs, the number of vehicles, the signaling guards. She wobbled off course, and the driver behind her honked his horn irritably. For a moment, she thought they were both going to fall off. She twisted the throttle, half by mistake, and the bike roared forward. The back of a bus loomed terrifyingly in front of them. She stamped on the brake, and the tires squealed as they jerked to a halt, a foot from the worn rivets on the bus's tailgate. The bus's muffler pumped fumes at them angrily. Rebecca was panting in alarm at the near catastrophe.

A red-headed guard came walking across to her, a clipboard in one hand, the other on the butt of his pistol. Rebecca clung to the handlebars, desperately trying to stop the disintegrating clutch from dragging the bike forward. She felt like a rabbit waiting to be shot.

The guard stared at them from behind mirrored shades. "Whoa there, ma'am," he said. "Don't cut in line."

"I'm sorry," she panted. "I skidded on some diesel."

"Take it *real* slow from here on, okay?"

"I will."

He nodded. They were out of line, now. The guard glanced around at the confusion they had caused, then waved the clipboard to indicate the lane ahead. "Take your bike down there, stop at the booth, and switch off your motor."

"Okay," she said.

She rolled the bike forward, the long forks wobbling. Under the leather jacket, sweat was pouring down her back, drenching her hair under the helmet. She stopped the bike at the booth and switched off the motor. She dared not get off. Her legs would not have supported her. She felt as though she were having a mild heart attack, her breathing ragged, her whole upper body tight and hurting. Against her back, Therese was trembling like a frightened animal. Surely their guilty terror would be evident to anyone.

The guard with the mirrored shades walked up slowly. He continued walking around the bike, looking at it noncommittally. Rebecca's attention fixed on the red hairs on his muscular forearms, the brushy little mustache.

He glanced up at last. "I need to see your passports and the vehicle documents, please."

Rebecca nodded. She pulled off her gloves and reached into the inside pocket of her jacket for her wallet. In it were their passports and all the documents Jiménez had given them. She passed it to him, uttering a silent, inarticulate prayer.

He flipped the wallet open and checked the papers.

"Wait here, please."

He took the papers and passports into the booth. Rebecca felt her heart sink into the pit of her stomach. Through the blinds on the windows of the booth, she could see uniformed figures moving around. Had he recognized their names? Was there something wrong with Jiménez's papers? Was this the end? She reached behind her and patted Therese's slender thigh in what she hoped was a reassuring way. Therese was motionless. She did not respond.

In front of them, a red-and-white barrier had been lowered. Beyond, the bridge crossed the Rio Grande, straight as a die, pointing to freedom. At that moment, Rebecca knew they would never attain that freedom.

The guard came out of the booth, accompanied by a second man. The second man, ignoring Rebecca and Therese, checked the bike over minutely, comparing frame and engine numbers to the documentation. Rebecca's thighs were strained and shaking. She realized she hadn't put down the kickstand. She was still holding it up. If the bike were to crash to the ground now, it would all be over.

The red-haired guard was looking through their passports now. "You need an entry permit to go into Mexico," he said shortly.

"I—I'm sorry," Rebecca stammered. "I didn't know. Where do we get it?"

"You can get it right here. How long are you planning to stay?"

"I—uh—a week."

"Plan on traveling farther than the border area?"

"We wanted to go down to Monterrey. And maybe come through the Sierra Madre on the way back."

He stared at her. She saw her own face reflected in his sunglasses, frightened gray eyes looking out of the opening in a black helmet. "Bogart fan?"

"I beg your pardon?" she faltered.

"*Treasure of the Sierra Madre.* Bogart's best film." She saw he was smiling slightly at her now.

"Oh. Yeah." She nodded.

He glanced at Therese. "Hi there, young lady. You're Teresa, right?"

Rebecca felt Therese nod yes.

"Are you two related?"

He had asked the question of Therese. Rebecca froze. There was a silence, then she heard Therese say, "She's my aunt."

The red-headed guard nodded. "Uh-huh. Do you have a letter from your parents saying they're happy for you to travel to Mexico with your aunt?"

Oh, no, Rebecca thought in horror.

"My mom's dead," Therese said. Her light voice was calm. "She died years ago. I lived with my dad for a while, but he kind of lost interest in me. He went to Canada. So I've been with Aunt Becky ever since."

The red-headed guard looked at his colleague inquiringly. The other man took the passports and studied them. He was clean-shaven, with thin features molded to his skull. "What's your dad's address?" he asked Therese.

Therese shrugged. "I have no idea. He hasn't written in two years." Her tone of indifference was perfect.

"Teresa lives with me," Rebecca said gently. "I take care of her now. We're just taking a week's vacation together."

"Camping out?"

"Only if we have to."

The red-haired man shook his head. "It says here you're a doctor. What kind?"

"I'm a pediatrician." She showed him her doctor's card. It occurred to her that her image of shabby girl-biker didn't quite square with her occupation.

"Do you have a contact address in Mexico?"

She spoke without thinking. "Dr. Ryan Foster, Hospital Santa Clara, Monterrey."

"A colleague?"

"A friend."

The skull-faced man wrote down the address, took her card, and, without a word, went back in the booth. Through the blinds, Rebecca saw him lift a telephone. Fear rushed up in her, as though she were drowning.

The red-haired man was watching her. "How much cash are you carrying for your trip?"

"Practically nothing," Rebecca said. "I plan to use credit cards."

"Can I see them?"

Rebecca showed him her American Express and Visa cards. At least the name on the credit cards corresponded with her passport and not with the name by which Michael Florio knew her.

The red-haired guard studied them. "Are you aware that gas stations in Mexico don't take credit cards?"

"No," she said, her lips stiff.

"It's a good thing to remember. You have an interesting machine there," he added, looking at the motor with distaste. "If you get into any mechanical trouble, you might have problems finding a mechanic in the Sierra Madre."

"It goes better than it looks," she said inanely. She patted the tank. "We've done an awful lot of miles together."

"Yeah?"

The skull-faced man came out of the booth. He was carrying a clipboard. He gave Rebecca back her medic's card. "You're going to need a thirty-day entry permit," he said briskly. "Don't overstay your time, Dr. Carey. You don't want trouble with the Mexican immigration authorities."

"I certainly don't."

"Okay. Sign here, please."

He handed her the clipboard for her to sign the entry visa. Emotions were surging in Rebecca. She could hardly believe it. Was it really all going to work out, after all? The skull-faced man tore off the slip and handed it to her. "Show that to the Mexican immigration officer," he said. "You folks have a good time now."

Rebecca tried to think of an appropriate answer, but both guards were already stepping back and reaching for the controls. The boom raised. The way was open for them to cross.

Rebecca kicked down on the starter. The Harley roared into life. She gave the border guards a big smile, and set off across the bridge.

The Rio Grande was wide, its water silvery under the brilliant sun. She slowed at the other end and stopped for the Mexican guards. They looked a lot more bored than their counterparts on the other side. Nobody made any comment as she handed them her entry visa. It was stamped and handed back to her. Nobody asked her where she was going, or for what purpose.

Then they were rolling into Mexico.

•   •   •

On the outskirts of Nuevo Laredo, once they had crossed the town, Re-becca pulled up outside a flaking cantina. She stopped the bike. They got off and looked at each other.

Therese yanked off her helmet. Her curls tumbled free. Her face was luminous with joy. "We *did it!*" she yelled, and threw her arms around Rebecca. Rebecca hugged her tight. They laughed together, breathless, hardly able to believe it. "We *did* it," Therese kept repeating. "We're free!"

"I didn't think you'd be so glad to get out," Rebecca said, smiling. "The way you were acting, I thought you'd lost faith in the plan."

"I just got scared," Therese said. "But I never wanted to go back to the U.S. I didn't want to leave Italy. Coming back was like the whole night-mare starting all over again." She stretched her arms up to the hot sun. "But now I'm free."

Rebecca glanced at her black plastic watch. "It's around a five-hour run to Monterrey, and it's getting late. Maybe we should eat, ride on till sundown, then find somewhere to sleep, okay?"

"Whatever you say," Therese said, still delirious with happiness.

They went into the cantina. The place was cool, dark, and relatively empty. Rebecca went to a corner table, and ordered a late lunch for them both.

"You were great back there, 'Aunt Becky'!" Therese said. "I thought they'd stop us for sure."

"So did I," Rebecca admitted. "You were great, too. You sounded so calm."

"I was ready to die." Therese giggled. "Now all we have to do is get Dad and Devvy out here with us."

Rebecca felt her heart turn cold at the words. She met Therese's eyes. "That was not part of my plan, Therese."

"You have to talk," Therese said eagerly. "All three of you. We have to get this ironed out."

"We'll discuss that later, okay?" Rebecca said, trying to sound light.

Their food arrived, a huge tray of fresh orange juice, huevos rancheros, refried beans, and tacos made with fresh, soft white tortillas. Rebecca was surprised by her own hunger. Therese obviously felt the same way. Tension had knotted up their stomachs, but now they ate eagerly.

Rebecca had expected a wave of relief on crossing the border. Instead, she found herself facing a whole new realm of problems. As to what Ryan would say when they arrived, what sort of future she and Therese faced, whether Mexico was far enough away to be safe, whether their journey would take them farther, to stranger and more remote places, she could not even begin to guess.

Anxiously, she got out the AAA Travel Guide and studied the map. The road to Monterrey looked awfully long, with barren spaces between the few towns. In a good car, it would be an afternoon's drive. But on César's chopper, with a failing clutch, they might never get there.

"We'll try and get as far as the Sabinas tonight," she said, "and hope we find somewhere to stay."

"Tell me more about my father," Therese commanded. She was evidently more interested in the idea of Ryan than in the rigors of the journey ahead. "You said before that he ran wild. You mean like me?"

"I guess so, in a way. Though Ryan never did anybody any harm." Tiredness had made her let the stupid words slip out, and she saw Therese flinch. "He was always in trouble with the police," she hurried on. "He used to hang out with some Hell's Angels for a while."

"Is that where you learned about fake papers and stuff like that?"

"Yes."

"So I've been following in his footsteps?" Therese asked.

"That's not genetic, either," Rebecca said, studying the map.

"How do you know? Everything else is."

"Maybe it is, I don't know. Therese, let's talk later. We need to get going. I don't want to be on the road at night, and even though we're in Mexico, I don't want any trouble with the cops, or they might just ship us back over the border. Okay?"

"Okay." Therese nodded, evidently reluctant to suspend the discussion.

"Now's a good time to make a bathroom stop," Rebecca suggested. "We've got a long ride ahead of us."

While Therese went to the bathroom, Rebecca paid up. They went out. She looked at the pool of oil under the bike grimly. More than ever, she was aware of the enormous trust she was asking Therese to put in her.

At least the machine started well. They rolled out of town and onto the freeway. The hot wind buffeted them. There was a lot of traffic, but they were on a good, American-style road, straight and endless, cutting through the wilderness. The thunder of the motor and the vibrations that shuddered up through her neck and back were numbing. She started to feel her mind drifting. She prayed Therese would stay awake, and not fall asleep on the back.

Long before La Gloria, the comfortable freeway ended. Once the slums and the billboards were left behind them, the road narrowed and the wilderness opened up, a vast plain covered by a vast sky, pitiless and unpopulated. Traffic thinned. The little groups of houses they passed were sunbaked and stark, an occasional lone figure on a burro the only sign of life.

Rebecca glanced at the landscape around them, where poverty and drought had cut deep channels, the way hard times will mark a human face. She was remembering that other trip she had taken with Ryan long ago. Was it only fourteen years? It felt like a lifetime. *Nothing ever turns out the way you expect,* she thought. The last time she had spoken to Ryan, he had been focused on his career, on becoming an eminent doctor. But instead of going to some celebrated hospital in Los Angeles or New York, he had chosen an unknown infirmary in Mexico. Instead of treating the rich, he had chosen to treat the poor. Instead of fame, he had chosen obscurity.

And yet, in some strange way, she felt she understood what had happened to him. Over the chasms of time and distance, had her heart not been walking the same sad road as Ryan's? She wondered whether she would still have rushed back to him if he had become, say, a plastic surgeon in Palm Beach.

This was a long way from Palm Beach. The sun started to slip down, a crimson ball that dazzled in her rearview mirror. The hot wind cooled. The Harley was terribly slow. It seemed unable to chug along at more than forty miles an hour. She had been hoping to make a place called Hidalgo, on the Sabinas. But when long purple shadows started sweeping across the road, she knew they would not get to Hidalgo before dark. The thought of riding at night was not attractive—there was a depressing amount of roadkill on the tarmac, and a wandering dog would be enough to bring them down. Away over to the right, she saw lights twinkling in the violet haze. Instinctively, she swung the bike off the road at the next exit, and headed toward the little group of lights, whatever they were.

A crowing rooster woke Rebecca early the next morning. She stared around the plain room, bewildered for a moment. Then she remembered where they were. They had been lucky to find this cheap *fonda* with an empty room. She lay listening to Therese's calm breathing, thinking back over the day before. In this hopeful light, the room didn't look quite as grimy as it had last night. She got up and washed her face. Therese was still asleep, so she put on her boots and let herself quietly out.

The barroom, where they had eaten a primitive supper, was also cleaner than it had seemed to her in her exhausted state last night. She pushed open the door and went out on the street. Their bike was parked where she had left it, but someone had left something pink on the saddle. She went to take a look. It was a perfect rose. She picked it up in surprise. The reason it was so perfect was that it was plastic. She recalled a group of shy young men staring at her and Therese last night in the barroom, and smiled. She looked up. The sky was the pellucid blue of a Mexican winter.

Today she would be with Ryan. Today she would be showing him the child they had made together, all those years ago. She went back inside to wake her daughter.

They were back on the road before nine. Therese was excited and cheerful now, and wanting to talk incessantly about Ryan. Her pangs about Michael and Devon were forgotten for the time being, it seemed. She had hardly mentioned them since Laredo.

The Harley fired up valiantly, but after a few miles, Rebecca found that the clutch was starting to disintegrate. After another hour of riding, the only way she could change gear was by stomping on the pedal without benefit of a clutch, which made the ancient machine jolt and shudder. She cursed César. Stopping and starting were going to be nightmares from now on.

But the motorcycle was starting to develop other and more serious infirmities. The mechanical innards rattled ever more loudly, and the exhaust was spewing smoke, showing that what little oil that hadn't already leaked out was now starting to burn somewhere in the combustion process.

They passed through Sabinas Hidalgo, and entered a vast salt desert. The only variation in the monotony was the black ribbon of the road and the telegraph poles alongside it. Everything else was the color of mustard. On the far distant horizon, something shimmered. Rebecca knew it was the mountain range that marked Monterrey. It looked frighteningly far away.

"This thing sounds sick," Therese yelled over Rebecca's shoulder. "What's wrong with it?"

"I'm a doctor, not a mechanic," Rebecca yelled back. The engine noise was now deafening. She knew that something dire would soon happen, and wondered how people survived if they were stranded in this place. Maybe they just disappeared, and nobody ever heard of them again. The next town they saw, they would stop and call Ryan.

Five minutes after that thought, there was a sudden billow of smoke from the machine between Rebecca's legs, and a blast of fierce heat. She looked down, and saw flames licking around her boots.

"Oh, my God," Rebecca gasped. She weaved onto the side of the road, squeezing the brakes. Without a clutch, there was no way of stopping the machine gracefully. "Hold on," she shouted to Therese, and cut the ignition. The bike crunched to a halt so abruptly that Therese almost fell off, and only saved herself by grabbing hold of Rebecca's neck.

"We're on *fire*," Therese said, disbelievingly.

"Get away," Rebecca commanded, dragging Therese away from the bike.

"But our stuff!"

"I'll get it. Run!"

Therese scampered off among the dry grass while Rebecca hauled at the fasteners that held their knapsacks on. The fire had started in some electrical component, and was blazing merrily. Pretty soon the carburetor would catch fire, and the tank would probably explode.

Panting, she dragged their backpacks off the bike and ran to join Therese at a safe distance. They stood together, watching the bike burn. The fire quickly got a good hold, and flames were soon shooting twenty feet in the air, sending black smoke billowing into the clean blue sky. The tank didn't blow, as she had thought. The machine burned brightly, and with a kind of grace, like a Viking funeral pyre.

"I guess that's it," Therese said.

"I guess."

"What do we do now?" Therese asked.

"Good question." Rebecca looked up and down the deserted road. "Maybe the smoke will bring somebody. All we can do is wait for a lift into the next town, and then call Ryan. I'm so sorry, Therese."

"What are you sorry for?" Therese demanded. "I'm having the best time of my life!"

Rebecca looked at Therese. "You are?"

Therese stretched her arms out to encompass the vast landscape around them. "Aren't you?" she said. "I feel like I'm alive for the first time. Like I really *exist*." She hesitated. "I guess I've been pretty crabby lately. In fact, I've been awful."

"No, you haven't," Rebecca said gently.

"I have." She lowered her arms. "I said some awful things to you in that hotel in Laredo. They weren't true. I've been a spoiled, selfish kid most of my life. It'll take me a while to grow out of it. But that doesn't mean I don't understand just how much you've done for me, Rebecca. How much you've given up. I don't just mean getting me out of Miami. I mean coming to find me in Italy. Caring enough to give up your whole life for me."

Rebecca felt a lump in her throat. She tried to sound light, but her voice came out husky. "Well, I figure I owe you a great deal, Therese. I have something to pay back."

"I don't see it like that," Therese said, holding Rebecca's eyes. "You didn't have to come for me. I didn't have to love you. The way I see it, we don't owe each other anything. Everything we give each other is of our own free will. There's no obligation on either side. I mean it, Rebecca. I want you to see it that way, too."

Rebecca looked at her daughter, a slight, brave figure standing in the middle of desert, with a motorcycle blazing behind her. She smiled. "Are you saying we're friends?"

Therese's misty eyes lit up. "That's exactly what I mean." She stepped forward and hugged Rebecca.

"I'm really confused," Therese said, stepping back. "I think I've been confused for a long time. At least when I'm with you, I can think straight."

"I'm glad."

"It'll take me a long time to get my head clear," Therese repeated. "About you, about Dad, about everything."

"You have all the time in the world," Rebecca promised.

She noticed the crackling had stopped. The fire had died down quite suddenly, leaving a smoldering skeleton. Their ears ringing in the silence, they walked cautiously back to the bike and looked at the machine. It stank poisonously. At least the tires hadn't caught fire, or it would have burned all day.

"The end, huh?" Therese said.

"Yes," Rebecca said. "The end of this old motorcycle anyhow. I guess we were lucky it got us this far."

Late in the afternoon, they reached Monterrey.

Monterrey was a large industrial town, covered with a pall of smog, set against remote, golden mountains. Rebecca stared out at the city. Therese was asleep, her head resting on Rebecca's shoulder. A cattleman had given them a lift from where their bike had burned to a nearby village, where they had taken a bus back to Sabinas Hidalgo. From Hidalgo, they had boarded another bus bound for Guadalupe. From Guadalupe, a third bus had brought them into the city.

As the bus pulled into the depot, she shook Therese awake. "Time to get off," she said.

"Where are we?"

"Monterrey."

"Thank God," Therese groaned. They shuffled off the bus. The concourse was windy and cold, the roar of diesel engines everywhere. "Are you gonna call him now?" Therese asked.

Rebecca nodded. It was finally time to call Ryan. "Yes, I'll call him now."

"Why are you looking so worried?"

"I'm not worried," she lied valiantly.

There was a public telephone against a wall, and Rebecca headed for it, her heart thudding dully. She called the number and asked the switchboard operator for Dr. Ryan Foster. After what felt like an eternity, she heard Ryan's voice come on the line.

"*Sí, digame?*"

She swallowed. "Ryan, hello. It's Rebecca."

There was a long silence. "Rebecca," he repeated, as if not quite believing it. "Where are you?"

"In Monterrey."

"Where, in Monterrey?"

"At the municipal bus station."

"So you came at last," he said quietly.

"Ryan, please listen to me. I have our daughter with me."

"Therese?"

"Yes. We need help."

"Hold on a moment." He sounded stunned. "You have *Therese* with you?"

"Yes. Barbara Florio, her adoptive mother, is dead. I've taken her away from Michael Florio, her adoptive father."

"When you say you've taken her away, you mean . . . ?"

"I guess the legal term is 'kidnapped,' " Rebecca said.

The silence was heavy, interminable. Rebecca felt her heart sink. She tried desperately to inject her voice with all the passion that lay beneath her weariness. "Ryan, I can't explain things over the phone. I wouldn't have done what I did if there weren't very strong reasons. Medical reasons. Humanitarian reasons. You have to believe me. Therese is in a very, very bad situation. The police think she killed her mother. She may have, I don't know. She has some complex psychological problems that I can't deal with yet. But I know one of the causes right off: Her father is in a long-term incestuous relationship with her adopted sister. We've been on the run for four days."

"Jesus, Rebecca. What have you gotten yourself involved with?"

"I've done what I had to do," she said forcefully. "I had to go to Italy to find them. The cops caught up with us. We just got back from Europe four days ago. Therese may have set a fire on the plane."

"She did *what?*"

"It doesn't end there. One of the cops got sick and collapsed at the airport. Heart attack. In the confusion, I took off with Therese."

"Rebecca," he said urgently, "go to the waiting room and sit tight. I'll be there in an hour."

"Ryan, wait," she said.

"What?"

She licked her dry lips. "Think about it before you come."

"I've done all the thinking I need to do," he replied tersely.

Rebecca felt tears swim into her eyes, blinding her. For the first time, she felt that she wasn't completely alone. "Thank you, Ryan."

"Is Therese okay?"

"Sure. She's just tired."

"What does she look like?"

"Curly hair. Slight build. Gray eyes."

"She knows . . . who we are?"

Rebecca looked at Therese. The cold wind was stirring her tangled hair. "I told her a few days ago."

"How did she take it?"

"She's up and down with me, curious about you. But she seems okay. In my humble opinion, that is."

"You're in way over your head," he replied, "but I guess that's where you've always done your best. I'll see you in the waiting room. One hour. Okay?"

"Okay," she said. She hung up.

"Is he coming?" Therese asked.

"Yes, he's coming."

"I knew he would," Therese said.

They went to the waiting room, and huddled together. The place was drafty and dimly lit; the people lining the benches looked poor and weary.

"I keep wondering if I'm going to recognize him," Therese said. For the first time, her voice sounded nervous. "I mean, a person ought to recognize her own father, right?"

"Not necessarily."

"I used to wonder whether I'd ever pass one of my parents on the street somewhere. Whether I'd recognize them, right off." Therese hugged her knees. "When you're adopted, you think about crazy stuff sometimes. I used to worry, what if I wound up marrying my own father? Devon told me she thought about the same thing, all the time. It has happened, you know."

"I know."

"There should be some special recognition between a parent and a child. I mean, not just that they look like each other. Something else. Something spiritual." She paused. "When you first met me, back in Urbino, did you . . . did you feel something special?"

"I sure did," Rebecca said. "I thought I was going to faint right there at your feet."

"Looking back, I think I recognized you, in a way."

They fell into a long silence, each occupied with her own thoughts. Suddenly, Rebecca felt Therese stiffen beside her.

"Oh, my God," she whispered. "I know that's him."

Rebecca looked up. Ryan was walking toward them. For a moment she felt it was a dream, and could only gape at him. His strong arms closed around her, lifting her up. Then it was real, and she was clinging to him, the way a drowning woman will cling to a rock in the current.

"Oh, Ryan," she whispered, her mouth pressed to his neck. "Thank God you're here."

His strength crushed her. At last he released her. Rebecca gripped his arms, drinking him in. He was thinner than he had been, and tanned a deep mahogany, which made the blue eyes even more striking. There were streaks of gray in his hair, and extra lines around his mouth, products of time and harsh sunlight. Therese was a silent presence beside them. She drew the girl in to share their space. "Therese, this is Ryan."

Therese's face wore the quivering tension that Rebecca knew so well. She was very pale. Rebecca glanced from her to Ryan, sharply recalling her own intense emotions on meeting Therese. But Ryan simply put his arm around Therese's shoulders, and pulled her close to his broad chest. He hugged her, kissing the top of her head.

"Therese," he said in a quiet voice, "I never thought I'd hold you in my arms. How are you?"

"Okay," Therese replied, her voice muffled against Ryan's chest. She sounded emotional. He let her go, and smiled at her tightly.

"You sure look okay. The last time I saw you, you had less hair."

Therese stared up at him. Rebecca wondered what Therese had been expecting. Ryan was dusty-looking, exotic. He wore boots, jeans, and a denim shirt with pearl buttons. The shirt was embroidered across the shoulders, and the boots had faded embroidery, too. His face was austere, but the ultramarine eyes were warm as a desert sky.

"Are you hungry or anything?" he asked gravely.

"No," Therese said.

"Let's go then." Taking each of them by the arm, Ryan headed them toward the exit. She had forgotten the quickness of his movements, the way his strength was concentrated, wasting nothing in pointless delay. Outside the building, the sun was already setting, the sky a beautiful abstract of ragged cloud.

"Here's the truck," Ryan said.

The dusty white pickup was parked right outside. The doors had been painted with the logo of the Santa Clara Hospital. Ryan unlocked the door and they climbed in. Therese sat between Ryan and Rebecca.

"We have about an hour's drive," he told them. "Gee, you're tall, Therese. You're going to be a beanpole like me."

Therese didn't answer, just looked away shyly. The girl's short life had been turbulent, Rebecca thought, but this was probably the strangest situation she had yet been in, stuck between natural parents she did not know, in a strange city, far from home.

She herself could not stop looking at Ryan. He had changed in so many subtle ways. He had passed through the fire in some way, and it showed. He was tougher, older, more in command. He had an added strength now that came of experience and maturity. Their eyes met for an instant. Rebecca wondered what they would be saying to each other if Therese weren't there. He smiled at Rebecca, then turned to Therese. "This isn't easy on you, Therese. I'm just here to help. There's nothing you can't ask me. I want you to know that."

"Okay," Therese said in a little voice.

"When we get where we're going, nobody's going to hassle you about anything. You can just be yourself, as long as you like. It's a nice place. You'll see."

Therese nodded again.

Rebecca watched Ryan's hands as he put the truck into gear and drove. She remembered them so well, their blunt strength, their sureness. He wore no rings. She thought of that passionate letter he had written her, of her own cool answer. She wondered whether he had someone new, someone he loved, who loved him.

"The hospital is up in the hills, outside Monterrey," he said. "It's beautiful up there, Therese."

"Am I going into the hospital?" Therese asked with a touch of panic in her voice.

"Oh, honey, of course not," Ryan said, smiling. "I didn't mean it that way. I just meant that you'll be staying at my house. It's a romantic old place. Santa Clara used to be a lung clinic for rich people, before the revolution. Nowadays, it's a no-fee children's hospital."

"You get a government grant?" Rebecca asked.

"A small one. Generally, we survive on private donations. Monterrey is rich, compared to any other Mexican city, and there's a long tradition of charity. Somehow we keep going."

"And you're the boss?"

"The big *tamale*," Ryan agreed. "I got a job under Luís Vargas, the old chief surgeon. He died a couple of years back, and they asked me to take over." He glanced at Rebecca. "So, how did you get to the bus station in Monterrey?"

Rebecca told him briefly about their flight to Texas, the purchase of the motorcycle, the long journey down. Ryan listened without comment, though his eyebrows lifted involuntarily from time to time.

While she talked, he drove them through the chaotic city center and out the other side, skirted the suburbs, and started to climb up into the mountains. It had been a long, long day. The world seemed to be whirling faster around Rebecca, everything around them turning into a blur over which she had increasingly less control.

In the mountain twilight, they reached their destination. The hospital was a large Colonial building, overlooking the city below. Arched colonnades made shady verandas, where Rebecca could see children moving and playing. The architecture was elaborate, and dozens of huge palm trees, obviously planted when the place had been built in the last century, were poised gracefully along the facade. The evening glow was kind to the dilapidated state of the building, giving it a romantic beauty.

"It's lovely," Therese said, looking out.

"I told you it was a nice place," Ryan replied. "I live about a mile from here. I'm going to take you straight there and let you start resting up. We'll do the grand tour tomorrow or the next day."

He drove on. His house was out of sight of the hospital, screened by trees, a simple but comfortable-looking adobe hacienda, painted a smart white, with a flat roof. A big clump of cottonwoods grew in front of it. Behind were two water towers, and behind them, an old barn. Ryan stopped the truck and they climbed stiffly out. The profound tranquillity of the place rushed around them. Rebecca stared. The setting was marvelous, mountain peaks all around, and the distant view of the city below. Ryan touched Therese's shoulder. "You okay?"

She nodded. "I'm okay." Ryan had made no attempt to impose any kind of special relationship with her. He simply treated her gently and kindly, as if he had known her all her life. It was, Rebecca thought, exactly the right approach.

The house had a gracious, simple feel to it, the ends of massive beams protruding from the outside walls, a creeper twining along the arches of the front porch, which overlooked the valley. A smudge of smoke drifted from the chimney.

Ryan led them in. The floor was tiled, and the walls were the same stark white as the exterior. All the furnishings were simple and austere. Rebecca stared around her with undisguised curiosity. The ambience was comfortable, but there were no discernible traces of any female presence, none of the touches a proprietress would have made. However, there was most likely a housekeeper. A fire was burning in a huge fireplace, a welcoming orange glow taking the chill off what must be cold night air up at this altitude, and a meal had been prepared for them—the comforting smell of chicken stew was in the air.

The rooms were decorated with simplicity and grace. The house was older than Rebecca had realized from the outside. The tiled floors were worn with the passage of years. The wooden furniture, too, shone brightly with years of loving use.

"There are only two bedrooms," Ryan said. "You and Therese will have to share. This way."

Dazed with so much travel, Rebecca and Therese followed Ryan. The bedroom furniture was heavy Colonial stuff—an elaborate mahogany four-poster, ornate wardrobes, a heavy brass lamp in the ceiling, all evidently inherited from his predecessor.

"The bed's a hundred years old, but it's comfortable," Ryan commented. Therese, taking him at his word, stretched out on the bedspread, groaning in bliss. Ryan smiled. "Don't you want to eat?"

"Later," Therese mumbled.

Rebecca pulled off Therese's shoes and covered her with a quilt. She and Ryan went to the kitchen together. She looked around the room, seeing the simple way of life depicted by the plain furnishings, the peace. "I envy you," she said quietly.

"You'd trade L.A. for this?" He smiled. "I don't think so."

"I'd give a lot to know what the best thing to do is."

"You've got her," Ryan said, nodding in the direction of Therese's room.

"For now. If she wants to go back to Florio and Devon, there's very little I can do to stop her. But I can never go back. I've burned every bridge I ever had."

Ryan considered her. "Don't take it too seriously," he said. "Every now and then, you need to slash and burn. That way life doesn't build up on you, and you don't lose the ability to develop, move on."

She smiled bleakly, not quite agreeing with his philosophy. "That's exactly what Therese accused me of, on the way down here—always moving on."

"Ah," he said. "She's angry with us?"

"From time to time. I'll just go and check on her."

When she got back, Ryan was setting out the dinner things. "How is she?" he asked.

"Fast asleep. I doubt whether she'll surface much before tomorrow morning," Rebecca judged. "Thank God we're off the road."

"Sit," Ryan offered, pulling out a chair for her. He put some food in front of her. She had little appetite, but knew she should eat something. "How did you find her?" he asked.

She told him about reading the report in Nepal, about her voyage to Urbino, how she had traced the Florios there, how she had managed to trick Michael into letting her enter the family. She described the weeks in Italy, the arrival of the police, then the disastrous plane trip back to the U.S. She told him how she had used Al Reagan's collapse to escape from the airport. She described how she had told Therese who she really was, and Therese's reaction.

She did not, however, mention the complication of her personal relationship with Michael.

"Are you sure Therese set the fire on that airliner?" Ryan asked.

Rebecca shrugged. "No, I'm not sure. I'm not sure of anything. But the burning cloth was pushed into the air-conditioning duct from one of the tourist-class lavatories. She was right nearby when the smoke started."

Ryan was silent for a few moments. "I can believe she might want to kill herself," he said. "I know how common suicide is with unhappy adolescents. But that she'd want to take you, Florio, and Devon with her? And three hundred other innocent people she didn't even know? That's almost impossible for me to believe. I've just met her, but she doesn't seem that crazy to me."

"But she's not herself when she does these things," she said sadly. "It's as if some kind of demon takes her over. It's hard to reconcile that Therese with the child I've been traveling with these last few days."

"If Therese is a serious arsonist, she'll need more than a lot of expert help. She'll also need to be watched. Teenage firebugs can be deadly. We've had one or two up here. One of them nearly burned down the hospital one night."

"She's not a firebug in a vicious sense, Ryan. She doesn't burn things out of spite. She seems to do it as a last resort, as a way of protecting herself when things just get unbearable. It's her last line of defense."

"She may have killed her adoptive mother that way," he said. "Don't lose sight of how serious that is."

"I never do," Rebecca said grimly.

"Another question," Ryan said. "Are you sure Michael Florio was completely fooled about your identity?"

"He wouldn't have let me within a mile of Therese if he'd suspected," she replied.

"I'm not so sure about that reasoning. He may have wanted to use you."

"In what way?"

"He's obviously a resourceful guy. And a determined father. You don't think you've seen the last of him, do you?"

"No, of course not. But right now he's under police jurisdiction. And I have weapons I can use against him when he does arrive. Remember what I told you on the phone?"

"You say he's in an incestuous relationship with the other child."

"Yes, with Devon." She rubbed her face wearily. "Oh, Ryan, it's such a ghastly mess." More than he knew, but she simply couldn't face telling him she had slept with Michael.

"You're exhausted. We'll talk about it tomorrow. Okay?"

"Okay," she said gratefully. She uncovered her face, and looked at him quizzically. "This is a strange situation, isn't it?"

In spite of the tension, Ryan laughed softly. "I guess you could say that, yeah."

"I feel *very* strange," she admitted. "So what do you think about what I've done? Am I certifiable?"

"Sure," he said, his smile deepening. "You're a certifiable mother."

"You don't think I'm crazy? You don't think I've just wrecked that child's life?"

"I think you've saved her," he said. He paused. "I think you've been wonderful, Becky," he went on more quietly. "You've shown tenacity, inventiveness, incredible courage. I could never have done it in a million years. You're remarkable." He smiled. "What are you sniveling for?"

"Oh, God, Ryan," she said, half laughing, half crying. "I wish you could have seen us on that Harley-Davidson!"

"I guess that would have been a sight to see," he agreed, amused.

"Talk about *Easy Rider* . . ." She groped for a handkerchief. He offered her one. Then he took her in his strong arms. She let him pull her close. His smell was achingly familiar, and yet disturbingly new. His body was lean and hard, but there was a place for her head, between his shoulder and his neck, which seemed to have been carved long ago, just for her. She rested her cheek against him, closing her eyes.

"I never thought I would be with you like this again," she murmured.

"*Cosas de la vida,*" he said. "What goes around, comes around."

"I never stopped thinking of you over these past thirteen years," she said quietly. "Of you . . . and her."

He was silent for a long while. "No," he replied at last. "You never do."

She drew back, breathing shakily. "Let me help you clear away this stuff."

"No. Bed for you. I don't expect to see you for another twelve hours."

"Thank you, Ryan," she said simply.

He took her hand and lifted it to his lips. His mouth was warm. "Thank you for bringing her to me," he replied gently. "I won't let her down. And I won't let you down, either."

Rebecca stumbled away to bed.

Rebecca awoke at seven o'clock the next morning, having slept intermittently for twelve hours, as Ryan had predicted. She felt as though sometime during the long night she had turned back into herself again. The three-foot-thick adobe walls kept the house as silent as a tomb. Therese was sleeping peacefully beside her, her lips slightly parted.

She slipped out of bed, showered, and dressed without disturbing Therese, and let herself out of the room. She walked through the silent house to the front porch. Through the glass, she could see that Ryan was standing there, leaning on the wooden rail, staring up at the mountains through binoculars. He was a tall, lean figure against the golden light.

She stepped out onto the porch, feeling suddenly very shy. "Hi," she said. "What're you looking at?"

He pointed. "Him."

She followed his gaze. An eagle was soaring among the mountain peaks, great wings barely moving as he rode on the thermals. It was a beautiful sight.

Ryan turned to face her. He wore jeans and a white high-collared shirt with antique silver buttons. The belt that cinched his lean waist was also decked with an old silver buckle.

"How did you sleep?"

"Like a log. I feel great."

"How's Therese?"

"Still dead to the world. God, this is beautiful. I've never known such tranquillity."

"You want a cup of coffee?"

"Yes, please."

"I'll get you one."

She waited for him on the porch, staring at the grandeur of the scenery. The air was cool and dry. In winter, the hills were tinged with green. In spring, this land would fill with wildflowers. In summer, it would bake golden. The isolation and peace were profound.

Ryan returned with a cup of coffee for each of them. They walked out into the garden. Ryan reached for her hand, and she let him take it, his strong fingers locking around her slim ones. The sky was huge and filled with fluffy white clouds, and the sun bathed the golden landscape. Despite all the horrors she had been through, Rebecca felt uplifted by Ryan's nearness.

"These fits of Therese's," he said. "Can you describe them for me?"

"They're frightening." Rebecca did her best to describe Therese's fits in clinical terms, recounting how they built up and what the aftermath was like.

Ryan was reflective when she had finished. "Does she have sleep disturbances?"

"Sometimes, apparently."

"Go into fugues? Forget who she is, and wander around like a zombie? Exhibit multiple personalities?"

"Not insofar as I know, thank God."

He sighed. "There are a couple of interesting features. As you describe it, she says things during the course of these seizures. And she hears what's said to her, and can remember it afterward?"

"Yes."

"And although there's some incontinence, it's only partial?"

"That's right."

"Those features show that her cerebral cortex is functioning right through the whole thing."

Rebecca nodded. "So it's definitely not epilepsy," she said. "I didn't think so either."

"No, it's not epilepsy."

"She's not putting it on, Ry."

"She wouldn't be able to put it on," he replied. "Ever dealt with hysteria as a clinical phenomenon?"

"I've seen children grow hysterical when they had to face treatment that was painful or frightening."

He shook his head. "True hysterics seldom have any conscious motive of gain. Therese wasn't putting on a histrionic performance. It was a violent escape from an unbearably stressful situation. It looks like grand mal, but it never comes on, for example, when the patient is alone, or asleep, or in some dangerous situation, like crossing a busy street. That happens to epileptics, but not to hysterics."

Rebecca was listening intently. "Then she'll never have another fit as long as she stays out of her stressful family situation."

"Or any stressful family situation," Ryan added.

"Hi," said a small voice. They turned.

Therese had emerged onto the porch, wearing a fawn sweater, evidently Ryan's, that came down to her knees. She seemed dazed, staring blankly at the sight of Ryan and Rebecca.

"I didn't know where I was," she said uncertainly.

Ryan smiled at her. "You're here. What else do you want to know?"

They ate breakfast together. As Therese's dazed air faded, she seemed to be floating along without too many questions, just expanding after the terrible pressure she had been under. Rebecca noted that she couldn't take her eyes off Ryan. This first meeting, Rebecca noted, was so different from her own first meeting with Therese. This time, Therese knew who Ryan was. She could make the observations, the comparisons, ask herself the questions in full knowledge that this man was her father, and that she was his daughter. She envied Ryan that. Looking back, one of the hardest parts of what she had had to do these past weeks was staying close to Therese without being able to tell her who she was.

Ryan offered to take Therese to the hospital with him. "I have to take the night nurses' report now," he said, "and go see my patients. Most of them are about your age, Therese. They'd love to meet you. Would you like to come along?"

Therese looked at Rebecca. "Are you going?"

Rebecca nodded. "Sure."

"You speak any Spanish?" Ryan asked Therese.

"No."

"It doesn't matter. Kids always find a way of communicating. Let's go."

The hospital was so much poorer a place than Rebecca's own hospital in L.A. that she felt almost ashamed. Here, Ryan had to make do with equipment that was outdated by twenty years, with overcrowded wards and barely adequate supplies of drugs. Yet, in another way, it was exactly the same. The same small, sick faces, the same rich rewards and tragic failures.

Ryan was a born pediatrician, Rebecca thought; not just a skilled doctor, but a charismatic personality whom children responded to. That response, she knew from experience, was sometimes half the battle, sometimes the added edge that made the difference between success and failure. His patients glowed in his presence, brilliant smiles lighting up at his word.

She envied him that, too. She knew that she herself possessed the gift in only a small way. No matter how skilled she was, she could not make patients light up the way Ryan did. She was too formal, appearing too cold. She did not know how to unwind for them.

For her part, Therese seemed to be enchanted with Ryan, her gaze following him everywhere.

Well, of course Therese would be dazzled by Ry, Rebecca told herself, but at times she wanted to remind Therese, *I'm also a doctor. I help sick kids, too.*

She seemed to have forgotten all about Michael and Devon, in the way teenagers will. But sooner or later, she would remember, and remember that she had a different life, that Ryan's world was not her world. The reckoning would come, and it might be a very bitter one.

"She seems happy here," Ryan said to Rebecca after Therese had gone to bed that evening. "I've seen no signs of mental instability. All I see is a shy girl who responds to friendship. You've seen her with these Mexican kids, Rebecca. There's instant communication. She reacts spontaneously, with smiles or sign language. She's highly intelligent, and she understands what the treatments entail, how medicine is meant to work." He spread his hands. "What else do you want from a thirteen-year-old?"

"You're seeing her out of the context of the Florio family," Rebecca replied. "When she's with Michael and Devon, she's a different personality. Completely different, believe me. She goes into some remote place inside herself." Rebecca shivered. The desert night was cold, and Ryan had lit a fire in the big fireplace. "That's partly why I took her away, Ryan. To give her a chance to grow into the light, because if she stays with Michael and Devon, she has very little hope of developing normally."

"Want a brandy?"

"Okay." She nodded.

He rose and got a bottle of Mexican brandy, pouring a generous dash of the rich brown liquor into two glasses. They touched glasses silently and drank. The brandy was fragrant and heady, burning Rebecca's lips pleasantly.

"At any rate, I think she likes me," Ryan said.

"Of course she likes you," Rebecca replied with a trace of sarcasm creeping into her voice. "You've done everything in your power to make her besotted with you."

"Come on." He smiled. "Is that the green-eyed monster peeping out?"

"She's a thirteen-year-old girl," Rebecca replied. "And you're a very attractive, charming man. It would be surprising if she didn't respond to you."

"I'm not Michael Florio, Becky," he said gently. "I don't want to seduce her."

"I'm sorry." Rebecca nodded. "I didn't mean to imply anything so hateful. It's just that, after it cost me so much to get to her, to see her throw herself at your feet makes me feel a little . . . jealous."

"You feel jealous because you refuse to see the whole picture," he said, watching her across his brandy glass. "We belong together. We need to start planning our future together."

"I came to you for sanctuary," she retorted, "not to be bullied."

"Who's bullying you?" he asked.

"You are." She watched him with ironic eyes. Against the darkly tanned skin of his chest, a small silver-and-turquoise amulet hung on a leather thong. "You've turned into a bit of a clotheshorse," she commented. "You used to be so unkempt. Now you dress like a country singer."

"Yeah?" he said, corking the bottle.

"Pearl buttons and hand-tooled boots and all. I just wonder who taught you such good clothes sense."

The dark blue eyes were tranquil. "I had a friend. A Crow Indian. She used to be a model. Now she runs a jewelry and fashion-design business in Laredo. She taught me all I know about pearl buttons and hand-tooled boots."

"She give you that piece you wear around your neck?"

He nodded. "She made it for me."

"And you still wear it."

"We parted on good terms," he replied. "Is this the green-eyed monster again?"

Rebecca drank the mellow, smooth brandy. "Did you marry her?"

He touched the turquoise amulet at his throat. "Yes."

She laughed softly. "I might have guessed you married her. It takes a wife to really leave a mark on a man. So what went wrong?"

"We just didn't make each other happy as husband and wife. We got divorced fast."

"That's when you wrote me that letter?" she asked.

"About six months after that."

"It was bad timing, Ry," she said quietly. "That letter arrived practically on the eve of my own marriage."

"I know. So your marriage didn't work out, either?" he asked.

"It never had a chance," she said.

He was silent for a while, his eyes smoky. "Becky," he said at last. "I never found anyone who could take your place. And that's the truth."

She reached out to him. She meant the gesture as one of friendship, but he took her in his arms like a lover. "No, Ry," she whispered, slipping away. "Not yet." She kissed his cheek. "I'm going to bed. Good night."

But she felt her heart pounding as she lay down. What she felt for Ry was not the raw hunger she had felt with Michael Florio. It was something much more familiar. What would happen if she let that familiar tide wash her away? How sweet it would be just to let Ry lift her high up above all her troubles! Then she reproached herself. Why did she keep letting those two impostors, sex and romance, derail her plans? She had to concentrate. It was not over yet, not by a long shot. The darkness came, and she drifted back into it.

The next afternoon Ryan suggested they take a walk up in the mountains. "There are some Mescalero Indian ruins up there," he promised, "and an interesting group of petroglyphs."

The three of them set out from the hacienda. Ryan led the way along a rough footpath, which cut through the hills in back of the barn.

As they climbed, the vegetation grew wild, fearsome agaves starting to produce the huge spikes that would blossom in spring. Cholla and other cacti tore at their denims, and the haunting smell of turpentine bush rose in the clear air. The golden swaths of the peaks above them were stark against the sky.

In an arroyo, they came on a group of six or seven wild-looking men at work. They had lit some small fires and were piling up heaps of vegetation, which they were boiling down in cauldrons. The resulting soup produced an astringent, not-unpleasant smell.

"It's a wax camp," Ryan explained. "They're gathering *candelilla*, wax plant. They boil down the juice to extract a wax, which they use to make shoe polish and candles. They also think it cures syphilis. It doesn't."

Therese stared at the men, who looked to Rebecca like something from the time of Pancho Villa. "I wish I could draw," she said to Rebecca. "I'd draw this."

They kept going, heading up to the ridge of hills that overlooked the hacienda. On the skyline, a group of paloverdes marked the Indian ruins. Only a few mud walls remained of what had once been a village.

It was a lot colder up here than down at the hacienda. A sharp wind swept across the rocks, reminding Rebecca this was still winter. But the views were spectacular, across the mountains and down into the valley.

"This must have been a beautiful place," Therese commented, pointing at the few remaining bits of wall, which were made of mud bricks. "Who were these people?"

"Nobody knows. Ancestors of the Mescalero Comanches, maybe. There's said to be a natural spring up here somewhere," Ryan added, shading his eyes with his palm.

"Where?" Therese demanded, panting with the climb.

"Nobody knows that anymore either, I guess," he replied. "The local Indians only built villages like this where there was a well or a spring. Ancient people thought springs were sacred. Besides, life was impossible up here without water."

"Let's go find it," Therese said. Her cheeks were flushed pink with the brisk wind and the exercise, and her eyes sparkled.

Ryan smiled. "We could try."

"Where do you think it is?"

Rebecca scanned the grays and russets of the hilltop, looking for an outcrop of greenery that might give a clue. "The village must have been built quite close to it, I suppose," she said. "But maybe it stopped flowing years ago. Maybe that's why the place fell into ruin, its water supply cut off."

"Oh," Therese said, sharply disappointed.

"Springs are capricious," Rebecca explained. "They'll stop flowing without warning or explanation."

"But don't they start again?" Therese pressed.

"Sometimes, I guess."

"I want to find that spring," Therese said urgently.

Rebecca smiled. "What for, honey?"

"I just do," Therese replied obstinately, her face set. She had obviously made her unpredictable mind up, so Rebecca indulged her. The three of them started hunting for any signs of water, wading through the brush and clambering across the rocks.

"Are there snakes up here?" Rebecca asked Ryan.

"Yes, but watch the cholla," Ryan warned. "They're a lot worse on ankles than snakes."

Rebecca watched Ryan's lean, athletic figure as he climbed. Every movement he made was so economical, so precise.

Suddenly, she heard Therese give a shout. She climbed across the rocks toward her. Therese was squatting beside a lichen-covered cairn of stones. Her head was cocked to one side, her face alight. "Listen!" she said.

Rebecca listened. From within the pile of stones came the faint sound of gushing water. "I hear it!"

"I think you found it," Ryan said, joining them.

"Let's uncover it," Therese said excitedly. She was already pulling stones away from the cairn. Rebecca looked up at Ryan. Together, they joined Therese in her caprice. Some of the stones were so heavy that it took the three of them to lift them away. As they made inroads, the sound of running water grew louder. When they had opened a cleft in the tumble of rock, Therese stuck her head inside. "Look!" she said triumphantly.

Rebecca peered in. The remains of a stone well could be seen, dark and in poor condition. But the dull light glittered on running water down there, emerging from the bowels of the earth and flowing off through some long-forgotten fissure.

Therese was bright-eyed with her success. "I found it! I found it!"

"Yes, you did," Ryan said. "You found the source." He looked around. "There used to be people here, children playing, life. I wish I could have seen it."

"You can't make the past come alive again," Rebecca heard herself say in a warning tone.

"You can if you really want to," Ryan replied.

Therese reached down and managed to touch the water with her fingertips. She tasted the wetness gleaming on her fingers. "It's good water," she said.

Rebecca felt Ryan's eyes on her. She met them briefly, feeling a shiver pass through her.

They climbed down from the ancient village, each wrapped in thought.

But as they approached the hacienda, Rebecca saw that a strange vehicle was parked out front, beside Ryan's truck, a white Land Cruiser. Two people were standing on the porch, waiting for them.

She grabbed Therese's hand on one side, and Ryan's on the other, squeezing tight as she recognized the figures of Michael and Devon.

"It's Dad!" Therese yelled. She tore her hand out of Rebecca's grasp, and before Rebecca could stop her, she was running toward Michael.

"How the hell did they find you?" Ryan asked.

"I don't know." Feeling sick to her soul, Rebecca watched Therese reach Michael. Michael's arms closed around Therese, holding her tight.

"Are you okay?" Ryan asked Rebecca quietly.

"No," Rebecca said. She was shaking.

"You want me to call the police?" Ryan asked.

She shook her head. "Not yet." *I should have kept on running,* she was telling herself.

They walked down to Michael. He was standing tall and straight, his arm around Therese. He was formally dressed, in a charcoal-gray suit, white shirt, and dark red tie. He must have traveled a long way to find her, but there was no hint of weariness around the powerful figure. Devon was holding Therese's free hand. Her blond hair was tied back in a ponytail. She looked exhausted.

Michael wore metal-rimmed sunglasses. He took them off now, and the dark, deep-set eyes met Rebecca's with a physical jolt. "Hello, Rebecca," he said.

"Hello, Michael," she said, her mouth dry. "How did you get here?"

"We flew to Monterrey," he replied tersely. "Rented the car and drove up here."

"I mean, how did you know where to find us?"

"Therese called me from Laredo," he said. "She told me where you were going."

Rebecca met Therese's eyes. She must have done it that first evening in Laredo, after that bitter outburst. She had gone out, leaving Therese watching TV. "Oh, Therese," she said gently. "I asked you to tell me before you did anything."

"You have to talk to each other, Rebecca," Therese said. She sagged against Michael, clinging to his arm. "You have to tell him who you are. You *have* to!"

Michael looked down at Therese's face. "What are you talking about, Therese?"

"He doesn't know," Therese said to Rebecca, her eyes holding Rebecca's with a kind of desperation. *"Tell him."*

Michael's eyes met Rebecca's. "Go on, Rebecca," he said quietly. "Tell me."

"I would have thought you'd have guessed by now, Michael," Rebecca said wearily.

"I haven't," Michael said, with a hint of impatience.

Devon was staring at Rebecca with a kind of fascination. "Oh, my God," she gasped suddenly. "She's Therese's mother."

"Yes," Rebecca said, nodding. "I'm Therese's mother."

Devon stared at Rebecca blindly. Her knuckles were white as she gripped Therese's hand.

Michael was frowning. "Therese's mother? What the hell do you mean, Rebecca?"

"I gave birth to Therese thirteen years ago. She's my daughter."

She watched the realization dawn on Michael. It seemed to be an effort for him to take it in. Like Devon, he had paled. "Why—why did you hide this from me?" he asked blankly.

"I'm sorry, Michael," she said.

" 'Sorry'?" he echoed in a flat voice. He seemed to sway. She felt almost sorry for him right then.

Devon spoke, her voice high and shaky. "We should have guessed. Why didn't we?" Her face was tight. The impact of the realization had shaken her to the core, too. "She even looks like Therese. The same hair. The same eyes. The same voice."

Michael cupped Therese's chin in his hand and pulled her face up so that he could look into her eyes. "How long have you known, Therese?"

"She told me after we ran away from the police. Dad, please don't be angry with her. Please, Dad."

Michael let her chin go. "You planned this from the start," he said to Rebecca. He still couldn't quite believe it, she realized. He was thinking out loud. "You set the whole thing up. Came to Italy. Laid a trap for me. Tunneled your way into my family." His eyes were suddenly flint-hard. "Did the police put you up to this, Rebecca?"

"Of course not," she said quietly. "Would I have run away in Miami if they had?"

"She's not a spy," Therese said. "She loves me, Dad. Just like you do." Her voice was breaking, and tears were making her lashes gleam. "Don't be angry."

"I'm not angry, honey," he said.

"I just wanted you to *talk*," Therese whimpered, frightened by Michael's expression.

Michael nodded mechanically. "Don't worry. You did the right thing, calling me."

"Michael, there's something else you have to know," Rebecca said. "This is Ryan Foster. He's Therese's biological father."

Michael stared at Ryan. He managed a death's-head grin. "I see. Any more surprises up your sleeve, Rebecca?"

"No."

Michael rubbed his face and neck with his palms, as if he felt ill. "I want to speak to you in private. Will you grant me that courtesy?"

"I don't have much choice, do I?" she said dryly.

"You do," Ryan said grimly. "I'd rather be present. I'm concerned in this."

"Not in what I have to say," Michael replied. "Right now, this is between me and Rebecca."

"It's okay, Ryan," Rebecca said.

Michael pushed Therese gently toward Devon. "Go talk to your sister," he said. "You two have missed each other. Can we go inside, Rebecca?"

Therese and Devon walked down into the garden together, while Rebecca went into the house with Michael. Ryan sat on the porch, watching over the girls.

She led Michael to the sitting area. She pointed to the comfortable, worn club chairs that flanked the fireplace, but he shook his head, staying on his feet.

"Why didn't you tell me who you were?" he asked.

"I wanted to, at times," she replied, her throat tight. "I was afraid of what would happen, if I did."

"Afraid?"

"Afraid you would throw me out. Or worse. And that I'd never see Therese again."

She'd expected him to be in a fury, but now he was almost frighteningly possessed, the cruel mouth steady, the eyes level. He had already assimilated the shock somehow. "Nobody has ever been able to deceive me the way you deceived me," he said, his voice soft. "You were very skillful. But things would have worked out a lot differently if you'd been honest with me. We'd all be a lot better off right now."

"I find that hard to believe. I don't know how you didn't guess who I was, in Italy."

"I was blind," he said bleakly. "I don't often make mistakes. But I've made several over you, Rebecca. Too many. You told me you trusted me. Why didn't you stick with that?"

"How could I trust you, Michael?"

"I trusted *you*." He shook his head. "Why did you run out?"

"To save Therese. I took the chance that offered itself. It wasn't planned, Michael. How is Detective Reagan?"

"He died," Michael said in a flat tone.

Rebecca felt her knees go weak. She swayed. "Oh, no."

"They got him to a cardiac unit in Miami, but he had another attack a couple of hours later. By the time Devon and I got back to San Francisco, he was dead."

"Oh, God."

"It's not too late, Rebecca."

"Not too late for what?" she asked.

"Therese has to go back. You both do."

She uncovered her gaze. "Have you told the police where we are?"

He shook his head slightly. "Not yet. When Therese called, we didn't even pack. We just got in the car and drove to the airport."

"Therese is never going back," Rebecca said. "I'm keeping her."

Michael's face hardened. "You can't keep her," he said. "She's not yours to keep."

"She is now."

He looked around the room, taking in the heavy pine beams, the thick walls, the simple furnishings. "What are you planning here, Rebecca? To set up house with this hippie doctor?"

"We're Therese's parents."

"No," Michael said. "He's not her father. And you're not her mother. I'm the only parent Therese has."

"You're talking about pieces of paper, Michael. We're beyond all that. Here, I'm her mother, and Ryan's her father. And nothing you can say or do will change that."

"If you had cared for her for thirteen years," Michael said, his voice low and passionate, "if you had housed her, and clothed her, and fed her mind and her body, and made her into what she is now, I would feel some sympathy with that kind of drivel. But you didn't." His hands were closed into rocky fists. "You abdicated all that before she was even born. So did Ryan Foster. You threw her away to follow your own selfish path. Barbara and I brought her up. Neither you nor Foster, in your entire spoiled, self-centered, irresponsible lives, could ever have the remotest idea what that means."

"How dare you? After what you've done to those girls, how *dare* you accuse us of irresponsibility?"

"What have I done to them, Rebecca?"

"Oh, come on," she retorted. "Hasn't Devon told you, Michael?"

"Told me what?"

"That I know about you and Devon. Your relationship."

His eyes narrowed. "Have you got some more surprises for me, Rebecca? What exactly has Devon told you?"

"That you and she have been lovers since she was nine years old," Rebecca said, nearly gagging on the words.

He was silent, staring at her. "And you believed her?" he asked quietly. "Is *that* why you ran out on me?"

"I heard you making love. I saw her coming out of your room, naked, in the middle of the night. She told me everything, standing there naked in the corridor. Why should I disbelieve her?"

"Because if that's what you saw, she set the whole thing up to suck you in," Michael replied. "It was nothing but a charade."

Rebecca held up her palm, as if to ward him away. "Please, Michael. You may be a lot of things, but you're not a coward. Have the courage to admit this."

He grimaced. "You were dealing with Devon's fantasies. Not with reality. Devon has a powerful erotic imagination. She can't always separate what's real and what's her own fantasy. And she regularly walks around the house naked at night. She always has, since she first came to us. Sometimes she's asleep, sometimes awake. She does come into my room while I'm sleeping. I don't always wake up. It would be easy for her to wake you, then stage a little sexual theater for your benefit." His calm was massive. It disturbed Rebecca deeply.

"Devon's fifteen," she said. "That's way too young to invent such vicious lies."

"You have a hospital two miles down that track," Michael said impassively. "Take her there and have one of the doctors check her over. She's a virgin, Rebecca. Medically, legally, and in every other sense."

She hesitated. "Sex doesn't have to entail penetration."

"I've never had any kind of sex with Devon," Michael replied. "Have you told Therese about this?"

She nodded slightly. "Yes."

Real fury flickered like lightning in his eyes. "You poured this filth into Therese's head, too? Hoping to alienate her from me? I can't believe you would be so vicious, Rebecca!"

She felt a pang of real guilt. She looked out the window. Devon and Therese were sitting together in the garden. The sunlight was bright on

Devon's hair. She was holding Therese in her arms, stroking her. "I felt she had to know," she said in a low voice.

"Barbara was unbelievably cruel to those girls," Michael said. "When we were breaking up, Devon told her that she and I were lovers, thinking Barbara would just let her go with me. But Barbara went crazy. She had Devon checked out by three doctors. The hymen was intact, they said. When they told her Devon was still a virgin, Barbara whaled her with the cord of a lamp. She still has some scars." His dark eyes met hers. "But Barbara never got the poison out of her system. Are you going to be the same?"

"You're trying to tell me Devon has delusions?"

"Devon used a lie to protect what was most valuable to her. She tried the same thing on you. It worked both times."

She felt her skin grow cold. Was it possible he was telling her the truth? She no longer knew what was true and what was false.

"If you don't believe me," he said, "ask for a medical examination to prove virginity. An interview with a psychiatrist. Anything you want."

"I don't want Devon interviewed or examined. Even if you haven't screwed her physically, you've screwed her mentally. You've screwed them both."

"Barbara screwed them," he cut in, his voice hard. "She was *sick*. All their problems started and ended with Barbara. Not with me. She did everything in her power to destroy our happiness. But she's gone now. We all have a chance now. Including *you*. Now that you know the truth, you have to come back." He walked toward her.

"Please stay away from me," she said, her voice tightening.

"I can't," he said, his voice suddenly rough. "I still love you, Rebecca." He was making an effort to control his emotions. "I love you, and I want you to come back to me. To marry me, and to be a mother to those two children out there."

"You're crazy," she whispered.

"No. You are, if you think there's any future without me. Ryan Foster could never be your man. He left you thirteen years ago because he was too weak to shoulder the burden. He's no different today."

Michael reached for her. She tried to evade his embrace. He pulled her almost brutally to him. As she gasped in shock at the passionate violence of it, Michael's mouth closed on hers. It was a kiss of blazing hunger, fierce and thrusting.

Rebecca felt herself respond to the blind, raw emotion in his kiss. She felt the fire awaken in her own body, an impulse that made her press against him, arching her throat. Her hand was on his powerful chest, and she could feel the wild thudding of his heart. This wasn't playacting. He loved her, wanted her with an overwhelming intensity.

For a few seconds, the kiss burned, as if the door of a furnace had been opened. Then she broke away. "Enough!"

"Come back with me," he said urgently. "For God's sake, trust me, Rebecca."

"How can you even *think* of taking Therese back to San Francisco? They'll crucify her, Michael! Is *that* what you want?"

"She cannot live as an outlaw for the rest of her life," he replied. "We have to deal with the truth, whatever it is, or she'll go insane. We'll all go insane."

"I thought you took her to Italy to protect her!" Rebecca said. "Now you want to throw her to the wolves?"

"I took her to Italy to give her breathing space. But it's over, Rebecca. We all have to see this thing through, once and for all. Trust me to know that things will work out!"

"You keep saying that, but it means nothing, Michael, *nothing*."

"It means something," he said quietly. "Trust me."

"How do you expect me to trust you?" she said, shuddering as she drew back from him.

"How do you expect me to trust *you* after what you've done? And yet I do. Rebecca, I love you. I don't want to do this without you."

She tried to turn away as he bent to kiss her again, but he pulled her face back, cupping her chin in his palm. His mouth was warm and tender this time. He took her in his arms, compelling her to accept his kiss. His strength was formidable. In his every movement, he was so sure of what he was doing, indifferent to her resistance. Was it passion? Or was it something much more calculating? Her body stiffened. She pushed away from him a second time, her breath rasping in her throat.

"Ryan!" she called. "*Ryan!*"

Michael stood immobile as they heard Ryan's boots thudding quickly down the corridor. He came into the room, his face dark. "What's going on?" he demanded.

"Nothing," Rebecca said, wiping her mouth. "We're through talking, that's all."

Ryan faced Michael. "You bastard," Ryan said. For a moment there was the red glare of physical violence between them.

"I don't want to have to hurt your friend," Michael said quietly to Rebecca. "Tell him to back off."

Silently, Rebecca put her hand on Ryan's arm. The muscles were hard with tension.

Michael nodded toward the garden. "Those are my daughters, Foster. They've been together all their lives. I don't intend to split them up—or to lose either of them—just because you and Rebecca are having second thoughts, thirteen years too late."

"You have no legal rights here," Ryan told him grimly.

Michael ignored him, concentrating on Rebecca. "If Therese wants to come back to me, you cannot stop her."

"No," Rebecca said, "but I would come with her. And whatever you and Devon plan to do to her, I'll fight you every inch of the way, Michael."

He stared at her for a long while. In his dark eyes, emotions were stirring, but she could only guess what they were. His face was like granite. At last, he spoke in a soft voice. "I've never admired any human being the way I admire you, Rebecca. You belong with me."

"No, Michael."

"For that reason, and no other, I'm not going to take Therese right now. I'm giving you time to talk to her. To explain that you're both coming back with me." He laid a card on the table. "We're staying at this hotel," he told her. "Don't try to go anywhere without telling me." Michael walked to the door. In the doorway, he turned. His magnetic gaze reached for Rebecca's. "I meant every word, Rebecca. I always will."

They followed Michael outside. He walked down to where Therese and Devon were sitting side by side. Ryan's eyes were bitter with hurt, and she knew why.

She took a shaky breath to steady herself. "I should have told you before, Ryan. I'm sorry. While I was living in Italy, I got involved with Michael Florio."

His mouth tightened. "I just figured that part out. What exactly does 'involved' mean?"

"I slept with him. Once."

She watched his eyes grow even bleaker. "Jesus. Was that smart?"

"No, it wasn't smart."

"I didn't imagine you could stoop to that," he said grimly.

"I would have stooped to anything to get Therese back," she retorted, angered. "But as it happens, I didn't plan sex with Michael. It just happened."

"Nothing 'just happens' to you. You're the arch-planner."

She watched Michael talking to the girls. "I'm just trying to tell you what happened between me and Michael."

"Are you telling me you're in love with him?"

"I thought I was, for a while. I thought I could love him, even if he was a killer. I thought that if he *had* killed Barbara, he'd done it out of desperation, for the girls. I could almost understand that. But then Devon told me about the incest thing. After that, I could hardly bear to look at him. I felt as though he'd defiled me in some way, as though he'd forced me to participate in his sickness. Now he says Devon was lying."

"And you believe him?" Ryan asked incredulously.

"I don't know."

"Are you going back to him?"

"If Therese decides to go back to San Francisco, I'll have to go with her."

"What did you bother to come to me for?" Ryan asked harshly. His face was as flinty as the craggy stone wall behind him. "Why are you here, Becky? Why did you bring Therese to me?"

"We needed help, Ry."

"Is that all?"

"I never promised anything else. I only asked for help."

"So this was just a stop along the way for you?"

She turned to him. "Don't be so harsh. Therese is the one who needs help. Not you. Not me." She touched his arm. "Maybe you'd be better off without us," she said, more gently. "We can only be trouble for you. Michael is very dangerous, believe me."

"I'm prepared to face trouble," Ryan said.

Michael and Devon were coming back up the garden path. Therese was left on the stone seat, huddled into herself. Michael paused for a moment to look at Rebecca. He said nothing, and made no sign, but Rebecca could feel his gaze strike into her. In silence, she and Ryan watched them get into the Land Cruiser and drive away.

Rebecca walked slowly down the garden path to Therese. The girl was sitting hunched in a tight ball. She touched Therese's shoulder. "How're you doing?"

"Okay," Therese said in a tiny voice. "Are you angry with me?"

"Of course not. You had every right to call Michael. I just wish you'd told me first."

"I was scared you'd stop me. Or run away. Or something."

"I'll never run away from you again," Rebecca said gently. "You can be sure of that."

Therese had picked a flower, from which she was shredding the petals, one by one. "I want it all, Rebecca. You, and Dad, and Ryan, and Devon. I don't want to have to choose."

Rebecca sank down on the bench beside her. She smiled sadly. "I don't think you can have it all."

"Why not?"

"It isn't that simple."

"Did you tell Dad what Devon said?"

"Yes."

Therese's face was pathetically eager. "And? He told you it was a lie, didn't he? Didn't he?"

"Yes. He said it was a lie."

"You have to believe him, don't you?"

Rebecca was silent for a while. "Therese," she said at last, "it may have been a lie. But there's too much that troubles me about Michael. Too many questions that have no answers. The truth is, I believe nobody can ever really know a man like Michael. He demands trust, demands love, but he never shows you his heart. I can't trust like that. And I can't love like that."

"Why not? I do!"

"Listen to me, honey. Michael has cared for you all your life, and that can't ever be wiped out. But you can't have it all. That isn't possible. You have to look back over your life, and decide whether you'd rather make a new start with me, even though you know very little about me. And even though you do know very little about me, I can promise you now that I love you with all my heart, and that I'll do everything I can to make sure you grow up happy, and able to fulfill yourself. And that goes for Ryan, as well. He wants to be a part of your life. Like me, he's spent the past thirteen years in pain, because we made the mistake of giving you away. He wants to make it up to you, in any way he can. Any way you'll let him. And neither of us wants you to go back to San Francisco. We don't believe you'd get a fair hearing."

"Do you think I killed my mother?" Therese asked at last, her voice still.

"Only you can know the answer to that."

"Yeah, but do *you* believe I did it?"

Did she believe it? Would she allow herself to? "No," Rebecca said, answering herself as much as Therese. "I don't. I think it was an accident. I think you have feelings of guilt and pain, and you're mixing them up with the idea that you were somehow responsible. Maybe there's even a touch of melodrama in it all. All those poems in your diary—I was shocked at first, but later on I realized I couldn't quite believe them. People of your age often feel emotions that aren't logical."

"But if I didn't do it, shouldn't I go back and face the police?"

"Therese, you don't know what you're saying."

"If I said I was going back to San Francisco, would you come with me?"

For a moment, her throat was dry, unable to produce an answer. "I don't want to lose you, Therese."

"Does that mean yes?"

"Yes, that's what it means. But I think you would be in terrible danger if you went back. And I might not be able to help you."

"I can't keep on running forever," Therese said. She was left with the bare calyx of the flower in her fingers, like some stark kernel of truth she'd uncovered. She twirled it slowly. "Sometime I have to face it."

"That's what Michael said just now. I strongly disagree. I think you stand to gain very little, and you could lose your whole life."

Therese said nothing. Rebecca did not want to pile any more pressure on Therese right now. She patted her shoulder and rose. "Let's go inside."

She awoke just before dawn, tearing herself out of terrifying dreams. She checked on Therese, who was sleeping peacefully beside her, then pulled on her wrap and went quietly out of the room.

She could smell coffee; Ryan, too, must be awake. She went to the kitchen, poured herself a cup from the machine, and went to find him. She knew where he would be: sitting on the porch, staring at the mountains. She pulled her wrap close against the chilly morning air as she opened the screen door. He was a dark silhouette against the velvet-blue sky.

"Hi," she said softly. "You woke early, too?"

"I haven't slept at all," he replied.

She sat beside him, shivering slightly. "I'm sorry, Ry. I should never have involved you in all this. What I've done is a hundred percent irresponsible."

"No," he replied quietly. "What we did thirteen years ago was a hundred percent irresponsible. We should never have given her away."

She clamped the hot cup between her palms. "Do you really feel that?"

"I didn't at first. At first, I kept trying to convince myself that we'd done the right thing, the *only* thing. But over the years, I had to face that I'd thrown away the most important things in my life."

"Ryan!"

"It's true," he said. "For years I waited for love to come. I married, and couldn't find it there. I looked for it in my work, and couldn't find it there. It took years for me to realize that I'd had all the love I was going to get in this life. And that I'd given it away."

He didn't need to say any more. Rebecca felt a lump in her throat. The sun was climbing over the rim of the earth, turning the mountains gold and blue in the crystalline air. "We can't go back."

"Can't we?" he asked softly. "Isn't that exactly what we should do? Go back and start all over again, the way it should have been?"

"How, Ryan?" she asked. "Michael Florio is just down that road, and he isn't going to let go. I'm so afraid of losing Therese. What if she decides to go back with him?"

"We can't let her make that choice," Ryan said.

"How can we stop her?"

"By showing her an alternative," Ryan said.

His tone made her heart lurch. "You mean . . . us?"

"That's exactly what I mean. The three of us belong together. If we show her that we're committed to each other, she'll know she has a real family."

"It can't be as simple as that," she said, her voice unsteady.

"Maybe it can be as simple as forgiveness," he said, laying his hand on hers. "Maybe all we need to go back is to forgive each other. And ourselves."

She was trembling. "Oh, Ry," she whispered, turning back to him blindly. "I forgave you years ago."

He took her in his arms, and started kissing her face, devouring her mouth, her cheeks, her eyelids. She arched her neck and he kissed the hollow of her throat, that favorite place he had always loved to kiss. She ran her fingers through the thickness of his hair, losing herself in the scent and feel of him. "I missed you so much, for years," she whispered. Her heart was pounding wildly.

He looked into her eyes. "We can go back," he said roughly. "Believe it, Rebecca."

"It seems impossible," she said.

"Parenthood is a two-person job," he said. "So is love. So is life."

"I know."

"Do you still care for him?"

"I can't forgive him, if that's what you mean."

"That isn't what I mean," he said. "And you know it."

"Ry, I've loved you half my life, if that's what you want me to say."

He smiled. "It's a start. If Therese chooses to stay, will you marry me?"

She gasped. "Jesus, Ry."

"Is that a yes?"

"It's a maybe," she said slowly.

"And if Therese chose to go back," he said, "would that change your maybe?"

She thought for a long time. "No," she said at last.

"Thank God," he said. "Then everything else follows from that."

"Oh, Ry," she breathed, as he pulled her against his hard body. "What if we lose her? What if we lose her again?"

"We won't," he vowed. "This time, we won't. You've given us a miraculous chance to put right what we did wrong all those years ago. I've been praying for this, without knowing it, ever since Therese was born."

She huddled against his strong shoulder, wanting so much to believe him, to believe that it could be as simple as that. After a while, he kissed her brow. "I have to operate at eight," he told her. "I have to get ready and scrub up. Drive me down to the hospital. That'll give us a chance to talk, and you can keep the car for today."

She nodded, and went back to her room. Therese was still asleep, and Rebecca had to shake her awake to tell her where she was going. She mumbled something, and stretched sleepily as Rebecca dressed.

"We can't let her go back to San Francisco," Ryan said, as Rebecca drove him along the dirt track to the hospital. "I can believe Therese has been a difficult child, maybe even a delinquent. But I can't believe she killed her mother. If she goes back, she won't just be going back to the sick family situation. She might be made a scapegoat for someone else's crime."

Rebecca nodded. "I know."

"Does *she* know? Does she understand the implications?"

"I doubt it. Think how devastating that would be for her."

"Then we have to talk to her, Becky. The first thing we have to do is to show her that you and I love each other, that we're planning a life together, around her."

She felt her heart lurch. Was this all going way too fast? Yes, it was. But what if it was going *right* for once?

"We need to show her that she's no longer in a vacuum," he went on. "That there is an alternative to what Florio is offering. You agree?"

"Yes, Ry. I agree."

"Then let's do it today."

She nodded without speaking, lost in her whirling thoughts. They pulled up in front of the hospital. "What have you got scheduled?" she asked him.

"Two orthopedic procedures. I persuaded a top bone man to come up from Mexico City. I'm just the assistant this morning. We're going to straighten a little girl's legs and try and help a curvature of the spine."

"Good luck," she told him, kissing him on the lips.

"Yeah. You, too. As soon as I get back, we'll speak to Therese. Okay?"

"Okay," she said.

She got back half an hour later to find a car parked outside the hacienda. Her heart jolted into overdrive.

It was Michael's Land Cruiser.

She skidded to a halt and jumped out. A blustering wind was surging down from the mountains, flattening her clothes against her body. She ran into the hacienda. The house was quite silent.

"Michael? Therese?"

There was no reply. She ran to their room. It was empty. She ran to the kitchen. It, too, was empty. Rebecca looked swiftly around the kitchen. A chair was lying on its side. In another corner of the room, a glass lay shattered on the floor. Then she saw that the shards of broken glass were stained with blood. There were more spatters of blood on one of the cabinet doors, a smear on the wooden counter.

She reached out and touched the blood with her fingertips. It was still wet, still red.

Fear ran through her like an electric current.

"Therese!"

The silence of the house mocked her. Had there been an accident? Or an act of violence? Had Michael done something terrible?

The kitchen door, which led out onto the back porch, was banging loudly. She saw that it was swinging open on its hinges. She saw another bright splash of blood on the back step.

She went out the kitchen door, hunting the ground for the red signs. There was a heavy spot in the dirt of the yard. Farther along, another. Her heart pounding, she followed them. On the rough grass of the path, another dribble of dark red. The drops of blood were leading to the barn.

"Therese!"

Rebecca ran toward the barn. It loomed on the brow of the hill, stark against the sky. The door was open, and she burst inside.

"Michael? Therese?"

The barn was big and cool. The whole place was piled high with bales of hay. Above was a loft, also piled high with golden bales. It smelled sweet and clean.

"Michael! Therese!"

Her voice echoed around the hollow structure. The silence rushed in after her words. She walked between the bales, her eyes slowly adjusting to the gloom after the brightness of the sun outside. The place was deserted. Her shoes scrunched on loose hay scattered on the wooden floor. She looked down at her feet. A dark spot lay on the boards. She stooped and touched it with her finger. It came away smeared with red.

"Therese?" she pleaded. "Michael, where are you? Are you in here?"

The door creaked behind her. She spun around. There was nobody there. The door was just swinging emptily in the wind. Filled with a nameless fear, Rebecca walked between the bales of hay, calling.

Then she saw them. Devon and Therese, sitting side by side on a bale. She ran over to them. "What's happened?" she demanded.

"Nothing," Devon said. Therese did not look up. She was sitting hunched into that miserable little ball, her head down, her tangled hair covering her face. Rebecca saw she was clutching a handkerchief to one of her fingers. There was blood on the white cloth.

"Have you cut yourself?" Rebecca asked.

Therese made no reply.

"She had a little accident in the kitchen," Devon said. "But it's nothing serious. Is it, Therese?"

"Therese!" Rebecca cried. "Therese!"

Therese raised her head slowly. Her cheeks were streaked with dirt and tears. Her eyes met Rebecca's for a moment, haunted and wild. Then she dropped her head again.

Devon looked terrible, too. Her normally pretty face was as white as paper, strained into premature old age.

"What are you doing here, Devon?" Rebecca asked.

"I came to talk," Devon said.

"Where's your father?"

"Back in Monterrey."

"Does he know you're here?"

Devon shook her head. "This is just between us."

"Devon," Rebecca said quietly, "let's go back to the house and call your father. You shouldn't be here."

"We have to talk," Devon said.

"What about?"

Devon jerked her head at her sister. "About *her*. You can't just *keep* her. You've got to give her back to Dad." Devon's hands were grappling at each other now, like two neat little animals fighting to the death. "You couldn't manage her."

"I think I could."

"She killed Mom."

"Therese, let's go," Rebecca said. "You don't need to listen to this. Come with me."

But Therese did not move, and Devon went on in a dead voice. "She burned Dad's car in San Francisco. We had a maid once, at home. She didn't like Therese. She slapped Therese one day. Therese nearly killed her. She put something in the woman's food so that she was doped. Then she set fire to her bed. She was so badly burned, she nearly died. No one except me ever knew it was Therese. She'll try and kill you, too."

Rebecca reached out to Therese. "Honey, please come with me."

"She won't listen to you," Devon said with something of a return to her earlier confidence. "You'd have to watch her every second. You don't know what she's like. You don't know what she's capable of."

"I'm her mother," Rebecca said simply.

"*That* doesn't count for much," Devon said, her voice full of thin venom.

"Maybe not," Rebecca replied. "Therese, let's go." She walked toward Therese, determined to pull her physically out of there, if she was too numb to obey.

"Stop," Devon said, her voice suddenly high and shrill.

Rebecca saw Devon reach into her jacket. She saw her pull something out, something snub-nosed and black. But she did not register what it was for a second.

Then she saw flame spurt from the muzzle, and heard the blast.

Something smashed into her leg with such force that she went down like a marionette, sprawling on the wooden boards. At first there was no pain, just an eerie numbness. She pulled herself onto her side slowly, and looked down at her leg. Something had ripped her jeans apart and gouged the flesh beneath. Dark blood was welling from the deep hole in her thigh. Blue smoke drifted in the air.

She tried to sit up, but the pain rushed in and seemed to crush her whole lower body. She could feel something jammed into the fibers of her muscles. She clutched her thigh, keening in agony, and wondered numbly whether the femur had been broken.

"Does it hurt?"

Rebecca looked up slowly, unable to move her lower body for the pain.

Devon held the pistol in both hands. The gun was shaking, but not all that much. Behind her, Therese had buried her face in her clawed hands, shutting out the horror.

"Does it hurt?" Devon repeated. "Dad taught me how to use this when I was twelve. I'm good, too."

Rebecca held out a bloodstained hand. "Why?" she whispered.

"I don't have any choice. You're taking my place. Therese is going to have her real mother. Dad is going to have a *charming* new wife. What place is there for me, Rebecca? Huh? What place for *me*? The nuthouse? The padded cell, where Therese belongs?" The passion in her eyes and voice was suddenly savage. She snapped the breech of the weapon. She leveled it at Rebecca. "I'll bet it really hurts."

Despite the wound, Rebecca tried to crawl back, away from Devon and the gun. But the pain in her leg seemed to paralyze her lungs, and she could do no more than shuffle a couple of inches.

"I never wanted to hurt her," Devon said. "I do love her. But she's younger and weaker than I am. When you get right down to it, it's survival of the fittest. That's the law of nature."

"What do you want?" Rebecca pleaded.

"I want what's *mine*," Devon said fiercely. "You're not going to take it away from me!"

Therese moved off the bale, her body trembling. "Devvy," she said in a whisper, "don't hurt her."

Devon reached out and gripped a handful of Therese's tangled hair. She jerked Therese's head back and thrust the gun into her face. "I'll kill you," she said through clenched teeth. Rebecca saw Therese's bloodstained hands curl into claws. Then her body went swiftly into the familiar fluttering spasms she had seen before. Devon released her. Therese's spine arched, and she collapsed onto the floor, her eyes rolling back.

"What do you think?" Devon panted. "What do you think of your wonderful daughter now?"

"What have you done to her?" Rebecca asked, her eyes fixed on Therese's agony.

"It's her response to anything she can't handle. Therese will explain it all. She's already written a suicide note. Actually, it's a suicide poem. A long one. It's about you. They'll find it when everything's over."

"Devon, no," Rebecca said in horror.

Devon's eyes were acetylene-hot. "You thought you could walk back into Therese's life after all these years, with your little sermons and your sickly-sweet smiles. You thought you could take Dad away from me. You're just another bad mother. Another selfish bitch who didn't care what happened to the children she brought into the world."

"I don't understand. What are you talking about?"

Devon loomed over Rebecca, her face darkening with passion. "You know what a bad mother does to her child? She makes the whole world evil. She has the ultimate power, and she causes the ultimate pain. You know what bad mothers deserve, Rebecca? They deserve to burn in *hell*."

She swung her boot and kicked Rebecca hard on the thigh, close to the wound. The explosion of pain sent blackness flooding through her mind. Rebecca felt her body curl up in a fetal ball, her fingers scrabbling as if to drag her to some place of safety. But there was nowhere.

The world stopped swinging after a long while. She groped herself upright, her vision still darkened. Devon was aiming the gun straight at her throat, her finger curling around the trigger. "Good-bye, Rebecca," Devon whispered. "I hope you burn in hell."

Then Rebecca heard a deep voice say, *"Devon, stop."*

She slowly turned her pounding head. Michael was walking toward Devon. He held his hand out.

"Go away, Dad," Devon said in a shaking voice.

"Give me the gun."

"She has to die," Devon hissed. Her knuckles were white around the weapon. "She has to!"

Michael had reached Devon. He kept his hand extended, but he was careful not to touch her. His voice was calm and very gentle. "Devvy, it's over. Please. Give me the gun."

Devon did not take her eyes off Rebecca. Rebecca's lungs had stopped breathing. For all she knew, her heart had stopped pumping blood. For a terrible moment, the world no longer turned. Then Devon started to tremble, and bright tears filled her eyes, spilling down her cheeks.

Michael stepped forward smoothly and took the gun out of Devon's hands. He checked the weapon, and put it in his belt. Then he whipped his knuckles, backhanded, across Devon's cheek.

Devon spun and almost fell.

"Are you insane?" Michael yelled at her furiously. Devon burst into violent weeping, covering her face with her hands and hunching over. Rebecca felt her own body twist with sobs she could not utter.

Ignoring Devon, Michael crouched beside Rebecca, slipping his arm under her neck to support her. He looked down at the wound. "Ah, Jesus." He groaned softly. "Has it hit the bone?"

"I think so," she gasped. "Oh, Michael, thank God you came!"

He kissed her brow gently. "My poor darling. Hold tight."

With infinite care, he lifted her in his arms, and eased her into a more comfortable position.

Devon was still sobbing painfully, hands clutching at her face. "Therese—" Rebecca panted. "Devon's done something to her. Please look at her, Michael! She's hurt!"

Michael went to Therese and hauled her to her feet. Therese staggered, struggling to stay upright. Her eyes were unfocused. Michael patted her cheeks. "Therese? Are you okay?"

Therese did not reply, but when Michael released her, she managed to stay on her feet, swaying.

Michael came back to Rebecca. He knelt down on one knee beside her. "I'm sorry," he said quietly.

She didn't hear the rest of what he said. She was sinking into darkness.

•   •   •

She came out of the swimming blackness, sound and voices echoing around her. Nothing was quite real. Even the vast pain was an unreal thing, a nightmare roller coaster on which she surged and sank.

She tried to sit up.

She was lying in a pool of dark blood. She laid a hand over the wound. The blood spread between her fingers, comfortingly warm. *Trauma bleeding,* a voice said calmly inside her head. *Intravenous plasma until cross-matched blood arrives. Watch for shock, hypotension.*

Therese was huddled beside her, crying silently. A shadow fell over Rebecca. She looked up. Michael was bending over, looking at her searchingly. "How are you, Rebecca?"

Rebecca frowned at him. "You have to get me to a hospital," she told him, trying to focus on the black eyes that stared at her. "You shouldn't leave me like this."

Michael nodded. "I'm sorry," he said. "This all got so out of control." He stroked her face tenderly. "My poor darling," he said softly. "I never wanted you to be hurt."

Devon appeared behind him. Her face was still clenched into that white fist, except that now there was a red mark on her cheek where Michael had hit her. "What are you going to do, Dad?" she demanded in a high voice.

Michael straightened. "You shouldn't have done this, Devon."

"I had to," Devon replied shrilly. "Everything I did, I did for *you*, Dad. You couldn't turn around and destroy me after all that. You couldn't."

Michael rubbed his face tiredly. "Shut up, Devon."

"What's she talking about?" Rebecca heard her own voice ask. "She's talking about Barbara, isn't she? *She* killed her! Not Therese!"

"We did it together," Devon spat out contemptuously. "I crushed up the stuff and put it in her drink. Then Dad came and lit the fire."

Rebecca groped at Therese with bloodied fingers, trying to draw her close protectively. "You've both used her," she said, her voice blank. "You've used her to cover the evil things you did."

"We didn't do anything evil," Devon said sharply. "Mom did the evil things. She wanted to ruin Dad. She decided to give the land away, so

Dad would lose his business. We tried to stop her. But she wouldn't be stopped. You know how primitive humans killed a mammoth? Spears wouldn't reach its heart. It was too big. Its hide was too thick. So they would dig a hole and cover it over. The mammoth would fall in. Then they would throw in sticks and leaves, and build a fire right on that sucker. They would burn it alive. They had no other way of killing something so big and strong. We didn't, either."

"You killed Barbara," Rebecca said to Michael. "You killed her for money. Not for the girls. Not for anything noble. For money!"

"Who the hell are *you* to pontificate about money?" Michael said with sudden savagery. "You don't know what real poverty is, Rebecca. You don't know what it is to claw your way up to the top of the pile, against the sneers of other people, against their hate, their prejudice. And then to have the drunken bitch you married drag you back down, tear it all away from you. You don't know!"

"And Therese was going to take the blame," Rebecca said, still holding her daughter tightly. "She was going to be sacrificed."

"Nothing would have happened to her," Michael said harshly. "Disturbed thirteen-year-olds don't go to jail. She'd have spent a couple of years in treatment, in some nice place with a lot of big gardens. And then she'd have been free."

"She'd have been destroyed!" The pain in her thigh seemed to be intensifying, suffocating Rebecca. Sweat poured under her arms and in the small of her back. "You told me you loved her, Michael. But all along, she's been nothing to you."

"She was nothing to *you*," Michael said bitterly. "That's why you gave her away. I love Therese more than you can ever imagine. But we all had to make sacrifices, huge sacrifices, in the war against Barbara. That was Therese's part. At least I didn't ask her to kill."

"But you asked Devon to kill."

"Devon's been there before," Michael said. "Haven't you, Devon?"

Devon flinched as though he had struck her across the face again. "Don't, Dad," she whispered.

"Devon's mother didn't die of leukemia," Michael said. "That was just the story the adoption agency made up. Otherwise, little Devon would never have found a home."

"Dad," Devon said piteously, "please don't."

Michael went on remorselessly. "Devon's mother was a prostitute. She couldn't even tell Devon who her father was."

Devon's eyes were slightly glazed now. "No, Dad," she begged. *"Please."*

Michael held Rebecca's gaze. "They were living up near Sausalito, in a wood shack she called a houseboat. Her life had no room for a child. She used to beat Devon. She used to knock the hell out of that child. She would have bruises, cuts, burns, a black eye. It was pitiful. But Devon got her own back, didn't you, Devvy?"

Devon started to cry in a thin, broken voice, like a much younger child. The air seemed to Rebecca to be getting unbreathable. The pain was strangling her.

"She had a party one time, and when she was through, and the men went back to where they came from, she beat Devon with her belt. It must have cut the child to the bone. Or maybe Devon decided she just wasn't going to take any more. There was a kerosene lamp. She just smashed the lamp down on her mother while she was sleeping, and ran out. The mother burned up, the houseboat burned up, it was all over in ten minutes. Just ash. They found Devon screaming on the beach."

Devon covered her face.

Rebecca cradled Therese in her arms, her muscles trembling. Her whole lower body was wet with blood. "Why are you telling me all this?" she asked.

"To show you that it isn't too late," Michael said.

"Too late for what?"

"Too late for you and me." He stepped forward, and crouched in front of her, so he could look full into her face. "Now I know who you really are, I can understand everything. I love you, Rebecca. I really do. And I respect your feelings for Therese. I won't ever ask you to let her go. You understand?"

His eyes had a cobra's fascination. "No," she whispered. "I don't understand."

"Devon set all the fires. Not Therese. She really did, Rebecca. She set fire to the car. She burned the maid. She started the fire on the plane, too. The police don't know about Devon and the houseboat. But when they do know, it'll all come clear."

"No, Dad!" Devon whimpered.

Michael ignored her. He stared intently into Rebecca's eyes. "She won't suffer. I guarantee it. A little therapy. A little treatment. She's smart enough to fool them all. She'll be out in no time. And then we'll all be together." He smiled tightly. "Happily ever after."

"*Don't do this, Dad!*" Devon's voice was the agonized sound of a rabbit in a trap.

"I spent the night trying to convince her," Michael went on. "I talked myself hoarse. I thought she had accepted it. I didn't expect this."

"Michael, you're mad," Rebecca whispered.

"You're still jealous of her?" Michael said. He shook his head. "She's just a child, Rebecca. What I have with you is so different. You eclipse her. She can't hold a candle to you."

"You *did* abuse her," Rebecca gasped. "You did, after all!"

Michael shook his head. "You don't understand. We played games together, that's all. A little fun for me, some good education for her. I never went over the line. Now that's all over though. I'll never want her again." Michael gestured at the wound in Rebecca's leg. "I'm sorry about this, Rebecca. But this helps us, too. Without this, it would have been hard to convince anyone what she's really like. She set all those fires. She really did. The only one Therese lit was the one with the dolls. That fire in the airplane—it was a big risk, but we thought it would be the final piece in the jigsaw—that, and Therese's little diary. When everyone hears Devon already burned one mother to death, though, nobody will believe anything else."

Rebecca was panting with the horror of it all. "Michael, stop!"

"Don't make the same mistake twice," he said urgently. "You nearly

screwed everything up once, Rebecca. Do it right this time. We get everything this way, don't you see? The money, the kids, *everything*." He smiled
again. "You even get Therese." He reached out and stroked Therese's
curls with his fingers.

Rebecca lashed out and knocked his hand away from Therese. "Don't
touch her," she gasped.

"Rebecca," he said, anger dark in his eyes again.

"Get away from me," Rebecca cried. "Get *away!*"

Michael rose slowly. He gazed down at her, his face terrible. "Is that
your final answer?" he said quietly.

Rebecca held Therese close, saying nothing.

Devon had uncovered her tear-streaked face. She was staring at her
father now, her reddened eyes wide. Swiftly, she turned and ran off.

"You're a fool, Rebecca," Michael said, and there was no more anger
in his voice, no more passion of any sort. "But you're right about one
thing. The money *is* the most important thing to me. I was wrong to hope
I could have it all." He stirred Therese with his boot. "And you were
wrong to think you could save her. You've only succeeded in destroying
her."

Devon came running back. She was lugging a plastic jerrican. "Dad!"
she called, her voice trembling with hope.

Michael turned slowly to her.

"Good girl," he said in a fatherly tone. "That's good. Go find another
one now."

Devon dumped the jerrican in front of Michael and ran off again.
Michael unscrewed the cap. He lifted the plastic container high over Rebecca and Therese, and started pouring.

The stink of kerosene was choking, oily. Rebecca could do nothing but
hunch her face down next to Therese's. She felt the greasy fluid streaming
heavily through her hair, pouring over her back, drenching her jeans. The
gurgling of the jerrican emptying was the only sound in the silence.

Then Therese screamed. "No! Dad, no!"

Michael kept pouring, drenching every part of them. Rebecca's clothes
were clinging to her. Her eyes, nose, and mouth were burning. The fumes

tore into her lungs, making her choke and gag. The dreamy effects of shock were receding as new fear clawed at her, new trauma loomed.

At last, the jerrican was empty. Michael kicked it aside. He picked up the second one, which Devon had brought, and poured the contents over the bales of hay. He wheeled, jerking the container so that the liquid flew and spattered.

"Using an accelerant is crude," he said as he worked. "You can do so much if you just understand how materials burn. But in this case, it has to be quick and obvious. There has to be no doubt." He emptied the last drops from the jerrican, then tossed it away. "We'll just let it all soak in for a while."

"Michael, listen to me," Rebecca said in a remote voice.

"I'm so sorry," he said softly, looking down at her. "But you made your decision, Rebecca. You made this inevitable. I have to finish what Devon started."

She tried desperately to push herself upright so that she could talk to them. "Please let Therese go. She doesn't have to suffer anymore."

"I can't trust her," Michael said. "Until you came along, she was so easy to manage. She was so mixed-up that it was easy to make her think she might have killed Barbara. But you taught her to think for herself. You taught her to fight back. So I can't trust her to say the right thing anymore." He touched Therese gently with his boot. "I'm sorry, Therese," he said. "You hear?"

Therese did not move. Michael stared down at her.

Then Devon took something out of her pocket. She clicked the thing, a little plastic cigarette lighter. "Dad. We have to hurry."

Rebecca thrust Therese away from her with all her force. "Run, Therese!" she screamed at her. "Run away from here. Go to Ryan. Go!"

She rolled Therese desperately away from her. Therese staggered to her feet.

"Please," Rebecca begged, her own voice shaken by sobs of despair. "Run away from them, Therese. Get Ryan."

"Her daddy's operating," Devon said matter-of-factly. "He's gonna be gone for hours." She pushed Therese. "It'll be over very soon. You'll see."

Rebecca saw Therese's body convulse. The scream seemed to be torn from her lungs. "*No!*"

She launched herself at Devon, hands clawing for the lighter. Devon was taken aback. She lifted her arms to shield her face from Therese's nails. Therese grabbed her arm and hauled on it. "No!" she was screaming. "No! No!"

"Devon," Michael yelled, "wait!"

More by luck than design, the lighter flipped out of Devon's hand and onto the floor.

Michael grabbed Therese's hair in one hand and spun her like a rag doll. But Therese was fighting like a demon, her slim body twisting, her small fists pounding at Michael. "No more!" she gasped. "Leave her alone!"

Devon stooped quickly and snatched up the lighter.

"Okay," she panted. "That's it." She flicked the lighter and thrust it at the nearest bale of hay.

The shimmering kerosene ignited with a *whump*, drowning out Therese's scream. The blue-and-yellow flame leaped around the bale, then sprang like a living thing to the next, and the next. Flame was suddenly roaring in a ring around them, enfolding the bales.

Then Rebecca saw Therese's thin, bloody fingers grasp the butt of the pistol in Michael's belt. Therese snatched the weapon away from Michael. But it slipped from her fingers and clattered onto the floor. Michael seemed not to have noticed. Rebecca forced herself into motion. She crawled toward the gun, dragging her wounded leg, which felt hugely swollen, a pounding hammer of pain. She tried to ignore it. She had to get the gun. Devon saw what she was doing. She kicked out at Rebecca, her boot grazing Rebecca's cheek. But Rebecca had the gun now. She clawed at the trigger, her eyes closing instinctively.

The recoil jolted her arm upward, and she dropped the weapon, her ears ringing. She opened her eyes. Devon was still standing, looking shocked. But Michael was now lying in a crooked, crumpled heap. He tried slowly to get up. Rebecca could see blood all over his chest.

"*Dad!*" Devon screamed, bending over him.

Therese ran to Rebecca, grabbing at her arms. "Get up," she screamed. "Get up!"

The fire was sweeping through the bales. The hay, dry as tinder, was literally exploding into flames. Sheets of fire were soaring up toward the wooden roof, the ferocious heat building up fast in the confined space. Any second now, Rebecca herself would explode into flames, her kerosene-soaked hair and clothing igniting. Rebecca forced herself upright, grasping Therese's slender arms. Her wounded leg was completely useless. It would not support any weight at all. Therese clutched Rebecca's waist, holding her upright. They staggered toward the door together.

Their progress was agonizing. In a blur, Rebecca saw blood spurt out of the wound with each step. She could not possibly make it. She would burn up, and Therese would be consumed in the same explosion.

"Go," she gasped, trying to push Therese away from her. "Get out, Therese. I'll follow."

"No," Therese panted. "I'm not leaving you."

The fire was roaring at their backs, acrid smoke billowing over them. Step by racking step, they blundered on. At last, they were in the doorway. They stumbled out into the cold, fresh air. The sunlight dazzled them.

Rebecca felt Therese's hands claw at her shirt, dragging it off her body. Buttons spat and cloth ripped. The wind was icy on her kerosene-wet skin. Therese's fingers tore at her jeans, trying to pull them down. The pain in her thigh was so terrible that Rebecca could barely stand any longer, even to save her life. She crumpled.

"Don't fall," Therese begged. "Don't fall, Rebecca."

She forced herself to obey Therese. Therese kept dragging her away from the barn. Rebecca could hear the breath rasping in her lungs. Behind them, the fire in the barn was roaring now, a deep, triumphant sound.

At last they were in the shadow of the water towers. Therese grabbed the hose that hung down, and swung the lever open. Cold water gushed over Rebecca, flooding her.

Therese thrust the hose into Rebecca's hands. "Wash yourself," she yelled.

"Where are you going?" Rebecca screamed as Therese started to run back to the barn.

"Dad and Devvy are still in there," she called over her shoulder.

"Therese, *no*," Rebecca sobbed.

But Therese was running, running toward the flames.

Rebecca lay back and sobbed. She had never felt such profound despair as now, watching her daughter run back to destruction. She sprawled helplessly under the shadow of the water tanks, clutching the hose, which spewed cold water across her thighs, winter rain mingling with the warm blood.

Somewhere in the world that is consuming itself, the sisters meet. Therese's hands claw at Devon's, grasping her, pulling her with violent desperation. Therese is smaller than Devon, but she has a kind of mad strength. She clutches her sister to her breast and lifts her off the floor.

The fire is bellowing all around them, searing heat reaching up to the sun, bursting through the roof of the barn. Burning things are falling all around them. The twine that secured the bales of hay has long since melted, and they are unwinding like fiery dragons, uncurling, unfolding in curtains of fire.

"Come on, Devvy," Therese shrieks. "Come on!"

Devon is in a daze. She crouches beside the man whom they have both called father. There is a dark stain on his chest. He is no longer moving. He lies quite still. Devon smiles at Therese loosely, the red light filling her eyes. "Leave me here with him," she says, so quietly, Therese can hardly hear the words above the roar. "Go to her! Get out!"

"I'm not leaving you here," Therese screams.

She starts to drag Devon toward the door. Devon resists. She pries Therese's fingers loose.

Therese will not allow herself to be shaken off. She crushes Devon's face against her breastbone, knowing if Devon breathes, the blistering air will shrivel her lungs. Her own lips are pinched shut. She can smell skin and hair burning, and does not know whether it is Devon's or her own.

She drags her burden toward the door. Devon fights, but her strength is now less than Therese's, though in the past it has always been greater. In the past, she has always been the one to move Therese, push her, drag her, carry her. Now it is Therese who moves Devon. She will not let her die.

The door of the abyss has opened. The fire howls like some huge creature in agony or rage. The very floorboards beneath their feet are hot. The air is searing skin, blistering lungs, scorching tender eyes. Therese feels flame lick at her very hands, and sees that Devon's hair is alight. She grasps the fire with her living fingers, trying to crush it out.

At the very doorway, when life is within their grasp, Devon puts up a frantic struggle.

"Leave me!" she is screaming. "Leave me with him!"

Therese will not let her fight away.

And then she bursts from the flames with her sister in her arms. The sky is above them and the clean air is in their faces.

Therese is whole. But Devon is broken. Something has broken inside her, and all she can do is cry. She stumbles like someone in a trance at Therese's side. Therese leads her away from the burning place, her arm around her sister's shoulders. Inside the barn, a whirlwind of fire dances around the bales.

Therese opens her eyes, as if for the first time in years. She opens her eyes and sees the world. She sees her mother lying there, her face wet with tears, her arms held out. She hears her mother call her name. She goes to her, pulling Devon along in her wake.

The barn is starting to collapse, wooden walls falling inward, wooden roof sagging down. The flames have triumphed. But they have escaped.

There is another roar, and Therese sees Ryan's truck careering across the meadow toward them. She calls to him. He leaps out and runs to her, to them. They are all converging in the same place. He reaches her. He helps her to shoulder the burden of Devon. Between them, they carry Devon toward where Rebecca lies bleeding.

And then they are all huddled together, under the shade of the water towers, the distant fire soaring back to the sun, God's great blue sky arching overhead.

EPILOGUE

SAN FRANCISCO

Ryan, Therese, and Rebecca made their way into the huge building, their pace slowed by Rebecca's limp. They took the elevator to the second floor, and walked down the corridor.

They stopped at the locked section marked SECURE ADOLESCENT UNIT, and handed their ID to the guard in the booth. They had been here a number of times over the past few weeks, but he still checked every detail thoroughly before he pressed the buzzer, and the electronic lock clicked open.

They had listened to the doctors' account of Devon's progress over the past days. It was evident to all of them that there was a long way to go, but they kept cheerful expressions in place, and said hopeful things.

The white paintwork on the walls and ceiling was dazzling in the fluorescent lights, and the atmosphere was relentlessly bright.

"Hi," the duty doctor greeted them. "She's out in the garden. She's been a lot better today. She read a little this morning, before our session.

Afterward she was upset, but that's natural—she's still grieving. She fell asleep just for a while, watching some TV. She keeps asking to speak to you, Therese."

He made it a gentle question. Therese shook her head slightly. "Not yet," she answered.

"No hurry whatsoever. You can watch her from my window if you want to."

They went to the doctor's office. His window looked down onto one of the enclosed gardens below. Devon was walking with a nurse beneath the spreading branches. She carried a book. Much of her blond hair had been burned in the barn, so the nurses had cut it short. She looked serenely beautiful, chatting to her companion. They stared at her for a long time.

"I blame myself," Rebecca said quietly. "I should have seen how Michael was manipulating her."

"Don't," Ryan said. "Psychopathic personalities can be so clever. They fool everyone—husbands, wives, parents, friends. Normal people are completely out of their depth. You have to be like they are, or be a trained specialist, to anticipate what they'll do. Michael was the only one who knew the truth about her childhood. He used that to turn her into his tool. That didn't make her any less dangerous. She would have killed you both."

"Yes." She thought of Michael's facile, callous view: *a couple of years in treatment, in some nice place with a lot of big gardens.* Looking at that pretty blond head, it was hard to imagine that Devon had helped Michael in so many unspeakable acts—in killing Barbara, in trying to brainwash Therese, even in setting fire to an airliner.

Devon looked up at their window briefly. She could not see through the bronzed glass, so they made no move. But suddenly, Rebecca wondered whether she could see Michael's handsome features embodied in Devon's face. Was there more to the houseboat story than Michael had told her? He had spoken almost like a witness when he'd described what Devon had endured. Was the tie between him and this once-glowing girl deeper even than he had admitted? She would never know that. Probably, nobody would ever know it. Best not to know. Best not to dig any more in that dark soil.

For a moment, his shadow was over her, and she felt fear and pain clench her muscles. She wondered whether she was truly free of him, free of needing to fear him, free of wondering whether she had loved him.

As if sensing her thoughts, Ryan put a strong arm around her, and drew her close. "It's all over," he whispered. "We're together now."

Slowly, she relaxed. He was right. Michael was dead, and there were no more questions to be asked. "I'm sorry," she whispered to the distant figure. She meant, for what she had done to Michael. "Forgive me, Devon. I hope you understand one day."

They crossed the city and drove out onto the Golden Gate Bridge.

Rebecca wound down the window to inhale the cold breath of the Pacific. Down below, a ship was forging its way into the harbor. Around it, she saw the exhilaration of yachts with drum-tight sails plowing through water layered with white breakers. The light was dazzlingly intense. But the pain of a too-bright sky was almost pleasurable. She felt like someone who had been underground too long.

"I always thought you were so fragile," Rebecca said, laying her cheek against Therese's. "A frail, vulnerable glass doll. But you weren't. You were tough enough to survive. Tough enough to save us all."

Ryan looked over his shoulder. "Want me to stop on the other side?" he asked.

"Yes," they both replied in unison.

He parked the car on the far side of the bridge. The immense sweep of the bridge, its huge span, filled Rebecca with a soaring sense of hope. It was a great achievement that told the heart all other achievements were possible.

"I love you both so much," she heard Ryan say.

Rebecca put an arm around each of them, and drew them in close. She felt as though a blessing were wreathing around them in that salty air, a spell compounded of Therese's flushed happiness, Ryan's quiet constancy, her own deep strength. The rolling music of the sea filled the silence.

ABOUT THE AUTHOR

MARIUS GABRIEL, author of *The Mask of Time* and *The Original Sin,* is a former Shakespearean scholar who left his academic pursuits to become a full-time writer. Mr. Gabriel is also an artist and musician. He lives in Spain with his wife and three children.